KU-312-103

BLOOD DANCING

Wanting to rid Manchester of evil, an assassin scours the newspaper headlines for his next victim... Meanwhile a young prostitute is viciously attacked, and Doctor Clare Burtonall has to decide whether or not to terminate her life support. As Clare contemplates the girl's future, her boyfriend – the handsome and intelligent Bonn – looks after the working girls on Manchester's seedy streets. A high-class male escort, he understands the tough and lonely world they inhabit, and he knows the imminent release of a paedophile back into the area will cause waves on streets already seething with suppressed anger.

For Jack

BLOOD DANCING

by

Jonathan Gash

Magna Large Print Books
Long Preston, North Yorkshire,
BD23 4ND, England.

British Library Cataloguing in Publication Data.

Gash, Jonathan
    Blood dancing.

      A catalogue record of this book is
      available from the British Library

      ISBN   978-0-7505-2628-9

ۑ\۱ﻟﻭ

First published in Great Britain in 2006 by Allison & Busby Ltd.

Copyright © 2006 by Jonathan Gash

Cover illustration © The Old Tin Dog by arrangement with
Allison & Busby Ltd.

The moral right of the author has been asserted

Published in Large Print 2007 by arrangement with
Jonathan Gash, care of Coombs Moylett Literary Agency

All Rights reserved. No part of this publication may be reproduced,
stored in a retrieval system, or transmitted in any form or by any
means, electronic, mechanical, photocopying, recording or otherwise
without the prior permission of the Copyright owner.

Magna Large Print is an imprint of Library Magna Books Ltd.

Printed and bound in Great Britain by
T.J. (International) Ltd., Cornwall, PL28 8RW

Acknowledgements

Ta, Susan

Note:
Definitions are given by known origin or the author's best supposition.

Chapter One

stringer – a street prostitute, of a group

Bonn walked among the traffic in Victoria Square, making the Rivergate corner before the tide of buses overwhelmed him.

'That's Bonn,' he heard one street walker tell the other. The new girl was called a goojer, as if everybody lightly tanned was from Goojerat.

'Him? But I thought Bonn'd be...'

Bonn reddened at the new stringer's surprise. He felt shame, knowing his appearance must disappoint. He vaguely recognised the experienced girl as Grace, but names defeated him because Grellie's working girls liked pseudonyms. He moved out of earshot in case more shame was to come. A baby's pushchair impeded him. He stooped to retrieve a stuffed toy on the pavement and handed it back to the mother, so caught the goojer's astonished question ('Women pay *that* much, just for him?'). The final shame, money purchasing women, men, people. And him too.

He walked on, unable to lengthen his stride because of the throng by the Weavers Hall Shopping Mall. Life was all embarrassment. Street girls kept wanting to buy him clothes – embarrassment. Martina, queen of the city centre, ruled against it – embarrassment. Fashion also embarrassed him. How was it that each prostitute *knew* that she alone could buy exactly the right garb for him to look stylish instead of nondescript? Females had such conviction. From where, though? He had none, not for anything.

His vestige of learning, from the seminary school, proved he lacked belief. Not just in personal relations, either, but in how he must seem. He'd opted for life in the streets and did not even know why. Life baffled him. Loneliness did not.

The next appointment was with a lady in the Time and Scythe Hotel, Mealhouse Lane. How strange, he thought, that the women who paid high sums to hire him for an hour seemed to have lost all feeling of home. How strange that transient sex, the most ephemeral of impulses, seemed to symbolise their only permanence.

'I'd pay him, Bally,' Grace said to her new street partner, now Bonn was beyond hearing. 'If that bitch Martina'd let me.'

'Why is he special?' Bally asked, for ever at her lipstick. She carried eleven colours in her handbag.

'Don't be stupid. We got to get four strides in before dark.'

A stride was one encounter with a john, not always easy in the swirling traffic. Four would be a rush, and Grellie who bossed the working girls had eyes everywhere.

Across in Central Gardens, Grellie and Rack were watching the old men play chess with huge plastic pieces on marked paving. Rack nudged Grellie and said, 'Them bints made Bonn go red. See it?'

'Yeh.' Grellie was spectacularly beautiful, slen-

10

der, twenty-three, and a control freak where her street walkers were concerned. 'I'm not blind.'

'It were that Grace said summert, right?'

'Yeh.'

'Fine her. Bonn's at the Time and Scythe next. Can't have his mind fucked up because some tart wants to show off to a new lass.'

'You do your job, Rack,' Grellie said, 'and I'll do mine.'

She never seemed to be looking, which showed how good she really was because she saw everything. If she didn't, and Martina found out, she'd not last a minute. She wished she still smoked cigarettes, but Bonn didn't like it so she'd stopped. She strolled off towards the two girls on the Rivergate pavement. Punishment time.

Rack went to extort money. His job, her job, same difference.

Chapter Two

rumming – to hunt in garbage for food or saleable detritus

Unbelievable that foxes roamed the inner city. Tennock hated foxes, thieving bastards filching garbage that was rightly his. The slinky swine got to rubbish quicker than any mumper could, faster even than rats.

Tennock stuck to his plan. Vagrancy had served him well for seven years, since he'd been evicted

11

and found himself a lurk among the street sleepers round St James's. Not that he had religion. Churches gave him one square a day, so he stayed fit enough to scavenge. Bin divers were ten a penny in the black-and-neon two-tone world of the city at night. He had an idea that cars and the girl street walkers kept foxes down. Chinese nosh places and Thai caffs, now mixed with Balkan skimmers – skim off anything, more guns even than Yardies – provided the best garbage, as long as you sorted through rotting offal to get it.

Survival was an art for a mumper. Forget the kerbside bins and small white bags from hairdressing salons. Even the fucking foxes left those untouched. Trendy sandwich bars gave little because the Italians were fading fast, losing in the city's mad daylight careering and clever night nudging. Tennock snickered. They couldn't hack it, these Italians who copied some film prat in the wrong trilbies. Good, sure, back when they were the only people who had guns. They lost the plot when everybody else thought, Hey, guns is good, let's go down Wardle Street and get a couple for two hundred and sixty-three zlotniks, another twenty-five for bullets that actually fitted. Faced with opposition shooters, the Ities started legit fitness-and-health gyms where they went home clean, the idle fuckers. Leaving mumpers like Tennock to go hungry.

He stood at the corner of Arkwright Street – two Malay caffs, one posh Goojer spot, four various and a caff for lorry long-haulers off the motorway because the city centre was cheaper than paying for a banger and beans in pricey Super-Service

Stations among coaches full of football rioters. Darkness never let him down. Starving, he would get some decent nosh by reaching in over the rim of the dumper and grabbing whatever lay on top.

Tennock heard a nearby girl giving her dickster a performance against a wall. Couldn't see them in the dark. She was going, 'Ooh, oooh, yes, yes!' like her feet weren't crippling her and her arse wasn't freezing. She was worn out, still needed to pull three more johns to make-up her strides so other girls on the Green string wouldn't blame her for not pulling her weight. Nobody could grumble like street tarts. They all said the same thing: they alone slogged under whichever bloke had enough gelt while other bitches smoked in the Central Gardens pretending they were trolling hard at it and doing sod all.

Another couple of minutes should see her finish the punter. They were in shadow twenty steps off. From habit, he stooped to see the distant lamp's feeble reflection off the damp pavement, the mumper's night trick to sort out people from buildings. Another black bin was within reach.

The lid came off easy peasy. Tennock reached in, felt a promising squelchy knob, ripped the black plastic with a quiet pull, and thrust in his hand. Another hand seemed to take his. For a second he stood wondering what the fuck, actually felt it – fingers, fingernails, palm, wrist, then nothing except frayed flesh and skin torn into flaps. He thought, hey, this can't be a ... then his hand came up tacky like that glue you could never get rid of.

He actually sniffed his fingers, thought a moment about reaching back in and pulling that

13

thing that felt like a hand, a fucking *hand*, out to see if it really was wrong. Then he screeched and yelled and ran wailing down the street, blundering into things and falling but keeping going, wailing and shouting meaningless sounds. His gammy leg didn't hurt one bit as he ran, knocking over two rubbish bins from the hairdressing emporium.

He heard the john exclaim, 'What the...?' and the girl call something but Tennock wasn't going to stop, not with things like that reaching out of tonight's garbage.

Chapter Three

prad – (street slang) to set up a scam

'What kind of a name is that?'

'I apologise, sir. My father gave it me.'

The car showroom man knew not to be taken in. Even killers could look benign. The man was old enough to remember when people who bought cars came in wearing suits, with collar-studs and cufflinks and shone their shoes of a morning.

'Ellston's odd, though, innit?'

Mr Ellston smiled, ever willing. He was not new to the north, so knew that money and crime flowed differently up here. The young man facing him with a buffoon's grin could be anyone. He wore a green eye-shade, striped shirt, jade-green singlet on an afternoon of bitter wind, an absurd shoe-lace tie and baggy Wild West jeans, and

14

looked simply ridiculous.

'I suppose it is, sir.'

'What is it, Ellston?' Shania Brownham came, her upraised chin and aggressive stride showing who was boss.

'Just attending to this customer, Ms Brownham. May I help, sir?'

Shania Brownham took in the newcomer, no more than a youth. The dolt was humming, looking round, kicking tyres on the display cars, snapping into a mime of a racing driver and making a child's noises of Formula One engines.

'Hey, Ello,' the customer said, ignoring her. 'Know why racer drivers never collect stamps?'

'I didn't know that was the case, sir,' Ellston said smoothly. 'Is there a reason?' His response had been honed over the years and did for any riposte, joke or not.

'That's 'cos you don't think, mate.' The youth's accent was Cockney, not local. Mr Ellston thought that interesting. 'Their eyes are set different van yours en mine, see? Know why? They's fastened different in their heads. Know why?'

'No, sir.'

'We are busy,' Ms Brownham interrupted, angrily pushing between them. Today was her debut. She hadn't earned promotion just to play straight man to some idiot scruff. 'Leave immediately or I shall call the police.'

The dolt ignored her. 'Who's the bint, Ello?'

'May I introduce the manager, Ms Brownham, sir?'

'She ain't heard what I come for yet. One per cent on this load of scrap, OK?'

15

'What are you talking about?' Shania Brownham demanded. 'You surely aren't asking for a loan?'

The youth eyed her in disgust. 'Tell her, Ello.' He revved an imaginary engine.

'Get him out, Ellston. I mean now.'

'See you in a week, Ell, OK? Tell her she's short on tit.' The youth said it over his shoulder, snapped pretended gears and then changed his mime into a foxtrot. And danced, literally segued and shuffled out, tunelessly lal-lalling then pretending to accelerate out by the immense glass pavement façade.

'Ms Brownham,' Ellston began, careful still. '"With respect, might I, ah, caution–'

'Ellston.' Shania tapped his chest, still furious. 'I'm putting you on official warning. I don't want layabouts in my car showroom. Do you understand?'

'He wants payment, Ms Brownham.'

She gaped. 'Paying? What for?'

'A guarantee of business.'

'Extortion? Call the police, Ellston.' She glared at him. 'I thought you had more sense. Have I to do everything round here?'

'Ms Brownham, perhaps it might be wiser–'

'I'll do it, Ellston. If you want anything doing, do it yourself!'

She was highly charged. Sheer ambition had carried her this far, and she was going to climb even higher. These new city showrooms were her third retail ladder, and she wasn't going to jeopardise her expectations for the sake of some exhibitionist moron and some creaking old yes-man.

Everything about Shania Brownham testified

16

to prowess. She behaved like a construct. The company demanded it. Great commercial destiny waited somewhere ahead, and she was on the move, way different from the seventeen dull sales people she had to manage here. They were born to servility. She wasn't. Personality was the driving force, aggression the fuel.

'Next time that low-life comes in, Ellston, take action. Police, then a company report.'

'Yes, Ms Brownham.'

She sent her clerk for a coffee, went into her glass pod office and sat facing her three flickering consoles. Ellston suppressed a sigh and advanced smiling to two new customers. It would end in tears. He'd seen this kind of thing before. What was one per cent, for protection from fire, injury, theft, anything from graffiti to even death? One per cent could always be concealed in the multiple transactions of a car showroom. It seemed cheap at the price.

He'd obey, though, because he lacked ambition. It was the best way to be. Safest.

Chapter Four

goojer – non-indigenous origin

Rack jived and bounced his way across the Central Gardens, switching from being a Western gunfighter to a ship's captain in a howling gale, rocks ahead and icebergs steaming up from

Biscay or those places on the weather forecast. By the time he reached Grellie at the Moorgate corner near London Road station he was a fighter pilot crashing in a screaming dive.

'Rack,' Grellie said wearily, lounging on the pedestrian pavement rail among passing shoppers, 'for Christ's *sake.*'

'Shut it! Bonn's here!'

'Where?' Grellie looked round guiltily before realising she'd been had. 'You sod.'

He went all indignant. 'I'm helping, you daft cow. You always want to talk nice when Bonn's around.'

'I hate you in this fucking mood.'

Rack leant on the barrier. He watched Grellie watching the girls. Gorgeous tart, best of all the street walkers, Grellie ruled Martina's syndicate girls throughout the city centre. It had been Grellie's idea to divide them up, each corner of Central Gardens named for a colour, so many girls in each. Martina, boss of the known world, delicate doll-like if lame beauty but vicious as any slag trolling her domain, had been reluctant but Rack persuaded her. Grellie's colour scheme worked a treat, which really narked Martina.

Main thing was, the stringers accepted most things, except for spats like once every fucking ten minutes, but that was par. There wasn't one girl Rack would call calm, not a single one. He didn't mind, as long as they behaved quiet with the punters and Grellie went along. Rack didn't mind a few wrinkles because he knew himself a genius, with a mind more brilliant than any scientist. He told everybody this. The girls pulled his leg. He

18

guessed they all admired him for his massive brain. Trouble was, Grellie was too efficient. Getting things right was like a fucking sickness with her, especially for someone who was only a tart. For one thing, Grellie behaved like every penny the marks paid over for a shag was her own frigging money. For another, Martina was cagey with Grellie, who returned Martina's suspicion back in spades. Rack knew it was only from them being female, because all birds fought, hate coming easy. Listen to them talk about other women's clothes, and there you had it. Rack's giant intellect had warned him that birds weren't like blokes, not one bit. He could prove it.

Grellie's clever control of the bints trolling for Martina's syndicate was a definite advantage, so that was one up to Grellie and Victoria Square. Rack believed the colour scheme was his idea, because tarts couldn't have a brilliant brain like him. A good system, it ran this way: Like, Moorgate corner was Yellow, should be sixteen working girls at full strength. Opposite, Grellie's Red string worked the Rivergate corner by the old Weavers Hall where bankers met to work out their latest frauds. South-east, Grellie only had nine girls today on the Green corner at Greygate, where the road dog-legged out of the city heading for London and the south. Only nine on any string was a definite calamity and Rack knew he'd get grief over it from Martina when he reported in later at the Shot Pot snooker hall, a right dump.

The most difficult was Deansgate, the north-west corner. Grellie liked a good fifteen or more Blue bints working by six o'clock. Fewer, the takings went down like a stone and Martina got shirty. It didn't sound much, but it could start Martina, blonde and lame and out-guessing everybody on frigging earth, sitting there just giving you the look. It was multo different, if you were on the receiving end, Martina's ice eyes and her terrible low blue look was the worst thing since the Black fucking Death. It was a well-known fact. Rack believed if only all the cunts in the world would leave everything to him he'd have the world perfect by Tuesday four o'clock, give or take. Them foreign wars would get straight in an afternoon, sack the fucking United Nations for a start. You saw these things clear if you had his giganto brain. He looked at Grellie.

A stunner, best twenty-three years on legs. Like the rest of the working girls she was crazy about Bonn. Rack warned her a year back she ought to get herself a tit job, a load of implants, really tactful, but the daft bitch went berserk, which only proved tarts couldn't see sense.

'What's the matter with our Red lot?' he asked, heart sinking, already seeing the signs across the Central Gardens square and knowing Grellie would pretty soon go ballistic.

There was always something wrong with one string or another. Last week there'd been a scrap after closing time at the Volunteer. Some goon actually called the police. Rack still hadn't found out who. Grellie lost two girls to the plod. One was still in the nick for trying to stab her mate with a screwdriver, which was really bad news. Martina fined the whole of the Greygate corner girls over that, which set the Green girls sulking

20

because they blamed the Blue stringers at Deansgate. Rack knew it was because females had no proper tunes in their heads, which was why they started street walking in the first place. If Grellie would only listen, he would explain his theory about thinking tunes, but she'd bitten his head off even though he tried to get her off the hook by taking it up with Martina. Rack was a martyr, an honest-to-God saint drowning in a sea of crazy bitches. He felt like that.

'They're upset,' she said, weighing up what was happening in the Gardens.

'Here, Grellie,' he said, thinking it was tact time. 'I reckon you not shagging Bonn is sending you miserable. Why don't you shack up with him? Martina wouldn't mind.'

Grellie turned on him with a snarl, ignoring the pedestrians crowding past.

'Don't you *dare* say anything to Bonn, Rack, or so help me—'

'I didn't! I didn't!' He held up his hands, all innocent, though of course he had.

'You've not? Honest?'

'Course not! Why should I?'

She leant on the barrier watching the traffic.

'Only, I reckon Bonn needs his own bint, know what I mean?' And when she did not answer, 'See, Grellie, a bloke wants his own tart, knock her about a bit, have a quiet shag, sleep proper, right? Bonn only shags them Agency cows, the ones with more money than sense.'

'Leave it, Rack.'

He admired Grellie. Even when he was giving her the benefit of superb advice like this, her eyes

21

were everywhere. Into the Gardens, digging out movements in the bus station, checking how long that pair of her girls had been in the public toilets, which Yellow stringers was taking an illicit smoke pretending to watch the old men playing Giant Chess near the Asda Supermart. Her eyes were like ferrets, always rooting, judging, working away.

Once, he'd tried it on with her because a bloke had to use girls he worked with because they expected it. She wouldn't. That proved she was a right prat, him being the sharpest bloke in the city. Still, Rack trusted her and she trusted nobody, which was the right way round. She loved Bonn but hated Martina, which was OK because women did that as a routine. One of his theories was that birds hated each other because they knew they didn't matter.

'Here, Grell,' sharing his genius. 'D'you know brains are all different? Like women's brains are brown, and brown never works proper, see?'

'And men's are better?' she said, still looking, questing, timing.

'Hey, you're learning, Grell!' Rack was pleased. Grellie was coming on, picking up education quicker these days.

Two cars paused opposite the Granadee TV Studios by Greygate and two Green girls alighted, one carelessly discarding a tissue as they strolled back to Mawdsley Place by the Textile Museum. The cars drove off.

'Thought so,' Grellie said. One was a tiny goojer lass from Ashton-in-Makerfield, wanted to be a croupier or maybe a singer in the Rum Romeo Casino up Mealhouse Lane. Some frigging hopes.

'Men's are different colours inside, see? Some of us are orange, purple, pink, all sorts, see? It gives bigger thinks, see?'

She said, 'I've often wondered,' but thinking of Neeta the new goojer girl who dared litter the street with her soiled tissues from a gob job. Grellie couldn't take cheek. She'd told the idle bitch on her very first day, and here she was bold as brass thinking she was Cleopatra because she'd earned a few notes sucking some punter off in a motor. It was breathtaking nerve. Neeta needed a talking to. Start as you mean to go on, with the insolent cow.

Rack was glad Grellie was willing to learn. 'Stick with me, girl, you'll fucking learn summat.'

'Please, Rack,' Bonn's voice said quietly.

Rack almost jumped, but turned with a beaming smile, pretending to shoot a six-gun from the hip. 'Barn! Barn! Wotcher, Bonn. Just telling Grellie—'

'Please abate your language in public, Rack,' Bonn said. 'Grellie does not want to hear coarseness.'

'It's all right, Bonn,' Grellie said, cheeks hot.

They waited. 'Rack,' Bonn said.

'Look, Bonn. There's a message.'

Bonn did not answer, just stood. Rack petered out.

'OK, Bonn. Sorry. I was just talking, see?'

'He was upset, Bonn,' Grellie said.

Bonn considered. Finally he gave an almost imperceptible nod and turned his attention to the lead girl.

'Upset.'

Relieved he was off the hook, Rack judged Bonn. Newly turned twenty, Bonn would pass for aver-

23

age on any northern street. Nothing flash, shoes off-the-peg, jacket routine stock from Oldfield's along the Deansgate mall, his tie so ordinary it might have come from a rubbish skip, shirt nothing special, and Mullgrave's least fashionable trouser style. Bonn was utter fucking dullsville. Trouble was, Rack wondered why he felt like crap just because Bonn told him off because he'd heard him use ordinary English words talking ordinary to the head street walker. It was fucking mad. Like, the passing heavy goods vehicle drivers would all faint away if they overheard somebody say fuck or shag, so refined were they wheeling through in their HGVs?

'Your hair never looks proper, Bonn,' Rack blurted out in his distress. It was true. Bonn washed it himself, never had it done by Roamin Combin down Waterloo Street by the Lagoon Casino. That right load of poofters were priciest in the whole city, but they did a good job if you threatened enough. They did Rack's hair once he'd got the lurks going in the Square of a Monday morning. And it was free, for Christ's sake, because Bonn could have anything free. He was the syndicate's top key. Except, unbelievably, he *paid* for everything himself. It was all wrong.

'Upset, Grellie.'

This was another thing. Bonn never asked a question, just stood there thinking you never knew what. Like you had to guess the fucking question as well as try and answer. Unless Grellie did a good guess and told him what Bonn wanted, he'd be there a fortnight saying the same thing.

'The girl in hospital, Bonn,' Grellie said,

24

prompting Rack so he could get out from under Bonn's terrible silence. Bonn looked at her and she went redder still. She was fibbing about something she really wanted to tell him.

'Girl.'

'She's in them tubes,' Rack said, quickly taking up Grellie's excuse and making it his own. 'Some paedo did her, lobbed her out on the ring road. It's been in the papers. She's well poorly, Bonn.'

Grellie joined in, keeping it going, 'The papers say she'll not come round.'

'Intensive care.' Rack was proud. Fat George had spelled it out in his newspaper stand by the Triple Racer, the caff where the message bikers sat all day waiting for jobs. Trouble was, Rack couldn't read or write, and pretended he could do both. People pretended to believe his pretence, under pain of getting themselves done over. 'She's dying.'

'Upset.'

Grellie wondered how much to say, and finally went for it. 'The girls over on Red string want to go to court over some perv.'

This was safer ground. Rack added, 'See, Bonn, I reckon the easiest thing is to have that perv blammed, see? He done the girl, right? And he's getting out from under, see? Law always lets pervs go. I think I should finish him, save worry.'

'Please do not say such, Rack.'

'Bonn, mate.' Rack was almost hopping from foot to foot, desperate to get it across. 'I'm only saying what everybody else is thinking. You want to hear our fu ... our bints on Deansgate. They're going spare.'

'That will do, Rack.' Bonn waited. 'This girl in hospital.'

'Only a kid. Fourteen or whatever. The girls say some perv trashed her, dolled her out on the Ringway, dying. The hospital wants to pull the plug on her 'cos she's done for.'

'And she is not one of your girls, Grellie.'

'No, Bonn. Too young for us to take on.'

Grellie looked away as she spoke. Bonn was against the syndicate using girls under age, so Martina said no kids. It was a constant topic at the Brown Owl mill, where Martina held her meetings. Fact was, a few juveniles got through, girls being full of tricks and going for what they wanted anyway.

'Your girls have very decided opinions, Grellie.'

Safer still. For a moment she was distracted by the way he spoke her name, slow, considering the syllables as if they had an actual taste. Nobody else did that. People just said her name like a grunt.

'Well, they would, Bonn.' She wondered if he listened to the way she said his name, quickly decided no. 'Some kid, after all.'

'Known to you, then.'

'No. None of the girls knew her. She's from Leeds.' She said it as if in exoneration, the next county nothing to do with anybody.

'Some of our girls dress, ah...'

'Punters like them looking young, Bonn. That's why–'

Grellie halted, stricken. A toddler clasped Bonn's leg amorously, its mother apologising and trying to disengage him. Bonn knelt to help, gently returned the infant to his pushchair.

He prompted, 'That's why, Grellie.'

'That's why some of the girls on Red think they knew the perv, see?' Rack said outright. 'He wanted only kid lookalikes.'

'There must be several.' Bonn waited until the young mother with the tot made it across the traffic lights, and relaxed. 'Yet the girls suspect only one.'

'They reckon they know.'

'The police might already be apprised, Rack.'

'Know,' Grellie translated for Rack. 'Our girls know better than the plod, Bonn.'

'No, Rack.'

'What?' Rack demanded, belligerent. 'I said nuffink, mate.'

'It is not for us to dispense justice, Rack.'

''Course not! I keep saying that, don't I, Grellie? I just told you before Bonn come, didn't I? I said we can't do nuffink, didn't I?'

'Yes, Bonn,' Grellie said, desperate to wax in the cracks. 'He did.'

'It's down to the filth, innit?' Rack continued, still indignant at Bonn's wrong think.

'Thank you.' Bonn glanced at the Central Garden clock. 'Message, Rack.'

'Eh? Oh, yih. Clare Three-Nine-Five at the Time and Scythe, eight o'clock. I'm your stander. Room 516, OK?'

'Very well. I shall be in the Textile Museum library, Rack, then to my room. Then the Worcester for a meal.'

'I'll be at the casino, Bonn,' Grellie said, and could have kicked herself. Bonn paused in mild surprise, said something noncommittal and left, walking along the pavement past the Butty Bar.

'Meet him in the Worcester,' Rack urged, seeing Grellie's face. 'It's posh there now the new cunt's taken it over.'

And indeed the Worcester Club and Tea rooms was looking splendid, newly decorated, its entrance grandest in the square.

'Don't be stupid,' Grellie said, and crossed against the traffic lights, annoyed with herself. She decided to give that goojer lass a right charring, serve the bitch right.

Chapter Five

pral – to beg (Romany)

Hassall hated waiting rooms. They showed the worst features of existence. Wherever you went, you were told to wait. Dismissive girls on the phone, bored out of their skulls, intoned, 'Wait, please,' and made you listen to an electronic *Für Elise* while they put you through to some other idlers who also couldn't care less.

'Come straight in, Mr Hassall,' Dr Burtonall called, a smile in her voice. 'I daren't keep you waiting. I couldn't stand another grumbler today.'

He entered the surgery and sat, hat on his knees, a supplicant. Doctors did that to people, made them understand they were here to beg for their lives. He said his good mornings.

Clare was finishing a note on a file, quite a

mound. Uneasily Hassall wondered if he had such a record. She told him she'd be just a second, her tongue on her lips while she concentrated. He looked round. New paint, glossy ledges, new instruments. A spirometric thing – it was labelled, curious tubes projecting. Everything seemed to consist of a cream-coloured plastic hollow wired to a midget black matchbox. When he'd started attending for routine police medicals, instruments were immense gadgets, mercury cylinders hard at it. Now, this young woman doctor he really admired was as likely to set him puffing into some mouthpiece or tightening a miniature belt round his forefinger instead of–

'Right!' Clare called through the hatch to Mrs Bowen. 'Could you please file these? I'll need them back this afternoon for Farnworth General.'

The middle-aged lady came for the documents, closing the door as she left. Clare caught the policeman's glance and grimaced.

'After the hullabaloo I decided on a complete change,' she explained. 'Mrs Bowen's SRN and a midwife, came back to work after her children left for university. I'm pleased so far.'

Hassall understood. The hatch was slightly ajar. Clare had not bothered to lower her voice so the receptionist could probably hear what was being said, a small office trick of approval. As he cleared his throat to begin, Clare slid the hatch shut.

'Trouble with the diet?'

'This diabetes.' He hesitated while she leant back to appraise him. 'Police Regs make you retire at fifty-five if you're a constable or sergeant. Sixty, if you're an inspector or higher.'

'Big noises, like you, go on five years longer?'

'Well, right.'

'Are you thinking of your pension?'

'It's a thought.'

'Pension being half the pay in your final year at any time after twenty-five years?'

'That's it.' He'd developed a pathetic habit of ahemming to give himself time to think. He did it now. 'I don't want to retire, Doctor. I'm fifty now, thirty years in.'

'Fifty-one,' she amended. 'One year with Type Two diabetes mellitus.'

He shrugged, caught out. 'Fifty-one, then. I stick to the diet.'

'Almost?'

'As near as dammit.' He tried not to sound defensive. 'I don't go over, not much.'

Clare considered. 'Your official medical board review is due in a fortnight, Mr Hassall. Are you anxious? Tell me, and I'll bring it forward to tomorrow, if you'll take any slot.'

'Yes, please.' He let her make a note then said, 'Is medication necessary? I'd like to avoid it if I can.' He had heard tales.

Clare leant back. 'Type Two diabetes is what used to be called the slow-onset version. Once, it was virtually restricted to adults. Now, children are pudgier, and some frankly obese, so they get it too. You're the traditional adult who over-ate and didn't exercise.'

He was slow getting to it. 'I read it can't be reversed. Your pamphlets.'

'True, in medical orthodoxy. Except it's changed somewhat lately.' She was quick to add, 'Don't get

30

your hopes up too much.'

'What do I have to do?'

'Inevitably there's argument. We all want our own beliefs to be true.' That was worth a smile, she thought, because nothing reassures a worried patient like self-deprecation. 'We all know a low-fat diet and plenty of exercise can lessen the likelihood of, say, some heart diseases. Now, many doctors think the same is true of Type Two late-onset diabetes, the kind you have.'

'I'm already on that diet.'

'I haven't finished. The current medical argument is between traditional diets which allow some lean meats, some dairy produce, and fish, on the one hand, and the flat out vegan diet on the other.'

'Vegan? Isn't that what girls do, to get too thin?'

'Not really. Beans and similar legumes, whole grains, selected fruits and tons of vegetables. In a vegan diet, meats of all kinds, dairy produce like milks and cheeses and including eggs, are dropped.'

'God,' Hassall muttered. 'What else is left?'

'It can be rather wearing at first. When you get into the swing, though, it becomes second nature to look at scones, cakes, biscuits, anything with dairy produce in, and simply wean them out. Patients allow themselves to be tricked, by misreading labels on prepared foods. You know those convenience meals sold as complete packs, pop-in-the-oven for twelve minutes? Some tend to spoil the vegan's plans.'

'And what happens?'

'Surveys are promising. Vegan diets claim your

31

own insulin becomes more effective. The final word isn't out yet.'

'And my blood sugar? I hate those tests.' He smiled, trying not to sound in a sulk. 'I can't help thinking I do them wrong.'

'You stick to the way I showed you?'

'Yes.'

'Then you're doing right. Have you brought your charts?'

'Not this time.'

Clare called through to Mrs Bowen and asked her to make an appointment for Mr Hassall, an official police medical.

'Arrange the time as you go, please.' She eyed the policeman. 'Unless you're particularly desperate to retire, Mr Hassall, I think it might be wise to continue working. You seem that sort of person.'

He smiled. 'Me too. Will you take me through this vegan grub later on?'

'Pleasure. It lowers blood glucose in many Type Two patients by a quarter, sometimes by only a tenth or so.'

She explained how the high fat content of meats and dairy produce was thought to reduce the effectiveness of a patient's own insulin. He nodded, his eyes occasionally straying round the surgery, taking in the instruments, the couch with the clean sheets and pillows, the scales and white trays.

'Thanks, doctor,' he said formally as she ended. 'I'll see you later this week? Oh, one thing, Doctor,' he said, far too casually, moving to the door. 'I gather there's a new police doctor in. Know anything about him?'

'Sorry. First I've heard of it, Mr Hassall.'

32

'Right.' Still he did not leave. 'Do you treat that girl in Farnworth General? Fourteen, found on the circular road?'

'On life support, in Intensive Care?'

'They're wanting to, well, take her off it.' He turned his hat by its brim, wanting her opinion. 'Was it you?'

'Was what me?' Clare was reminded how often she had had this discussion before about patients, a policeman asking for information she could not disclose.

'I mean was it you who wanted her life support terminated?'

'You know I won't answer, Mr Hassall.' He knew the rules as well as she.

'I could commandeer the clinical files,' he said, knowing how feeble his threat was.

'Get on with it, then, Mr Hassall.' And she added as he finally turned to go, 'If you're sure you know where they are.'

He halted. 'The thing is, Doctor, I'd like her to stay alive as long as there's a chance of nailing the paedophile that committed the crime.' And into her pause said slowly, 'The predicament's mine, see?'

'The predicament is the patient's, Mr Hassall,' Clare said evenly, 'nobody else's.'

His pause was barely perceptible. He left, sure he had enough to go on with.

For a moment Clare stared unseeing at the door, then checked her booking diary. So far, Mrs Bowen had been meticulous with her entries, and Clare had not yet been misled. She still had consultations to do, two street girls and one dosser, then she would be free to head to the Farnworth General in time for the clinico-pathological conference. Today's subject was the treatment of serious head injuries, to be presented by Dr Bernard Wattisham, a sober-sides but one of her staff favourites.

Her hand hovered over the telephone. She wondered whether to call the agency Bonn worked for, but decided against dialling for an appointment. It would be two whole days before she would see him, an intolerable delay. Her conduct would have been shameful by anyone else, and it was even worse for a professional with clinical responsibilities.

She sighed, thinking of her family. The risk of a visit from her mother lurked constantly in the background, a great worry since Bonn had become part of her life. The danger had increased sharply with the move to Salford from Charlestown, where she had lived in a flat above the surgery. Mother especially was eager to come and see the place, and cast her usual death-ray judgement on every aspect, deploring her wayward daughter's inability to 'get back with Clifford'. She would add, 'Make a proper try at marriage, Clare, instead of just wandering off.' Her perennial grousing litany.

Calling for Mr Hassall's official police medical file, kept separate from his incidental notes, Clare made a brief entry about his request for details of a vegan regime, and began to peruse the notes of the next patients. Hard work helped.

Chapter Six

tad – (Tale, Alibi, Drink) successful completion of a crime

The assassin said to the mirror, 'I'm lethal.'

The reflection seemed to be in no doubt. The killer pondered. How could a reflection be truer than the person whose reflection it was? The killer said, 'I mean it. I know what has to be done.' The next assassination was now essential, no backing out. Decisions made themselves. Anybody with half an education could see that. The killer's own school had been the pits. For a start, there was all that religion. The one benefit was, you got morality. You took a definite stance, like not letting criminals get away with vile things. They had to be stopped. No good thinking criminals might give up and shazaam into honesty. Evil people were going to do evil anyway.

Morality was sensible stuff. Look at that Boston prelate, in America, condoning wholesale sex abuse of Massachusetts children. The entire diocese was virtually bankrupt. Facing catastrophe, he was whisked to the Vatican out of harm's way, 'relocated' as tabloids told it.

Was that justice?

The assassin happened on the next weapon by pure chance. The die was cast, the Rubicon crossed, all those tiresome archaic clichés meaning that someone had actually decided to *do* something at last. The killer had been walking by the canal that day. Like it was God-given. A pleasant day, bees about, weeds along the towpath. The killer had noticed a plant with purple berries, automatically pulled it up and left it for dead among the undergrowth.

A true assassin recognises portents, like from some benevolent deity. You need not accept such an offer, but it was at least a contender. The killer had been seeking a foolproof method for months. Lethality for the deserving, the killer corrected sternly. Nothing stupid, nothing random. That's what murderers did in their ignorance, picking out some innocent child almost by chance from maybe a shopping mall, anywhere they hoped they'd not get caught. The terrible things they did to children were unthinkable, which is why perverts had to die.

The house had a workshop, in the garden for safety. A hobby was a hobby, fair enough. But a risky hobby – fire, possibly an electrical short starting wood shavings smouldering, and the noise from dinky rolling stock and railway tracks – would bring unwelcome attention. Last thing an assassin wanted was complaining neighbours or a visit from the fire brigade.

The best of the scheme was its cover, selling miniature engines and giving the proceeds to infant schools. The government was full of liars, despite their colossal majority after that massive political landslide. Education was always the orphan child of policy.

Spare time had to be measured out as an aliquot,

making diminutive railway scenes, whole trains even, and station platforms for the local model society. Enough to be convincing should anybody come asking what the killer did to while away time.

Most were built from kits, of course. Painting was the killer's real forte. Brushes were superb these days, and acrylic paints were child's play. Quick drying, smooth, and realistic. Children adored them. Collectors now looked out for the killer's minuscule assemblies. The killer never signed them, just put a plain B monogram underneath, no deception. Deception was wrong. No passing the miniature railways bridges off as original work, oh dear no! There was enough dishonesty in the world.

The latest works-in-progress were a scenic backdrop to the Stockton-on-Tees culvert that had taken the killer's fancy some weeks previously in the *Railway Modeller*, and a newly-completed signal box of the LNER railway. Possibly the mid-1950s? Dates were a worry. Terrible to be asked by some enthusiast the construction date of, say, a Salford or Pendleton railway platform and be unable to answer! The killer shivered. Standards, keep up the standards, you wouldn't go far wrong.

One thing, in class, if a child was unable to reply when asked anything, anything at all, the killer always simply smiled and said, 'Oh, don't worry. Things often slip my mind too!' and move on to something else. Teachers could be too harsh. Mr Joachim, next class, subject chemistry and mathematics, was given to bawling his head off at the slightest thing. He'd do better taking his time and easing his way past obstacles. The whole school would be the better for it, and the children would learn so much faster. Education shouldn't be cruel. That's how trouble started.

The next model railway exhibition was in just under three weeks. The killer would have possibly eleven items for Harry Entwistle's stall, not enough to justify the expense of a separate display. Each stand consisted of a trestle or crate up-ended with a beige cloth for stall-holders' wares. Various clubs arranged superb demos across the hall, crowds admiring them and commenting on the authenticity of the constructs. The killer never did anything so ostentatious. Old Harry Entwistle, school helper, his sons now fully grown, helped out, which was how Harry came to know the killer, who had expressed interest in his models, and so it began.

The route to being an assassin?

No, think executioner, not killer. Killers were illegal. They did wrong, being murderers. Their acts were random. They were simply wrong-doers, though the most malevolent kind. An executioner, on the other hand, was a loyal servant of morality. In a way, executions were God's work.

The killer only realised this by accident, once having come across a newspaper blowing about the pavement. It had been natural to pick it up thinking to put it in the litter bin along Albert Street. In remaining daylight – it had been getting on for dusk – a headline caught the eye: *THE WORK OF GOD*. The article concerned an executioner in the Middle East.

Senseless to go about wanting signs. Only

mentally sick people did that. Omens were for the imagination alone. Figments, jokes, or fervid wishes were for inadequate personalities unable to cope. Nothing wrong with people who worked in dead-end jobs, of course, and nothing against people who found solace in mysticism. Whatever turned them on, as long as their weird pursuits didn't harm others.

The article, though.

This Middle Eastern man was forty-odd. He slept well of a night, and used either a sword or gun to kill his victims. Except, the killer immediately thought, were they victims as such? Weren't they simply people who had *created* victims of innocents? The man's condemned prisoners were society's outcasts, who had forfeited the right to decency. Indeed, the condemned had turned a boring world of normality into an evil maelstrom, thinking evil people get away with anything.

No. God's work was perhaps a bit teleological, yet there was a respectable point here. That foreign executioner was at peace. He said so, and blithely reported to the newspaper columnist how he said prayers with the prisoners and gave them the choice of being executed with a gun or sword. Was there some religious basis for the sword method in some religious text? In other circumstances it might have been worthwhile looking it up. Countries with strong religious leanings and mores saw their executioners as respectable heroes, it seemed.

In the western world, liberalism had spread to mean absolutely anything goes, whatever you could get away with. You had the right to escape the consequences of your own actions. However mindless you were, you could claim you were depressed, scarred by anything that seemed an excuse, and you were given counselling, chats with social workers until the cows came home, and monetary support until you were sufficiently bored to try some other evil.

The killer had the right logic. Somebody *had* to take the responsibility. To put it another way, the necessary sanction. And what was the sanction? The truth stared any right-thinking person in the face: execution. The newspaper was taken next day to the city council rubbish tip.

Now, the killer was almost ready. The lethal dart was almost perfect. The killer had made it, and very beautiful it was. The poison was perfect, had to be. The information was available and succinct. Public libraries were a godsend, full of information. They did not ask why you wanted details.

The garden shed was a perfect place to work, and the hobby a perfect cover. Naturally, the killer had gravitated to constructing scenes, because not everyone had a natural skill in working with miniature lathes and special steels such as, say, a retired engineer like Harry Entwistle possessed. No, it was simpler to go for railway embankments with decorative foliage, miniature gardens along platforms, trees and figurines. The killer really loved making those. It showed true artistry, like the poisoned missiles.

Sometimes, at model engineering exhibitions it was really satisfying having coffee while crowds went from stall to display, tableaux to layouts, and relishing the comments people made. Folk

40

often exclaimed aloud, and of course the models always sold. Harry Entwistle would bring the money over. The killer would say, 'Oh, thanks, Mr Entwistle. More for the children's hospice!' or perhaps, 'Towards the next bit of equipment for St Alban's Infants,' or some such.

Others would often add to the money, with, 'Oh, yes, of course, you collect for the babies' school. Here, let's chip in.' The killer would decline, and never take as much as a farthing, adding with a smile, 'It wouldn't be right. They would assume I was making a bigger donation that I actually was.' And quickly the killer would then deflect the interest by some remark like, 'What about the Britannia engine? Do you think the scenery quite right...?' and so on.

The façade, behind which the killer would operate and perform the execution, was in place. The means were on hand, completed and lethal. The dart was perfect as any skilled miniaturist could make it. The poison was prepared and, the killer trusted, sufficiently potent to result in death in short order for the average seventy-kilogram standard male pervert.

The question now was who.

The killer had taken to having a daily newspaper delivered, and perused the columns at home of an evening. Making selections was not easy.

The choice seemed endless, except one perv seemed to be asking to be the next candidate. Lawyers were appealing for him to be released on some legal technicality, oldest trick in the lawyers' books. And let's face it, lawyers were as guilty as the evil perverts they defended.

Chapter Seven

blood fifteen – sexual murder of the under-age

'Foreign,' Rack said as Bonn stepped into the hotel foyer.

Bonn said nothing. He strolled, almost as if about to ask for tea. It drove Rack wild.

'She's foreign,' he repeated. 'The bloke won't be around. He's Latin, see? Latins make sure they're somewhere else when you do their missus.'

'Language, please, Rack.'

'What'd I say?' Rack asked indignantly.

Privately, he was sure Bonn was going mental. You couldn't say a word without Bonn telling him to say something different. Silence was Bonn's problem. All those years in that crappy seminary had done Bonn's head in. Learning did your head in, as Rack had found at his own school.

'Top suite, Angelica Five-Five-Oh. I put Rooky on the landing just in case.'

'In case.' Bonn pressed the button. Gears creaked and illuminated pointer flickered.

'In case he's murderous, mate.'

'Very well.'

The previous month they'd had such an instance. Den, a goer from Wigan, had been attacked as he'd serviced a visiting Baltic lady at the Time and Scythe. The incident still smarted, because Rack had trusted Den to have the sense to check the car park himself. But once a dickster, always a thickster, meaning a thick-headed dickster, Bonn excepted of course. The woman's husband came at Den with a sort of machette. Rack had had to deck him, break a few sticks and get him to hospital.

The way Rack saw things, blokes shouldn't go hiring other blokes to shag their women as a treat, then go berserk in car parks waving them bent foreign sword things. It wasn't respectable. The man had several operations in that big Liverpool bone hospital, serve the mad bastard right. Rack had made the injured man pay quad what the Pleases Agency, Inc., charged. He'd told Martina to keep the man's credit and debit cards and run them dry, but she had accountants and who knew what they'd done?

'Like last month,' Rack said, still narked as the lift began its ascent. 'Frigging Baltic. Latins don't think straight. Know why? It's the way their hair grows.'

'Excuse me, Rack.' Bonn paused. 'I wonder if the Baltic is a Latin region.'

Rack stared. The Baltics not Latin? Who gave a fuck?

'Right,' he said, keeping calm. 'He's still in dock. I reckon he'll lose a leg. If doctors keep you in hospital more than four weeks, they take your legs off. Know why? Air conditioning.'

'Rack,' Bonn said quietly, and Rack shut up.

Rack was only going to tell Bonn he had fifteen minutes before this woman Angelica was due, but subsided in a sulk. One day, he'd let Bonn do a stand on his own, see how he liked the risk. Maybe

43

the woman would start screaming blue murder, yelling she didn't want fucking, only talk and tea with Peak Frean biscuits and a slice of a Dundee. She might howl there was some young maniac fornicating in her hotel bedroom, and bring police and riot squads when it should just be a goer doing his stand and the bird going home well shagged. Except the thought of Bonn in trouble was mind-bending. Martina would see that heads rolled, mostly Rack's. She could do it. Rack would go to the wall for letting Bonn down. As if anybody would. He'd be in there at the finish scrapping for Bonn because that's what meeting Bonn made you do.

Glancing at Bonn's calm features, he tried to work out what was in that mind of his, but you couldn't. One of the girls in Grellie's Green lot, other side of Victoria Square, paid a photographer to snap Bonn for pin-up pictures to enlarge and stick to her wall. He'd heard it from Womp who touted fake first-night tickets – Rack got Martina's syndicate fifteen per cent, because fair's fair – and had given the girl a straightener. She was a nice Wolverhampton lass, trace of goojer in her with big brown eyes. Martina had fined her a whole fortnight's money, which most of the girls thought a bit thick and caused Grellie a load of grief for two nights until she'd threatened to fine the whole Green string a day's full gelt. The other three colours went smug about it, and started sniping at the Green streeters until Rack put a stop to it. He hated that bitch stuff. Things should run smooth. It had happened once before when two Red working girls started buying Bonn pullovers...

'Eh?' he said, for Bonn had said something.

'Her husband is a gambler,' Bonn said again.

Rack was amazed. 'How'd you know that?'

'Angelica was Angelica Five-Four-Nine, same date of last month. Previously, Angelica Five-Four-Eight on the equivalent date before that.'

Rack thought hard. He didn't know numbers or words, and couldn't write or read, so he was always a lap behind until he made people put the pedal down and bring him more news. He still should have spotted it because it was his job, being the head stander for the whole syndicate.

'You will tell me if that is correct, please.'

'Right, mate.'

'The same suite, same hotel.' Bonn added as the lift gates slid back, 'It's possibly the poker heats.'

'Right.' Rack pretended he knew all the time, stepping out to suss the corridor. 'I wondered if you'd spot it.'

'I am tardy in street matters, Rack. I envy you your perception.'

'No problem.'

Rack gave a nod, seeing Rooky flit silently into the service door so it was safe to let Bonn walk down the corridor and keep the appointment. Bonn reached the end suite and opened the door with Rack's the electronic slice.

The poker heats were eliminators for the World Series, the first six heats on the same date of each month. Knock-out competitions left contenders who would go to the world championships proper, in USA. The ante was enough for an average new motor, which wasn't much as money went. Rack had theories about gamblers but nobody would

45

listen, gamblers especially being dim about advice even from a genius with a brilliant brain like he was.

Rack paced the corridor listening at every door. He sussed the plant stands for electronics using the new Atlanta gadgets – he'd had to pay extra for two batteries, and it still rankled – and checked that Rooky had disabled the fire alarm at the corridor intersection. Done, he leant against the wall thinking about his Mama, an angry church-going saint who dreamt of going back to Sicily, until a lift crashed distantly and began its upwards journey. He eeled silently to the service stairs. Rooky would have belied him had there been any strife as the lady arrived. It looked like being normal. Angelica Five-Five-Oh would get her money's worth. Rack wondered if her husband, the Latin gambler, would be as lucky.

Angelica entered in a flurry of gift-wrapped boxes and a froth of ribbons. Her scent enveloped Bonn as he stood to welcome her. She advanced, arms outstretched and scattering her shopping like largesse. She was all colours, her scarlet skirted coat a cascade and her immense powder-blue capelone hat flapping as if in some secret gale. She hugged him, her cheek pressed to his, and crying, 'Mind my lipstick, darling! It took an imbecilic girl a *whole hour*, and still I had to go somewhere else! How are you, darling? Pierre is at his cards. We had masses said for his success, can you imagine?'

And so on. Bonn listened with grave attention, helping her to stack her packages in two separate tiers according to her directions then taking her

46

coat. He was often astonished by the multitude of colours, quite like emotional rainbows, women displayed as they settled down. He wondered if Angelica's entry was some kind of performance planned on the way in.

'...my friend Beatrice who is one of those embassy people, y'know, darling?' She grimaced, asking Bonn for a dry vermouth and flounced down on the couch, whisking her feet up beside her with the impossible grace of women. 'I'm beginning to hate – *hate* – Beatrice. Her husband thinks nothing but documents, treaties, figures for the sale of coffee and cotton and... Dry, darling. Did I say?'

Her eyelashes projected so far Bonn was almost mesmerised. He stuttered, 'I'm afraid I'm not quite certain, ah, that is, not really.'

'Don't you, darling?' She held his eyes, looking up at him and smiling. 'You know so little. Then gin and tonic, with ice.'

He coloured slightly and went to pour the drink, which took some time while she rabbited on about friends among visiting trade legations. There was a large selection of gins. One was blue, even, or was that just the bottle? He couldn't tell. He poured a little away, and it came out colourless just like the other London gins. He felt despair. Which was correct, or did it matter?

'Have you succeeded, darling?' She was mischievously amused when he returned with her drink and sat beside her. 'Shall we try?'

She took the glass and touched it to his lips. He turned aside. 'No, thank you, Angelica.'

'You didn't last time, darling. Nor the time before. Why?'

47

'I drink little.'

'When you are not ... working? Is that it? No drinking while you are...?'

'I was never used to it.' Bonn wondered how to sound firmer, dominant. He might ask Posser, if Martina's dad was well enough after supper, but to that sick old man everything seemed self-explanatory, as the world also was even to Rack with his demented theories.

'Is that what you call it, darling, working?'

'Whatever the lady wishes.'

She sat sideways. His earlier thought, that perhaps her entrance and postures were planned, was unkind, and he mentally apologised. To harbour even fleeting suspicions was a form of treachery. Women had the right to be taken as they wished to be seen, and not with suspicion. Bonn was starting to wonder if he had a carping mind. He would have to reason through this difficulty in a quiet moment, and see where blame lay. Guilt was a corollary. How to apologise, except by doing her bidding?

'Pierre spends a fortune on mystics.' She was into sudden bitterness. He listened, astonished. Why bitter, if her husband's prowess at some card game, plus his workaday efforts, gave her everything she wished? 'Do you know how much he spends on his lunatic cards? Enough *in one month* to buy a house in Los Angeles! Can you imagine?'

Another problem. Bonn sat in mystified silence. How did one reply to that? Was it rhetorical? Did it need some general agreement, of the kind he worked through in the seminary, or was one supposed to counter it with a different proposition?

48

And who exactly was Pierre? Presumably the husband, hard at his poker somewhere. Bonn's tutor in his final year at the seminary – before it closed, that was – Father Thom, insisted that all questions required answers, spoken or not. It was a moral duty imposed by the very fact of listening. Why else had God given us speech? Once uttered, even a badly formulated question became the listener's responsibility. The hearer had to compose his very best possible reply. If Father Thom spoke the truth, how on earth did one work out a response? Did one have to know all about the husband to reply? Bonn could, yes, imagine a man spending enough to buy a house in America on something so pointless as gambling. Even during his short time in the street, he had seen truly large sums wagered on cards, roulette, even horses. The apparent unconcern of regular gamblers about the money they lost was a perennial surprise to him. Sooner or later they came back, evidently with the purpose of losing still more. That part he could not quite 'imagine', as this Angelica asked. Honesty took hold.

'Yes,' he said with great diffidence.

She drew away the better to inspect him. He saw her surprise, and guessed that she usually wore spectacles or contact lenses. Was that too unkind? Thoughts were hard today.

'You're a gambler?' She sounded thrilled. A smile lit her features.

'No.'

'Then how do you know.

'They all appear the same.'

Was that true, though? He remembered a

49

woman who sat at a slot machine tapping the spin button, the orange numbers clicking away her tokens bought from the cashier. It was in one of Martina's casinos behind the Rum Romeo where the homosexuals assembled after nine o'clock of an evening. Bonn had passed that way three hours later, after having visited an Argentinian lady in the Royal and Grand Hotel near London Road mainline railway station. The fruit-machine lady had still been there, spending one token at a time, dabbing a finger on the illuminated rectangle, and losing, losing. She had seemed merely a woman loyally at her post, dedicated to a task.

'Come.' Angelica finished the glass and held out her hands to be raised. 'Tell me more afterwards.' She unfolded with the woman's singular grace, smoothly as if elegance was beyond conscious thought. Men could not do that, he'd often noticed. Men stood in a series of marionette processes, sections jerking upright in sequence as if on pulled strings. A woman rose with fluidity, uniquely whole.

'You stare at me. Why?'

'You are beautiful,' he said frankly after a moment. 'The way you stand up. We can't do it. We come without grace.'

'What does this mean?'

'I can't say it in any other way.'

She stood facing him, so close he had to step back to avoid falling backwards onto the couch.

'I like that. I remember before. You always look at me.'

'I apologise if I give offence.'

'I like it.' She went past him, drawing him after.

50

'Come and find something else I like.'

For a brief instant he felt a flicker of disapproval. Crudities disconcerted him, the more flagrant worst of all. Girls who spilled from the night boozers along Liverpool Road, shrieking obscenities and sometimes actually fighting, in particular caused this feeling, almost as if he were responsible. Often he crossed over the road to get on. But pleasing this lady was his appointed task. Had he not wished to be employed in this fashion, as a goer, he ought to have refused when Posser invited him to join the Pleases Agency. He was committed.

'Yes, Angelica.'

'Darling,' she commanded, pausing with a frown. 'Say darling.'

'Darling,' he said.

Chapter Eight

tanker – one who hires out to assault another

Hassall watched Rack cross Victoria Square. He remained on the bench near Bradshawgate among the traffic fumes. Time enough to do Dr Clare's prescribed two-mile trudge, but it was easier to sit. Traffic was getting out of hand, carouselling round in clockwise madness. HGVs should be banned, like in New York, the city council just too damned idle to pull their fingers out.

From the street behind him emerged an elderly

51

man – well, Hassall thought, peeved, not exactly as old as all that, but still getting on. The man walked with a stick, pausing every few yards to get his breath. Posser still hard at it, then, the policeman thought with gratification. Long the boss of the Syndicate, Posser was easier to tolerate than challenge. Hassall's grandma's philosophy was to leave in one piece things that would shatter if tinkered with. OK, so Posser's daughter Martina, lovely and lame, hadn't quite the same firm hand on the tiller as Posser used to have in his day, but at least she was an identifiable boss. That showy git Rack was her glove bloke, the yob who kept her empire in order.

The police still couldn't quite work out the relationship between the two, barmy youth and beautiful lass. Spider and fly? Hardly. Crime maven and humble serf? Most unlikely, for Hassall had had Martina's syndicate investigated by Customs and Excise audit teams, and the even idler Inland Revenue Tax mob at Lytham-St-Ann's. Nothing. Martina was St Cecilia as far as they were concerned, for she delivered her taxes on the nail, never a day late and every groat accounted for. No, more like a small business, say the manageress of a toffee shop and her assistant. That was Martina's façade, though he was sure the police knew less about some local deaths than Martina did. Hassall's way was to keep crime within bounds, sort of. New police graduates occasionally upset the handcart, going through the city like a dose of salts, but they came and went. He had no illusions. Best way to be.

Several young stringers were out, some garish,

some prim, all hawkish of eye and focussed on passing cars. It was time Hassall got a new count of Grellie's street walkers in the Square, keep a check for sanity's sake.

He settled back. Posser raised a hand to a passing saloon motor. The car turned left into the traffic. It would be Posser's daughter Martina, heading to her office behind the car park. Hassall sighed with a sense of peace at the normality. He wondered where Rack was, what that crazy idiot was up to on a nice day like this.

Two tankers sat in the Butty Bar.

By habit and instinct they chose a grotty caff, and sat at its grubbiest table. Both were heavily built, and spoke with pronounced Leeds accents, crew-cuts their trade mark and leather jackets and frayed jeans their uniform. Tankers hired themselves out to chastise, on the orders of whoever rented their services to correct injury. They spoke to their client, the wallet who sat opposite, almost as roughly dressed as they were.

'Money, innit?' one said. He wore pure gold earrings. Neither of the tankers had a full set of teeth. Their features looked corrugated.

'Yes.'

'How much?' Into the silence, the stockier tanker said, 'That decides how much we charge, see?'

'A lot.'

'What we mean is,' Earrings explained patiently, seeing they'd drawn a real thicko, 'if you want us to damage the mark to the tune of, say, the cost of a whole house, it'd cost you a good wadge. If it's only that somebody keeps on nicking your TV or

53

letting your tyres down every night and you want them warned off, then it'd be cheap, get it?'

'I want somebody topped.'

The two tankers exchanged glances. Earrings cleared his throat. Nobody was near enough to hear, and the Victoria Square traffic was noisy enough.

'Topped? As in...?'

'Right,' said the wallet. 'He is in prison, and will be released soon. I want him done before he gets out. Once he's released it'll be so much harder, you see.'

'Why?' They were surprised. 'Outside is easier.'

'I haven't the resources to have somebody followed.'

'If you haven't the bunce, how come you're asking us to do it?'

'We need paying, see,' the older one said. He kept his eyes on the tattoos on his forearms as if figuring out redesign work.

'I know that. Only, I heard having somebody killed in prison is quite difficult.'

'True.'

'He's a paedophile.'

'The one we keep hearing about in the news?'

'Yes. He'll be released on some legal technicality.'

'The lads inside might do it for nothing, given half a chance.'

'Then I want them to get that half-chance. I'll pay. I just want you to see it gets done. If they're going to top him anyway, where's the problem?'

Earrings sighed. He heard somebody come in, a noisy young sod shouting and joking, pretending

54

to sing some music-hall song with gestures, various blokes calling and clapping as he waltzed among the tables, the counter girls laughing.

Earrings said, 'The problem is, we leave the nick to others. We just steer clear. Prisons have their own systems, mostly drug-pay. We're strictly street tanking, see?'

'You mean you won't do it?'

'Can't, more like,' Tattoo said.

'Is that it? You'll let him to come out and do anything he likes to any child he can grab hold of?'

'No good going on at us.' Earrings hated this side of things, when a wallet meant well but had come to the wrong people. 'We do an honest job. We stop half the frigging felons from robbing everybody blind. That's why streets aren't worse.'

'That's a fact,' Tattoo said, looking across at the noisy newcomer, now miming some actor. 'Tell us if some neighbour's kids torch your pets or loot your house, we'll damage them on a scale of charges. Their nuisance stops, and you sleep sound. That's it.'

'Can't do anything about some git inside, though.'

'Sorry.' Earrings waited. 'Got the money?'

The wallet stared. 'I thought you said–'

'Fee for coming. Like lawyers, we charge expenses for interview, see.'

Earrings made sure nobody was watching, and spread his fingers. 'That's each. We always do the first talk together. It costs.'

'Right,' the wallet said. 'I can't pay you here, can I?'

'The bus station in the Square. Drop a news-

55

paper with it in.'

'Right. I'm very disappointed. It would be so beneficial to society.'

'We're sorry too. Ta for asking.'

They waited until after the wallet had gone into Mealhouse Lane and the door pinged shut, then rose and left.

Rack was interested, but only mildly. The first person to leave was evidently the wallet. He knew Leeds tankers when he saw them, stood out a mile. His antics hadn't stopped him from watching them in the steamy mirrors.

'Your coffee, Rack. How's Bonn?'

Kizzy was the pretty one, but she narked Rack by forever asking after Bonn. The Square needed some fucking newspaper, like when a king is poorly, Bonn Is Well Today in its headline, shut the fucking world up.

'Stop asking, you stupid cow.'

Kizzy went laughing. Rack pulled out his cell phone.

'What?' Grellie sounded well narked.

'Two tankers, one covered in tattoos, bus station. Talked in the Butty Bar. Have a gander, OK?'

The phone went dead. He felt double choked. Grellie, in another of her sodding moods? Maybe it was time he straightened her, like he had to sometimes straighten the street girls, keep things civilised.

Rack crossed the Butty Bar to where Elfon was doing his music. Elfon was writing a symphony, always was, only you'd to say composing because it was rotten tunes nobody'd ever want. The old man was thin, stubbly chin, and pretended he was blind to cadge from passengers off the commuter trains, London Road Station, except when he was having his tea and waffles. He was about ninety. Fat George was running a book, odds thirteen to eight Elfon never finished his daft music. Rack sat, kneed the old man.

'Elfon. Get over to the bus depot. See where them two tankers go.'

The composer found his white stick, stuffed his grubby papers into his manky duffle bag, and left arranging his sun specs. Rack admired Elfon. He had a really good blind man's walk once he got among people, really convincing, his battered cup dangling and his card asking a coin for a blind man who was a war hero. Rack liked a pro. He finished Elfon's waffles and drank his tea.

He wished he could count proper, like he saw threadbare blokes doing the football pools and horses in the far corner. It would save having the girl Eleanor at the Palais Rocco to do his sums before he saw the money safe to Martina. Everybody else had life easy, except for him. Life was a pig.

Three people to see today, before he could stop for a pint at the Volunteer and have a dinnertime talk with Bonn. One concern was drugs, the second importing more tarts for the working house in Bradshawgate, Posser's special project. The brothel was well short, needing another six bints. The cost would be crippling. Martina would probably go up the wall and put her blue-eyed stare in your skull for fucking days. The third problem was some cretin who fancied himself for a goer. Word had passed from some lass on the

Red string who had a degree from Manchester University, the bloke her relative. Rack would concoct a pack of lies and chuck him out. The trouble was, once a yobbo heard blokes actually got paid a fortune to serve women, they like went sort of mad. They only saw the cream, never the job. Give them half a minute facing one of Bonn's terrible silences or Martina's baby blues, they'd soon get life's fucking worst nightmares.

It was a hard frigging life, that's what life was.

Chapter Nine

key – a goer who controls a group of goers, usually not more than three in number

Bonn had his evening meal at Posser's home later than usual. The housekeeper Mrs Houchin kept it back so he was saved the worry. He had personal reservations about wandering the city centre during the dark hours, though he would be sacrosanct if he went about. An air of subdued violence was everywhere after nine, pubs and clubs spilling drunks onto the pavements, girls shrieking, the usual hullabaloo.

He read while he ate alone. He could hear Martina and Posser talking in the living room, the faint noise of a television, and occasional wheezing from the old man. Bonn went upstairs afterwards to replace his book, *The History of the Templar Knights.* So sad, everyone misunderstanding everyone else through centuries, the constant feature of mankind.

Collecting himself, he went down to join Martina and Posser, knocking politely as he entered.

'Good to see you, son.' Posser was already using his inhaler. Martina was sitting on the carpet, legs curled beneath and her blonde hair shining in the firelight.

'Good evening.' Bonn positioned himself facing the old man, and smiled tentatively at Martina.

She was probably the bonniest girl in the whole city. Though often saddened by some of her decisions, he was never surprised. Rack was her lieutenant, in control of the Pleases Agency syndicate. The violent young eccentric saw her as the ideal ruler now Posser himself was too much of a casualty.

'Tell us where we're going wrong, Bonn.' Posser gave him an outrageous wink, chuckling himself into a fit of coughing.

'Can I get you anything?'

Posser shook his head, sucking on his inhaler.

'Dad's asking about new girls.'

Martina had ice in her voice tonight, and barely gave him a glance. She had changed into a light floral house coat, the father and daughter making a comforting picture against the dark oak panels. Posser was addicted to his tall rocking chair.

'We're short,' Posser rasped. 'Grellie's working out numbers. She'll get them over tomorrow.'

'I wonder if she can suggest a legitimate means,' Bonn said. Comment required effort. He paused, making certain Martina wasn't going to speak first.

'What's your question?' Martina snapped.

Bonn reddened. Questions were of two mutually exclusive kinds. One was the blunt interrogation, an affront, to him almost verbal abuse however gentle the format. Direct questions felt unpardonable. The second kind was an offer of debate, the kind he had been raised to see as common sense, and invitation to analysis. The world's troubles, he often thought, were attributable to one type of question being mistaken for the other.

'I was not asking, Martina,' he said. Asking something outright was an admission of failure. How much better, to respond by a meek offer. If only people would listen. He mentally apologised to the beautiful girl for that critical thought. If she took umbrage, his phraseology caused it.

'Leave the lad alone, Martina,' Posser said in his gravelly voice. 'Thing is, Bonn, we need more girls. Grellie's going frantic, and next door's lot are all but done for, the rate they have to slog.'

Next door was the brothel, consisting of terraced houses conjoined into one functional working house. Nobody in the girl trade used the terms brothel or prostitute. A brothel instead was a working house, a prostitute a working girl. Grellie had drawn blood insisting on that. The house, functional six months, was roaringly successful.

'Rack guesses she'll ask for six more,' Martina said.

'Think that'll be enough, son?'

Both looked at Bonn. He said nothing. No, that was wrong; he failed to answer, silence as his response. This was a constant error. He wondered if his reticence was the reason the street

60

girls seemed to seek him out, deliberately make a point of finding him in the Volunteer, sometimes simply standing there half-smiling, in quest of something he failed to understand. They found a deal of comfort in the spoken word, the very means of contact he found a degrading risk. Conversations made him feel thrust onto a stage before a demanding audience, each of whom had just asked some unheard yet vital question.

'Well?' Martina demanded, closing on fury, her habit when he proved useless.

Posser made a placatory gesture. The old man almost understood, Bonn imagined. As it was, Bonn could not respond enough. He looked at the carpet, a pseudo-Persian of reds, ochres, blues, browns any woman would scream at. Posser had inherited it from the first lady he had taken money to sleep with, when he had begun the Pleases Agency so long ago. Posser often told the tale.

'Rack will say when he comes.' And Posser added when Bonn lifted his head to look, 'He'll be along presently.'

'There are new applicants for goer,' Martina told Bonn. 'I want you to see them, with Den and myself.'

Posser ahemed, shrewd. 'Why Den?'

Bonn returned to the carpet, that odd onion shape the Persians seemed to love. Lotus, was it? Some leaf thing in symbolism of regrowth? Den was a goer, lately rumoured to be Martina's lover. Bonn had once or twice – thirteen, in truth – made love with the beautiful girl. Easy, for he lived in the very top room above her flat. Posser lived along the second-floor corridor in the same Victorian dwelling, so many more rooms than the exterior might suggest. Martina should not be enquired into, not even to explain her precise needling. Posser must have heard the same rumours.

'I'd like *him* for an opinion.' Meaning Bonn offered none.

'What about the rest?' Posser persisted.

'Too many irons in the fire, the lot of them.' Martina raised her eyes to Bonn.

'The girl,' Bonn said into prolonged quiet.

'A new girl?' Posser asked. 'Who?'

'Thought we'd cleared all that up.' Martina was ready for combat. Bonn wondered whether he had a right to continue, then made a swift plan to raise the terrible subject.

'The sick girl.'

'The one in hospital?'

'Is she one of ours? I haven't heard.'

The old man looked from one to the other, suspecting he was being talked out of events. It happened to old lions, Bonn found in desperate analogy, testiness setting their hackles and bringing them back to a war zone they'd last experienced when young.

'A child. I believe it was in the newspapers, Posser.'

'D'you spend your time gossiping?'

'Martina,' Posser said.

Bonn felt his face colour. The carpet seemed not to have changed. He assumed Persians dyes had developed from their local plants, perhaps with earth colours? He could look it up.

To gossip, though. The thought engaged him even as Posser began to speak about the need to keep the herds full, the old man's phrase. (Odd that his daughter, so given to belligerence often over details Bonn missed, never rounded on Posser for his derogatory terms.) Gossip seemed to be so gratifying to many; men in pubs, women on buses, students from the Arts and Design College. He assumed that relaxation pleased most people. How did one go about it, though? He had seen strangers, even, start casual arguments leading to laughter over virtually no points of view.

He abandoned the notion. Perhaps there would be relaxation in Paradise, always assuming. Someone had spoken. He pulled himself back.

'Rack must suss out a single batch,' Posser repeated, waiting for Bonn.

'Batch,' Bonn managed after a lull so prolonged Martina began to stir irritably.

'From one source, a shipment.' She almost spat the words.

'It would be easiest, Bonn.'

The doorbell rang and Mrs Houchin went to answer. Words cascaded down Bonn's mind: easiest for who, doing what, who and where lay these sources, was six a finite batch of girls, and who decided what to do if there came one too many, would the girl trade be improved or worsened. He resisted the temptation to bring in the money question. That would be self-indulgence, at the expense of the shipped girls. Posser's scheme must be nullified.

They heard Rack's gusto entrance, Mrs Houchin squealing and Rack bawling, 'Put me down! You're nothing but an animal! I'll report you for mauling visitors!' with the housekeeper

63

laughing and flustered as she showed Rack in.

'Time you got rid of that woman,' Rack called. 'She always tries it on. Next time, Posser, I swear it's resignation time, OK?' He turned and bawled into the hallway, 'Did you hear that, missus?' and came in grinning.

Immediately he began speaking in his normal voice, plumping himself down on the settee and kicking off his shoes.

'Thing is, they're bringing in Macedonia bints. They got loads. Some's broken in, Italy way, some's not. Way I sees it, we pay on the nail so we decide, OK? Hungarians are best cheapos. They got most of every kind uv tarts, and will deliver where we tell. The Germans mostly drying up, France is useless except for older girls who won't do for us. Like, some of them are twenty-five, twenty-six, what's the point of them?' He glared round indignantly as if outraged at some con trick.

'Cross Channel girls are all North Africans, Rack?'

'Too many, Posser. Anyhow, everybody's sick up to here with them. We got enough North Africans to fill a sack. I say buy Balkans.'

'Brazil?' Posser said.

Rack grinned. 'You been reading bad mags, you naughty old devil, aincher, guy?' Rack's Cockney accent tended to surface under the impulse of anger or humour. 'How you say it, them *meninas?*'

Posser took to his inhaler for a few wheezes and rested a moment. 'The contact people are that lot in Braganza, in Portugal somewhere.'

'Traz-oz-Montez,' Rack said unexpectedly but with a certain pride. 'Askey took word from a courier, dunno who.'

Posser nodded. He knew Rack kept his sources to himself. It was all right with Posser, who had originated this selfsame enquiry over a new intake three days earlier, and anyway had learned Rack's news the previous day. Askey's newsagent's shop served the city as courier station, paying the syndicate fifteen per cent of gross for the privilege, though Rack thought it too cheap. Bikers lounging about waiting for swift dash across the city with hot documents ought to pay through the nose.

'I heard they come through Paris from Brazil,' Martina said.

'Paris doesn't mind, is what I heard. That right, Rack?'

'Always Paris,' Rack said, pleased to be the one who mattered. He felt like the Sundance Kid. He'd get one of them hats tomorrow from Fair Wear or Spats-N-Hats, maybe visit the phoney Western rancho out near Wigan where they had a street complete with saloons and horses along hitching rails. You could get six-guns and holsters for shoot-outs while they filmed you from a covered wagon. It would make for a great Christmas present to Grellie's teams of street girls, who'd love to see him on video, him being naturally photogenic. The stringers deserved a treat like that.

'How do they stay?' Martina asked.

'Come in on some tourist visa,' Rack said. 'When time's up, flit to Spain somewhere or go back to this Traz dump. Must be hell of a place, I reckon big as Manchester.'

Bonn gently cleared his throat. Martina ignored

him and returned to her question.

'But how? Money? Permission? The lizards?'

Lizards were traffickers who brokered the deals to supply children, women, or even migrant workers to particular industries. All Europe was a porous compound where wages and illegitimate money provided justification for any population movement.

'I'd sort all that.'

'Are you sure you can?' Only Martina would dare to ask such a thing directly from Rack. Only key-of-the-door in age, Rack still had done more straighteners in Posser's service than anyone except the old man himself.

'Easy-peasy, boss,' Rack said, swallowing his annoyance only because Martina was a bird and they hadn't much of a brain. You had to make allowances for them, like when some kid with a gammy leg tried to get up the station steps and you had to make some passerby give it a lift. Rack was kind, so thoughts like this came natural instead of to other bleeders who'd take no notice. There were too many rotten bastards about, Rack believed. Everybody should be like him.

'Do they come sight unseen? We take them on trust?'

'Leave it out, boss.' Rack was disgusted. 'Think I'd be that dumb?'

'How if we managed with locals instead?'

'See, I don't mind,' Rack said, back on the rails now Martina was at last being sensible, leaving it up to him. 'As long as Grellie doesn't give a tinker's toss.'

'Rack,' Bonn said. 'Please.'

Rack stared from face to face, wondering Christ's fucking sake, what now? He struggled to recall the words he'd used, then thought back to tinker's toss. Is that what Bonn meant? He fought to keep explosions within.

He said, 'Sorry. I meant, er...' Jesus Aitch. What the fuck would do instead? As long as Grellie doesn't give a gob in a mob? Fart in a gale? What? He felt sure tinker's toss was in the fucking bible.

'It is not up to Grellie,' Martina said, her voice sleet. Now Rack's spirits really did plunge, because Grellie and Martina should sort out their differences once and for all. Their difference was only Bonn, and which one of the two got him sticking her regular. It didn't take a brain surgeon to work that out. He saw he'd have to put it straight to Bonn, move the silent bugger to jamming one of them then everybody could cool it.

'Right, boss,' he said. 'Want her boned?'

Dog-and-bone, phone in Cockney rhyming slang.

'Keep off phones,' Posser ordered, conscious of these fireside ripples. 'Let's sleep on it. I'm allowed a sherry about now. No smokes,' he added for Martina's sake, who gave a satisfied nod.

Bonn rose to bring the drinks trolley, to save Martina, and, frowning with concentration, gave Posser his glass of Montilla before asking if the girl would like a glass of wine.

'Red.'

Only one bottle on offer, so everything had been planned to come out like this. He took it to her. Rack meanwhile filled a pint glass from bottled beers. Bonn had mineral water. Nobody suggested a toast. Rack said, 'Cheers.'

'I hear there are enough locals,' Martina told Posser, which probably concluded the matter. 'We can rely on those. Grellie,' she said, chill returning to her voice with the name, 'must find out how soon she can bring them in.'

'Their ages might be more reliable if they are indigenous,' Bonn said mildly.

'That goes without saying,' Martina said, though it didn't.

Rack looked at her wondering if he should chance his arm. He'd argued before that it wasn't wrong to forget they had a couple of fifteeners or fourteeners in a string, bring in more custom. Bonn had gone quiet, and Martina flared up which made Posser tell them all no, no under-agers. Pleases Agency working girls were legal age, and that was that.

Bonn said nothing more. Posser began to speak about the finance of the Rum Romeo, the Palais Rocco and the casino, and the advisability of allowing another bar to be opened in the Shot Pot snooker hall in Settle Street. Rack instantly weighed in with a theory, weather stopping Salford snooker lads from winning, and they settled for that. Bonn felt exhausted. They had ignored the problem of the dying girl in hospital. It hung in the air as the conversations finally petered out.

Chapter Ten

larper – (Live Action Role Player) one who dresses up as a fictional character

The Palais Rocco had seen better days. To believe the local rags, it would soon be 'restored to its former glory', with rumours of millions being spent. Like the dancehall itself, all was pretence. Hassall sat to watch the tea dancing from the end balcony. Serious couples, in ordinary clothes for their practice, stood in seeming fright while the dance teacher bullied them. Hassall had never danced, though his missus had once earned a putty medal for it. Too late to begin now.

'Listen, tout le monde,' Hiplips carolled, spinning in his tight jump suit so the sequined collar and bertha glittered. 'I'll say it once, ferstayhenssee?'

He paused dramatically. The couples waited, ready to start.

'The answer, O riff-raff, is a mighty Yes, Hiplips. What is it?'

'Yes, Hiplips,' they muttered.

'There! Not too difficult, was it?' Another pause, then a pouting, 'No, Hiplips. What is it?'

'No, Hiplips.'

Hiplips signalled to Quopper the afternoon pianist, a morose tipsy chain-smoker, slouched forward over the keys.

'I think a slow waltz, Quoppie, dear.'

Hassall heard Hiplips start to count, making the dancers clap to the beat. He wondered why on earth a queer like Hiplips – really Fred Allidyce from Tunstall – resorted to this extravagance of speech, eccentric mannerisms and show. The silly bugger wore mascara and false eyelashes, high heels, great cuffed sleeves, and shone like Bonfire Night. His ponytail hair seemed a wig, but Hassall could never tell wigs. What for? Like murder, like damaging children, like cunning lawyers getting killers off the hook on technicalities, it was simply what people did. The maniac sham tart down there was now teaching them the rudiments of mogga dancing. Hassall had never got the hang of that, either, though he'd seen it done often enough. God only knew why they couldn't dance in time.

'Mogga dancing is special, tout le monde. What is it?'

'Special, Hiplips.'

Then tell them to dance a fucking waltz when they're playing a waltz, wack, Hassall thought irritably. A foxtrot to a foxtrot, you'd not go wrong. Instead, this gunge, every dance mixed in.

'One melodeee, different dances. What is it?'

They muttered. He screeched, 'Again!' miming stricken by a headache. They looked at each other in embarrassment. Hiplips burst into tears and had to be comforted. Two dancers found him tissues and paracetamol.

Hassall heard three girls talking along the balcony, one explaining the dance in a foreign language. Five days before, he'd asked somebody

70

along the road at the Salford Late-Ed College how to tell Brazilian lingo. The woman had laughed. 'Think Spanish, make it slithery, and there's your Portuguese!'

How to think Spanish though? And he hadn't asked for Portuguese. She had realised his difficulty.

'Brazil speaks Portuguese. Think Jamaican English, and there's your idea of distance.'

'Oh, right.' Hassall hadn't known that. The balcony girls seemed to be waitresses coming on duty. One went through swing doors, the other pair sat looking down at the dancefloor.

'Tout le monde!' Hiplips warbled, clicking his powder compact away and smiling roguishly. 'We're not going to *assault* our beloved teacher any more today, are we?'

'No, Hiplips!'

'When the waltz starts, we dance a waltz, capeesho?'

'Yes, Hiplips.'

'Then on my signal you change to a foxtrot, capeesho?'

'Yes, Hiplips.'

'Then on my next signal, to a quickstep.' He pirouetted, arms out and graceful, smiling with approval at his own elegance. 'And we're all going to do the sequences brilliantly, aren't we?'

'Yes, Hiplips.'

'And off ... we ... go!'

What a mess people are, Hassall thought. The talkative girl emerged in a waitress's uniform, saw him there alone and came over. Haltingly she asked him if he wanted anything. He didn't, but asked for tea, please, and a toasted teacake. No chance of Dr Clare spying on him here, though he had seen her once before on this very balcony. The girl seemed pleasant and smiled, fluttered her fingers at her two girl friends, had difficulty noting his order then went towards the serving hatch. Hassall worked out how to chat and ask something useful. The piano started. Brazil. Then Portugal, then Paris, wasn't that what gossip said? Easy from there.

He wondered how the investigation was getting on. A vagrant called Tennock, rummaging for discarded grub in the bins behind the city restaurants, had pulled out a hand. Hassall hoped the reject Scotch git, transferred from Glasgow, wasn't going to be the named officer for it, or nobody would get anywhere.

Chapter Eleven

butty (b brief) – a beginner lawyer (who survives on cheap sandwiches – butties)

Before the prison interview Toofy refused to go for a shower, in case he got knifed with a sharpened spoon. That was the destiny of a paedophile in prison. Thoughts of release made him feel sick with anticipation. The water in the lavatory pan had gone red during the night – how did other prisoners *do* that? It was their threat. He was allowed no company, no messages except verbals

72

from Mrs Horsfall his solicitor, and the screws. They all hated him, though Mrs H was full of triumph. She wanted applause.

'I can always make a fist,' she told him often enough. 'Here's a tip, in case you're arrested again.'

Next time, she almost forgot herself enough to say, *if you don't get me the next time you're arrested and charged for your despicable crime.* But she was his brief, the mouthpiece he'd drawn, legal aid being what it is, and the honest old taxpayers forking out countless fortunes on his trial, God bless their stingy-bastard hearts.

'What?' he asked, just to keep on the right side of the smarmy cow. Once a dud, always a fraud. Briefs were all alike, gelt first and justice coming nowhere in the two-horse race they jockeyed all their miserable lives. He kept his adoring eyes on her. Who the hell would touch her with a barge-pole, teeth of a dead sheep?

'I go for the Achilles heel of the legal processes,' she said. Buck teeth and saggy breasts, wedding ring like it was from her grannie and shoes a mile thick, Argyle stockings hoping for the fashions to come back if the wind changed, and skirts matching disastrous opal and ecru colours. Her shape thudded the eye as she shed her coat. What a mess. She could at least have done her nails, the money she was milking Legal Aid for.

'The Achilles heel,' she said, louder. 'From the Greek story. He was dipped in the Styx to make himself invulnerable, y'know?'

What, chat now and all pals together so he'd recommend her to peedie friends? *I'm not illiterate, you ugly cow.* What was she, thirty if she was a day? He loved – that's *loved,* dear – fresh flesh, winsome smiles, the first groping doubtful blissful touch. The paedo was one of the elite, a devoted craftsman. He pulled himself together and smiled.

Achilles heel? What is it?' *Like he didn't know?* Any minute now, she was going to say procedural technicalities at arrest point.

'Technical procedures, time, place, date of arrest. Formalities.' She trotted it out like the Neck-Verse, that ancient snatch of Scriptures that proved you were a cleric and thereby immune to law. Incidentally, bitch, he thought smugly, it is the beginning of the Fifty-First Psalm. He could recite it for her, if the old hag ever got stuck.

She closed the interview, said she would be waiting to accompany him on his return to freedom, har-de-har, her phraseology but his snigger. He put mistiness on, smiling soulfully into her with utter gratitude.

'Thank you, Mrs Horsfall,' he said, making sure he hesitated, for sincerity. 'You must have harboured some doubts about me, but I'm so grateful. And I admire you. I'd never met anyone so clever and with such ... breeding before.'

'Oh, come *on!*' she trilled gaily, touching her hair and rising. 'You're just a bit overcome, that's all.'

'I am,' he said candidly. 'I confess it. I just want to say...' He thought that was maybe enough for the repellent crone. Besides, it kept her in his mind. It was a psychological fact, something unfinished was better remembered than completed acts. And who knew what acts might have to be completed with her, at some time in the future?

No, not that, Ricky, he told himself in case his mind got the wrong idea, *Jesus Christ, not that, no, never.* She was old, old as old. How on earth could some blokes actually stroke that, and eventually strip it down and, strap-shaped udders coming at you, reach for that crinkly skin...?

'Are you all right, Ricky?' she asked, concerned.

'Yes, thank you, Mrs Horsfall.' He sat, smiling wanly at her.

'Could you please get my client a drink of water?' the solicitor called to the attendant warder. 'He's feeling a little faint.'

'Yeh, right.'

The warder went for a paper cup and used bottled water. The perv was lucky to survive in the nick, and that was a fact. The screw had seen all manner of releases, and this was as transparent a phoney as they came. He deplored the law. It sent pervs out to do it again, and again, and...

'Thank you, sir,' Ricky said with a wink at the portly uniformed screw.

He sipped, held out the plastic cup. The screw ignored him. Ricky really relished these moments, each one a drama in miniature. He had no illusions. The screw would have to come to this charade tomorrow morning. Ricky would be free as air, having played the system and got out to ... well, let's not think too closely of the enjoyable days to come.

Gourmets must feel the same sense of brimming anticipation, choosing some delicious food item from the shelves. Pleasurable to be out among other connoisseurs, selecting from the most choice delectables. He almost moaned aloud, saw yet

75

more consternation on the brief's ugly visage, and smiled bravely, nodding to reassure her.

'I shall be with you at the point of departure, Ricky.'

'Are you sure, Mrs Horsfall? Only, I don't want to inconvenience you. You've already done so much for me.'

'I shall, Ricky,' the lawyer said, nobility all over her scrawny countenance. 'It's my last task for you.'

He smiled, a hint of sadness. He was really quite good at that, holding her eyes for a moment before looking down shyly the instant her eyes met his. Not wanting to reveal how attached he had become, you see, to the horsy old tart, because that might expose his deep affection for her, and leave himself open to being hurt in his very soul. He was pleased to see her cheeks colour.

A buzzer sounded. The screw told him to stand.

'Your gear, Grobbon. Time to leave us.'

'Thank you, sir.' Ricky stood, taking Mrs Horsfall's hand just a fraction of a second too long. 'You've been very kind, sir. I appreciate your charity towards me.'

That, to the uniform Ricky suspected of pissing in his stew three days before, and doing worse at other times.

'Not at all, Grobbon,' the screw said, knowing exactly what the perv meant, and vowing to cause him serious agony the next time they met. The inmates did far worse, and would compound them with topping the perv bastard if they could. Pervs, destroyers of children, lasted no time behind bars, and good riddance. 'Don't let's see you again. That advice is for your own good.'

'Thank you, sir.'

Mrs Horsfall was not entirely clueless. She allowed Ricky to go first, coming close behind. It was a lesson learnt from several of these episodes. All too often some departing prisoner heading for release might unaccountably stumble and fall, damaging himself severely on the way out. A lawyer's presence meant he would be safe.

They went to the door, ready for the signing ritual that meant Ricky 'Toofy' Grobbon was legally entitled to walk free, and not a stain on his character. Mrs Horsfall had already prepared a recommendation – she called such legal folderol insistences, meaning she wanted her client to be smuggled into a waiting car. She had her cell phone ready to send instructions to the driver waiting a mile away in the crowded city.

'Don't worry, Mr Grobbon,' she told the ex-prisoner formally. 'You will be got away safely. It is all arranged.'

'What is, ma'am?' the screw said, pausing at the next intersection.

'Mr Grobbon's mode of departure,' the lawyer said tartly. She also had no illusions about the trustworthiness of prison staff or prisoners. A word could be passed quick as electrons. She wanted the waiting paparazzi left staring at their own stupid selves while her client got away. They were utterly irresponsible people, and had to be hindered at all costs. Her client was innocent because the law said so. After due legal process, whatever suppositions of the case might be, he was now a declared innocent.

Across the road two men sat in a lifting cradle, ostensibly mending a neon road light. The vehicle was legit. The council workman smoking his head off in the cab below also authentic, having signed out the whole shebang two hours before was an essential job. Police had been along, smarmy bastards, checking on the driver's worksheet and even phoning the council service department to make sure.

'Watch them filth,' the pale young man said. 'Busy, busy, busy. Makes you sick.'

'They're eating our frigging taxes.'

The older man with the dreadful scarred face told his mate to pass a coil of wire. It was unnecessary, because the trade union insisted that nobody actually mend any light. Work was for union-registered labour force only.

'Them down there are worse,' the pale man said, indicating the tangle of cameramen and reporters below. 'They make *me* sick.'

'If they hadn't made a fuss, we'd not have a job on.'

'Reckon the briefs will slide the perv out the side door?'

'If they've any sense.'

'How many cars have the news-prats got staking the place?'

'I counted three on the way, round Tibb Street.'

'They'll have him clocked before nightfall.'

They made a show of whistling, passing each other tools, shouting down to the cab man vague sets of numbers. He answered randomly, not taking his eyes from the racing page of his newspaper.

'I think we'd do a sale with a Harris,' the scarred man said casually. 'That Ultra Light should do the perv anywhere.'

'Two thousand yards for a point fifty round?' The pale youth chuckled. 'No sights, has it? What d'you do, guess? Point and hope?' They always differed on weapons.

'Telescopic sight's fitted, you barmy sod.'

'No good having a twenty-round cartridge sack when you're too busy working its silly fucking bolt.' He mimed losing some quarry peering along a wrench. His mate nudged him.

'Them buggers might be filming us. Watch it.'

The mutters below rose to a babble as a hooded figure emerged from the main prison door between two warders, policemen clearing the way to a waiting black saloon car.

Other cars started up along the thoroughfare. The man was bundled into the motor, which tried to make headway through the press of photographers and shouting reporters. Police shoved a path through.

'That's it.' The scarred man downed tools and pressed the signal button. The cab driver's voice crackled in response.

'Right, mate,' the scarred man said. 'We're done here.'

'Was it the perv?' the pale youth asked.

'Leave off,' the scarred man said disgustedly. 'In that hullabaloo? Nar, the legals will owff him by the old postern in Silken Street.' He watched reporters pile into hired motors and rev off.

'Just look at the silly sods. Taken in every time, they are.'

'Shouldn't we just leave it to Holly?'

'We already have. She'll stop at every traffic light and lamppost, always let other cars go first. We'll take yours and catch up once this idle sod gets us down to the ground.'

'Then what?'

'Then we sell the wallet the best weapons money can buy, and wait for the evening news, nine o'clock on ITV.'

'Same as always,' the pale man grumbled. 'They never want us to do the job for them. It's boring, this is. I'd thought it'd be more exciting, like.'

'It's where the money is. Don't moan.'

The gondola reached the ground. They nodded to the council workman in the cab of the vehicle, and strolled off to collect their car. Holly would be close behind, and ready with her cell phone. If, the scarfaced man thought, the silly bitch remembered to switch it on.

Chapter Twelve

fest – source of annoyance

Hassall did not have to wait in Dr Clare's surgery. He remembered the faces of girls who left just as he arrived, and clocked them for two street stringers for Grellie's Red string in Rivergate. He was sure somebody was waiting for them outside. He tried for confidence during the preliminary chat and weighing, the sample and the stethoscope bit, the offensive intrusion of the light in his eyes, the discomfort of the auroscope.

'Your weight, Mr Hassall,' Clare said. He dressed.

'Yes.' Then sadly, 'Yes?'

'Over 210 pounds. I'm afraid it won't do.'

'I've been trying.'

'Mr Hassall, excuse me.' Clare leaned back, her tactic to show she was ready to talk. 'Whatever you've been trying, you have not succeeded.'

'No, well, you see, Dr Clare, I've been working out how to judge what I eat and compare...'

He halted. She was shaking her head.

'You remember we spoke of the vegan diet?'

'Well, yes.'

'Did you begin to move a little towards it?'

'Not really. I tried. I got lost in grub at midday. You know the sort of thing.'

'No. Please tell me.'

'Well, you're rushing, got to be somewhere, and realise you've not had anything to eat for a few hours. So you stop.' He looked put-upon by all this. 'You know that once you're there, scene-of-the-crime, all go, no chance to grab a bite. So you stop on the way.'

'And have what, Mr Hassall?'

'Well, whatever's going.'

'Could you be more specific?'

'Look, Doc, I know how busy you are.'

'I have time. Would you buy what Mrs Hassall would make for you, the same kind of supper she would do?'

'Well, no.' He shifted uncomfortably, and realised he was looking at his fingers. He was sur-

81

prised by their appearance. He hadn't inspected them so minutely for a long time. Fat, almost podgy. He put them away, concealing the evidence.

'Give me an example, Mr Hassall. No need to be exhaustive, just so I get an idea.'

'Well, a couple of pasties, maybe a cheese and potato pie, a jam roll, tea, maybe a block of chocolate.'

'To tide you over?'

'That's it.'

'For how long?'

'Oh, some hours. Maybe three or four.'

'And then home?'

'Late, always later than I'd planned.'

'And what does Mrs Hassall say?'

'Nothing. She expects it. I get her on the blower, tell her what time I'll be coming home.'

'And she has prepared you a meal?'

'Well, as a rule.'

'Do you tell her you've already had a bite or two?'

'Not usually.'

'Why, Mr Hassall?'

'She's gone to all that trouble, hasn't she? Cooked, maybe got special stuff in if I'm working late. Depends on the weather.' He tried to smile, feeling he was ducking flak. 'Last week I had to stay–'

'So you have a bite on the way to something urgent. Then you have another meal when you get home?'

'Only because I'm unwilling to say I've already had a mouthful.'

'How often is this, Mr Hassall?' The silence continued, so she prompted him. 'I mean how often do you have two main meals instead of one?'

'Oh, now and then.' He sounded lame, and tried to make it easy for Clare. 'See, you lose track of time when there's crime to consider.'

'Once a week? Twice?'

He shook his head, pursed his lips. 'Maybe three times.'

'Or even more?'

'Sometimes, yes. You can never tell.'

'And fill in between times?'

'I usually stop at some caff, a couple of cheese rolls, maybe a hot dog.'

'Your increased weight, Mr Hassall. It seems no mystery, does it?' She saw he was shocked by her bluntness. This was the moment to suppress pity for the man. 'It must come from somewhere. Increased weight has been eaten and kept on board. It cannot be inhaled, or acquired by touch.'

'I haven't had time for much exercise, Doctor.'

'What exercise?'

'Oh, I walk a great deal.'

'How long in a day?'

'Oh, two, three hours.'

'Have you tried climbing stairs rather than use the lift? Walk to work rather than drive?'

'We've been pretty busy.' He tried to think up convincing explanations. 'The business with the perv is taking time.'

'You must rescue yourself, Mr Hassall.' Clare made notes, giving herself moments to gather thought. 'I want you to survive. Would you agree to a course of activity therapy?'

'Jumping about in a leotard, Doctor?'

'No. In solitary if you wish. You can enrol at the Bouncing Block. Do you know it? Moor Lane, near the street market?'

'Yes.'

'I can give you a certificate showing it is recommended on medical grounds. You being part-time, you have ample time.'

'Is it really necessary?' The thought of being among all the gymnasium queers made him feel awkward.

She let the significance of her deliberate pause, intended as a rebuke, sink in. 'Did you read the information I gave you? The pamphlets? Any of the charts?'

'Some, yes.'

Clare smiled, so friendly to a backsliding patient, but making no bones about the lesson that had to come.

'You're a classic example of diseases waiting to happen, Mr Hassall. You already have diabetes mellitus. Gall-bladder morbidity, strokes, hypertension, osteoarthritis, heart diseases, various cancers. You can conjecture about many others. You are not helping yourself. I intend to make you lend a hand, to delay the onset of some of these ailments.'

'I appreciate it–'

'Please.' She held the quiet then, 'Some fifty thousand years ago, our physiology became set in its ways. We burn and metabolise now in, more or less, the same way we did then. But there's a huge behavioural difference. In geologic time, our ancestors foraged. They searched and grubbed

84

all day long, moving, digging, reaching, climbing, gathering edibles. They had to, or they starved. They burned off any excess just to stay alive. If they didn't, they had nothing to eat, and they and their children, the entire tribe, died.'

'I understand all that.'

'Sugars from fruits were valuable energy-providers. We inherited the craving for sweet things. Now, Mr Hassall, we live in warm surroundings. We do not have to keep on the go. If we travel, we sit in a warm train or over-heated car. If we're hungry, we don't need to clamber and root. We stop and buy a cheese and potato pie, with chocolate rolls and pasties to be going on with.'

'That's all very well, Doctor, but–'

'So, Mr Hassall, you eat an excess. I intend to register you at the Bouncing Block gymnasium, and require you to make three visits there a week.'

'Look, I don't quite have the time–'

'You must, Mr Hassall.' She let the implied threat sink in. 'If you default on a single session, without prior explanation made directly to me, I shall write you off my list, and you will need to report to the police surgeon with all my notes on your case.'

He felt she was being truly cruel. 'That will mean my medical discharge.'

'Indeed. And it might be the saving of you. You must go down in weight, down in hypertension and the need for serious drug control of your blood pressure. I shall then stand a chance of getting your diabetes under control.'

'You're being unfair, Doctor. I've been trying.'

'No, Mr Hassall. *You* have been *failing*. Two

million years ago, our ancestors found they liked meat. The tribes learned how to develop a hunting skill. It furthered their racial development. Their brains grew, and biochemical pathways evolved into what we have now, except we still love the thing our earliest primate ancestors felt were tasty and essential. Some of those foods contain the sugars we all still crave.'

'I don't eat much sugar,' Hassall complained. He felt he was letting her have all the argument. 'I miss sugar out. I have diet cola.'

'Please. In the reign of Queen Anne – think, say, the start of the eighteenth century – our countrymen ate seven pounds of sugar each. Now, some western nations consume over twenty times that much per annum. Why? We don't need it. We simply *like* it. We have lost the knack of doing without tasty things. So we – you, I – are addicted. You must get off the sweet carousel. I insist you attend the Bouncing Block.'

'It seems a bit unnecessary.'

'Your body – mine, everyone's – keeps reminding us that there is a long hard cold winter ahead during which our tribe's food will be scarce. It keeps telling us to eat fat, to stock up. It nudges our minds to prepare for a long delayed spring season, when survival will require us to travel enormous distances in search of food. You spot the mistake, Mr Hassall? There *is* no period of starvation ahead in the West. We get reminders from our metabolism, so we obediently stop the car and walk across to the fast-food van and buy enough to feed a regiment.'

She clicked the computer. 'Your first session is

tomorrow, Mr Hassall. Please ask for Jeremiska.'

'Is this a threat?'

'Yes, Mr Hassall.' She set the printer to run off a sheet, tore it off and gave it to him with a radiant smile. 'I'm determined to keep you alive. And police-employable, of course.'

He accepted it with ill grace. 'Thanks.'

She watched him rise and start to go. 'Are you any nearer with the girl injured on the by-pass, Mr Hassall?' she asked on the spur.

'Not really my bag.' He stopped at the door. 'One thing. Do the girl patients only come in when you send for them?'

'No. They can walk in here any time. That's the idea of this surgery. Why?' She was surprised by the question.

'Just some friend of one of the girls I saw leaving, I suppose.'

He left, and took his time outside in the dark Raglan Road, putting on his hat and checking the hour, glancing about as if hoping for a taxi before setting off at a slow walk towards George Street and the lighted area of Central Gardens and the bus station. He saw nobody, but knew they were there, definitely there. They were simply as wary as he was. He decided some kind of watch on Dr Clare might be worth while. He would attend the Bouncing Block gymnasium in the morning, deliberately get the time wrong and upset this Jeremiska. He was not going to give in without a scrap. He did not look back down Raglan Street as he turned the corner; he had more savvy than that.

Chapter Thirteen

glove man – main doer/the chief one who executes violence to order

Akker was a thin, almost cachectic man chosen for his nondescript appearance, his evident weakness and his killing ability. Rack liked a pro. Secretly, the only thing that got to Rack was that Akker worked for the Pleases Agency before Rack came on the scene, which meant maybe Martina knew him. That meant Posser, who was pretty open about things with Rack, also knew him, which was OK except for one thing, which was this: maybe sometimes Akker sloped off somewhere and talked to Posser on the quiet, and maybe even Martina on the sly too, which was a right fest calculated to get up Rack's nose. This sort of thing really mattered, because Rack had to keep the Square in a state of respect.

There was something else Rack hated. Akker came too sudden for Rack's liking. Send for the shifty bugger and he'd suddenly be there at your elbow, just flitting along saying nothing, and you'd have to say, 'Shot Pot, ten minutes,' so he'd nod and be at the snooker hall pronto. He was well weird. Down south among Cockneys this sort of carry on wouldn't be tolerated, but Rack knew these northerners talked loud and showed off something chronic but deep down held onto something silent and deep. It was a right frigging pest. Except for Bonn, who wasn't noisy at all, just quiet, which was also a frigging ruinous way to behave.

So here they were in the Shot Pot before the snooker really got going, just three or four Ganja Petes from Oldham showing off their trick shots, blue-then-red-then-pink with one white ball like they'd invented the wheel. Rack decided to have a word after seeing to Akker, tell them too much pot stinking the place out was a right needle if the filth came calling so keep it down a mite. Much notice they took until he'd put the straightener on one or two. The Yardies liked Rack which, he thought, only goes to show. He had a theory about their trick shots and gambling needing special food and eating it in time to the noise in boom-boxes, them massive black trannies they hauled everywhere turned on max.

'See,' he told Akker, the glove man still in his shabby raincoat like it was some uniform he couldn't get off, 'I'm sick of two fucking things, Akker, capeesh?'

'Cap what?' Akker asked.

'It means see,' Rack told him, well narked. Cockneys'd know what he meant straight off because they said it on the pictures in them Hollywood gangster films. 'I'm sick of never hearing things till the last sodding minute.'

'Right,' Akker said, never knowing what Rack meant, but keeping in.

'Like, where's the paedophile? I told you to keep an eye on him and nobody's telled me a dicky bird.'

'He's at a house in Newcastle, Rack,' Akker said it like everybody knew that. He always sounded far away, something of the echo in his voice, like his voice come from some empty drill hall. 'Want him?'

'Not yet. Tell me if anybody else is keeping tabs on the pig, see?'

'Yeh,' Akker said. Rack wondered if Akker had ever been young and gone to school, or if he'd started off in that lousy mac and tatty shoes, born in the frigging things. 'Two blokes were making like council workers in one of them lifting gears outside the prison when they released the perv. They had legit passes and the right tackle. They had a girl called Holly in the next street, a tubby lass, fake blonde, drove a red Ford Escort. They went after Grobbon to Newcastle.'

'Then why,' Rack said through his teeth, 'didn't you tell me straight off?'

'Want him topped?' Akker asked tonelessly. He only ever cared for the next job, what was it and where, no chat mattered. 'Except they're already taking him out, I heard, with some sniping thing.' He went even more distant and Rack thought he'd better listen, Akker giving good value. 'I thought snipering went out after them Yank goings on, like you lose fashions in clothes. Then Yanks started buying that Israeli stuff, them angle cameras they use on the West Bank against the poor 'Stiney bleeders. All that ninety per cent concealment is serious crap. It just can't do it. Christ, they cost enough. Just adverts, I think.'

'Yeh, well,' Rack said, not having the faintest what Akker was on about. Something to do with killing, which wasn't allowed except where Martina said, and she'd not given any orders yet though the working girls were all up in arms about the perv and it was going to get multo fucking worse. He'd heard something about the Green walkers wanting to send word to Bonn, get him on their side, which would hit the fan sure enough and get Martina coming unglued if she got wind of it. Like Rack hadn't enough on his mind.

'What you want with the perv, then?'

'Them others going to top him, d'you reckon?'

'The two blokes and that Holly girl. Mebbe.'

'Do we know her?'

Akker paused while Geronimo, a lanky Barbadian, chose a different cue. The Baddo had lucky cues for different shots. Akker thought them all barmy, putting money on coloured balls on a flat table with holes at the sides. Life wasn't for things like that.

'Yeh,' he said. 'She did a short spell from that shopping mall in Old Trafford. You warned her off over it three months back Don't you remember?'

'Course I do, prat.' Rack was especially narked because he didn't, but that was why he hired Akker.

'She's stayed off your strip ever since. Nice lass, gives to the hospice in Charleston. Has a kiddie in Cheadle Hulme. It dances. She's only five.'

Rack marvelled at Akker, including other people. Who'd think that some folks' minds were so empty they could store facts like that, a five-year-old kid in Cheadle taking dancing classes?

'What's this Holly doing with them, then?'

'Hires out as cover, see? Always carries boxes of

stuff, legit dry goods for showing to women at home, boxes and lipsticks and them. Careful bint, does nothing out of line.'

'Holly, eh? Can we use her?'

'Take too long sussing her out,' Akker said. Then, careful not to give offence because Rack was the paymaster where jobs like this were concerned unless Akker secretly got higher orders from Posser or, more likely now, Martina. 'Unless you tell me different.'

'Hey, Geronimo,' Rack called, 'a tenner you don't make it.'

'No, man,' the lean West Indian answered, eyes on the white, 'I'm useless at this fucking game, man.'

Grinning, he struck the white perfectly and a ball rattled into a pocket.

'Lucky me, eh?' Rack laughed, miming paying out vast sheaves of notes. He nudged Akker. 'The perv going to stay in Newcastle, then?'

'Dunno, Rack. The plod's doing dropsies.'

'Police surveillance? Let me know if he moves, OK?'

'Right.'

'Anybody else, is there?'

'That Hassall keeps dossing around, but he always is. He's a sod. He's gone half time from being poorly. He gets on my nerves, him.'

'Don't I know it, mate,' Rack said with feeling. 'What else?'

'Get word from Elfon,' Rack said, eventually making up his mind. He was getting interested in the snooker now, though he didn't want to because he was due at the Rum Romeo Casino.

'He'll tell you. Two Leeds tankers. A wallet was learning how to hire them, wanting the perv topped.'

'Amateur, or somebody who matters?'

'Find out,' Rack said tilting his head to show Akker should be halfway there by now. He had to do every frigging thing in the city. They'd have him carrying the pots and pans next. That's why layabouts like Akker and others had life easy and he didn't.

Half an hour later, Akker found Elfon begging outside the London Road mainline station concourse, white stick and sun specs in evidence, his medals the only thing shining about him. Akker was pleased so much gelt was in Elfon's cheese-cutter cap because it showed folk were really nice deep down. You only had to give people half a chance to show charity for the afflicted.

It took ten minutes for him to get the description of the wallet who'd sat opposite the two tankers from Leeds in the Butty Bar.

'You sure, Elfon, wack?' he asked, just making sure because the description didn't sound what Rack would normally worry about. Except, with a city perv now released under police protection, Martina would go berserk if anything happened on her manor, and that was God's truth. Elsewhere was in the lap of the gods, but in the city centre, no, no.

'Positive.'

'Rack know about this, does he?'

'He was in the Butty Bar when he sent me after the tankers. I clocked them all in the Central Bus Station.'

'OK, keep your hair on.' Akker dropped a few coins into Elfon's cap, to encourage people to give even though Christmas was a mile off. It taught people to think of giving to sad causes, like the phony old soldier who was only twenty-eight but did a really good act with his sun specs and white cane and really did close his eyes when begging so he deserved charity if anybody did.

Akker drifted through the crowds, apologising if anybody bumped into him. Politeness mattered. He wondered if Rack knew the message he'd just got from Martina, to see her at nine-thirty tonight for a special order. Maybe not? With Martina, the only person except Bonn who made Akker feel uneasy, it would either be a pizza or something more serious like death. Either way was OK. He made his meek way through the concourse, saying he was sorry when people blundered into him, going, 'Sorry, miss, sorry, sir,' as he went.

Chapter Fourteen

red walk home – murdered to order, for street transgression

Three of the street girls were talking by the Volunteer, Sorella brashly dominating the other two. Or so she thinks, little Anjie told herself, her smile so sweet. She'd been being Greek and exotic all until she met a real Greek talker from Bury, who always came into the city when United played at home. She then had to revert to being a simple Scunthorpe girl innocently blinking her false eyelashes. Muna knew all about Anjie, and cracked on she was stupid and from somewhere in Bangladesh, a place she couldn't even spell in its original lingo, the easier to earn more from the punters than she admitted to Grellie. She and Anjie were friends, did an occasional twosie. Anjie took on the lezzies who came trolling round the Green corner, but they weren't often except on holidays. Muna didn't know why, though Anjie had school terms marked on a big calendar from a garage that sold discount tyres and car exhausts.

'See, it's all right for you Muzzies,' Sorella declared, know-all as ever, 'because you're not Christian.'

'Why's that all right?' Anjie asked, keeping an eye on a motor slowing at the intersection.

'We're Christian,' Muna said. 'Aren't we, Anjie?'

'Yeh.' The car suddenly accelerated into the traffic. Anjie was disappointed. She'd only done three strides since dark. Punters hardly stepped out some nights. She blamed the weather. 'Yeh, we been to school.'

'Yeh, but you Muzzies don't really count.'

Muna hated Sorella in this mood. The bitch confused what the girls pretended to be and who they really were. Deep down under the working girl crap they were all different. Sorella was thick as a lamppost.

'We're not Muzzies,' Anjie said, 'except for Muna.'

'So what? I've better tits than anybody on the street.'

95

That was true. Muna's figure was sound and all her own.

'It's the dead girl, see.'

'She isn't dead.'

'She might as well be.'

They brooded on that for a moment. Two cars slowed, one sporting a football scarf trailing from its open window, lads hanging out shouting obscenities. The three girls strolled in the opposite direction away from the Volunteer, hoping Grellie hadn't spotted them chatting. Grellie's eyes were like a hawk's, everywhere at once, and Muna had already been fined half a night's personal the previous Tuesday for idly watching disgorging buses in the Central Bus Station, which was unfair because she'd had to go to the loo twice and anyway was only making up her mind. Grellie never listened. She hated excuses. You were tons better off just saying sorry and paying up. Grellie had moods galore lately. Jenny from the Red girls across the other corner reckoned it was because Grellie was set on Bonn, like all the girls hadn't already thought of that.

'Well, I think we ought to get somebody to give her...' Sorella's theology ran out. She groped for the word.

Her second cousin Gord kept telling everybody he was a committed Christian, like it was a palace award. She might give him a bell and ask, except that would set her brother on her tail, and maybe he'd find her and then Dad would come steaming up the motorway and haul her back to school, a fate worse than death.

'Last rites?' Anjie said timidly.

'Last rites, that's it.'

'Don't you have to be awake when they do that?'

'No, because what if you have an accident?' Sorella could be a snooty bitch, like she'd proved something by brain power alone.

'I'm not arguing, Sorrie,' Anjie said, meek to the last. 'I don't know what it means.'

'They rub stuff on your head that makes you holy,' Sorella said with scorn. 'They say Latin over you and you go to heaven. It works whatever you've done, see.'

'Don't they do that anyway?' Muna asked, having lost the plot. 'Hospitals, I mean.'

'Like on the National Health?'

'Yeh. They ought to, because what if...?'

They slowed, waiting as if to cross to the Central Gardens. There was a path through, so it was quite legitimate even though it had gone dark two hours before. Cars were slow taking off from the traffic lights, as possible punters caught sight of girls along the pavement.

'Well they don't,' Sorella snapped, so that was that. 'What we need, seeing they're going to switch all her tubes and wires off, is somebody to do it.'

'A priest!' Anjie exclaimed, light dawning.

'Of course a fucking priest,' Sorella said. 'Trouble is, we can't go up to one and say will he do it for us, can we? Unless,' she went on, uncertain now, 'we know any priests?'

'The hospital might have already done it.' Muna could never let a thing go if she thought it a good idea. 'She's only a kid.'

'The family?'

'She's got nobody. The papers were on about it.'

They thought hard, ignoring a car now halted ten yards away, the punter looking back in his driving mirror. The same thought occurred to them all.

'Look,' Sorella said after a protracted pause, 'Bonn were a priest once.'

The other two looked at her, knowing this was where it had been heading all along.

'He's only young. You have to be old to get priested.'

'You're stupid.' Sorella could be a bossy bitch. She was angling to be Grellie's seconder at the Green string, double her take, because she had a musician in a Rochdale club, hoping to be a part-owner soon. 'Somebody's got to ask him. It should be you, Anjie.'

Anjie paled. 'Me? Ask Bonn?'

'One of us has to. You must.'

'I can't do that. It'd be like...' She ran out of extremes. 'I couldn't, Sorrie.'

'There'd be no harm in just asking.'

'What if somebody heard me?' Anjie went giddy, like from spinning round and round in the schoolyard. 'Rack'd go fucking mental.'

'Well, talk to the rest of the Greens and see what they say.'

'Why me?' Anjie wailed, losing her protective veneer of timidity. 'If you think I'm going to walk up to Bonn and tell him he's got to give that last rite thing to the kid, you're off your fucking trolley. If it got back to Martina she'd have me topped.'

'No. It's a good idea,' Muna smiled reflexively at the driver of the first car. 'I mean, there can't be much time left.'

'What d'you three think you're up to?' Grellie said, stepping out of the first car's passenger seat. The girls hadn't seen her in the shadow cast by the street lights, and they yelped in alarm. 'Standing there yakking. Get to one side and wait.'

The three girls moved close to the wall as Grellie wiped her mouth on a tissue, folded it meticulously and placed it in her handbag. She joked a second with the punter and waved, smiling, as the Rover pulled away. She kept her smile on until the motor had gone, then came to the girls.

'Get separate, you idle bitches. How often do I have to tell you? Three girls trolling on a pavement counts as a fucking brothel. That's the law, see? I learned you that when you three first started, you lazy slags. Keep separate and get working. That's the rule. You.'

Muna stopped, stricken. 'Yes, Grellie?'

'How many strides you done tonight?'

'Two. I've a gobber due in an hour.'

'You idle cow. Do less than four by knocking off time, you're fined. And you two,' she told the others as Muna moved away, 'be at the casino midnight.'

'Yes, Grellie,' they chorused, watching her leave, her quick noisy heels rattling the pavement as she went to the Volunteer. Anjie was frankly envious of Grellie's figure, really neat, always looked smart no matter how many jobs she'd done in a night. Whatever punishment Grellie might do to her and Sorella later, you had to admit Grellie was real class. Not many working girls had it like her, and that was a fact.

Chapter Fifteen

zok – a fool

Bonn knew it was Clare the moment he heard her open the door. Rack was doing the stander's routine, monitoring the corridors out there, checking the lifts, using staircases. Rack spared himself mundanities. Other goers were on a scale of significance only Rack knew. He even drove Bonn to dommies himself instead of sending Bonn with a driver. Domestic visits were what some women wanted. He did that for no other goer. Bonn didn't know if Martina had laid down a law about that particular quirk. This hotel go should be routine.

Clare came in, smiling to see Bonn. He always found this moment particularly difficult, words being what they were.

She held him, and he clasped her so hard she grunted from, what, ache, pleasure? That too was unknowable, except she always smiled as he released her. He took her coat, rescued her gloves from the cushion where she'd dropped them, and put them on the hall table then hung her coat. It was scented. Words and scent. Those and drinks were his difficulties.

'Remember how awkward I found it, when we first...?'

'Yes, Clare.'

'You were so kind, so understanding.'

100

Bonn truly found this a surprise. He could not recall being understanding or kind. Polite, yes, and possibly helpful to the lady, yes, because those were always aspects of which he was particularly anxious. But kind? Understanding? He knew so little of women, what they thought, the extraordinary motives that surfaced as antagonisms, even hatreds, for each other set them off into accusations about unknown friends. He heard it among the street girls, who could be the souls of charity one minute and harridans the next.

He clearly remembered Clare's bitterness at her then husband Clifford when she'd learned that he was involved in deaths, extortion, the criminal life of the city. Still around, and she'd kept Clifford's surname for, as she admitted, simple convenience.

'I have made tea, Clare.'

'Let's do without, darling, unless you...?'

'No, thank you.'

'I have the new flat. Lease signed today!' She was so pleased.

This was her project, settle into a small apartment close to the city centre where he could visit and, she hoped, eventually do more than just call. She had quizzed him on the matter. Were goers allowed to have a woman of their own? Maybe even a family, as long as they did their work, if work it was to them? Not for the first time, Bonn was taken aback by a woman's determination when setting her mind on permanent union.

She knew about Martina's empire, of syndicate, working girls, teams of people with hard hands on the city. Not as well informed as she might think, but certainly enlightened now she had finally broken with working for Martina's charity and was going it alone.

Bonn had suggested they avoid mention of the street's activities, and so far she had complied.

'I can't exactly ask you if you've had a hard day, can I?'

She had not quite come to terms with Bonn's employment, and found it hard to accept. Once or twice she asked how some girls managed, if they had their own man as well as ... and here she petered out. Bonn did his best to reply, but trying with words often made things worse. Women found them so easy.

'Bonn, with you being a key – is that the word? – means you can have a place to stay besides where they, *they*, say, doesn't it?'

'Yes.'

'Is it the same for all the, ah, goers?'

'Usually, yes.'

And there would really be no objection if you came to my flat?'

'Probably not.'

'Could you decide for yourself, or is it up to somebody else?'

He knew she meant Martina. Clare had met her when she worked for the syndicate's charity for the city's homeless months before. Martina had sacked her, knowing she wished to take her relationship with Bonn further than that of hireling and client.

'Myself.' Unless, he perhaps might have added, there is some overriding obstacle.

'That means yes? Your decision alone?'

'Yes.'

'That's what I wanted to hear.' She pressed her face into the side of his neck. 'I hope you like my new place. It was one of three in a small block of flats, and I chose the second floor. One was by the entrance, ground floor, the other right at the top. I went for simplicity.'

He said nothing. She drew back to look at his face. 'You now say it sounds delightful.'

'It sounds delightful, Clare.'

'In the centre.' She smiled, trying to exude confidence. 'I hope this is one last time in a hotel. We should have it furnished soon, then you can come round to me.'

'I hope so.' He tried not to sound full of doubt.

She took his hand and drew him down beside her. 'It's the reason for my return. Why would it be wrong?'

'It might look bad.'

'Neighbours?' She laughed, shaking her hair out. He admired her conviction. Not all clients showed her sense of purpose. 'They're nothing to do with us.'

Us. We. The plurals came easily, but full of assumptions. If carelessness spoiled her plan, it would be his fault. He had read of people whose gentle deceptions were exposed. The more sensitive the soul, the more terrible calamity could be. Would he wound her if differences developed?

'People might criticise.'

She finally understood. 'They might know what you do? Is that it?'

'Perhaps.'

'Are you reluctant?'

'No. I would be glad at any time.'

103

She sighed, examining his expression. 'Shall we?' she suggested, touching his face.

'Yes.'

He brought her to her feet. They moved into the bedroom. It was warm, the curtains a darker grey and red than previously, she noticed. Soon, they would not have to rely on some hotel girl entrusted with the décor of anonymous suites. And about time.

As they slipped into bed she tried hard to remember the first time they met in this fashion, but failed in a glow of satisfaction as he brought her close. She realised she'd forgotten to ask him something important, but there was too little time for talk. One hour was always too little. She wanted whole nights, whole days too, in her own place, and Bonn a permanence. She would try everything, then who knew where life might lead?

It was not going to be smooth. A twenty-year-old from some seminary engaged in servicing bored or tortured women, and herself – what, nine years older, holding down a difficult professional job with its own problems. But it was the right way round, she told herself fiercely, the woman still young enough, the man on a par with her longevity, perfectly matched if you thought statistics.

Still not easy, though. Odds were still on her side, as long as others kept out of it. For the while, she would bear the worry and the risks, if he promised to stay. His commitment to Martina's syndicate was a problem she could confront later, once they started life together. She too could be resolute, and was more determined than most.

She turned to him, lips parting.

Chapter Sixteen

mother – information to be trusted among criminals; a warning

'Rack,' Bonn said. 'I should please like to see the street girl.'

Rack was surprised but he beamed, feeling God was finally on his side, making Bonn see the light. He wondered which bint Bonn had finally picked.

'Yeh. Which one?'

'The one who was, ah, busy in Arkwright Street when the vagrant found the remains in the waste skip.'

Rack thought, Christ Almighty. 'Oh, her? I think maybe she's moved on somewhere. I'll have to ask...' He petered out because it was Bonn he was talking to. He already felt rotten and hadn't even got to the end of an ordinary lie. Truly not a lie as such, just an explanation that did just that little better than the truth, and where was the harm? Bonn looked so sad.

'I'll try and find her.' Rack always perched on the edge of the balcony so he could look down at the dancers. They were training for the mogga dancing, six pairs, ordinary clothes with Fag Scanlon on the piano smoking his head off, against by-laws, and Beldam – for Belle Dame, which was like French for queer – who was the Palais Rocco's nearly-strangest dance instructor.

105

Bonn was at a table looking down.

'Why d'you watch them lot, if you never try, Bonn?' Rack's delaying tactic.

Bonn's sorrow was like a shine but without the gleam, just a darkness slowly shoving at how you think. Rack felt sad too, which was a right fucking bastard because honest blokes who did a good job shouldn't be made to feel like that for sweet fuck all.

'They seem so peaceful, Rack.'

'Here he comes.' Rack liked this bit, when Beldam came sweeping onto the dancefloor. The dancers shied nervously. Beldam was dressed in spangled military dress-uniform tights on high heeled silver boots. He was naked to the waist except for a rainbow-striped sequinned gilet with a flare collar. His blond hair was heaped in Carolean profusion.

'Spread,' Beldam shrilled at the learners. 'You're a positive herd. No nearer than ten paces – can we count to ten, tout le monde? No collisions like last Friday, or I'll get one of my heads.'

'Same patter as the other teachers,' Rack said. 'They catch it from each other because they've all had polio. Know why?'

'Please, Rack.'

'Now?'

'I have a lady this evening, I believe.' It was four o'clock, mogga dancing class time in the Palais Rocco. 'Seven-thirty. Aqua One-Seven-Eight-Two, a first timer, the Ramona Hotel. Soon, if possible. Please do not let it inconvenience her.'

Rack went sarcastic. 'Like, it's OK to bugger up everybody else's day, but not a tart's?'

106

'Language, please, in public.' And after Rack said sorry, 'I do not mind waiting until later.'

Rack went for Bryl who he'd had loitering at the balcony bar for two hours, wasting his frigging time, knowing that what troubled Bonn would sooner or later come out. He wondered how Bonn had known there was some Green stringer doing a stride in Arkwright Street that night. This was unexplained, Bonn picked up odd bits he shouldn't even know. There was a word for it, Rack'd heard, where people understood things without having to find out. He'd have looked for the word in a book if he could read.

'Bryl?' he said to the shadows near the bar. 'Get the tart Tennock said about.'

Bryl appeared suddenly behind the locked grille. 'We told the plod there was none of our bints there, Rack.'

'Bring her here.' A bar girl rose sullenly from somewhere and faced Rack through the grille. 'Get this open.' Bryl muttered and she raised the grille with a clatter. Rack indicated Bonn. 'I'll have a Magees and don't ask for change.'

She brought him a bottle. As she lifted the counter flap for Bryl to go, she asked, 'Is he the one they call Bonn?'

'Shut your teeth,' Bryl told her. 'On my way, Rack.'

Rack went to watch the mogga dancing with Bonn. 'I like this bit,' he said, resuming his perch. 'They all say the same thing, notice that? Reason is, they're not titted enough milk when they're horned. Know why?'

By the time Bryl brought the girl, Bonn had begun to doubt, despite Rack's promises. The girl was sent over on her own and Bryl left to go back on stand for the money with the Lagoon's all-nighter card players in Waterloo Street. Rack was hardly distracted from laughing at the dancers. He pointed at the chair near Bonn.

'Just listen to the burke!'

The girl was slightly older than most of those on Green string, Bonn saw. He felt guilt at the awareness of her age, for what right had he to recognise the feature of life called age? Her appearance was her own concern, as was her age, and should be none of his. Except, he worried as she sat nervously facing, how could one apologise for a thought? He felt obliged to make redress, but how?

'Hark, hark, trogs,' Beldam was shrieking in his weariest voice. 'Do we have ears to hear? Do we know what mogga dancing actually is today? Like, it's the same as *ever*. Even troglodytes know that. So why are you Neanderthals still ignoramosis-simi?'

Silence. Rack laughed. 'They're too shit scared to talk back.'

'Rack,' Bonn said.

'Good afternoon, Bonn,' the girl quavered. 'I'm Cilla. Really Drusilla.' She twisted her handbag strap.

'Excuse me please, for a moment,' Bonn said. 'Rack.'

'Eh?' Rack, still laughing, looked down from his perch, then from Bonn to Cilla. 'Oh, did I talk wrong?'

'Mogga dancing,' carolled Beldam, doing fancy wriggles, 'is six bars of one tempo then six bars of another, and so on, all to one melody. Cap-head-aching-peesh, oh ignorant trogs?'

'Yes, Beldam!' the dancers cried nervously back.

'Well, I was doing this stride in Arkwright—'

'Excuse me, please, a moment,' Bonn said. He sat in silence. Rack sagged, sighing.

'Sorry, Bonn, if I said summert wrong. Only I was laughing, see?' Bonn said nothing. Cilla felt so sorry for Bonn. It must be terrible for him, she thought without wondering why she believed that.

'To the lady, please,' Bonn said.

Rack stared, seemed about to explode at the ceiling then looked at her. 'Sorry, Cill. I didn't talk proper.'

'It's all right,' Cilla said, not seeing what was happening but wanting really desperately to agree if it would stop Bonn feeling sorry for things. She wondered if he didn't really like the Palais Rocco, but you couldn't ask him something really personal like that.

Rack wanted to challenge Bonn on it, say, 'See, mate?' or some such, teach him sense, but instead went back to the barminess on the dance-floor where music had begun and the dancers were moving to Beldam's shrieks.

'Thank you, Cilla,' Bonn said. 'Arkwright Street, you were saying.'

'Yeh.' She loved the way he said her name, like he was trying it out for the first time. She wondered if he had ever talked to a Cilla before, or even a Drusilla.

'You often, er...'

'I don't usually work there. I hate the smell of them caffs, all them bins.'

'You prefer to go elsewhere.'

'Well, anywhere the stride says.' She worried stride would offend, but Bonn said nothing. 'Cars I don't like. Best is when they want a lay down and you can charge them for the room. It's safer, because standers are about.' Why didn't Bonn know all this? She almost asked him outright, except he seemed so concerned. Feeling, she decided, it was some feeling he was getting.

'The Green stringers have seven or eight different places.' She tried to be helpful but not knowing what he wanted to know if he didn't come right out with it. 'I haven't got them writ down. Grellie keeps a rota with times and things. Or she sometimes sends the stride to the working house instead. It depends on their gelt. I don't like getting behind with the money or Grellie goes mental.'

'One night you did go down Arkwright Street, Cilla.'

'Well, yeh. The stride said it had to be there, see?'

'The stride wanted it to be in Arkwright Street.'

'Yeh. He was...' She caught herself, remembering Rack's ordeal with ordinary words a minute since. 'Drunk.'

'Yet he knew exactly where he intended to, ah, be with you, I suppose.'

'Yeh. The right door, too. It were odd. Never done that before except like in a room and you've to dress up how the stride says. Like a nurse or a teacher. I once had to dress like a nun.'

110

'I wonder if you could point the, ah, stride out to Rack or one of Rack's friends, Cilla.'

'Well, yeh. I haven't seed him since.'

Rack, listening, exclaimed impatiently, 'Tell him how you trolled him.'

Cilla looked her surprise. 'He come up to me at Greygate, Mawdsley Street. Why?'

'Ever seen him before?' Rack could see where Bonn was going, and it made him mad. This would entail endless work, have the boys scurrying every which way for fucking days.

'No. I think maybe the other girls have, from what they were saying.'

'Right.' He slid off the balcony rail as Beldam went into a shrieking fit and the music below faltered. 'That enough, Bonn?'

'A description might be of help, Rack.'

The chief stander laboriously questioned the girl for an account of that night and the john she serviced, until even Rack could see she was becoming increasingly scared. Bonn smiled then and said he would accompany her out, as Rack was busy with important work at the Palais and needed to stay.

Bonn left with Cilla, and talked with her in the foyer for some time. He waved her off at the entrance, saying he regretted not being able to walk with her up Quaker Street. He had said he would be disappointed if she told her friends about their conversation in the Palais Rocco. Cilla said she wouldn't tell, and meant it.

111

Chapter Seventeen

PLP – Play-Lay-Pay; the sex trade

The new applicant for goer came into the Shot Pot and stood looking. Rack liked to boss these new-comers, show who was in charge. Let them discover Martina later, then take in Bonn, see how the job was done proper, like. They'd learn decent.

'Mate,' this idiot began, trying casual man-of-the-manor and all-pals-here, 'I've come about a job.' At least he'd had the sense to see that Rack was the man, not one of the clowns loafing among the cones of light over the green beige.

'Wrong,' Rack said, pretending to write.

He couldn't, but moved the pencil like he knew what the marks meant. He was in the alcove, curtain pulled back. You could get a drink there, a new girl waiting on like it was computer science. She'd worked in the Shot Pot five days, not a smile yet. Rack reckoned she was overcome with lust for him, which only went to show. Today, he wore his green eye-shade with the inbuilt flickering yellow lights for effect, and his four-tone silk shirt. No wonder she was impressed.

'What?' the goon asked.

'Wrong.'

Rack didn't look up but had already sussed him from the glimpse of shoes, corner of his eye. Drainpipe jeans, would you credit the cret, strapped – *strapped!* – underneath, something out of Great-Grampa's time back before some frigging war. Who let these blokes in out of the rain?

'They told me to come here.'

'Wrong.'

'What's your game?' the nerk said, coming close. Rack wrote on, pausing to peer at the pencil point like he'd seen an actor do in *Oliver Twist*, an old picture that had made him nearly, almost but not quite, cry. Well, have to blot his eyes with his sleeve in case anybody saw. It was about a kid who got lost. Rack knew he'd have acted it better if he'd still been a kid. He grew bored. This prat couldn't appreciate fine acting when it was there right in front of his face.

'Who you for?' Rack said. There didn't seem to be much of a point on the pencil, just a smoothed bit where the lead had gone flattish. Well, well. Couldn't depend on a frigging thing.

'Rack.'

'I'm Rack.'

'You're Rack?'

Stymied. The youth hadn't the sense he was born with, stood hesitant and wondering if he'd been given the run-around.

Thing was, new blokes came thinking because they'd got some relative to put the word in, that they'd get stuck on some gigantic payroll and any number of shags a day, women provided by the Pleases Agency, Inc., protected from the law and other hoodlums, happy ever after. They'd heard of how some blokes got paid for just doing some crusty rusty old bird, or maybe some younger rich tart full of doubts, willing to pay for a dip-

113

and-scratch. They decided, hey, I'll have some of that: play, lay, pay.

Rack had seen this burke dawdling outside the Bouncing Block in Moor Lane, the fitness centre Martina had established some months back. The idiot had heard of it from his relative, was it one of the fifteen Blue string girls, Deansgate corner? Rack'd forgotten. If he knew how, he'd have written her name down, except he always remembered names. Folk who could write sometimes forgot them. Odd, that. He'd work the theory out.

'I come about the job.'

'Wrong.'

This was where the goon got sore because he wasn't getting it large when he'd come expecting free cunt, booze and tickets for the match.

'Look, mate,' the nerk had the fucking gall to say, perching on the edge of Rack's desk and disturbing these essential papers, 'I come to see your boss. Like,' he said loudly so everybody heard, 'the organ-grinder not the monkey.'

Rack leant back, gazing at his pieces of paper. Two were blank, and one with his scrawls of pretended writing. He could hardly see from pure white-heat rage, this toad coming mucking his papers about. What if there was something really important there, some vital code to save the world? No wonder Bonn got sad.

'See these papers?' Rack said, looking up at last, giving the zok his best stare. Bardie, a lanky yardie from St John's parish in Barbados, once People's Churchwarden there, emitted a grumble of laughter, not needing to look to know what was going on.

The duckegg stood slowly, looking at Rack, at the three pieces of paper. He knew things had gone weird but hadn't the sense to do more than say, 'Don't frig about. Am I in the right place?'

'Eat them,' Rack said.

The youth didn't get it.

'Eat what?'

'These papers, and say sorry.'

The lad's incredulous stare almost changed to a grin. He said, 'You're off your nut, mate,' and turned to go.

Rack laughed and resumed writing, pencil or no pencil, shaking his head. The visitor walked out, saying to Bardie as he passed, 'Snooker behind the pink, mate.'

Bardie grinned, eyes on the white, cue on the long rest.

'Too late now, prole. You com – puh – *leet.*'

'See,' Rack said to nobody in particular as the double doors swung to with a thump, 'people haven't got manners nowadays, right?'

Several snooker players grunted assent. Rack sighed. Somebody comes in and disses a bloke, what's a bloke to do except get him tarred? 'My hands are tied, see?' he explained, feeling a little anxious, quite as if Bonn himself were standing sorrowfully observing these goings-on.

Rack shouted to Bardie to see to it, and stood for a good stretch. All that writing couldn't be good for your muscles, could it? That was how back-bones got wonky, spoiled your aim spitting at moths on the way home in the dark summertime's street lamps. He decided to ask Bonn if he ever spat at fluttery insects. If Bonn said no, that would

115

prove Rack's theory, writing spoils your aim.

Bardie said, double bass, 'Done it, Rack,' and left his cue on the green beige, accepting the three pieces of paper Rack handed him as he went.

Some thirty minutes later, the reject waited on Liverpool Road for the traffic to ease. He wanted to see his cousin, who'd suggested he apply for a goer. She gave him lurid tales of free sex, money galore, yet hadn't warned him about this daft bastard.

He watched a massive pantechnicon rumble by heading for the canal bridge, the traffic not slackening. He decided to walk to the end of the Deansgate shopping mall. Sandra had put him up to it, silly cow. That prat, his flickering eyeshade lit up like a Christmas tree, arm-bands and a waistcoat full of fluorescent playing cards. What a minger. His stare was madness but straight, nearly scary enough to get up and run. Eat the bits of paper? A freak, a maniac. He'd ballock Sandra for leading him on.

A gap appeared among the vehicles ploughing out of town. He decided to cross, then tried to halt as something massive revved and moved nearby. He'd stepped confidently off the kerb but was too slow getting back onto the pavement. He was impeded by somebody close, got struck by a heavy goods wagon and mown down.

It was moments later that he came to, people milling about and somebody shoving stuff into his mouth, somebody saying, 'He'll be fine if we can just get him to hospital,' and somebody else saying, 'Please keep back. Give him air. Anybody see what happened?'

He couldn't breathe for the stuff in his mouth. His head was spinning. He tried to shove the blockage out, get his breath.

'Why's he got paper in his mouth?' a uniformed copper asked, kneeling and forking the stuff out with a finger. 'Who the hell put that there?'

'Dunno, constable,' an emergency bloke said, kneeling, his fluorescent orange jacket a-dazzle. 'He was like that.'

The victim tried to tell the copper no, it was the ambulance man had shoved the papers into his mouth, but somebody pressed a mask over his face and a rush of cold gushed into his lung.

'We've got the bleeding under control, constable,' another voice said. 'We'd best get him to the crankie. Can you get us clear of this frigging traffic?'

'Right, pal,' the constable said. 'Make way there, please, all done here, on your way, people...'

The victim was lifted. He saw a big coloured geezer just like that snooker player he'd passed in the Shot Pot, standing smiling among the faces to one side. The bloke grinned with a mass of gold teeth, and gave a jaunty salute as he caught his eye.

'Any witnesses, please?' the constable was calling as the ambulance door slammed shut.

Chapter Eighteen

cushy, cushty – good, easy (Romany)

Hassall spoke to Sergeant Heghorn, a pallid youth who looked too weak to have made the physical at the Palace of Varieties, as Hendon Police College was known in the Force. Yet he seemed wiry, and Hassall was as surprised as the rest to discover that Heghorn still coached an amateur boxing school out in Moses Gate. Looked like the gloves would weigh him down, so spindly was he.

Heghorn – bet there are just as many puns on his name as on mine, Hassall thought – was waiting with a plastic case containing three pieces of paper, just when Hassall thought he was making progress with the problem advertisement.

They were in the canteen, ladies clattering and phones ringing.

'It gets me down,' Hassall told the sergeant as he came to join him at the Formica table. 'Why does every nick deafen you with phones? Even on the bog there's phones playing tunes and SOS. Don't even ring properly any more.'

'It's the canteens, Mr Hassall,' Heghorn said gravely. He was a grave man. 'The other five or six nicks in the city have to economise on grub. It's the cutbacks. If they can save, like, eight per cent on the cottage pies and fifteen per cent, like, on the chops, then they swap the food

118

among themselves.'

Jesus, Hassall thought, hark at the bloke.

'This advert,' he said. 'See it? Today's *Journal and Guardian*?'

'I heard, Mr Hassall.'

'What do you think?'

'It can't be a nutter. It has to be taken for real.' And Heghorn said, going a bit embarrassed at Hassall's long look, 'Punctuation is correct. Spelling is right. Phraseology's a cut above, isn't it, for somebody who's forgot their education at school.'

So Heghorn had read it, and also wondered. Hassall decided not to ask if the sergeant's attention had been drawn to it by others or if he'd spotted it himself.

Hassall read it again.

Wanted: A reliable gentleman able to handle a long arm, and who is able to supply the implement, for a specified purpose. The fee, payable on completion of the assigned task, will be exactly equal to the national living wage as stated by the Bureau of National Economics at the time of going to press. It will be handed over in cash in one sum. Proof of execution of the assignment will be expected. Please answer to Box 451.

'Anything else?'

'Yes. It's a cut above the national reading age.'

Hassall pondered. 'What?'

'It's meant to select out a particular social band.'

He decided to listen. 'It is?'

That hadn't struck Hassall. He re-read it slowly.

'A colon, Mr Hassall. Who uses colons nowadays? You can read that entire newspaper and won't find a single one. And it's used correctly. And the mention of that Bureau place. I gave them a call. They do publish figures about wages. Like, how much money the average fishmonger gets compared with greengrocers.'

'What else?'

'It has the ring of somebody maybe once used to authority, maybe an old soldier type who's bedridden now and can't get about like he used to. And that *long arm* suggests the advertiser wants to avoid mentioning a rifle in plain words.' Heghorn waited. 'That's what I think,' he finished lamely.

'Nothing else?'

'Well...'

'Spit it out.'

'That word execution came over as a bit, well, definite, didn't it?'

'So it did, sergeant.' Hassall rose, spilling the rest of his tea into his saucer. He always had to hang around until the tea got cold, not having an asbestos gullet like other cops. 'Let's go.'

'To the newspaper?'

'Right.' On the way out, Hassall glanced down at the sheets in Heghorn's plastic folder. 'What's that?'

'Three pieces of paper. They were stuffed in some young bloke's mouth who'd got himself knocked down on Liverpool Road.'

Hassall paused, blocking the way in the canteen doorway.

'Mouth? In his *mouth?* Some barmy first aid tactic gone wrong?'

'Nobody knows, nobody saw. The accident looked genuine. A heavy goods vehicle by the canal bridge. Bloke didn't seem to look, witnesses said. And now this.'

'Worth fingerprints?'

'I thought that. I've got the lads taking witness details and looking at CCTV cameras.'

'Good. Let's see if the newspaper's had any-thing like this before. Shouldn't take more than a few minutes.'

Hassall felt pleased with Heghorn. You could never tell, callow extroverts fresh out of the Palace of Varieties, you could finish up with the Crazy Gang if you weren't careful. On the way out Heghorn handed the plastic folder in for dabs.

Chapter Nineteen

zomb, zombic – unthinking

'It's not the money.' Rack often said the opposite, but today was a Wednesday and he had theories about Wednesdays.

'No, you're right.'

Akker, Martina's glove man, and therefore Rack's, always agreed. Sometimes, though, he did different to what he was ordered, but not much because he knew Rack would go ballistic if Akker ever dissed him or the syndicate, same thing.

'It's being dissed.'

'Well, yeh,' Akker agreed, though not knowing with what.

They were watching a Gay Day parade across the end of Rossendale Road, just beyond where the circus arrived every Easter. Rack wanted to tax the city's queers, seeing he had the right. They carried on like some poxy religion, which he hated. Posser gave Rack a flat no on it, which really narked Rack but he just said OK. Reason being, Posser wheezed, knowing Rack got really burned up when he thought locals were taking the nonce, he allowed the Rum Romeo where the gays congregated after dusk, and they saw it now as a kind of right. And who knew, maybe they were allies. Rack told him OK, OK, don't go on. Martina gave Rack her blue-iced stare at that, which shut chat down about it. Posser's daughter's cold stare was getting multo fucking worse, and Rack blamed Bonn for not taking her on as his regular.

'I told them the percent clear as day, Akker. That old geezer knew straight off.'

'Good.'

'That manageress was trouble. I knew it.'

'What, then?' Akker wanted to be off and doing. Rack wasn't usually like this, round-the-houses. Something more important was on the chief stander's mind, which didn't bode well.

'Don't tell me,' Rack said in disgust. 'You want fires, doncha?'

'Not unless you say. Fires is obvious.'

'I never said fires, did I? No.' Rack grinned. 'They've got a frigging band, them queers. Just take a look at the prats, half of them in effing pink. Know why?'

'No.' Here it comes, another cret theory.

'No pets when they were kids, see?'

'Never knew that, Rack.' Get on with it for Christ's sake, Akker thought. A car showroom defaulting on paying across, where's the problem?

122

Gelt, or bye-bye buggerlugs is all it was. Everybody knew that, except this new car place's
manageress.

'Nick all their cars.' Rack liked to shock people.
Trouble was, Akker looked fed up whatever you
told him to do, never smiled then went and got
on with it, did the crisp or the tank then come
back and said it was all done and could he go
now. A good glove man, the best, but Rack would
have liked a bit of contact instead of all this
zombic yeh-OK stuff.

Akker gave a nod. 'All of them.'

'They come in, unlock the place ready to start
selling and all them lovely motors are gone. A
right laugh. No damage, nuffing.'

'You want them sold or kept?'

'Use that Belgian dealer, Liege or somewhere.
Tell him he underpaid us last time for them Land
Rovers, ten per cent.'

'Did he?' Akker was surprised. First he'd heard
of it.

'No.' Rack thought, give me fucking strength.
'No, see, I just made that up. It gives us another
dollop, see?'

'Right,' Akker said. Rack could tell he was well
impressed. 'When?'

'Couple more days.'

Rack nodded so Akker knew he could get on
with it. He stared at the gays dressed as baton-
twirling American girl cheerleaders in tinsel.
Allowed to parade like that in the city, on Martina's patch, and not pay a decent penny to Rack
for permission? It was corruption or something,
and not even decent. He wondered how to talk

123

Posser and his frigid daughter round, make them queers pay an honest fee for carrying on like they did.

'Right, then, Rack.' Akker didn't move, guessing more was coming.

'That mumper. Found some hands or summink.'

'Yeh.'

'Arkwright Street.'

'Yeh.'

'Tennock, bin diver.'

'The plod have it in Forensic.'

'Word is some bint saw Tennock.'

'I heard that.' Akker was cautious because Rack could go into one if he thought you were out-guessing him. 'Except I wondered if it was true.'

'Green stringer. Put the word round a bit, but make it like from out of town, not from in the Square, right?'

'Yeh. When?'

'Straight away.'

'Right.'

'Thing is,' Rack said, 'the bint was posh, like, not one of our tarts. Like, Cilla did the punter, but who was the civvy bird?'

'Dunno. I'll try.'

'Go on, then.'

That was it, Akker decided, feeling better now it was all out in the open. One thing a glove man learned fast was to leave nothing undone, no frayed ends, no cottons hanging to get caught in the machinery.

'Ta-ra, mate.'

'Ta-ra.' Rack stared in rage at the last of the

124

Gay Day procession, some frock-legs walking back then spinning and pretending to dance. He noticed Hiplips from the Palais Rocco among them, leaping and showing off. Rack could hear his squeal. It wasn't decent. It wasn't even like learning people summink. He'd have another word with Posser and Martina, maybe try to talk Bonn into seeing his point of view.

Second thoughts, he decided not to. He went off to visit the Arts and Design College, deciding to put a little extra business their way.

Chapter Twenty

easy work – same-gender sex, esp lesbian, for pay

Mrs Horsfall was thrilled at her legal success. Some people, she knew from rabble-rousing newspapers, argued that Ricky Grobbon should be gaoled for life. They meant literal life, never let out again. They wanted vengeance, instead of true justice from courts of law. She protected honesty by defending the accused.

Her car was at the police station, for safety. She collected her keys from the desk constable, a really offensive man who showed displeasure. Hadn't she served due legal processes, as established by society? If only the police were as steadfast and noble! She never succumbed to uneducated whimsy, having long since learned that it was wrong to surrender to silly feelings just because

125

ignorant people glared. They even blamed her for the plight of that child on life support machinery. As if she, a respected lawyer, had anything to do with crime! No, her purpose in life was to argue the accusation away, using correct legal procedures. She had successfully defended Ricky Grobbon.

Of course, visiting the hospital had been a due part of the legal process. Shocking to see the Intensive Care Unit, the girl nesting in the centre of flickering medical gadgetry. Naturally, an evil photographer from some chip-wrapper, along with her lying sidekick reporter, had snapped the woman doctor – Dr Clare Burtonall, was it? – on duty. It was in all the wretched penny-a-rag shrieking headlines. They simply wrote down whatever emotional assumptions they made up, then claimed they represented God-given truth. And people believed them!

No, she thought angrily, driving her car out of the police yard. She always felt relief at this point, mercifully one of the crowd. Women were the worst, their eyes full of hate even in the supermarket where her husband Ben ruled his retail empire. The Horsfalls lived two floors above the actual sales area, in an expansive flat with its great bay windows, quite beautifully appointed. For the next few days, until the newspapers and broadcasters moved on to parade other lies, she'd get Ben to arrange delivery. Careful, though. She'd give the delivery girl plenty of time to return to the main shop floor before taking the groceries in.

Disgusting, of course, for a lawyer to have to lie low for a week, and only go out in her car when she judged the coast was clear. Criminal for society to behave so misguidedly, but it was only to be expected.

She drove down Liverpool Road into Deansgate and continued on to Station Approach. Lots of evening traffic, two HGVs swinging – such carelessness – from lane to lane when they had absolutely no right, as she continued round Victoria Square. She made for the Greygate exit, marked *To London & The South*, following a massive furniture van, the sense of repletion returning. Many people hated driving. After her fantastic success, she found it relaxing.

Inevitably, the traffic lights were against her at Mawdsley Street. She waited, traffic and buses in her rear-view. She smiled to herself. Tonight she was booked for her first serious encounter in the city. It cost a fortune, but so what? Law paid well. Ricky Grobbon had been tried with due process of law, and she had done her civic duty. Her profession made it her responsibility to stand up for the accused and argue his case by all legal means her education conferred. Society made the rules, not she. Parliament decided the laws, adding to the precedent and the tenets of natural justice. She, Jessica Horsfall, had been *entrusted with the law,* and she kept the process clean and untainted. In short, she had faithfully done her duty. Society should be grateful.

Several motor horns sounded. Most unfair, that she should be blamed. Green! She moved off quickly not to give offence, smiling. A female clerk in chambers had given her the idea of private, very personal solace. The Pleases Agency,

Inc., was in the phone book, broad as day. Fascinated by the outrageous idea, she had had a high old time of it, charging herself up to call asking for terms, methods of payment. She even rehearsed her questions using a tape recorder. Easy in one sense because a highly skilled lawyer could use the skill her legal training had drummed into her over the years.

The lady taking the call sounded quite elderly and discreet, wanting to know how she had come by the recommendation. She explained she had simply overheard a clerk talking, and used the telephone book. That had been sufficient. Jessica hadn't believed it could be so simple. She had prepared a list of seven difficulties, and simply went down the list to the last, the question of a domiciliary visit.

Yes, she was told, domiciliary visits were possible. She gave her credit card number, arranged details and asked if there were any problems she might expect.

'None,' the dry old lady replied.

'Do I have to confirm nearer the time?'

'No, ma'am. That is sufficient. Do you wish to apply special conditions?'

'No. None.'

Both she and the Agency lady said their thanks. That had been it. A young man called Bonn would visit.

Jessica Horsfall felt her mouth go dry as the traffic got clear of the city and she settled down for the short drive to her lovely flat. Her husband Ben was so understanding. There had been one or two previous occasions elsewhere, so Jessica was

128

not quite a novice. He had allowed them. Not all had been satisfactory, though a little dalliance – without causing gossip – was always a thrilling personal entertainment. This time, he had already said how she deserved a special treat when this important case was finished. And indeed it had taken it out of her. Naturally, Ben knew she would need the flat to herself for the evening.

He was so sweet, Ben. He quite understood. How strange it was, yet seeming such a precise routine. Quite agreeable, really, and so routine. That elderly-sounding lady on the telephone, so respectable, so businesslike and reassuring. Since first hearing of the Agency, she had picked up more snatches of gossip from other women, in hairdressers, shopping, even in a restaurant, and once while waiting in a court anteroom. It emboldened her. Examining the impulse dispassionately, it was clear that she only made the arrangement in a spirit of natural enquiry, that's all it was. If it turned out too strange, then she had simply learned a new aspect of life and could move on. If on the other hand it turned out as she hoped, then she had a perfect right for a lovely interlude. Heavens above, people went out to the theatre, didn't they? And sometimes they saw the most improper movies, didn't they?

The supper ordered from the caterers would arrive at eight. This Bonn, strange name, was booked for eight-fifteen. She would be home before seven. Ample time.

Rack drove Bonn out through Hardwick.

'Easiest this way. It's above a big megamarket.'

'Above, you say.'

'Why don't you fucking ask, Bonn?' Rack burst out. He was irritated, being nagged by a slick swerving Porsche. It had tried it on at the last traffic lights. 'Did you hear that goon revving?'

'Apologies,' Bonn said. They were unaccompanied, so it would have been pedantic to correct Rack for using such atrocious lingo. 'Above, you say.'

Rack pulled away with maddening slowness riling the frantic Porsche.

'Justina Nine-Six-Oh. I sussed her out. Manager's missus.'

'Perhaps investigating her was unnecessary, Rack.'

'I knowed you'd say that,' Rack crowed, triumphant. 'I had a feeling, see?' He changed down to crawl pace, the cars behind making a cacophony. Bonn appeared not to notice. 'She contacts the working house. Mavis says she wants easy work, just getting up the nerve.'

Easy work meant same-gender booking. Mavis kept six girls on her list of samers, two of them wholly just that, and four either way, about average for working houses.

Bonn looked. 'Yet she books a domiciliary with me.'

'That's what's skew, see? I've this sixth sense. Know why some got it and others not?'

'No.' Bonn was resigned.

'Fathers in the wrong job too early leaving school. Take me, for instance...'

And Rack was away, explaining electrons and cheap foods and street lamps too near your front

130

door, while cars risked themselves at Amen Corner coming up the slope and Bonn reflected on Martina's casual use of Den, the Barrow-in-Furness goer.

Highly gratifying, Bonn imagined, for Den to be booked by the head of the syndicate herself. Bonn was naturally pleased for him, such progress. Den made key less than a year since, and before that had been a goer two years. Very rapid. Yet why was Martina so sour each time she arranged for the tall, presentable and well-spoken Den? He so wanted to ask. Turning to Rack's hunch about Justina Nine-Six-Oh, what had been the clue suggesting something might be awry this time?

They turned down a side street, Rack slowing, the procession of vehicles honking, liberated at last, and Rack grinning from having angered so many motorists at one go. Minutes later, the car drew into the megamarket car park among hundreds of cars, shoppers pushing loaded wheelies through the glaring illumination.

'We're parking round the far side, Bonn. Banco's done the CCTV.'

'Not the lights too, I trust.'

'Nope. Folk might get hurt, see,' Rack said, pious because Bonn frosted him for that kind of malarkey. 'They have new TV search cameras. They're bastards, mend themselves if you crank them out. Security boss here's a rotten sod, won't be greased or pushed. Got religion, stupid bugger.'

'I trust he will not be harassed, Rack.'

'I trust so too, like,' Rack said, smug because he knew something he hadn't yet told Bonn, see how he liked it. 'Her flat's two floors up.'

131

Typical Rack, matter-of-fact, the job in hand. They parked in a free space between two dark saloons and got out. Two banks of lights shone down. A railing surmounted by barbed wire ran round the periphery.

'One thing, Bonn. She's that lawyer.'

Bonn paused and looked back. Rack was disappointed. Was that it?

'Got that perv off on a techie. The paedo who put that kid in hospital, the one the Green bints are on about.'

'Thank you, Rack.'

'Only, I didn't want you saying summat wrong, see?'

'Thank you.'

'Two hours,' Rack said, telling Bonn the time.

Bonn was the only key never wore a watch, which was stupid when any of the girls would do their nappers to choose him one. It narked Rack. Any case, he could buy any he wanted on Martina's creddie same as the other goers. Rack's theory was, Bonn let the syndicate down not showing off by spending. What did a few notes matter?

'Very well. I do hope you have some means of occupying your time, Rack.'

'Yeh, ta, mate. Don't you worry.'

He went with Bonn to the single door, opened it and went in first, scooting silently up the stairs ahead of the key. Rack didn't trust lifts, not even single-person size like the one provided here. Having a giant brain was good.

Chapter Twenty-One

sol – Space-Occupying Lesion (medical slang)

Dr Terry Elphinstone met Clare on her way to Cardiology.

'Waiting for me?' she said, trying mock coquettish despite the maelstrom of visitors and staff in the corridors. She liked him.

Terry looked sheepish. 'I'm trying to dump a problem on you, Clare.'

'What now?' They were friends, so she could pretend irritability without being misunderstood. Once, and only once, they had made more than just pleasant time together, but that was in the past, such things coming about under the pressure of frantic hospital work. Some thoughts lingered, though, and did not need to be erased. Terry had a wife, and two children in school and a third on the way. For a moment she felt a pang of envy, but quickly put it aside. She had Bonn, and soon would possess him for ever.

'It's a nurse. She's got a black eye.'

'And you did it?' Clare joked, but saw how uncomfortable he was. 'What?'

'Another nurse did it. Scratches, hair pulled.'

'Fighting?' Nurses had rows, of course, but matters did not usually reach fisticuffs.

'It seems so. I saw the injured one in at ten past nine.'

133

'Staff surgery, is it?'

'Yes. I'm sorry, Clare, to ask, but...'

'I'll do it.'

She could understand Terry's reluctance. All doctoral staff took turns on the Staff Welfare rota, and anyone falling sick could simply use their power of veto, not wanting to be seen by Dr X because he's still angry with me over something I did in Paediatrics, that kind of thing. Similarly, doctors could feel prejudiced and ask to change slots. This was usual when the Hospital Admin Unit, a ferociously parsimonious bureaucracy given to claiming non-accountability at every juncture, were too stingy to allocate a separate (paid!) doctor to look after Staff Health And Welfare. This was the sign of the times. Terry saw her expression change.

'I know, I know, Clare.' He sighed. 'It shouldn't be our duty, on top of everything else. I had a go yesterday at Mrs Temter but she was adamant.'

'Pope Joan still refusing to appoint a staff health service doctor?' Clare smiled to put him at his ease, using the Chief Administrator's nickname.

'She says it won't even go into the "topics for later discussion" list.'

'She hopes to get on some New Year's Honours List by spending less.'

'Possibly.' Terry was always benign in his criticism. Too kind by far, Clare thought, though that was part of Terry's attractiveness. 'About the girl, Clare.'

'I heard she's comatose. Doesn't seem much likelihood, does there?'

'Not really.'

134

'The force of being thrown from the car, after all.'

'Or fall.'

'Whatever it was, the trauma completed the process. Her family?'

'The mother was last heard of in Portugal.'

'No trace?'

'We had a social-service report mentioning Brazil, nothing substantial.'

Terry Elphinstone paused. 'I always dread this.'

'Don't we all.'

'I always imagine some long-lost brother walking in the instant we pull the plug, yelling blue murder and it shouldn't be allowed, all that.'

'Everybody thinks that.'

'It doesn't make it any easier.'

'Have you had your conference?' The hospital ethical responsibility committee, of which Clare had been secretary until four months previously, ruled that three consultant doctors should confer at the bedside before taking so drastic as step as ending life support. Relations were to be invited and given an opportunity to decide. Surprisingly, most objections tended to come from the doctors rather than relatives.

'One this morning, then a couple of queries from the media. I told them we were trying to trace relatives.'

'The perpetrator's been released, I hear.'

'Alleged perpetrator,' Terry said drily. 'On a legal technicality.'

'Whatever. He's under police protection and moved out. The local rags said.'

'It's been on the TV.' He smiled with some

bitterness. 'Anyone could find him in ten minutes if they really wanted. He's the sort they'll hunt down after a year, and then release a series of outraged rehashes, working up indignation.'

'It's only newspaper copy for blank spaces.'

'The public never forgives us, though.'

Life was always hell in hospitals after a patient was removed from life support systems. Clerks and ancillary staff were worst of all, and went about full of outrage, their snide remarks epidemic until they forgot all about it.

'They never do,' Clare said. They paused by the main entrance where incoming patients separated for Out Patients and the Triage Appraisal door. 'Can I help, Terry?'

'Yes, Clare.' He had difficulty getting the words out. 'What would you do, left alone?'

'I'd say do it.' Clare felt saddened. 'I took the liberty of going over her notes and looking in on her. There's no absolutely sure proof, but every criterion seems to point that way.'

'Seems?' He picked up on the word.

'You know what I mean. You asked me for a prognosis.'

'Right,' he said, indicating his folder. 'Would you do a clinical appraisal of her?'

'Of course. Someone has to.' She gave him a smile and told him not to worry and hurried off to shed her books and coat before seeing these two warring nurses.

They were waiting seated across from each other in the ante room of the Staff Surgery. She gave them both a bright good morning. The staff nurse who had caught the SHAW rota was already wait-

136

ing, surprised that Clare came instead of Dr Elphinstone.

'Dr Burtonall? I thought–'

'He's in Intensive Care. I offered.'

Sister Mahon nodded her understanding, having been here before. 'Nurse Bingley has a black eye. She was seen earlier this morning by Dr Jettson, the new Australian registrar on Orthopaedics, who passed her fit. The other, Nurse Keveen, is complaining she was abused and attacked.'

'The loser won and the winner lost, then?'

'The fight was in the ward.' Sister Mahon's lips set in a thin red line, and Clare's heart sank.

'Union trouble?'

'It's beginning to look like that.'

'Any idea what they fought about?'

'It sounds highly improbable.' Oh, dear, Clare thought, registering Sister Mahon's hesitation.

'Very well. I think I had better see them both together.'

The two nurses came in, both full of aggression. Nurse Bingley had a swelling on her right eye. The other had scratches down her cheek and a slightly puffy mouth. She must have taken a blow.

'Could you please tell me what happened?'

Both started speaking together, neither giving way until Clare clapped her hands together to make sudden report. They quietened, glaring.

'Now, ladies. I wish to know if you have anything else physically wrong with you that Dr Jettson or anyone else might not have been aware of.' And into the silence she said, 'Nurse Bingley?'

And got a silent denial.

137

'Nurse Keveen?'

'No.'

'So you are here to discuss your reasons for having become physical, in the ward. Is that what happened, you actually fought in plain view of patients?'

'It was her fault,' Keveen said through her swollen lips.

'That's what she always says!'

'Please. You say first. Nurse Bingley?'

Both wore the uniform of third-year nurses, plain sky blue with leg-of-mutton sleeves and white starched pinafore. Caps had long since gone, yet more economic paring by Admin and, if older nurses were to be believed, marking the downfall of proper standards.

'We were making beds on Seven. She was on the other side. She said I was pulling the sheets too tight so she couldn't do the hospital corners right.'

'That isn't true!' Keveen shot in, almost starting out of her chair.

'It's absolutely true,' Nurse Bingley said with a face of stone. She did not even glance Nurse Keveen's way.

'Please. Carry on, Nurse Bingley.'

'At least I know how to make a bed. I always get *my* hospital corners right.'

'Except today!'

'Nurse Keveen, please.' Clare saw she was going to be late for the CPC, the usual Tuesday clinico-pathological conference. Today's problem case was the young girl found by the roadside in the dark hours, evidently of no fixed abode and seemingly

138

brain dead. Newspapers were already maniacal about the patient, who had figured prominently on the previous night's local TV news. 'Give me your summary, please, Nurse Bingley.'

'She thinks she's a cut above the rest of us, when she's had *no* practical training. Just comes in deciding she knows it all. I'm not the only one to say this.' Clare held a hand out to restrain Nurse Keveen who was bursting to interrupt.

'You were to make some beds, is that so?'

'That's right. She decided I was to do the other side with her, and then starts telling me off when she's the one can't do it properly.'

Nurse Keveen stood, pale with anger. 'I'm not staying to listen to this junk, Doctor Burtonall.'

'Please. One minute more. So you disputed each other's ability over making beds the right way?'

They signified a yes, opting for silence. Clare thought quickly. Nurse Keveen was evidently the senior, though they both wore the same uniform. It could only be that Nurse Keveen was one of the new breed, those nurses who had first entered university to gain a BSc degree in nursing studies, while Nurse Bingley must be one of the direct entrants. The former group were disliked by the latter, for assuming a superiority that the indigent nurses hated. Friendships never formed between the two groups. Nurse Bingley's lot had ward experience, been through the hospital and so knew where instruments, linen, drugs, were kept, and were privy to hospital folklore and badger runs of the whole complex. The Keveen category were wide-eyed, often having to ask the way to departments and having to stare at layout charts and the

139

authority trees papering the Admin corridors just to find out who was who. It was a long-running dispute as to which were better. The eternal question of whether the BSc group were cost-effective was always bitterly fought. Worse, all the hated Admin senior staff were derived from the university-educated group. The unions were continually invoked to support one or other lot, to nobody's gain. As ever, patients bore the brunt of the crossfire. Services deteriorated while Admin argued and held costly meetings arguing about saving pennies and paper-clips.

Clare mentally called herself to heel.

There was only one way out of this, to look foolish by trying to put herself into the camp of some imaginary idle elite, the popular image of the doctoral staff. Terry Elphinstone had been right to deputise her to this task, for as a female she could readily assume the role of the inept without taking sides, whereas these two young harridans would each have competed to get Terry on her team.

'What exactly is a hospital corner?' she asked innocently. 'I've seen it done a million times but am never quite sure if I could manage it myself.' And as they both started up, she patted the air with both palms to ask for silence and nodded to Nurse Bingley.

'When making beds, Doctor, you have to make sure the sheet is pulled over the mattress quite firmly,' the nurse began, darting a glance at Keveen, 'so as to put the end flap in so it holds. If you don't, it works loose and causes trouble when the patient is being treated.'

'How?' Clare asked innocently. 'Can you give

me an example?'

'Well, like in a lumbar puncture, it can ruck over the corner and work down and cause the doctor to have to disentangle himself. It's important,' she lectured the other nurse sternly, nodding to confirm how right she was.

'And that's what you do?' Clare said to Nurse Keveen.

'Yes. Only—'

'No wonder when I make my own bed it never stays straight!' She gave a wry smile, placating both, hoping to ease them out of their intransigence. 'We medical students did only one day's nursing.' Nurse Bingley gave her a more confident look as Clare added, 'And most of us didn't turn up for that. You probably do more to save lives in the hospital than we doctors do in a month of Sundays.'

She allowed no time for either to reply, going quickly on to forestall some partisan comment.

'Would you prefer me to make some kind of report suggesting you be returned to different wards? I can easily do that, make it simpler for us all, or maybe put a couple of days' break into your schedules and then recommend you come back to the same ward?' She shrugged, showing as much doubt as she could without going over the top and alerting their suspicions. 'Only, I have to put down something. Seeing you're each twice as expert in these, what are they, hospital corners as I could ever be, it seems a bit of an imposition for me to make any firm comment.'

They reflected. Clare hoped. Neither seemed willing to offer a reconciling glance towards the other, but the tension had relaxed somewhat.

'Were I to write a screed, I'd be compelled to appear before some terrible assembly drawn entirely from Admin.' Clare rolled her eyes in graphic dismay. 'While I should absolutely *love* to enjoy their company, it would be a terrible waste of time, seeing I have to evaluate a case I haven't even yet seen.'

She tried to look distraught, and was rewarded by the nurses' sudden interest.

'It's some girl – evidently no more than a child, what, fourteen? – who was found by the roadside. Some kind of street walker, if I've guessed right.' She paused, mildly curious. 'Do either of you know anything about her?'

'I do,' Nurse Keveen said. 'She was found on the by-pass and is brain dead. I heard.'

'Fourteen is right. The police said so,' Nurse Bingley added.

Clare pursed her lips to show dismay. 'Were you on duty when she arrived?'

'She's in the next ward, ICU. One of our set's on duty there this morning.'

Nothing travels faster than doom on the nurses' grapevine, Clare reminded herself with satisfaction as the two before her began offering what little news they had. She already held in her folder a transcript of the girl's notes from Dr Elphinstone, so was more or less well apprised about the poor girl.

'Thank you. You're both a real help. At least now I shall not be completely taken by surprise.' She saw satisfaction appear in the nurses' manner and felt more confident offering her final

142

question. 'Well, ladies. What do we do, the three of us? Sentence me, a poor old working doctor, to explain all kinds of bother to our perfectly splendid Admin staff...?'

They almost smiled, for Clare knew she could only look her true age, twenty-nine on a good day, or thirty-five on a positively dire evening after slogging eighteen hours on the go.

'Or give me an easier sentence, let me see this poor girl, and make possibly some fatal judgement?'

Now they did shoot a glance in exchange, swiftly looking aside. Clare saw she would have to take the risk of forcing them to leave together, to curtail gossip.

'Can I suggest we sleep on it, and maybe let it drop if I can talk Dr Terry into making a decently tailored report in the accident book?'

Both nodded and Clare rose, wanting out by the fastest route.

'Then I thank you both. And I pay well, if you would wrestle my mother to the ground if she dares to come visiting. She makes me bleach my teapot.'

They smiled now, both standing and leaving together. Nurse Keveen, she noticed, held the door for Nurse Bingley. Maybe they had learned a little sense.

Clare sighed and thought, ah, well, at least they'd both now be speculating on whether she and Dr Terry had any kind of relationship going, and ... and all that jazz, Clare added to herself.

She gathered her things and hurried out heading for ICU where she wanted to examine the

143

moribund girl. I need to see Bonn, she told herself, and be properly used soonest. And try to gain a little more understanding of the seemingly transparent individual she now loved. If only she did not have to buy his time from the Pleases Agency, Inc., life would be almost perfect.

Nearly. Maybe. Perhaps.

Chapter Twenty-Two

dommy – (ex. domicilary) paid visit for hired sex

The meal Justina Nine-Six-Oh provided disappointed Bonn. Or, rather, he quickly amended, he was rather sad that she had gone to the bother of insisting they have a meal together. Having supper was an impediment, with rare exceptions. Clare Three-Nine-Five was one with whom having dinner seemed natural. He did not understand why.

Nor did he know why some needed to lay on a feast. Important, he was learning, to share a meal with someone close. Maybe this was a private signal within to some women. Even though, as seemed the case with Justina Nine-Six-Oh, the meal was brought in prepared by caterers. Charming for the lady to be so concerned, but why?

He wondered about this as she provided him with more than he normally ate in a day. She served hors d'oeuvres first, her brow furrowed as she poured wine, looking anxiously at his expres-

144

sion as she replaced the bottle in the wine cooler. He said with regret that he knew next to nothing about wines, but its taste was wonderful. She was relieved. He admired her furniture, truly pleasing and restrained.

'I was on edge coming, Justina,' he said.

'You were?' She seemed astonished.

'Yes. I felt I might say the wrong things.'

'I can't understand that, Bonn.' She repeated his name as if trying it out.

'I wish we had met before.'

'What, by ... arrangement, you mean?'

'In a way, yes.'

'I didn't think a man worried about meeting another person,' she said with a hint of bitterness. 'All too often they're aggressive. They're bullies.'

'Bullies.' His distress was so obvious she flew to make amends.

'I don't mean you, Bonn.' She judged him anew. 'No. My profession, what I do, seems all manipulation.' She was reluctant to eat while he seemed so slow at his plate. 'Do you recognise me?'

'No,' he said carefully.

'Not even a hint that you might have seen me before?'

'I have never seen you before, Justina.'

'Don't you read the papers?'

'Rarely.'

'Or watch the television news?'

His pause was so prolonged she began to think she had given offence.

'I defended the man they freed. The one involving the girl?'

'Your past is not my concern, Justina.'

145

She loved that Justina. It had been an inspired choice of name, culled from the public library.

'I imagined you people ... you, I mean, were taught how to approach these situations.'

'No.'

'Are you not shown, well, what to do?'

'What to do,' he said hesitantly.

She caught time by serving the main dish, a chicken casserole, potatoes, carrots, broccoli, and diced parsnip. He had barely touched his wine, and she asked about it.

'It is exactly right, Justina.'

'I only meant you must have some kind of training in, well, think of the situations you might...' She had dug herself into difficulty.

'You see, Justina,' Bonn said into the silence, 'I believe a lady has the right.'

'The right?'

'Yes. The lady has the right. Not just because hers is the invitation. But because she is she. I am merely the one who visits.'

'The right to...?'

'The right to decide what happens before I arrive, before I speak, before anything transpires. All events are within her gift. In fact...'

She felt mesmerised. 'In fact what?'

'She determines events. Here in your lovely flat, you make the decisions and I must comply. It is my duty and privilege, because you are the one.'

'But I...' She fingered her double-choker pearls, a last-minute choice she had already begun to regret.

'It is always so, Justina.'

'Always?'

'If we had met by some chance encounter, I would feel the same.'

'Do you go about–?'

He saw the mistaken implication shocked her and said quickly, 'Of course not! I have never gone this far in any chance encounter. In fact, I have never had social contact with a lady from a chance meeting.'

'Never?'

'True. I couldn't even begin to imagine how to. Though,' he added thoughtfully, 'I do know it happens. I am fairly certain I've seen those kind of incidents taking place.'

'They occur everywhere, Bonn.'

'I am unsure of what I see.'

She began to explain about her profession, how she had organised the defence for the man 'arrested in connection with the injuries sustained by a young girl'. The girl was on life support in the Intensive Care Unit at Farnworth General. She went on about the public, letters of condemnation and anonymous threats against her life.

'The police have been marvellous.'

'Good.'

'I felt the trial would never end. The public abuse! As if I was getting away with fraud, when it was simply the law being applied.'

Bonn considered the image, she supposed, then said, 'The public.'

'Yes.' She spoke with feeling. 'So angry without thinking. And so uneducated, determined to get worked up. They're a mob. I mean, wasn't it in Wales that those people stormed that poor woman doctor's house because she was a *paediatrician,*

147

and they misread it for paedophile?'

'It must be hard for you, Justina.'

'Can I tell you something, Bonn?' She sipped her wine, and he refilled her glass. 'We used to live in Derbyshire, I won't say exactly where.'

'And you came here...'

'My husband's job.'

He nodded, taking his time, wondering where the conversation was going. Justina gathered herself and spoke.

'I used to, that is occasionally, *went* to Wolverhampton.'

'I do not know Wolverhampton, Justina.'

Her cheeks were touched with red as she said, 'I sometimes, only three times really, had a similar thing there. We had a service flat over one of the supermarkets. My husband operated three small ones for a multinational. There was a service flat with each. I could use them if I wanted. He didn't mind.'

'Didn't mind.' It needed care.

'Workaholic, you see. He makes allowances. For me, you see?'

'That is kind.'

'I worked for the Crown Prosecution Service then. Are you not curious about who I...?' She took a breath. 'I don't know if you talk to each other. Like, do you have friends who do the same thing, become special escorts in other places?'

'No, Justina.'

'Don't you talk among yourselves?'

He laid aside his knife and fork, and reached for his glass. 'I speak with nobody about this visit. I mention you to no one. I never shall. My duty is

148

a lady's privacy. I can never tell.'

'Is that true?'

'As God's my judge.'

She wondered if he might be slightly offended, even angry. Then he smiled a little and resumed the meal, and she saw he might actually never become furious, only saddened by wrong assumptions people might make.

'I sometimes went further than just having a dinner,' she said after a few moments.

He seemed unfazed by that, too. 'It is your privilege, Justina.'

'Justina isn't really my name,' she admitted recklessly, feeling hot and noticing her wine level had gone down of its own accord.

'It is, Justina.' His eyes met hers. 'If you say so.'

'It feels odd, saying it like that.'

'Unusual. Not odd.'

His smile seemed to start slowly, then extend almost imperceptibly. She watched, feeling rather woozy. Was the full smile reserved for later? She judged the time, saw how it had flown and almost exclaimed with disappointment.

'They used my real name,' she confessed, almost abandoning reticence now trust was in the air. 'You know what it is?'

'Justina.'

'Millicent Jessica,' she admitted bitterly. 'Have you ever heard such?'

'It is beautiful, Justina. So famous, such an old imperious name. It is pretty. Even Millicent's diminutives are pretty.'

'You make love to some,' she heard herself say.

'I never disclose confidences,' Bonn said.

149

'No, please, as a friend. Do you?'

'A lady has a right to silence, Justina. I can't reply if you ask me.'

'I'm glad,' she said at last. 'One of the other people in the Midlands used to tell me sometimes, if I asked him.'

'I should be sad if you asked me, Justina.'

'I won't!' she blurted out, desperate to please of a sudden. 'Honestly.'

'I know,' he said gravely, rising and taking her hand to lead her to the couch. 'I hope you have a few moments to rest a while.'

'Yes, Bonn.' She went with him. 'How long have you been doing this?'

'A short while.'

'Before that, where were you? I mean what you used to do.'

'I rarely remember.'

'You won't tell me?'

His reply took its time. 'You have a right to better subjects than me, Justina. This is time for you, not for me.'

The second hour had begun to tick away, Bonn noticed. Justina started telling him what a hell of a time she had had on the Grobbon case. He listened, nodding and putting in small prompting phrases. If this was how she chose to spend her hours, so be it. His being here belonged to her until the clock ticked time away.

Chapter Twenty-Three

Iole – an indigenous person

Heghorn did the donkey-work at the newspaper office. The advertiser was a woman bank worker. Even before they entered and asked to see her, Heghorn knew she must be unbelievably docile. He fretted at Hassall's insistence on what would be a wasted journey.

'She's a regular churchgoer, Mr Hassall. Spinster, hospice charity fund-raiser.'

'Let's make up our mind when we see her, eh?'

They interviewed her with the bank's branch manager and a glowering trade union rep in attendance, the latter obviously convinced the police were inventing dubious charges against an innocent colleague.

Erica Knott was a plain but interesting woman, say thirty-four, give or take. She wore her hair in a dated bob, her blouse high and tight at the neck. Everything was subdued about Miss Knott, the sort you'd never notice without a photo taken with skilled lighting. Mundane? Hassall told her, his manner quite friendly, placing adverts for assassins around the city simply wasn't on. This caused the branch manager to pale, and the trade union rep, a breathlessly stout chuffer like something fresh out of an engine shed, to ask for a postponement so he could call up two trade

151

union lawyers. Both stared at the benign Miss Knott as if seeing her for the first time.

'We shall be gone in a moment. This is not an arrest,' Hassall told them amiably. 'It's just that your Box 451 advert, Miss Knott, might be construed as disturbing the sovereign's peace. People become unstitched and worry for no reason. We don't like that.

'So a pervert can get away scot-free after killing some poor girl?'

Hassall sighed. The last thing he needed today was an argument on the morality behind criminal law. 'She isn't dead, Miss Knott. The law freed Ricky Grobbon.'

'On a technicality!' Miss Knott said, full of reproach.

'He was declared innocent.'

'So you say, Mr Hassall! Everybody thinks otherwise!'

'Then they are wrong, Miss Knott.' Hassall kept his patience.

The bank manager and the union rep were still gaping at her.

'What *is* this?' The manager, Frederick Wilberforce, had his quarterly report to head office to think of. Should he report this incident in full, or smooth things over? His ulcer was playing up.

'Miss Knott placed a notice in the paper. The sum is considerable. A year's free living.' Sergeant Heghorn handed each of the two men a photocopy of the newspaper advertisment.

He must have felt left out because he spoke the precise figures, the average national wage adjusted for inflation but before Inland Revenue tax and NIC deductions. Both observers looked with awe at Miss Knott. Was this Erica's first revelation of independent decision? Mr Wilberforce's fingers rippled in suppressed anxiety.

'I have the money, Mr Hassall,' she said as if challenged on the point. 'I have no intention of defaulting. All I require is—'

'All the police require, Miss Knott, is for you to obey the law, and not to go about disturbing the peace. I don't doubt your intentions are honest, as far as the money is concerned. What you propose, however, is an encouragement to commit murder.'

'There you are quite wrong, Mr Hassall,' Miss Knott said gravely. 'I am merely proposing that society redresses the wrong done to that poor child.'

'The policeman means it might reflect on the bank's good name,' the manager said anxiously.

'The policeman doesn't mean that at all,' Hassall said heavily, not welcoming the interruption. 'The policeman could not care less about the bank's name. The policeman wishes to nip this in the bud, and have Miss Knott's promise not to carry it any further.' He turned to the clerk. 'Did anyone put you up to this, Miss Knott, or did you think of it yourself?'

'I thought of it all by myself, of course.' She seemed affronted, her hands primly checking the hem of her tweed skirt.

Heghorn asked, 'Doesn't it concern you that you were doing something illegal?'

'I have behaved perfectly properly. Somebody has to settle that pervert's hash. Why else would I go to such expense? After all, it represents my life savings. I can't throw it away on a worthless cause.'

Hassall began to wish he hadn't come in today. His missus wanted to go to the new Horsfall Megamarket beyond Hardwick, and he was here with this claptrap. He should have left it to Heghorn, who'd have loved doing this on his own, something to chat about in the cop shop.

'You intended to have this man murdered?'

'Of course.' Hassall waited for her to make some qualification, but the woman seemed adamant. 'Everyone wants that, except you.'

'What you propose is against the law, Miss Knott.'

'What I have done, sir, is public-spirited.' The woman was unfazed and quietly spoken. She faced them with docility, hands clasped on her knees, skirt tucked well in. 'If the law will not defend the children of this city, then ordinary citizens must. I have twice written to the Home Secretary, without even the courtesy of a reply, Mr Hassall. I can furnish you with copies of the originals.'

'What gave you the idea, Miss Knott?'

'A film I saw. It was on television many weeks ago. Rather too violent for my taste, but I like watching late TV. It was the story of somebody who decided to take vengeance over a similar issue in America. The police favoured the perpetrator instead of the poor victim, just,' she added primly, 'like you.'

'You decided to do the same thing?'

'Yes.' She adjusted her spectacles. 'I know nothing about weapons. I took a book from the library, but found it hard to understand. They call rifles long arms,' she explained helpfully. 'I shouldn't be

154

able to do it, so I clearly had to advertise.'

'It was very wrong of you, Miss Knott,' Hassall said gently.

'No, Mr Hassall,' she said firmly, fixing him with startlingly clear blue eyes. 'Everybody in this city thinks as I do. Listen to them on the Number Twelve bus out to Salford College, and you'll hear whether people approve or not. The judiciary was wrong to free the murderer. It is that simple. You police had no right letting the court free him.'

'We can't go against the law, Miss Knott.'

'So he is under police protection?' She glared up at him. 'Free to kill again? Some other innocent child is out there thinking itself safe while he stalks...' She broke down. The men remained silent as she gathered herself. 'I'm sorry, Mr Hassall.'

'I need your undertaking that you will not repeat this kind of thing again, Miss Knott.'

'I have already received four replies.'

'You've *what?*' Heghorn exclaimed then halted, conscious of Hassall's irritation.

'Four replies. I have them in my handbag.' She looked up at Heghorn. 'It is in my desk.'

'Might we see them, please?'

'Why, yes. One is very strange. I couldn't understand the second. The other two seem sensible. One says he was a soldier, but is only free to do it at weekends.'

Hassall hated shopping, but the megamarket beyond Hardwick now seemed to beckon like a pleasant holiday camp. He nodded to Heghorn, go and get them, let's take this further. He made a slight chopping gesture, the universal police sign

155

to keep the paparazzi out of it. He thanked Mr Wilberforce and even shook hands with the trade union rep, all good friends here even if their colleague was barmy. While Heghorn accompanied Miss Knott to her desk to collect evidence about the city's cohorts of eager assassins, he smilingly assured the two officials that he would see that the events of today would not reflect either on the bank's good name or the union's character.

They were relieved. Everybody parted as adults should.

'See, sir,' Heghorn said on the way back to the nick, 'for every Miss Knott in the country there's thousands think the same.'

'Get away,' Hassall said, morose with sarcasm. 'Get everything?'

'She carried them in their envelopes. I bagged them. I got a sample of her fingerprints.'

'Hers won't be evidence, not in those circumstances.'

'No, sir. I'll run them just the same, eh? For exclusion purposes. They're probably only nutters, wanting to be the Hooded Avenger.'

'Let's hope none of them takes himself seriously.'

'Or herself,' Heghorn surprised Hassall by saying, because he'd just been thinking the same thing.

'Right, right.'

Chapter Twenty-Four

sezzer – a know-all (from 'Says I')

Magazines often said it was a question of personal choice. Choice, as if the very act of looking at furniture was an accomplishment. It wasn't. Clare knew that from being a girl.

Logically, you choose between alternates, this against that. Blue or green, then on to compare Sap with Leaf Green, thus considering different leaf greens. And so on. That's how a choice is made, this side of madness. Too often she had come unstuck, she remembered, as she drifted round the space that would be her home. Tempting to gather every possible career move, estate agent brochures, whatever, and finish up exhausted. You simply wore yourself out, switching from one temptation to another.

The flat – very well, 'apartment', as estate agents now said – was above a retail newsagent's. She had chosen well. She told herself this. The view into Raglan Road was possibly a little grim, just a triangular piece of grass with swings and roundabouts. The noisy children were reassuring. To the left, by craning from her window, she could glimpse the old converted mill everybody called the Barn Owl. Clare knew Martina met her syndicate leaders there, including the main keys like Bonn, when making decisions. Fine, let the malicious bitch limp on to her evil destiny. For the while, the blue-eyed blonde sociopath could hold her position, but before long Clare would have Bonn out from beneath Martina's wing. After that decisive step, things would be in the lap of the gods. It would all be down to herself, and how Bonn would respond. He had more or less agreed to come.

More distantly, she could see a line of six lock-up garages, the bus stop opposite, and beyond a horizon view of moors marking the Pennines, with smudges of industrial smoke. Well, you couldn't help those, you lived with the rest of the city. Her own garage was adjacent. A young couple who ran the newsagent's on the ground floor had already spoken to her about customers parking there of a morning. Clare couldn't worry about such things. Who can make rules for the world? Life was as it was. She was long past joining crusades for insignificant causes.

Two bedrooms, one with an en suite bathroom, a small shower room and loo, handles set in the wall showing where a former occupant, maybe disabled, had found help necessary to get about, and a living-room of a surprisingly decent size. The bay window was above the newsagent's display place, sweets, papers, dry goods. The entire building had recently been re-wired, so the electrics were sound, the plumbing lately checked in detail, and boisterous delivery men were available from the furnishing warehouse at a day's notice. The decorators would come this afternoon, with their inevitable radios, sandwiches, insatiable demands for flasks of tea, and requests about the nearest betting shop. They could get on with it, she had other things on her mind.

Colours worried Clare. This was it. Her furniture was chosen, the die cast, no way of going back. Her mother and father would come early Sunday, Mum frosty with disapproval about her status as a divorced woman, with her repetitive grumble: 'You're a *professional* lady, Clare, and don't forget you are back to being *single...*' in aghast tones, while Dad would hum and ha, speculating on the BTUs from her radiators and the wisdom of under-floor heating. Clare had never quite worked Dad out, whether his tactics were simple evasion or complete lack of understanding. Now, she thought she knew: Dad kept out of it.

One of Clare's choices was eggshell or sheer matt for the walls. Bonn, educated in a seminary, had no real awareness of life outside. It was only a chance encounter with Posser, Martina's ailing father, that had kept Bonn from travelling south to London looking for a job. He was then recruited by Posser. Bonn's continual doubts, and withdrawals, from the mass of people in Martina's syndicate, were still there. She returned to the decorating problem.

So far, she had decided on an eggshell finish, though one of the younger decorators had grimaced. The older man made some joke, evidently an old squabble. Her selection of different pastels had surprised the foreman, but he had given the typical gaffer's head-tilt to show he didn't quite go along but would comply. It was Dad's sort of noncommittal comment.

Sometimes she wondered if her parents knew about Bonn. Dad often heard more than he let on. Sometimes she was taken aback by an occasional flash of understanding in his eyes as he turned away humming and pretending not to listen. Once he realised, though, what would his response be? Mum would do everything but swoon, and she'd probably do that too if the vapours threatened to come back into fashion.

Clare consulted a colour chart. She went from room to room, to see how the colours might look with lights on then lights off. Music was essential, for Bonn loved to listen, his reserve masking a fascination with the art. These things were important. Not that Bonn had to be pleased on every single count, the way some women submerged their own personalities into their man's likes and dislikes. Bonn would hate that. No, Bonn often marvelled at her, just looking, preoccupied by her movements, her face, seeming anxious to get in her mind. He found her alluring. The danger, never far from Clare's mind, was that he developed the same interest in every woman he met, young or old, in his bizarre occupation.

That was the question. She halted, thinking. Occupation? Was it truly that, or was it a kind of addiction? A salaried job could be forgiven, whatever form it took. After all, a man must pursue his trade, profession, vocation if you liked. As, nowadays, most women did too, and nobody was the worse for that. Reasonable to expect decent money for your hours and work. Fair enough. But addiction, obsession? He might never be able to rid himself of it. There lay the one-way street to

160

madness. She worried, thoughts coming full circle.

Luckily she was never without a small notebook. She brought it out and with the lights still on decided to make a new list of colours. The decorators would be cross if she changed her mind, especially over the bathroom, but heavens above, she was paying them enough. And the ganger had a lad along who could make a dash for new supplies to the Deansgate shopping mall across Victoria Square, fifteen minutes there and back.

Rack met Sonz at the Textile Museum corner. The electrician was having a smoke, his missus busy inside copying some drawings for her nightschool class.

'Got it done?'

'Yeh,' Sonz said. 'You didn't say about the shop downstairs.'

'Leave it.'

Rack could have grown heated, a dead-leg like Sonz checking whether he'd asked for the right thing or not, but he had things on his mind. One was the Green stringers going ape over that girl deaded in Farnworth General's Intensive Care Unit. Some photo in the papers sent them into orbit. It was getting so you couldn't go for a pee without the world taking off and riot squads about.

He decided to tell Grellie to rein her fucking herd in. It was coming to something. Life had no time for essentials, and here came dross like the stringers spoiling his day.

Trouble was, Rack was hoping to use a new girl. She looked like a goojer but was broad Brummie

161

with an uncle said to be a Methody minister in Newcastle – a place soon to be much in the news, Rack hoped fervently, because of an unexpected death coming up soon. Well, this lass called herself Chloe and had gone blonde, the changes all in two days. Rack fancied using her maybe the once, see how she was shaping up. Always worth a try. He hadn't had a regular girl for a fortnight, that cow Hannah from the Wirral who'd once been a nurse, she said, and tried to get him to fork out money for some habit she'd acquired. She'd been useless. He was glad she had to go, like some beers made you glad you'd had enough.

No, he wanted straight things today so he could get his head round too many happenings. Like the car showroom he'd heard nothing of when he should have. What was Akker playing at?

'I put them new San Francisco gadgets in,' Sonz said, indifferent, flicking fag ash every-where, which really narked Rack. 'Good enough, last for ever, the batteries they sell now. Nice flat, she's got. Ghange them every three months, say ten weeks on the safe side.'

'Right. The decorators know?'

'Not from me, Rack,' Sonz said, who knew Rack's reputation though this was only the third lecky job he'd done for the syndicate's chief stander with the evil temper. 'I sez nothing.'

'Better not, Sonz,' Rack said, pleased at the answer, because it went to show that some of these northern prats weren't as thick as they looked. 'See you change them regular, right?'

'Right, Rack. Who do I tell?'

'Fat George, newspaper-seller at the corner of

Bolgate Street. Check with him before and after, OK? If you can't raise Fat George for some reason, then leave a message with Askey at the Triple Racer. Never through the street girls.'

Rack didn't want Grellie's Blue string, who worked the Deansgate corner centred on the Volunteer pub, being disturbed by the thought that Dr Clare's new flat was bugged. But this was Martina's orders, and you couldn't go against those or you got your head bit off for nowt.

'Do I collect the tapes, Rack?'

'Did I tell you to?'

'No, no!' Sonz almost backed away before Rack's stare. 'Sorry, chief, I meant nothing, honest.'

'Don't not never mean nowt, Sonz,' Rack said, deciding to be kind because Chloe, the new girl he wanted to try, was strolling among the Square's traffic, doing a stroll knowing the traffic would slow in appreciation. Twice she'd glanced over to where Rack was.

'Course not, Rack.' Sonz wished his missus would come out, with her sketches of them bloody frocks she kept drawing. 'Exact as you say, chief.'

'Right,' Rack said. 'See yer.'

He liked it when people saw they'd no right to sod about making up their own minds. It was more reasonable to do as he told, because life got easier then. These were important things for people to learn.

'Ta-ra, Rack.'

Rack walked casually towards the pedestrian crossing at George Street so he could follow Chloe into the Central Gardens. He had more sense than try to cross in the middle of the traffic, like Chloe did. The cow simply took no notice of traffic lights and irate motorists, knowing they'd crawl to watch her move and never a horn parped. Rack felt bitter waiting to cross. If that wasn't discrimination, what was?

Chapter Twenty-Five

tool – gun, weapon

The assassin was collected at the railway station in a remote part of Suffolk. The American was smiling as they met and, careful ambassador for his country that he was, made only the usual we're-in-public welcome. His automobile's military registration made him conspicuous. The chat on the way to the squadron's base was all routine.

'Lot of rotation,' Hal Weatherton said. 'Always trouble. We get seven queries for every notification.'

'Good heavens.'

The assassin was smiling at the superfluous conversation. They often put this act on during previous visits. Such was Hal's status as special enquiror on the American Air Force base that almost everything he did or said was recorded as a cautionary measure. Like the White House presidential tapes.

'Hardly time to do any modelling work on the railway series at all.'

'Never mind. I've brought one or two things to interest you.'

'Really?' Hal smiled, his voice becoming husky at the casual promise.

'Five or six. You can keep only one. I'm helping at an exhibition for a children's hospice and they'll need them there. We've been let down by those suppliers.'

'I thought the Swedes were good.'

'They have their moments. Two deliveries of copper tubing for the smallest gauge railways – you know, the one you criticise? – haven't arrived.'

'What did you do?'

The car approached the checkpoint. Two guards appeared. The passenger presented the pass. This was taken into their booth for validation with the assassin's passport. The assassin approved. All too often, systems forgot the importance of security. Things could easily become sloppy. That was how child molesters escaped.

'OK, major,' the guard said, returning the document.

'Thanks, sergeant.'

'Have a good visit.'

'Thank you.'

The assassin smiled as the car moved on through. Each visit, all details had been cross-checked and duly registered. Good to see standards upheld.

Next morning, Hal and the assassin visited the military firing range. Hal was always pleasantly surprised by his friend's handling of the weapons.

As ever, they talked at length about a wide

selection of killing devices used by marksmen who trained at the base. A sergeant instructor joined them.

'No, sir,' Sergeant Alvarez said firmly when the major tried to respond to his visitor's question about the rounds used. 'The 0.50 BMG calibre cartridge – stands for Browning Machine Gun – came about when John Moses Browning designed the machine gun, and made the round just for that.'

'That's who our marksmen call Saint John Moses!' Hal put in, laughing. 'At least, those of our marksmen who prefer using such a monstrosity!'

'All marskmen are capable with all weapons supplied, major,' Alvarez said soberly.

'I'm sure,' the assassin said politely. 'Can a weak-kneed teacher like myself give one a try?'

'It's heavy duty,' Alvarez warned.

'Isn't it still in use in NATO?' Hal asked.

'Correct, sir. Some armoured vehicles, and aircraft, are capable of using it. I prefer the old bolt-action long arm with the 0.50 BMG round. Here we use a standard training distance of 1,500 metres, virtually one imperial mile, for snipers.'

'If you have an entire month to spare,' Major Weatherton said, grinning at his visitor, 'listen to the marksmen arguing their favourites!'

'The Harris weapons stand out, sir,' Alvarez said without humour. 'The IMI Israeli weapons are supposed to be as good, but I doubt it.'

'I'd like to handle at least one, if that's allowed.'

'The major can sign you in.' Alvarez rose. 'I have an Ultra-Light M-95 Harris. It carries a tenor twenty-round bank. You might find the bolt-action something of a haul, but seeing you coped well enough with the standard issue NATO toy last time...' He winked at Hal Weatherton and the assassin smiled along as they followed the instructor to the military firing range. The lack of any civilian firing range of appropriate size and security in the country had made this endless pantomime of visiting Hal Weatherton necessary. This would be the last time before Ricky Grobbon was dispatched to his ancestors.

'Weighs just over eight kilos, the Harris M-95,' Alvarez was saying as they approached the issue counter. 'The trouble is its lack of sight, but you can stick on your usual telescopic sight when called for.'

'All black, I see,' the visitor said, drawing breath with suppressed excitement as the weapon was issued against signatures from Hal and Sergeant Alvarez. 'Is that usual?'

'Standard, though some of the boys dislike the glass-fibre pistol-grip configuration of the stock. I love it. Best yet made.'

'Of course,' the assassin concurred politely. 'May I handle it, please?'

'That's why we're here,' Alvarez said. He liked enthusiasm, and the major's visitor certainly had that in abundance. The soul of a true craftsman.

Chapter Twenty-Six

twoc – Taken Without Consent (police slang); twocker

Akker tended to lose patience, but not so anybody would notice. He just seethed inside, standing there in his drab raincoat looking bedraggled.

'Got the Gets?' he asked Penk, his main car mover.

Penk, a local, from Moses Gate, snorted.

'I can't be doing with these gadgets, Akk,' he said, but nodding. 'They cost the fucking earth. We got them, so what?'

'Show.'

'I don't hold with all this lecky crap.'

'I want to see you got them all, Penk.'

Penk, who hated electricity, brought out the receivers. Akker looked at them with interest. The Garmin Etrex Global Positioning System units were small. He marvelled at American military bosses. If these little things were so valued by the Yank rank-and-file soldiery, why the hell couldn't the USA manufacture a few million more? Their own troops couldn't get them issued, and resorted to buying them privately over the Internet. Barmy.

'And the Motorola Talkabouts?'

'Them and all.' The lightweight two-way radios were standard thief's toolery and everybody had them, not to mention the plod. Penk produced them as proof.

'Owt else, Akk?'

'Yeh. Who's your oppo?'

'Got Bondi from the 'Pool.'

Akker was impressed, for Bondi, the fattest Australian known to civilisation, had once competed in the World's Strongest Man heats. Never got beyond the first round, but was the fastest car thief in Liverpool, which was like saying you could give him a light year start to anywhere and he'd still have the kettle on when you came puffing in.

'Truckers?'

'Two blokes.' Penk shrugged. 'Bondi speaks for one, me the other. They know the drill.'

Odd, a trucker was always the least important of any motor nicker, no more than a dogsbody despite his title. Truckers often couldn't even drive, just came along to perform menial tasks. They rode with the driver in the car transporter and simply did his bidding.

'Either of them drunks?'

'No, Akk. Honest.'

'Better not be.'

This was another of Akker's phobias, that some goon would come staggering out of the vehicle-shifter wagon on the motorway and get the whole scam taken down because they stank like a brewery. It hadn't happened yet, which was all the better reason to see it never.

'Whose transporters are they?'

Akker was in a service station on the M6 motorway.

'They're clean, booked out of the depot in Macclesfield less'n an hour since.' Penk eyed the camera on the service station building. He too had his foibles. Akker saw the glance.

'They're seen to. Think I'd forget?'

'Just a thought.'

Akker looked about and gave Penk the nod. 'Go in. You'll be met by two plod outriders on standard issue filth motorbikes. A third'll follow you.'

'By the time we get to Victoria Square it'll be dark, Akk.'

'I know.'

Akker thought, Jesus, you really need patience in this frigging game. Like, he'd remember everything from the proper cop bike outfits, paperwork all done and dusted, and he'd forget when daylight faded?

'Where's that queer bird, bosses the showroom?'

'None of your business.'

'And the alarms, the rest of the staff?'

'Gone or unavailable.'

'Right.'

'And no talking, not a single word out of the lot of you, right?'

'I already told them.'

'One word, one name, and our fee gets chopped.'

'Quartered?' Penk was horrified. He vowed to repeat his threats to his team of three. To chop, except when gambling, meant to decrease a fee to three-quarters of the previously agreed price. 'The transporters need to be back at the depot tennish, Akk. I got blokes there to scour them clean.'

'Your drop's fixed. Wait for the signals. They'll be on the M16 for the lead wagon, on the M6 for the second.'

170

'Reet, Akk.'

They said so-long and Akker went to fumble with the door of a Toyota Yaris. Its owner had not long before gone inside for a meal. He prised the window and sat in the driver's seat as Penk's two giant car transporters rumbled into life and rolled massively from the car park.

He waited a few minutes then left the Yaris and went to the petrol pumps. His own car was in a CCTV blind spot near the pay desk window. You couldn't be too careful.

The time had gone about right. Another thirty minutes, and the sabotaged auto-cameras would flick miraculously back into life, the gap inexplicable to the authorities but making his meeting with Penk's team unrecorded. He decided to drive to the outskirts of the city, wait a bit, then spend a good hour or so going ahead of the immense wagons.

Two decoy wagons, legitimately hired from elsewhere, would soon start for Liverpool. Their drivers would be pulled in, baffled, in a couple of hours and taken in for questioning by the plod. Their descriptions were already being learnt by heart, two strawmen – actually women on Rack's panel of standby perjurists – allegedly returning home from Blackpool after an evening out at the South Pier, ready to complain about the maniacs who drove two loaded transporters hammering their way to Liverpool at the motorway interchange. They would rant and rave, demanding to know what were the police going to do about it, dangerous driving ought not to be allowed, etc, etc.

'Yackety-yackety,' Akker said to himself.

He often thought Rack went a bit over the top insisting on arrangements down to such detail, because after all who cared? Once a load of posh saloon motors were owffed and sent winging on their way to France for a significant wadge, all was peace and light, right? Out of sight, out of mind, Akker always told himself. Still, why not stick to Rack's image of perfection?

Akker drove contentedly on his way, going over the phoney orders, the sham coppers, the borrowed police motorbikes, the cones ready to be placed outside the showroom to warn traffic about a shipment of new cars being loaded up. It was foolproof. Yet, just when you thought that, sure enough sod's law would come into play. He could remember a dozen scams that had gone amiss. Overconfidence did it.

For an instant he was tempted to crack on, catch up with Penk and Bondi and see they did right, but kept control. No good worrying himself sick. It was all done now. Planned right, things should follow like clockwork. Faintly anxious he'd missed something, he stayed at fifty, clocking the white-on-blue direction signs flicking by. If he got edgy, the others would become the same.

He switched on his own Motorola Talkabout, staying in touch with the two giant vehicles rumbling north, and tried humming some song.

Chapter Twenty-Seven

payhem – illegal damage inflicted in return for offence or injury

Martina had a small flat in Quaker Street. She thought of it as her reservation. It was nothing more than a couple of second floor rooms, kitchen, bathroom, served by a private lift from the ground floor. Officially it was designated accountancy office. Taxation people listed it as such, and charged Value Added Tax as a legitimate expenditure on her syndicate's books, the legitimate versions of course.

Outside, Quaker Street was at its usual bustle, being one of the hectic thoroughfares every old city in the kingdom seemed embarrassed by yet never knew what to do with. These narrow lanes were a problem for city councillors, and could not be altered, redesigned or changed. Traffic ingress was strictly controlled. The Palais Rocco stood at the nearby junction with Moor Lane. Within a stone's throw, the Bouncing Block gym, the Café Phrynne, the card-sharp alcove locals called The Lagoon, the mighty Worcester Club and Tea Rooms, all fell into Martina's feifdom, and functioned in various states of elation and despair. Vehicles dashed clockwise round Victoria Square and were always audible. The Pilot Ship, a casino serving as Martina's control centre, was within a hundred yards beyond the dog-leg of Waterloo Street.

She lay replete in Den's sweat. Strange, this episode. She wondered if it was so for the man, decided no. How could it be? They slept after orgasm, then rose with different degrees of alacrity, and were off into life. The woman simply lay, contemplatively willing to speak, maybe even analyse, usually against the man's instincts. Did it take so much out of them, literally and metaphorically? She supposed it must, for they provided the musculature and the spillage, however much the feminists insisted that sexual intercourse was a mere 'exchange of fluid'. The donation was the male's. Except, of course, emotions were paramount for both. With feelings, anything could happen.

Den was pleasant, jocular even. He was willing to chat, and smiled a great deal before, during, afterwards. He watched serial TV programmes she too made sure of catching. She found herself laughing at amusing things he said, caught on to the characters he imitated and actually enjoyed his company, even scoring how long it had been since she had felt so entertained. The thought was inescapable, of course, and only came when finally she let it in.

Was it a performance, from one so practised in the art of performing? Was it a show put on by a showman? All right, carry the sad thought to its conclusion: *was it an act?* Who knew this? And did they themselves – she had accepted a few, over time – did *they* know for absolute certain if their eager love making was sheer pretence? She stared

174

at the ceiling. The one lover she had taken, since assuming charge of her dad's syndicate, who uniquely had not left this anxious residue, was Bonn. There was no answer. Den was amusing, attentive, and roused her, brought her off, in the vulgar phrase. He worked tirelessly, left her satisfied, so what was wrong? Nothing. Which, she told herself slightly sourly, only meant there actually was something amiss. Den had been a pleasure.

So?

She listened to the traffic, people calling and two of Grellie's own girls shouting crudenesses across the alley to some shopkeeper's helper – possibly Deepo, who should by now be sweeping out the newsagency below, and having an illicit fag while his boss Vitak wasn't looking. That they made such casual exchanges confirmed for Martina that her secret nook was still unknown to her employees. She did not stretch when coming to, though she always did after having Bonn. Why was this? She had made it evident to Bonn that she would have Den, and got no response. Did she expect any? Bonn had made no sign of disapproval or jealousy. There was not even a sign of acceptance, as if he were inert. A woman wanted responses and looked for them. It is in our nature. Men gave few signs, hardly any clues to how they were thinking.

Bonn, though?

How many times had it been with Bonn? Only after the most careful planning, making sure Posser was well out of the way and Mrs Ogden and her two busybodies who did for Posser's family home in Bradshawgate were off duty, did she see Bonn. After Bonn something different

175

happened. Odd signs tipped her off to this. Like having a good stretch, for instance, after Bonn but never after Den or others. Not much in itself, but it was something to be explained. Another change: she once had told Bonn to get her a drink, please, with both of them still lying in bed, and he simply shook his head, no, pondering away. Now, nobody ever told her no, except for Posser, and he after all was Dad, who had a right. And unbelievably she had not insisted, behaved quite as if she understood he was away in that mind of his and could not be disturbed for the moment. Amazed at herself, she simply got out of bed and limped – as in *limped* on her gammy leg within plain view if Bonn had as much as glanced at her – and got the drink herself, even turning to ask if he wanted one too. He had said a polite, 'No, thank you.' Incredible for her to be so passive, though she thought nothing of it at the time, only being astonished at herself afterwards.

Another oddity was when he slept. She watched him, something she never did with others. And she enjoyed watching him sleep, before or after didn't worry her. She almost purred, as if he were some infant she was watching over while he slumbered. Sillier still, she counted his breaths, wondered how he had been at puberty, who had been his first, why he seemed so stricken by everyday details of life. Even now, Den's sweat drying on her skin, she found herself wondering why Bonn never asked a question outright, just stated a problem as if for himself. He only offered words to the world Out There, positing them for others to answer or ignore. Was it that he was strange, and others more manly, more outgoing, dashing, daring, sporty even? They enjoyed her, for Christ's sake, she thought angrily at herself, and Bonn seemed to ... well, worship. That in itself was difference enough.

Her cell phone rang. It could only be Posser, for nobody else had access. The one hacker who had somehow culled her number from the ether had suffered badly for the intrusion, and would never, never ever, do such a thing again.

She picked up. 'Dad?'

'Hello, love. The TV news, if you can get it.'

'What channel?'

'Don't know, love. It'll be on the radio. Got one there?'

He didn't know where she was, had been left to make supposes, and understood it was private. He never enquired.

'Maybe. What station?'

'Dunno. Bound to be on local, what is it, Radio Piccadilly?'

'Right, Dad.'

'See you later. All right, love?'

'Fine, thanks. You?'

They made reassuring noises and rang off. Off? The thought gave her a clue about herself and Bonn. The physical act of sex might be the same with the dashing Den. The difference was, she suddenly felt, that afterwards, coming down to earth, with Den it was simply over. They had done it, got or given whatever passion, and the world went on.

With Bonn, though? Had she accepted Bonn for the past hour, and watched him leave, he would

177

still remain here with her somehow. There was still Bonn somewhere beyond the physical. He would still be on some road as a consequence of having had sex with her, and her alone. It was intolerable that he would travel it alone, meaning without her, as if she was deprived of what came next. However intense the orgasm, whatever the satisfaction, Bonn continued questing on, and she wanted to be there. Love, though? She reached out and switched on the radio, hardly willing to listen. Love was something else. She had spoken only once with Bonn about the nature of love. She'd claimed that love was comfort, friendship, warmth, support, help. He had turned his intrusive look on her, and she fell silent.

'Comfort is comfort,' he'd told her, as if he had already got this far in thinking it out. 'Friendship is friendship. Warmth is warmth. Love needs to be more than its subsidiaries, just as a river is more than its tributaries and the sea is more than the rivers flowing in.'

She'd thought it juvenile, and said so. Then he had said it, shocking her. 'Love is unconditional desire to do another good.'

Unconditional? She was outraged, and they had separated in silence, a clear hour before Posser came home. Was that another clue, that she had accepted Bonn there, in Bradshawgate, her home? Nobody else was allowed that privilege.

Unconditional, she thought, deciding to rouse and bath while she listened to the wretched news. It came on as she ran the water, and she hurried back into the bedroom to hear.

'...from the life support machines at the hospital.

178

The Hospital Ethical Committee has received protests from religious sects, and demonstrators are gathering outside the central offices of the Area Health Authority in Markland Street. The fourteen-year-old girl was found on the by-pass, apparently after being flung from a car travelling at speed. The incident was witnessed...'

Great, Martina thought. That's all I need. Grellie's girls were already in orbit about the girl. She knew of their wish to have the apparent perpetrator straightened. Rack had told Posser about it two days back, and Martina had asked Rack to make sure no mayhem-payhem resulted from the girls' outrage, especially after that Toofy Grobbon was released on some legal technicality.

She turned off the hot tap, limped for her dressing gown and rang Posser.

'Dad? What now?'

'Phone, love,' he wheezed. He sounded particularly breathless. Taking time away like this was always attended by the risk that Posser tippled some whisky against Dr Winnwick's orders. She was sure he hid a bottle or two about the house and suspected Mrs Ogden of complicity.

'Still,' she said, accepting his warning. 'The question is, do we do anything.'

'I reckon not. There'll be grief enough.'

'That's what I think, Dad,' she said, easier now. 'Let the newspapers and the telly newscasters get on with it. What's it to do with us anyway?'

'Glad we see eye to eye,' Posser said. 'Home soon?'

'I'll drop in. Did you remember your tablets?'

'Yes, yes,' he said testily, and said so-long.

179

She looked at her image in the full-length mirror. The leg deformity gave her body a tilt, utterly hateful, and would never be corrected. Posser still blamed himself for her childhood injury. Another point of difference occurred to her. Bonn never even truly noticed her limp, her stilted dot-and-carry-one walk. Others, Den included, painstakingly stared elsewhere as if clearly announcing they were ignoring her lameness. It was twice as bad as telling her outright, 'God, that's a limp-and-a-half you've got there, Martina'. Bonn did not pretend. With Bonn, she was ... *with Bonn she was whole.* Almost as if Bonn made her whole by some inner transcendental power. Seen this way, sometimes she grew disturbed, even slightly frightened, as if in the presence of one thought insane.

'Love,' she said to the reflection, 'is maybe in the eye of the beholder. Is that it?'

She told herself off for becoming insufferably fanciful, and got into the bath. She would have to speak to Rack. It was time she told him the perp, that Toofy Grobbon, was to be topped. Someone would have to do it. She wondered who.

Soaking, she decided she would send for Akker. Before suppertime, when Rack was hard at some lunatic business or other. It had to be done, or the whole syndicate, Grellie's girls included, would come apart.

Chapter Twenty-Eight

slitterati – hired killers of questionable allegiance

Hassall watched the men crane the giant screen in place. He could have found a better place for it than right in the middle of Victoria Square, spoiling the view of the bus depot, the gardens and the all night caff, the old geezers' massive plastic chess game and new crown bowling green. He said as much to the drab bloke standing there.

'Football,' Hassall told him. 'It's for the big match.'

'Is it?' the bloke said.

'The gardens'll be littered with tins and plastic,' Hassall complained. 'Fast food.'

'Mmmh.'

'Not from round here?'

'Sort of,' Akker said. 'Is it worth their while?'

'Who?'

'City council. They'll have to take it down on Monday.'

'Publicity, see?' Hassall had a thing about publicity. Too much was counter productive. It was a phrase he'd heard on Talk Sports Radio. It had stuck, this counter productive.

'I used to see a man prune trees as a lad.' Akker hadn't taken his eyes off the crane swinging the enormous television screen. Hassall noticed he only looked at the derrick, not the men guiding the huge object onto its supports. 'He had a block and tackle. Chainsaws were new, back then. He did the little branches first.'

'Then what?' Hassall kept the suspicion from his mind, that this might be the glove man he'd heard about. Rack's, Martina's, the syndicate's. If so, what the hell was he doing gaping at workmen for?

'He tied ropes round big branches. Lowered them once he cut them free.'

'Then the trunk?'

Akker was some time answering. 'No. Left it standing. I asked him why. He told me he was giving trees a hair cut.'

'Local, was he?'

'I hated him clearing up. Logs, twigs, leaves. All gone.'

'They've done it.'

The men were shouting. The crane driver, so high up, was nodding to their signals. The ganger yakked at a mobile phone. His workmen unhooked the chains and swarmed over the screen's supports. The clusters of spectators began to move.

'Must cost the earth,' Hassall started to say, then realised the drab man had left.

Akker walked towards Greygate. He hadn't once glanced Hassall's way which, Hassall thought, was odd. That was the tactic of people who were partially sighted or blind. Or of blokes who knew you anyway, and had no need to fix you in the mind.

Just for the hell of it Hassall strolled in the same direction. The dowdy thin bloke passed several of Grellie's girls as he crossed near the caff and made his way through the traffic to the far pavement. Waterloo Street, by the Lagoon all-night card place? Or George Street, passing Reel's ticket agency and the City Textile Museum? Anyway, Hassall thought, finally turning away, none of Grellie's girls had propositioned Drab. It was as if he wasn't there, drifting casually like a ghost among the Green stringers.

Then it struck Hassall. Shouldn't at least one of the street walkers have offered her services? None had as much as eyed him. They hadn't shunned him, not quite, just ignored the thin man. So they knew him, but not to speak to. None solicited. Hadn't smiled or nodded. *They were careful.* He ambled on, into Mawdsley Street by the Granadee TV Studios. Turn left, you'd be at the Shot Pot, the snooker hall where everything, it was said, happened or wasn't allowed to happen at all.

Hassall was disappointed, for the drab bloke paused, read a poster outside the Granadee's impressive portico, and turned back. He went into the bus station and caught the Number Eight bus to Bolton-le-Moors. Hassall waited to make sure. It left after a few minutes, Drab on it.

It was never Hassall's way to chat much. Asking fellow officers if they knew this or that low life was the way of dull scripters of TV bang-gang yawners. Hassall sometimes heard the lads in the ward room having a laugh at the taut faces and grim antagonisms of telly coppers. Emotions caused most hilarity. Routine TV soap phrases became catch-words you won points-for-pints in ordinary conversation, like, 'Can we talk?' and 'What's going on?' Hassall thought a ploddite really needed to become tired, practically done for, to be any use. You proved your worth by shutting up and getting on with it. Growing up, in a word.

First, though, you had to listen, not saying anything. Best of all were caffs, nosh bars, bus queues, benches by the bowling green, then – very far down the list – pubs. Next to last, the police canteen. Last of all, official police incident rooms, should anything become political enough to deserve such a load of crap.

He looked at the time, and went to the Butty Bar in Mealhouse Lane to listen some more.

Chapter Twenty-Nine

soshe – social services

Toofy Grobbon got the local cop lawyer off his back by pleading lawyers might be a security risk. The filth had finally come round, and decided to let him be. They insisted on a cell phone, which they provided, and a reserve cell phone he had 'to keep on his person at all times', as they put it, writing some Magna Carta.

'Pathetic,' he announced to the little flat in New-castle-on-Tyne. 'The filth are fucking pathetic.'

That was for the benefit of the ploddite on earwig duty. The poor sad bastard would have to log that in, spell it correctly, keeping a report of everything ex-perv releasee Grobbon had said or done since being spirited away from that cockroach infested nick across the Pennines.

'They think this is frigging luxury,' Toofy told his new living space. 'It's a right wank-hole, a fucking pit they shouldn't give a dog.'

He allowed them time to smoulder, get them really steamed up, then muttered, 'It's in all the newspapers. Police are all at it, shagging each other's missuses while they're supposed to be working. No wonder the papers keep on about it.'

That would shake the bastards up. He almost burst out laughing. They'd waste umpteen man-years of their valuable time scanning print for reports, which constable was dicking whose wives. Toofy hadn't read any reports, of course, but it all helped. Keep them on their toes, keep them thinking he was a rebel against all society. He was one of the elect, a higher thinker who reached a more elevated plane of exaltation that any of those thick uncomprehending thickos who were the plod.

Time was of the essence, though. Isn't that what poets said? He would give them three days of unspeakable boredom, somehow falsify his presence here, then do a flit, and unite with some young angel who didn't yet know she was going to become elevated to his own high plateau of mysticism. OK, society called his activities perversions, but he could escape their absurd laws any old time. He'd proved it, too clever for them by far.

He had it all worked out. He set his wrist watch for a series of reminding bleeps. The idea was keep the filth listening as he established the most boring routine in existence. That would lull the thick bastards into doing exactly as he wished. It would take no more than four days at the out-

185

side. The plod were all mental defectives, unable to plan longer than a week. Their success rates for SAs, meaning Social Aberrances such as they classified Toofy Grobbon – like they alone knew what levels of thought should exist in the whole fucking world – stood at no more than three per cent. One, two, three, that's *three*, in a hundred.

Toofy longed to meet up with others of his own kind. He lolled on the bed, thinking dreamily of the chats they could have, him and his other devotees. There must be plenty, judging by the hysterical press headlines, and those endless fucking talk shows on the idiot box where young fathers went berserk at politicians giving it gavotte, like, 'When are you going to put all these perverts behind bars?' and their stupid wives complaining, 'It's all right for politicians and MPs. You have special guards for your kids, but we people who pay taxes... Yakkety-yackety.'

He could compare notes with other mystics like himself, talk through how he'd actually felt that very first time. Purity expressed it, purity that came when the... No, he was becoming excited at the images flashing through his mind, and that would never do. No, stay in control. That was his means of access to the sacred portals through which he would take flight, leap into his brilliant world of mysticism. And return again to that sacred land where perfection lay.

It was easy enough to do, establish a ritual so mind-dulling that nobody with half a brain could tolerate. Three more days, the earwigger would be falling asleep or turning to see how the match was doing. Toofy had done it once before, and had his reward. He might go out and get a newspaper, see how the planet had managed without him, burn an innocent hour or two. He would read bits out aloud from the newspaper, ten minutes at a time, see how they liked that.

He almost roared with laughter. He'd start with the classified adverts, read them lists of cars for sale, or maybe flats and houses in nearby districts, though that was maybe a bit risky, for what if he accidentally hit on some victim from such an area? No, best give them lists of supermarket produce, special offers. They'd have to log every mutter, look for codes, expressions of intent the headshrinkers called it. Think of the doctors' fees, as they analysed every syllable! He'd read out holidays. That was it! The holiday firms, Come To The Algarve and all that crap, let the filth think he was aiming to abscond. Mixed with sports results, teams, arguments over a footballer eager to be sold, hired, picked, whatever, would drive the police listeners barmy.

His watch vibrated. He felt the thrill of the hunter return. This was how it was done. He picked up an old newspaper, already in the flat when he'd arrived, and began to read out special offers, starting with Austria, skiing, then snorkelling in the Red Sea. Laughing mustn't give the game away, though. He imagined a lovely victim, up there ahead, her features blurred but soon to be defined and beckoning, promising. I'm coming soon, he thought, very soon, the moment this stupid ritual is over and done with.

'Special Offers this weekend...' he read, gravely adjusting his tone.

Chapter Thirty

plazzie – police identity (warrant) card

The story was, Shania Brownham arrived just as the cleaners were about to leave. She stared at the vacated showrooms, unable to grasp the immensity of the crime.

'I asked where the cars were,' she'd told the investigating officer. 'Then I sent for Mr Ellston.'

Hassall wasn't the Scene of the Crime Officer, nor was he some unsworn layabout doing sweet sod all to bulk out his police pension. By avoiding glares when some phone boner took the 999 call and tried to pass the job, Hassall had developed superb dexterity at avoiding being landed with the city's crud. He kept responsibility off his shoulders, saved on desk donkey-work, and had time to see what the hell was going on. Being part-time from his health problem made this adaptation a whole lot easier.

Hassall wandered through, saying sorry for getting in the way, shaking his head at human perfidy, the missing motors. All had been new, except for one reconditioned thing, three thousand legitimate miles on the clock and going at a discount.

'Sixteen, then, Eric?' Hassall had asked Chancer, who'd drawn the short straw.

'She's not said anything much since we got here.'

'Good pro job, eh?'

'Looks like it.'

'Got photos?'

'The cars? Aye, Hassy, that folder on the desk. For a brochure.'

'Any idea?'

Chancer hesitated, and Hassall understood his difficulty. SOCOs, the Scene of the Crime Officers, were mostly ex-police nowadays. To appoint genuine sworn-into-the-book police would cost a few more groats than authorities wanted to spend, being stingy and spendthrift rolled into one caring police authority. So SOCOs tended now to be ex-police, earning a few zlotniks on the side, using the police club facilities and nicking the odd perk – free parking, financial entitlements, subsidised nosh in the canteen. That meant they could not push their minuscule weight around as if they were still the city's finest. They tended to be mucho careful, and didn't stir hornets from nests.

'She said somebody called round. She had him moved on.'

'Name? Description?'

'That's the point. No name. A youth, mebbe in his twenties, flashy, gabby, pretended to be a gunfighter, kid's stuff.'

Hello, Hassall thought. 'And?'

'That's it. She's got standing orders to have him collared if he shows again.'

Oh, dear, Hassall thought. 'No more?'

'She said he demanded payment.'

'For?' Like drawing teeth. Eric Chancer pursed his lips and shrugged.

'No services were mentioned.'

"Witnesses?'

'To the chat? Aye, deputy showroom manager. Mr Ellston. She doesn't think much of him.'

He told Hassall about Ellston, whose day off it was. He got Ellston's address and called round, guessing from the toys in the front garden that Ellston was off out with some infant. He got a likely direction from the daughter hanging out washing. It took two minutes, but Hassall hated flashing the plazzie. He always felt he was acting out Dick Powell in one of those old black-and-whiters, was it *The Big Sleep?* For a few moments he watched the little boy try to sink his model boat on the pond in the park. It was a while before Mr Ellston noticed Hassall.

'Mr Ellston?'

'This is my grandson Denny,' Ellston said, instantly nervous. 'I'm his grampa.'

Hassall crouched down. 'OK. Your motors are all nicked.'

'Nicked?' Ellston stared about as if expecting SAS teams of masked raiders. 'Stolen?'

'My name is Hassall. I'm police.'

'Stolen? Taken away? They can't do that, because...'

'Because what, Mr Ellston?'

Little Denny threw gravel at his sail boat, but missed.

'You missed,' Hassall said.

'I'll do it, I'll do it!'

'Because...?'

'There are so many.' Ellston kept hold of the boy, a careful man. The pool was barely a foot deep. The sail boat drifted ever further away. It could have been reached easily, by tearing a small rhododendron branch from one of the nearby bushes. Hassall guessed Mr Ellston was too careful a man for that kind of hooliganism. 'Sixteen. I have their photographs. It cost the earth, a special display for the *Chronicle*.'

'Seventeen, Mr Ellston. They took the recondie too.'

'Oh, dear. Ms Brownham will be furious. She'll blame me,' he added rather pathetically.

'Any ideas, Mr Ellston?'

'About what? Who would do such a thing?' He shook his head, passed Denny a few bits of shingle from the path for the lad to hurl at his boat. 'We've only been open a short while. Ms Brownham can give you all the dates. Has she been told?'

John Ellston was scared of Shania Brownham, then, despite his years in the trade. Ellston sighed. Denny crowed as one of his pebbles struck his boat. It moved further away.

'Yes. She's shocked.'

'Poor lady. She's just been promoted. This will be a terribly sad set-back.'

'Who was the bloke, then, Mr Ellston? Youngish, acted foolish like playing games.'

'Who?' Ellston guided his grandson's hand, trying to set the sail boat rocking, appearing engrossed. 'I'll have to try to find a stick. We'll have a job getting it back, Denny. Who?' he repeated.

'Some young fool. Ms Brownham barred him.'

'Oh, him.' Ellston paused, still holding the child, and frowned at the ornamental gardens. 'Can't say I paid much attention. Last week some time?'

'It was ten days ago. Can you describe him?'

'Can't say I can, much.'

'He wanted money. To guarantee your firm's business.'

Ellston was puzzled. 'Don't remember that. Did I make a note in the log?'

For one disorientating second Hassall had the mad idea Ellston meant the incident log, created by police the instant an emergency 999 call was received.

'We keep a log of daily enquiries,' Ellston explained, seeing his difficulty. 'It's a running-incident book. I still keep it in longhand, not on computer,' he added with pride.

'Not seen it, Mr Ellston.' Hassall rose with a grunt. 'If you remember anything, give us a bell.'

'Shall do, Mr Hassall.'

'The cleaners all new people too, are they?'

'Ms Brownham hired them herself.' Ellston's eyes showed a flash of humour, his face impassive. 'She trusts her own judgement. She is the boss, after all.'

'Ta for the help. Good luck with the boat.'

Hassall said so-long and left. Nothing more from that wise old bird. Ms Shania Brownham could whistle for her motors. They were long gone, and likely to remain so. The job had Rack's hallmarks, so there'd be no joy there.

He wondered if he should talk to Martina, Posser's daughter. Maybe it was high time he met her face to face. Charm her, he thought with a grimace, by my handsome visage and splendid physique. To what purpose, though? In any case, he needed to get to the Bouncing Block Gymnasium and Fitness Centre in Moor Lane before the city's finest fouled up every single thing.

Chapter Thirty-One

thumb – investigation of the means for an illegal act (as robbery, murder)

The assassin loved libraries. Warmth was unimportant, the inviting spectacle of books ranked on shelves was the real enticement. The book was a work of devotion. The pages turned, endearing to the assassin's eyes.

Charles Waterton, born in 1782 at Walton Hall, Yorkshire, was one of those spectacular men who became truly notable. From being a mere rat-catcher, he wandered into world history, exploring the Orinoco River and delving with single-minded devotion into the furthest reaches of the mighty Demerara River. In 1812 he hunted with tribes, patiently making notes of their plants, sketching animals and – this was it – poisons. Frequently young Waterton took ill. Riddled with tertian malaria, he bravely soldiered on, scribbling his *Essays on Natural History* and liberally sprinkling his notes with epigrams from Virgil and Ovid. The assassin finally came to it, barely repressing a thrill of excitement: the account of the Wourali vine, among the most virulent botanical poisons known.

Reaching the remote Macouchi tribe after a slogging one hundred and twenty days through tropical jungle, the intrepid young Mr Waterton

193

noted the tribal hunters' precise techniques to purify the poison. You must keep the arrows dry, for moisture somehow corrupted the vital principle. Correctly prepared, the wourali poison acted gently and imperceptibly. The assassin read this with regret, for a perv should suffer horror as he faced death in those last minutes, but you couldn't have everything. The assassin could accept that the Macouchi tribal hunters would need a 'sufficient quantity' of the vine, but why add two species of stinging ants only found in the steaming rain forests of what once was British Guiana? (The famous Sydney Smith said they were superfluous; the assassin checked this and other references.) Extra ingredients – fangs of the Labarri snake, plus strong Indian Pepper – could also be rejected, same reasons.

The vine and roots were to be heated in a new pot, and filtered into a thick glutinous syrup. The arrows were only prepared when women of the tribe – the assassin smiled – were excluded. The hunter must frequently wash his hands and face, and fast two days beforehand. The blow-pipe was made from a bright yellow Ourah reed of perfect cylindrical shape. Well, the assassin thought wryly, that was out because even the plod would spot somebody carrying *that* around Newcastle-on-Tyne. The arrow was a standard nine inches long. Would some kind of miniature air gun do? It would need thinking over. Lastly, noted the meticulous young Charles Waterton in his unexplored jungle, the Macouchi hunter carried a quiver of some *six hundred* poisoned arrows. Good God. To kill just one living thing, or fight a war?

Phew, the assassin thought. Well, cities are not jungles holding plenty of prey. Modern civilisation required the death of only one, the perv all right-minded citizens should be out hunting. One arrow, maybe two, would have to do. The arrow's tip was made of Coucourite wood, tightly fitted into a long feathered arrow. Four coats of poison were put on by simple dipping into the brew.

'And that is that,' the assassin said, closing the book and returning it to the shelves. Mr Waterton had meticulously observed the action of the poison and recorded the details in his journal. Animals from fowl to dogs and three-toed sloths died fairly peaceably in three minutes, a massive ox weighing a thousand pounds in four. That would give an assassin just enough time to catch the bus home. No secret jungle hideouts in sunny Newcastle, right?

Chapter Thirty-Two

git-mit – chit-chat (Punjabi slang)

'I say Bally talks for all the girls.' Milly liked the Punjabi, who was shocked.

'Christ, Milly! What do I know?' The three prostitutes from Blue string were talking outside the loos by the Volunteer.

'You got to. You're schooled and that. We're not.'

'Speak for yourself, bitch. I'm educated too.' Grace could be belligerent when she wanted,

195

which was often. She'd had a row with Milly anyway, because the Walkden girl wanted to buy Fallon, a key goer they all fancied, a bishop-sleeved shirt. In fact she was so narked she was rumoured to have told on Milly, so of course Grellie went spare and ballocked Milly because she hadn't asked Grellie. Working girls weren't allowed to cross over, as they called giving prezzies to goers. Shagging in the syndicate was strictly forbidden. That's all there was to rules. They were either there or not. Grace wouldn't ever forget, because hate was her way. This was a special occasion.

The three girls were restless, because nobody was any nearer solving the perv business. It was the dying girl in hospital. All the girls in the Square were in uproar. Soon it would come to a scrap. Red stringers at the Rivergate corner were already talking bottles, which was the way rumbles always started. Then if Grellie couldn't shut the girls up she'd talk with Rack, and then where did that always end but some girl taking the red walk home? It's what had happened before, when Sybil, a Liverpool girl really from Albania, tried to go indie with herbal stuff some boyfriend started on the stalls down Market Street hoping to get the Bouncing Block trade. The Bouncing Block was the gym in Moor Lane where the muscle husslers congregated and it was stuffed with idle money. Rack had gone spare. They mentioned this to each other but only as a caution. They knew violence, part of the game.

'See, Bally,' Milly put in reasonably, 'you're out of it, sort of.'

'What's that supposed to mean?' Bally was furi-

196

ous for being put in the firing line. 'This is only git-mit, right? Now you're sending me to talk to Grellie?'

'Everybody says so.'

'Grellie'd go berserk.'

Bally never dressed Indian, not since she'd rebelled against the Gurudwara's elite controllers who'd decided one day that girls in the local Punjabi school were learning loose ways and had to wear a salwar kameez. Bally sulked over that and kept inventing accidents until everybody gave up on her. In time, meaning once she'd grown, she chucked all that up and got herself broken in. She earned twice what most did on the Square, and Grellie approved. It was the approval that enticed Bally more than anything, though of course there were spin-offs like money. She shunned drugs, having seen too much among teenagers, loles, windies and goojers alike, though nothing to equal the balkies who came from those countries too small even to have proper names somewhere beyond Greece.

'Just say it's for the poorly girl.'

'That's right.' Grace wanted to egg Bally on. Getting Bally into trouble with Grellie would be one in the eye for Milly, serve the bitch right. 'You're out of it, sort of.'

'How'm I out of it?' Bally knew what Grace was up to. She often wanted to start smoking, but hated the stink of fags and it cost a fortune which made her shy clear. In times like this it would be an advantage, direct the git-mit like starlettes did in movies. Fags were really graceful.

'You're a goojer, see?'

197

'I'm not from Goojerat. Dad's Punjab.'

'Same difference.'

'Rack'll go spare if it gets past Grellie.'

'It'll be OK. Grellie'll see sense.'

'They're on about it on Moorgate. I'll bet you ten quid they'll talk to Grellie. Then we'll look stupid.'

Noisy youths teemed from the Volunteer and started banging their way among the waste bins on the way to the narrow car park, yelling and shouting. They whooped at the sight of the girls, then all chat ceased because it was work time and Milly and Bally got carried along, which truly narked Grace who had to go back into the street lights by the Central Gardens. She hated that, because somewhere out in the darkness Grellie's eyes would be counting and clocking every girl's strides, which was a right pain. She'd not been told off this month, and didn't want to get fined like she had four weeks back

She resolved to work on her friend Maureen, who had the gift of the gab and would talk Bally into making the plea to have the perv topped. One of the Green girls was trying to get a subscription at Reel's Ticket Agency down Greygate, say some holy masses for the dying kid in Farnworth General. Grace thought of Bonn. Would Bally really be gormless enough to talk to Bonn direct?

Her spirits rose. She'd wait for Bally. She was only doing a car job, probably a gob or two max. Say fifteen minutes with luck.

Chapter Thirty-Three

owff – to steal

'He charges us a deposit,' the girl told Rack. He'd had her dragged in from the Weavers Hall Shopping Mall because she'd been crying near the Argyle Street entrance.

Rack hated the design of the mall. If he'd been able to write, he'd have written to the dumb builders and told them they were thick as pig turd. He couldn't, so just went on hating. She couldn't tell him what was wrong. Typical bird, all guess and no think. Fat George had seen her crying up Bolgate Street and sent a runner with word of some landlord's scam.

'He charges you? Who's this he?'

'Landlord.' She was still sniffing. She wasn't bad, fusty in an off-the-peg way, hair done by herself in her sink after beans and toast, on a wage you wouldn't pay a Blackpool donkey. She worked at Fleeters in the station. What, twenty-three, and already defeated? Rack wondered who shagged her. 'He gives us a contract, charges us a deposit.'

'Us?' Rack's interest quickened. Now, this was really interesting. He'd ballocked Fat George for interrupting his boring non-existent work. Now, it seemed Fat George had guessed right. Us all? It sounded like plenty of tarts were being rooked. That meant more money was being owffed than

Rack could ignore. If money changed hands, Rack ought to have a 'centage. 'How many of you?'

'There's thirty-seven flats in the buildings.' She looked about for somewhere to sit. Rack ignored that. Tarts always wanted to get you doing things, fetching and carrying. They got on his nerves sometimes.

'Buildings?' Rack thought, Bonn wouldn't have asked a single question, and still got more out of her than anybody could, but then Bonn was mental. Rack reckoned religion turned you mental. You wanted proof, look at Bonn.

'Mr Iffy owns seventeen, they say.'

'Buildings or flats?'

'Flats.'

That wouldn't get Mr Iffy off. Rack glowered, now throat-thick with rage. The girl, thinking he meant her, burst into tears again. The Shot Pot was in a hell of a state because of a fire the previous night which Rack had started, to help the turn-over which was falling short last quarter. Insurance would pay. That meant he had to use the corridor by the loo and cleaners' cupboards for interviews, which he hated because it was where he straightened trouble-makers when necessary. Also, there was a risk of Bonn walking in, and Rack had sworn blind that he never, honestly hand-on-heart, never would belt people who'd made simple mistakes, God's truth. Except what he told Bonn and what really happened were sometimes almost nearly virtually sometimes practically the same. Also very fucking different. Like last week he'd had to have Jaker done over here, and the cleaners still hadn't cleaned the marks off the wall, idle bitches. He began to hate cleaners, and began to wonder who the idle fuckers were.

'It's all right,' he told the girl, and she stopped sobbing. 'Not you, OK? Only,' he said with swift invention, 'we're Inland Revenue Customs, see? That's why we have to go under cover. Like here, see? I'm vexed Mr Iffy hasn't, er...' There was a word for telling them tax bastards what you earned, wasn't there? With forms. Martina's butty briefs filled in forms every year and sent in a fucking fortune. Rack had offered to sort them out so Martina needn't pay tax at all, but she just told him no, leave it. He'd fumed for days over that. What did the idle thieves do for all that tax money? Rooked the whole syndicate year after year. The government should do something. Odds on they were in on the tax scam.

'Er, his forms, see?' He didn't know what happened to forms.

'You're from the Customs?'

He leaned back, nearly went over backwards, forgetting he wasn't in his usual nook. He righted himself, now truly narked with whoever this Iffy geezer was, making him nearly unbalance like that.

'Course.' And he'd forgotten the green eye-shade which changed him into Cool Hand Luke. His temper worsened. His voice changed. 'You're due a rebate, love.'

'What?' She stared, looked round. The corridor was a ruin, buckets and charred drapes in a tangled heap, old wooden stepladders leaning on the door, sounds of the snooker hall beyond the tatty green felt, blood stains smeared on the wall.

'Before you go, give us the name of his agents. And where you live, OK?'

She felt in her handbag. No paper, no pen. She looked at Rack.

'We're not allowed things to write with,' he invented. 'Under cover, see?'

'This is a doctor's note,' she said. 'Can I write it on the back? I've only lipstick.'

'That's allowed.' He felt really grand, never having been an Inland Revenue Customs man before.

He watched her write Mr Iffy's details. He took the scrawl and examined its hieroglyphics, thinking how strange it was that writing had got off the ground in the first place. People should be satisfied with talking. 'What's it say?'

She stared. Her gormless gape was starting to piss him off. 'It's for the recording machine,' he said, doing his brooding stare, Bogart in *The Big Sleep*.

'Oh.' She read him her address and Mr Iffy's one-room office over the Liverpool Road bridge. Rack seethed. Now he really was fuming. So near the Square, some bastard was running a rent-deposit scam without asking? Worse than the bitch who managed that new car mart.

'You can go. Tell everybody from tomorrow they don't pay anything for three months. Then a different rent collector'll come round, OK?'

She halted, staring back at him. 'What?'

He felt drained. Had he to tell everybody everything ten times over, Christ's sake? 'Piss off, love,' he said. 'Not that way. Door behind me. Tell nobody you come here, OK?'

202

'Yes, sir.'

She went out almost on tiptoe. Rack liked that. So she wasn't so stupid. He liked being called sir. He revised his opinion. She was brighter than she seemed, and her arse wasn't bad. He speculated on how she'd look tarted up, but finally stopped all that because he wanted to stay fuming. He went into the snooker hall and told Sonz to find Dabbo and Clithero, who'd be just right for this Iffy job. And no, he said when Sonz asked, you can't finish your game first, go now.

Chapter Thirty-Four

carnie – grave injury, a wanton brawl

Gertie spoke to anyone in the laboratory. She was very loud. 'Ever since that polyacrylamide-gel business, I've been sick of forensics.'

'Fine time to discover that.' Pat was the lab's veteran, joined on leaving school. She loathed youngsters. They all grumbled. Gertie, on the Forensics and Analyses staff less than a year, had come from 'a year off' after some crummy school science course, a bare D grade. Of course, she knew everything. Yeh, right.

'I think it's going to come up this time.'

'How many tries is that, Gert?' Pat said drily. She knew Gertie hated the abbreviation.

'Seven hundred and twenty.'

'Good luck, Gert.'

'I feel a positive's on it's way.'

Gertie had a tendency towards bikers in black leathers, studs, and alchemic jewellery. Pat was dying to know how Gertie managed when she had a cold, or spewed up her previous night's booze, what with silver studs in her eyelids, lips, nose, tongue, and heaven only knew where else. Pat thought the fashion revolting. Pat was into her boss, a taciturn but charming man who was tied to a desperate family he'd inherited from a neighbour who'd walked out. She was on a loser, but what could you do?

'You always say that. Let me know if it does.'

Pat made sure that only she did the records. On average, four per cent of all documentary systems across the nation were wrong – *Medical Register*, church listings, police lists of course, paedophiles, registers of electors, the lot. Meaning one in twenty-five. Police data were nineteen per cent wrong at input. Meaning one in five, and that was after corrections made at desks during canteen chat and arcane comparisons of tales in assorted boozers. At the outset, it was one balls-up in two. Therefore you had as much chance of guessing right/wrong or wrong/right as if you'd spun a penny and called heads or tails. The info came, of course, from bored and gormless squaddies out on the plod in the dark. The range of error was com-pounded by the honest old public who gave false names, denied they were even driving their car at the time, lied they were racing some poor lady to hospital when in fact they truly were creating may-hem at the football match and, yes constable, that's me caught on camera right there and I'm guilty so here's the fine and sorry I'll not do it again, Your Honour.

'It does!'

Gertie gave a yelp about ten minutes later as the auto-scanner whirred its pack of lies. Pat came to see. Joanie from across in Blood Typing walked over and grimaced in envy. She only ever got positives, what with the narrow possibilities in bloods. She hoped it meant tons more work for Gertie, whom she hated for the ironmongery crusted round her features. Joanie, mum of three, saw Bad Example everywhere. Gertie was a prime instance of the disorder menacing Joanie's infants later in life.

'Where's the fucking code then?'

'I've got it.'

'You should leave it around instead of keeping it separate,' Gertie groused.

'You'd lose it,' Pat said. 'I've got to know where it is.'

The code book was an old-fashioned dip-and-scratch soft-back ledger bought with Pat's own money. She'd been caught out too many times by misbehaving computers, electricity that blanked just when you needed its vital power, and the carelessness of other lab staff who entered any old scrambled admix of numbers they imagined were hard data. She got the code book from her case and sat flipping the pages by her console.

'You sure, Gertie?'

'Clear as day.'

Joanie smirked, liking that little bit of doubt creeping in, and returned to her racks of boring positives.

'He was Birmingham weeks since.'

They considered the news. Pat repeated the checks. The screen showed the same conclusion, Gertie happy, Joanie sulking and Pat frowning because a stack of trouble was coming up on the flat-matt screen.

'Name of Blendix. Pervo freed on a mistrial. Tons of stuff. They'll have a field day.'

'What else?' Gertie secretly believed Pat wanted her out of the lab and mistrusted everything she did. Pat saw Gertie as a threat to position, like all elderly crones with no future. Pat was thirty-four, so clearly past it, having nothing to live for except her miserable little life with its part-time shags with the boss.

'He was under police protection. Safe house and all.'

'Oh, dear!' Joanie carolled, bright as a button. As long as things didn't go smoothly across in Tissue Typing and its Genetics sub-section, it wasn't altogether a wasted day. She felt chirpy. 'How on earth will you break the news?' she cried with sympathy, and turned up the volume on her Jimmy Buffet record that everybody hated except the boss.

She started to sing along. Pat went into her office to dial, in a dreadful sulk because she was the only one dedicated enough to be overjoyed at a technological breakthrough, proving the hand in the bin was a perv freed on a legal technicality in the Midlands.

Chapter Thirty-Five

slab – death, to kill

The assassin watched from the street. The easy way would have been to rent one of the hotel places nearby while the perv made up his mind. That sort of info was worth paying for. Nothing like reliability. Reliability was dependence. Trustworthiness led to order. In a well structured society, no child would be importuned or injured. Neglect and cruelty would, frankly, be out for ever, and children could grow up in peace. The perv must go. The assassin had paid for the guise of a news reporter from a TV cable network, using an American accent, and had done a convincing job, confessing doubt about the money, notes, how much one converted from the dollar. It had given the man from the police's data network some amusement. Quite the actor, the assassin thought. Was there a hint of a new career in there?

The American military depot's weapon was safely stowed away at home. The home-made weapon in the flat customed leatherette case, form-hugging for the sake of concealment, sat quite lightly on the hip. Plenty of excellent reasons, however, for borrowing a weapon then not using it for execution. It would give the police a thrill – what was the name of that sorrowing part-time loser, Hassall? Flab on wheels, with mental alacrity to match.

This was the third night the assassin had waited for the perv to make his move. He would, he would, and soon. Twenty to nine, just when the assassin was thinking doubtfully of going to have a pee and risking losing the perv, a shadow slipped round the end of the street. The only way for a pedestrian to come from back there was a small row of lock-up garages. No car had gone down in forty minutes, except the police protection's stake motor, and they stood out like beacons on a moor. No, it must be the perv finally making his run to some new form of malice.

The assassin readied the weapon. Its slip-catch had proved a serious difficulty. Made of the lightest alloy possible, it would wear as quick as dough. Hopeless. With the best Swedish tungsten, though, several replicates proved acceptable. Open and shut the weapon case twice, you had to replace the catch. Four spares in the left pocket, one final reserve poison dart in the butt cap.

Time to go. The perv could only be making for one place, the disco bar. Its lights flicked the dark clouds on and off in multiple colours in time to a faint thump from percussion. The assassin fol-lowed. At the corner secrecy was irrelevant, for now the perv was in the sights. Let the shoes clack on the pavement, and all the better if the perv, coming into clear view, heard a fellow human being walking along to the same entertainment. Hold that zero, the nought at the centre of the marksman's sight mechanism. Wasn't that what the veteran American quartermaster sergeant said snipers did?

Grobbon was strolling, taking pleasure in being among others in the evening, looking with interest at passing buses, staring in particular at one carrying several children, the swine. He crossed over by the two corner pubs, carrying on to where brighter shopping malls crystallised in the precinct. Nice, the assassin thought pleasantly, for Newcastle to have so many pedestrianised shopping zones, CCTV cameras showing exactly the nil reliability citizens could place on the vigilant police. A real laugh. A few simple adjustments to gear, attire so speedily converted so as to be different for each unavoidable camera angle, with the right amount of oh-so-accidental facial masking and turning aside from that one vital camera scan. The assassin made it with hardly a single frame caught on the tracker tape. Time, though, Newcastle invested in one or two of the newer versions like the Mark O-XL5 auto, a bastard Californian auto-sector camera that didn't let go until it finally got a clear view and, should you prove too wily, had the sinister knack of communicating to other cameras to pick you up before you left an area. The cameras in situ were almost on the road to redundancy.

The perv was looking round now, close to the bus station. There, plenty of people despite the hour. Nine o'clock bar five minutes, or as the military might say, twenty fifty-five hours. A city bus pulled out, and the perv hesitated – first pause – at the sight of the crammed caff holding families, workers, shoppers on their way home. More cameras, though, so the assassin was pleased when the perv headed for the glowing neons of the disco bar across the pavement. The assassin walked quicker, cutting across the traffic lights as if seeing a bus depart and hesitating in apparent disappointment. Give the police something to waste their valuable time on – was that person really intending to sprint for that bus or not? The assassin smiled, imagining the irritable exchange of shouts there would be across the police call centre, see if that passenger can be traced, all that malarkey.

By the time the perv reached the disco pavement, the assassin was ahead of him, approaching casually yet out of sight of the camera sweeps – only private set ups, so they were el cheapos. Only two showed signs of still working. Four bouncers stood before the double swing doors, hands folded and wearing the dark stretched-stitch suits of their trade. The assassin paused and lit a cigarette as the perv came by. The weapon was simply activated, the high-pressure air bulb emitting a discreet pop as the metal dart shot through the jacket fabric and into the strolling perv.

'What the fuck?'

Toofy swatted, thinking he'd been stung by a wasp, then walking on towards the bright doorway, too cool to show worry. If you've been In, you never showed signs of anything.

The assassin knew the dart was too small to project, when delivered into the skin at such short range. What was it, the assassin wondered idly, maybe three paces? The cigarette drew well, though it was a filthy habit. How strange that folk paid for the right to pollute themselves, their lungs, their children, making their clothes and hair stink. You could always tell a habitual smoker by the advanced ageing of their skin far beyond their chronological years.

The assassin put the cigarette lighter away and walked on as if about to cross the road. Toofy was now behind the sight line. What, a hundred yards from the bouncers at the disco admission bar? Toofy seemed to be slightly puzzled, judging from the assassin's reflection glimpsed in the brightly lit shop window.

'That bastard drunk, or what?' a Geordie voice growled.

The assassin turned, saw that Toofy was still only a mere ten paces away. A marksman would say it was almost within reach! The perv had paused, leaning towards the double window of the jewellery shop, though of course the display had been removed and the iron grille was down. For all the world it looked as if the perv was about to sit. The assassin saw the bouncers were showing wary interest but were still several paces off, so it seemed worthwhile to make a show of wondering whether to return and offer some help. The poor man was now decidedly listing. Another press of the thumb, and the second dart popped across the intervening space, unfortunately catching Toofy somewhere in the arm, which even the police, blind as bats, couldn't miss. The first dart had gone into the perv's leg, a lovely shot. In fact, the assassin wondered if the dart might even show reflected light from the disco's dazzling light display. Too late now. Let the police guess.

The assassin walked away, clearly a reserved individual deciding not to risk offering assistance to a drunk in a public place. The bouncers approached the slumping figure of Toofy, already loudly speculating on his ailment, one reaching for a cell phone to call the security centre to come and get rid of another wino.

Walking to the densest crowd in the bus station through the late-night shopping mall, the assassin bought a cup of coffee and sat at the open spread of tables among the shoppers, reading a paper. Waterton had to be admired. Such a great traveller, to explore the deepest rain forests of British Guiana, as it was named. Two centuries ago! The intrepid young man had endured impossible hardships to experiment on the Wourali extract, using it to kill chickens and other creatures, timing the deaths and measuring the distances each doomed creature managed to travel before collapsing in a kind of doze.

Nice and convenient that the vine was cultivated in Kew Gardens. Civilisation, the assassin thought with a glow of pleasure, was the dissemination of vital knowledge for the good of society. Three minutes, then, if the dose was sufficient and the preparation had been judged perfectly. A man ten doors away from home kept pigeons, but what had those pigeons ever done to be sacrificed? No, Toofy, perv who deserved to die, and his execution could be regarded as a trial of the experimental method. If the perv died, then it was all worthwhile.

By midnight, the assassin was back in the city, reflecting on a task well done. The morning headlines would show nothing. Maybe by tomorrow night, TV newscasters would be reading out details of the perv's calamitous death, using of

212

course their appalling grammar– 'more easier' and 'as equal as' were the assassin's particular hates of the illiterate TV babbling crews. For once it would be pleasant to hear.

Chapter Thirty-Six

upper – a female who hires a male for an episode of sex

The lady had lost conviction, Bonn knew. Marvellous she had come at all. He smiled as best he could, aware smiles were dangerous entities starting wrong patterns of behaviour.

'Miss Dacie Two-Two-One? I am so sorry.'

'Sorry?' she said, startled.

Dacie wore what Bonn guessed were daring clothes. Her hair was almost stage-set, probably her wish of a former style that convinced her she was being the flamboyant creature she perhaps always wanted to be. Her wedding finger showed an almost imperceptible paler band. She had removed her rings in yet more concealment. Was she all disguise and no reality beneath? Yet, Bonn thought with sadness, how many out there in Victoria Square were truly themselves and not simulants made up to impress others at work, in marriage, in gangs, clubs?

'I was so worried coming here, Miss Dacie.' Bonn felt his smile give out, like a leaking tyre, and abandoned it. He felt immediately restored.

'Thank goodness. As soon as I saw you I felt such relief.'

'Why?' Her eyes became round. She had chosen earrings longer than she should have considered. They touched her shoulder. Her blouse was risky, her skirt tight enough to show shape. She felt certain her appearance was what a hired man would recognise as effective, usual, determined. Bonn thought it charming.

'I don't know, Miss Dacie.' His wan look needed no acting. 'Perhaps it was the Miss. I have never had to meet someone titled like you before.'

'Oh, it's just...' She would have become flustered, so Bonn moved slightly.

'I was almost scared,' he admitted. It was no lie. He often was apprehensive, and usually more than a little disturbed by the fragments of information Miss Hope or Miss Faith cobbled together to accompany the booking.

'Scared? You?'

Slight, with a figure any man would have liked to escort. Strange how women failed to see their own worth. Bonn could never understand. It was as if, say, they had all the attributes of speed and talent with which to become natural Olympic champions, then talked themselves into anxieties. The way women thought of themselves, and the way they came over, were irreconcilables.

'Yes. I suppose it must seem strange.' He let his non-smile sink into oblivion. They were still standing like strangers in a bar wondering how to order supper. 'It only happens to me, losing heart just when I'm about to meet the person I've been looking forward to meeting all day long.'

214

'Oh, that's me all over!' she exclaimed.

'I don't think so!' At last his smile almost began of its own accord. 'I'm the one who is uncertain – at least, until I see the lady concerned, then I'm fine.'

'But surely you...'

He saw her sudden terror of committing some awful gaffe.

'No, Miss Dacie. It can be a real ... they say cliff-hanger. Hazard. Only when the lady finally appears, and the moment is there, does it make sense and becomes brilliant. Like you, coming as if out of the blue, so capable and reassuring.'

'It's my first time.' She blurted the words, almost fearful.

He looked about. It was one of the best suites in the Time and Scythe. The old hotel stood at the junction of Bolgate Street and Mealhouse Lane, near the Rum Romeo casino and, further down, the infamous Butty Bar where highly mannered gilded youths assembled of an evening. Listen from the bay windows of any of the front suites in the hotel, and the thump-thump of music from the main square was clearly audible.

'Perhaps I might make you a drink, Miss Dacie.'

'Martini, please,' she said. Bonn's heart sank as he wondered if she knew cocktails. Posser had given him lessons – a dash of this to that, a half-measure of mead, a lick of Cointreau and so on – to no avail. He was lost. So many types, and so little certainty. Cocktails were religious ritual without the conviction.

'I'm not very good, Miss Dacie.' He went to the drinks cabinet in the kitchen and opened a cab-

215

inet. He had been in this suite before, but been disconcerted when Rack told him on the way up that Miss Dacie Two-Two-One had insisted on being there first so she could open the door on Bonn's knock.

'It's an anniversary,' she said after him.

He turned politely, waiting for more. The glasses were chilled, so whoever prepared the suite had done well. 'Anniversary.' He was pleased about the anniversary, for no reason. 'I'm glad.'

'I had hopes it would be ... different, you see.'

She meant this time it had to be different. From before, maybe when something had gone terribly wrong? That must have been the source of his tremor when entering. He was to be cast in the role of someone in whom she had placed trust or loved and then died or....?

'I hope it will be perfect, then, Miss Dacie.'

'Thank you,' she said reflexively, then coloured slightly and stammered. 'Oh, I didn't mean how that came out.'

'I hope this isn't too dreadful, Miss Dacie.' He brought the drink with a frown of concentration, moving slowly as if trying not to spill it. 'I once went over with a lady's drink. She was so cross, then laughed and laughed. I was ashamed. I'm rather clumsy. Like the Queen Mother's waiter.'

'The old Queen Mum?'

'Yes. A waiter spilled a drink on her dress at table, some public gathering, and he froze. She laughed and said, "Never mind. It was quite refreshing!" And he kept his job.'

Miss Dacie smiled a real smile and took the glass. Bonn returned for his. He had no intention

216

of even taking a sip, but would act tasting it with appreciation, unless Miss Dacie hated hers. He would agree. The thought came, even at this juncture, of how much was an enactment. Only in the final throes, when beauty soared into perfection and ecstasy assumed one of its six dazzling colours, would he be released from the doubts. The blessing was, all women gave him bliss, having the same stupendous power to lead a man from mundane life into that passionate serenity.

'I was in two minds whether to come or not,' she said, her lips on the rim and almost wrinkling her nose in disapproval. She seemed unused to the drink. Had she tasted it at the event this hiring was to commemorate?

'I am so glad you did.' Bonn was sincere.

'Because...?'

'No.' Others would have laughed at the wrongness of her assumption. He wanted to show the lady that his delight was nothing to do with money, as she seemed to be wondering. 'Money is always second to everything. Always.'

'Always?' For the first time humour showed through. 'One so old?'

It was a brave speech. Bonn looked at the carpet in embarrassment. 'Wealth is of little consequence, Miss Dacie. I once had nothing.'

'Are some, ah, very rich?'

She was asking about other women. 'I have no right to answer, Miss Dacie, or form opinions of any lady. It would be unjust. Do I sound high-handed? I don't mean to be. Only, a lady has a right to silence. Even if a lady hires me a second time, or a third, I must not even recollect the previous encounter.'

She looked at him. He shrugged. It had to be that way. A different key might have said that she paid for silence. Truth, yes, but still he could not say outright. Later, he might be tempted to consider the derivation of that treacherous word *admission*, as he had been forced to in the now-defunct seminary. You cannot, said the great synonymnist Crabb, *admit* without an associated idea of what was being admitted. The danger in such thoughts, pondered over when he was alone in his sparsely furnished room in Martina's home, was the serious comparison with *receiving*. The latter is always positive, and has no relative idea of the receiver or the received. He caught himself wandering, wrong when she was reaching some inner resolve.

'I'm glad you say that, Bonn.'

'Your anniversary. I'm always sceptical, in case they turn out like reunions.'

'Don't you go? Reunions, I mean?'

She was pretty, yet here she was, worried she was ageing fast. All women did that, he believed. Hence her attempted quip about his comparative youth. Had it startled her when he arrived?

'No. The place I was raised has closed down.'

'I did well at school,' she said, gazing past him. 'I met somebody after I got married. I wanted to be different, you know? Like women in stories, out-going and doing things.'

'People have more choice now, they say.'

'I haven't. I went with him. It was a failure, all my fault. He was a traveller. He came from, well, abroad, and wanted to meet. We agreed a place. I had a child by then, and I made arrangements for my sister to take care of her for the day. I made up a story about a job interview.' Her smile became rueful. 'It wasn't too far from what I intended, I suppose. We met in...' She seemed to cast about in her mind for a fictitious town and shrugged. 'By the sea, y'know?'

Bonn said he knew. He had only seen the sea twice. Once was a domicilary, with an aggressive lady who did accounts for a funfair hotel chain. He sighed inwardly. There he was again, registering judgements of that seaside lady. Most unfair.

'I called myself Dacie. He said it was an interesting name. He'd never met a Dacie before. Have you?' Bonn tilted his head in demur and she pinked slightly. 'Oh, yes. You are not to say.'

She had almost sipped her drink now, he noticed. His own was almost untouched. His lips were stinging where he had pressed them to the glass. He wondered how people had come to brew and ferment the first spirits. Accidental lodgements in, say, maple trees? He imagined tribes coming across alcoholic puddles in the boles of leaning trunks.

'He must have been delighted, Miss Dacie,' he heard himself say.

'You're so kind. He wasn't. He wanted ... well, you know. I grew frightened, and left too soon. We hadn't even...'

'Well, a lady's privilege, Miss Dacie.'

'I cursed myself for a fool. I didn't want to leave my family, just have something. Do you understand?'

'It's quite natural.'

'I became scared life was passing me by. A woman does. Look what they say in magazines. Everybody has a right to everything and all that.' She was reminiscing unaided, Bonn forgotten. 'I think of it often. D'you know what, Bonn? I think fantasies. Daydreams. In them I'm always so cool, so brilliant.' She almost giggled. 'I actually take the initiative, tell him what I want and how far he can go. He just goes along because I'm so sure of myself.' Her gaze returned to his. 'I'm not really like that, otherwise I wouldn't have run in the first place, would I?'

'You regret it, Miss Dacie.'

'Oh, a million times. See, I could have gone to meet him in Canada, had a holiday perhaps. My husband works overseas sometimes, and the children are at school now. I could write, but what if he's moved? Or the letter be intercepted by...' She looked her horror at Bonn. 'It doesn't bear thinking about.'

'That's why you are Miss Dacie.'

'Yes. I imagined hiring somebody, like an actor. Just to play the role of Charles. I would be just as I should have been, that day I met Charles in Boulters Lock. I would make him do what I wanted, and he wouldn't step out of line. So many dreams.'

'They must have been beautiful.'

'In them, Miss Dacie did some really terrible things.' She looked at him. 'Do I sound horrid? It's a perversion, isn't it?'

'No, Miss Dacie. It is as you wish, and only what everybody does.'

'Do you, Bonn?'

'I do what the lady wishes. Just like your Charles, I suppose, in your dreams, when you meet him and give him your instructions and decide how far you wish to go.'

'Exactly what she wishes,' she repeated. 'You see, that's it. In a dream, you can be in control.'

'As you are here, Miss Dacie.'

'Like, you being Charles. In a way.'

'I know. You can see how the reality would be for a moment, without going any farther.'

'We could.' She glanced towards the bedroom. The door was firmly closed. Bonn guessed she had gone round the whole suite beforehand, making sure no gremlins were in the wardrobes or listening devices in cupboards. He felt such compassion for Miss Dacie, creature of her own longings. 'There would be no harm in that, would there?'

'None at all. As you wish.' He took her empty glass and asked, 'Would you like another drink, Miss Dacie?'

'Can I call you Charles?'

'Of course.'

'You don't mind? Yes, please, then.'

They made incomplete, though not partial, love, in the hour, her drink untouched by the bed. She wanted to talk afterwards, explain her intentions and how she first heard of the Pleases Agency. Time ran out, and Bonn had to explain how extra time had to be ordered beforehand.

Leaving after Miss Dacie had gone, Bonn asked Rack to avoid accepting bookings where the lady wished to be first to arrive in the suite.

'Domicilary calls are different, Rack,' he countered when Rack protested.

'Why? Look, Bonn, mate. They're all the fucking same. Like doing somebody over because they've dissed you. Summat's got to be done, or it all goes bad. It's a frigging law, innit?'

'Language, Rack.'

Rack danced in outrage, careering along the pavement nearing Foundry Street. 'Christ's sake, Bonn. You've just shagged some tart's arse off, and now we can't even talk proper?'

Bonn stopped on the pavement. 'Rack, I shall return unaccompanied. Please walk elsewhere.'

'Martina wants you, about that dead girl. I'm to bring you. She's in the Pilot Ship casso.'

'Thank you for the message, Rack. Good day.'

Bonn crossed over immediately and headed towards the Square. Four Blue girls of Grellie's watched him and made signs to each other. One walked along to speak with him. He slowed to match her pace while Rack glared and held up a finger to the others in warning. They pouted and dispersed, but kept looking across to where their friend was walking with Bonn. She spoke, and Bonn seemed to not refuse whatever she asked. Rack leant on the pedestrian railings by the Warrington turn-off traffic lights. It was becoming too much.

He still hadn't got the money for the motors he'd sent Akker and the boys to nick, and now some plod squaddies were creating merry hell because a dead bloke's hand had been found in a refuse skip. Naturally, the plod being thickos trained to avoid thinks, they blamed anybody and sent sniffers round the syndicate's legit businesses, which meant Martina was going into one.

And now Bonn takes umbrage and tells you off because you cut a few corners with some bint who wants a quick shag? He wondered if he should go to church with Mama next Sunday, do Confession and everything for a special deal, but Mama was even thicker than the police and would have him on a lifetime nine-to-five. He'd told her he was a computer programmer for ICI, head of a section, and she believed him. She did a novena when he lied he'd got promoted. Mama was so stupid she asked where his ICI works actually were so she could come and visit. Everything was fucking trouble.

He decided to do some stonking, fix a few faces, put some blood on a couple or three paving slabs, and feel better. He'd restore a bit of order round the Square, get back to common sense.

Chapter Thirty-Seven

cilop – Civilian In Lieu Of Police (police employee)

Hassall borrowed the Yellow without asking. He'd had his eye on the file for an hour, biding his time, knowing that sooner or later the section leader would call his mob to a coffee chat. Henderley was a squat Bristol geezer who lived for peg-to-peg indoor bowling and craved international status in that art. So far he'd managed to do no worthwhile police work, precisely zilch, since his transfer from the south-west over a year previously.

'You allowed to do that, Mr Hassall?' a CILOP officer called Vaughan asked, not even bothering to look up, noticing the garish file disappearing.

'No,' Hassall told the Civilian-in-lieu-of-police clerk.

'Right.'

Vaughan was a pale clerky lad – well, twenty-three – who looked a right misery but who did comic turns on the pubs and halls of an evening. He was said to be a riot, very popular with female audiences. Rumour said he'd just got an agent. He was a whizz at data banks, and a cynic. Hassall admired the former skill, and approved the latter.

'Any copies gone out?'

'Two to Brum, one to Bristol, another to Newcastle.' Vaughan chuckled. 'Newcastle, Mr Hassall.'

That was surprising. 'Why Newcastle?'

'Dunno. Somebody surfing the web. Maybe they've hundreds of staff, and are trying to find them something to do.'

'Like us, eh?'

'Mr Henderley'll be back in about forty minutes, Mr Hassall. He's started smoking again. It was the new ruling that did it.'

Smoking was forbidden everywhere on earth now and enforcement disputes were everywhere, police and pollution being synonymous.

'Wonder he can afford it. I'll have it back in no time.'

Hassall sat by the lift outside the office by the staircase, where he could hear people returning, and opened the Yellow, catching the flimsies from

224

the lab reports as they fluttered in the draught. Air currents always blew a gale by the main doors, nobody knew why. Women on the staff were always on about it, nothing ever done. He read of Blendix's career as a perv.

The man was forty-two. He'd so-say fathered two children of his own, becoming a full-time predatory paedophile some four years prior to his arrest in Wolverhampton. A dark, specky bloke, he preyed on children after being hired as a van driver on school runs. Hassall sighed at the sequence of police mistakes, vaguely remembering the political fall-out and the public meetings with angry parents and bewildered school staff. Some local copper had managed to bat out time until all the perv's false names had been excavated and the crimes more or less detailed. Clever lawyers had managed to get Blendix off on some technicality.

'Story of all our days,' Hassall muttered, thinking of the recent local case. 'One balls-up after another.' He blamed computers, which promised not only secrecy but infallibility when they actually delivered no such things.

Blendix evidently had some insight into the workings of police – what, a friend? – for he'd boxed clever and managed to stay one jump ahead. Legalities were no interest to Hassall. The addresses, however, called his attention. He clocked the names and status of investigating officers where the man had lodged. All the time he was thinking Newcastle and wondering how near Bristol was to Wolverhampton. The latter was of course stuck onto Birmingham, or was it? Still no sound of Henderley and his merry mob returning, well nicotined up by now after a few snouts. Hassall photocopied two or three lists and a couple of flimsies from the Yellow, and dropped it on Vaughan's desk. The clerk didn't look up.

'You'll get in trouble one of these days borrowing files without a proforma, Mr Hassall.'

'How much do you get for a turn?'

'Your use of that term is ambiguous, Mr Hassall,' Vaughan said with dignity. 'You mean how much do I get paid for a pub gig. Am I correct?'

'Well, yes.'

'Half a week's wage, Mr Hassall.'

Hassall was astonished. 'Just for telling jokes?'

'It's going to be more soon.' The clerk glanced round, saw nobody was in earshot and said, 'There's a new Yellow coming from Brum later, Mr Hassall.'

'Do they have the same system as us, files and all that?'

'No. Once it gets here it gets a stripe, but on our colour's background.'

'Right. Ta.'

Vaughan watched Hassall move away across the office and called, 'I'm ranked fifth.'

'Eh?'

'Fifth. I'm fifth comedian on the city circuit. I'll be on telly one day. Everybody says that.'

'Oh, great. Right.' Hassall didn't know what to say. He ambled off, thinking it was people's hobbies and ambitions that caused the problem in life, not the jobs they got paid for.

Chapter Thirty-Eight

Palace of Varieties – Police Training College (nickname for an old comedy music hall)

Hassall met his old friend at the London Road railway station.

'Lousy weather you've got here, Hassie.'

'Brummies never stop grumbling, Jeff.'

'Now, then, Hassie. Where we going?'

'Football ground.'

'Standing in the wet, cold tea from plastic?'

'You know better than that.'

They talked transfer lists, young hopefuls for the league, who would play against Arsenal, Villa, Liverpool the coming season. Jeff Merston was always pale, forever sprouting stubble, but the trendiest suited bloke in the Midlands. He was known for his dapper shoes, slender form, and trilby hats worn at a rakish angle. He hated smokers, was the only bloke Hassall had ever met who measured out his booze. As in measured, with a gadget from his waistcoat pocket. He had only so much white wine of an evening, no more. Hassall and Merston had gone through the Palace of Varieties police college in the same intake.

They drove through Victoria Square and out towards the famous ground. Hassall explained he'd scrounged a couple of perk slots in the hospitality restaurant.

'No game this week. Away to the Wanderers.'

'Still go, do you, Hass?'

'Too old. No, I stop home and do pretend gardening. I go mall shopping with the missus. You?'

Jeff told Hassall about the changes in staffing in the Midlands, complained it was a nightmare of cutbacks, everybody writing to the newspapers and their MPs if they got a speeding ticket, magistrates on the blink. 'Half of them have never read the Manual, seems to me.'

They made the ground in good time. The taxi dropped them at the staff entrance and they went straight up to the restaurant where some young bird met them and showed them in with a brilliant smile. She wore the team's home colours. Hassall explained it was the new Continental manager's rule. A score of diners were already in, talking football over cholesterol and hooch.

They ordered, Merston placing his measurer ready on the tablecloth. Hassall waited until they started their meal before asking about the hand in the bin.

'This bloke Blendix, Jeff. Did he really have so many frigging aliases? Sixteen's a bit much.'

'Plus one official. Changed his name before coming south.'

'Coming south from where?'

'That's just it. He put it about he was from a village near Kendal, actually from Edinburgh. Changed his name a time or two even there.' Jeff Merston nodded. 'Do yourselves proud up here, Hassie, eh? Grub like this, all free.'

Hassall pulled a face. 'Just a social, Jeff. Nothing official.'

228

'Blendix was his preferred name. Said he got it from a kid's comic years ago, but I don't think anybody ever tracked it down. The comic, I mean.'

'Got some wordsmith on it, did you?'

'Aye. Bonny OED lass called Judy, used to check quotations, can you believe. She couldn't raise a rumour, so his name was made up. His others were all dumbo words – *Beano, Dandy,* girlie mags. That bloody Internet's a criminal past-time, you ask me. Half the lads down our way haven't a clue what it's for except selling sport memorabilia.'

'You need a dedicated lass on the job.' Hassall knew the difficulty. 'Young women only stay eighteen months before they're off with some boyfriend getting wed or for supermarket wages.'

Merston cleared his throat and waited until they were served the main course. He smiled at the football ground below through the panoramic windows.

'Don't say it, Jeff,' Hassall cracked. 'You could have been a contender?'

'No, Hass. Too idle to play seriously. My brother now, he was a real flier, could catch pigeons, a twinkletoes.'

Hassall nodded. The midlander's brother had been involved in a pursuit and died in the execution of his duty, years ago before Jeff entered the police.

'Wish I'd seen this Blendix bloke. You got our Yellow? We got yours.'

Neither spoke a moment, watching the groundsmen move machines about the touch-lines.

'Surprised you're on fish, Hassie. You were always the big raw meat bloke.' Merston lowered

229

his voice so other diners wouldn't hear. 'When it was a free nosh, like.'

'I'm trying veggie.'

'Nothing wrong, I hope?' Merston judged his old friend. 'Only I had this mate – not on the force, just a pal in the chapel me and the missus go to. His quack made him go veggie because he was working up to sugar.'

'There is that,' Hassall conceded. 'A doctor warned me about diabetes. I had a check before the official medical board. Dogs are a good thing, some magazine said last week, gets you out round the park. Like I didn't do enough when I wore a funny hat and carried a truncheon.'

'Good luck, then. Aye, I'll have a drink, please, miss. White wine.' Jeff did his magic with the measuring thing, watched critically by the waitress. Three middle-aged diners nearby were fascinated.

'Sir, we can do that for you if you'd only asked.' The waitress was miffed.

'Sorry, love. My doctor's given me strict instructions.'

'Oh, right.'

They were left alone. Hassall cleared his throat.

'But I'm OK.' He hated skin on fish, and had a pathological fear of fish bones, so took some time with his sea bass. He would have grimaced at the spinach if he'd been at home. Here he stoically tackled the meal. Jeff ate with gusto, sipping his measured wine. 'This Blendix. Did you send everything we asked?'

'All of it. Check the contents page if you think we're that bloody sloppy. Hassie, you're getting picky. Doesn't do. My sister-in-law's like that,

230

keeps wondering if she did wrong. No future in it.'

Hassall agreed. 'You're right, Jeff.' The thing was, there had been no contents page in the Brum file because Hassall had looked for it. In itself, it was a small incidental you could forget, and in any case the pages were numbered in sequence and full of cross-references so nothing could have gone missing. Possibly. 'Blendix's destination, though,' he said after a moment. 'What was your distribution list?'

'It's in the file, pal. You always were a sloppy sod.' Jeff started laughing at some reminiscence, which took about ten minutes while their minds frolicked through aged pastures. Hassall had almost finished his light-weight calories by the time he got his friend back on the rails.

'The previous attempts on Blendix's life. Any you didn't actually list or investigate?'

Jeff put down his knife and fork and examined Hassall critically. 'Aye. One. He claimed he'd been poisoned, something he ate at a fairground. You know the sort of thing, cake stalls, carousels, kids galore and vicars making speeches about the church tower. I think it was a blessing. Travelling fairs are the paedo's happy hunting ground.'

'Anything proved?'

'Not even dug into. Some doctor put Blendix back on his feet. No specimens. I mean, why would there be?'

'Bloke answering to his description got run down near the motorway, M18. It fits. The hand was typed. It matched. Not often somebody goes to the trouble of providing you with original fingerprints, eh?'

They gave semi-chuckles for a moment, unsmiling. 'So how come, Hassie?'

'Dunno. Another question is who.'

'He had a sister in Penrith. Moved down with some garage owner who did shop fittings, then went into road haulages. Small fry.'

'What gives with you in that Victoria Square?' Merston tore another bread roll. 'When we came through, you were like a cat on hot bricks. Never seen you look so edgy. Like you were expecting an abduction.'

'Street girls are acting up, pickets at the hospital over that girl. Did you hear about it? It got to the national press. A tame perv dumped her from a motor. Got off, after some lawyer jiggery-pokery.'

'Another ride-and-hide,' Jeff said sourly. 'Rather you than me. Keep yet another perv in a multi-million safe dwelling, change of identity? Just what the tax-payers love. Do they let you employ extra staff to answer the complaints about police wastefulness?' Before Hassall could reply to such a stupid question he went on, 'I put in for five more clerical officers – temps, school-leavers – in case some admin goon hadn't taken his tablet that morning and let it slip through. Got myself reprimanded. Official too, the bastards.'

'Bad luck, Jeff.' Hassall was thinking that Penrith wasn't far from Newcastle, but then nowhere was any great distance from anywhere. 'Here, one thing.'

'Yeh?'

'Have you a list of your prison visitors?'

'You kidding? They're always in local papers.'

'How do you appoint them?'

'We don't. Local do-gooders have a selection panel. Anybody can attend, pick a row about somebody being the wrong religion, different ethnic, too frigging tall or not hating fox-hunting. The usual.'

'What is it, three-yearly renewal?'

'Dunno. I'll send you the stuff if you like.'

Half of it missing, no doubt, like last time. Hassall thought this but did not say. They talked of the coming football season, the trickiness of managers, and the absurd wages paid to up-and-coming stars in the leagues. By the time they went for a walk round the pitch and chatted to the groundsmen, Hassall had extracted a promise for Jeff to send him a full repeat copy of the Blendix file separately, to his home address only, by one of the Yankee rapid hand-to-hand parcel vans.

Chapter Thirty-Nine

key – a goer who controls a group of goers, usually not more than three in number

'Excuse me, please. Are you Bonn?'

Bonn looked up and rose. Bally was nervous, having less idea of the keys than any of the working girls, but Grace had kindly explained he wasn't to be taken much notice of. Just be yourself, Grace had counselled. Bally thought Grace really kind for telling her that.

Bonn waited. For some reason, Bally dried. He

stood in the Butty Bar by his chair. The place was suddenly quieter now than when Bally entered. The counter girls were still, watching as if unusual things were going on.

'Excuse me, please. Have I interrupted?'

'No, miss.'

She noticed he did not glance about as most would when somebody spoke. He didn't even ask what she wanted.

'It's about the little girl.'

'Please sit, miss.'

Bonn watched as she sank into the chair facing, then he too sat. His tea was pale, no milk, no sugar crystals scattered on the Formica. Desultory talk began among the customers as if things were resuming. Bally now felt seriously nervous. The counter girls slowly got back to work, exchanging glances. She wondered what she had got into.

'Tea,' he said.

She waited. Did he want fresh tea pouring? She had three brothers at home who did nothing, and she always had to pour them tea, fetch and carry everything. That was the way on the Indian Subcontinent, males do nothing at home, females do the lot. Here, there was just Bonn's cup in a saucer. She had never seen this before. Mugs, for the Butty Bar, were the rule. Then she realised he was offering, did she want tea?

'Oh. No, thank you. It's the kid. The girls said I should say please can...'

'If you're sure.'

Still the tea? She shook her head, and he leant back as if at some problem newly settled. The counter girls resumed their routine. The eight or nine customers in the place went back to their sports pages and fry-ups. Bally thought, Bonn's not in his right place; he should be somewhere else. He was unremarkable, but she felt in some presence and wondered what she had done. And Grace had been so helpful.

'I'm sorry. I don't think I should be here.' As if making amends, she added, 'I'm Bally. That's what they call me. The girls.'

'Bally.' He took his time saying it, his eyes on her, her forehead. Seeking a bindi? 'You were to ask, ah...'

'If you'd see she got priested.' Bally made sure her words were almost inaudible, speaking of spirits after all. Bonn's gaze never left her.

'The girl.'

She got the hang of Bonn's speech. He simply spoke. If his words chose to form themselves into a question, that would be fine. If they didn't, well, that was nobody's fault. The world was simply choosing to be a little different round Bonn and that was that.

'Is it all right to speak here?' She didn't look about, Bonn noticed, so she had some street experience, which was all to the good.

'Of course, miss.'

'There's a little girl, they say thirteen, in hospital. Some perv, excuse me, got off on a legal techie after leaving her dead on the by-pass. She's going to be cut off.' She thought in amazement, I just apologised for mentioning a pervert to this bloke I've only just met, when all the girls seem to know him and the entire Butty Bar can't finish their racing pages if his cup of tea, in its saucer, is interrupted.

'God help the child.'

That's not the point, she almost blurted out, quickly donning the street girls' rage. His eyes lifted. They were different now, sorrow filling them. Strangely, it seemed he was sorry for her. Why? She stumbled on, wanting out from this and the quicker the better.

'And they want him topped.' She gave a shrug, disowning her message. The incongruous notion came to her, what if he was some kind of under-cover policeman, such as she often saw in the late-night TV blockbusters? 'They say, Tell Bonn it's only fair.'

'You are only recently at work, Bally.'

'Two months.' Relieved to be on safe ground, she tried a smile at his unwavering look. 'I did six weeks in the working house, Number Fifteen. Kate looked after me. I was happy there, first time in my life.'

Posser's first working house near Victoria Square backed onto the Volunteer. Now, the three houses, Numbers Eleven, Fifteen and Seventeen, were linked by causeways and fire escapes newly installed.

'Kate is pleasant, Bally.' The way he spoke her name warmed her. Maybe it was the mention of Kate, a forty-plus woman from Pendleton who ran the working house. She had been trained up by Posser, and did night school classes in hand-ling accounts. She once knifed somebody and earned a short stretch, had done her probation before Martina said she was OK enough to take on running Fifteen.

'The girls love her. She stands up to everybody. Except Rack, that is.'

He said nothing, didn't even nod to show it was all right to keep on talking. His silence unnerved her a bit. She decided to go for it, and asked what should she tell the girls.

'Grace said I'd to say they had to get an answer because the girls are really...' Bally didn't want to use Grace's crude expression, but why not? Even in the short time Bally had worked the streets she had seen the Butty Bar ransacked in some brawl over that pole dancer who called herself Ermine. Now even ordinary slang felt wrong. She looked with respect at Bonn. Why wasn't he drinking his tea? 'Upset,' she finished lamely.

'Thank you,' he said. No answer? She didn't know what to do. His eyes wanted to take in the distance. Was she to wait until he finally told her she could go, or was that it?

'Am I to tell Grace and Milly anything, please?'

Her chair scraped the pocked lino. Customers looked round.

'It was kind of you to come, Bally.'

'Ta-ra, then.' She felt stupid, but didn't mind.

Which made things all right, she thought in relief as the door pinged behind her. She made Foundry Street and headed for the Square. Had he meant brave? She was almost back on station with her string when a word came that she had felt lacking. Almost, she thought, *almost* made things all right.

Back in the Butty Bar, Bonn wondered if Bally believed in ghosts. People sensed these things, and perhaps the others in her team had chosen her to come and make the plea for the little girl in hospital because they guessed that, as Hindi, Bally might be outside their normal terms of reference. Or maybe it was some kind of argument, and Bally was simply being bubbled, put into harm's way to get even. He gave up, finally let his eyes go into distance, and in his mind saw a mumper groping in a huge waste bin. He wondered whether to tell Rack he wanted to know details. Or Martina? Then decided no, to both. Best if he asked himself. Fewer ghosts, perhaps.

Chapter Forty

pom, pommo – Prescription Only Medicine

'What now?'

Rack was in the OB van borrowed from the Granadee TV Studios, *OUTSIDE BROADCAST* glyph on its side to tell the plod to sod off while he got his end away. Lara had only just got going when somebody knocked the side panel. He opened the door thinking, Christ, do I have to do everything?

Dabbo and Clitheroe were standing sheepishly on the pavement in the dark.

'Sorry, Rack. You nivver said what we wus to do.'

'Give me frigging strength. Get the gelt, duff him and whoever he's got with.'

Dabbo tried to see round Rack into the van. Rack pulled his jeans up. He'd been wearing a gunslinger belt, no holster.

'Do we top him, like?'

'You think it's going to get that far, you come and tell me.'

He slammed the van door, rotated the handle and sprawled on the couch he'd installed. Lara was still kneeling. Rack liked one light, a small round thing, not those long flickery glims that hurt your eyes and took forever to light up. He slid his kecks and lay back, cuffing her head to jump-start where she left off.

He felt the glow begin as she bobbed and jawed. He thought what a pleasant way it was to spend an evening, even if the two burkes he'd told to do the job were thick. Yet, he thought, getting steamed up in anger, they could probably read and maybe write too, which only went to show what dumb fucks made it through schooling when decent people like himself couldn't tell what a letter did, or why black bits stuck out of some letters and not others. He caressed Lara's head as she worked. She was said to be Russian, Ukraine was it or was that somewhere else? He stared at the single bulb, his mouth opening and breathing getting hard to do. She'd cost, sorting through the passport malarkey, but thanks to Martina's supposed lawyer supposed uncle it had only taken three days and here she was behaving proper.

Idle thoughts of Dabbo and Clitheroe intruded but he only got mad at cackhandedness so he shelved them and concentrated on giving Lara a good choking. Second time round he'd make her look at the light so he could tell if she was thinking. Above all, Rack wanted the street girls happy, sort of.

Rack sent Lara off, to report to Grellie's Yellow corner. Grellie would be sure to change her from the Moorgate girls, but so? She knew best. Dabbo was standing at the Warrington exit when Rack hit the pavement.

'Trouble, Rack. Mr Iffy got five honchos with.'

Rack sighed, jauntily acknowledging the silent applause of imaginary but invisible crowds. Dabbo watched the useless fucker doing his clasped-hands bit while late-night shoppers stared and thought what the fuck. Dabbo was used to it and walked alongside the boss stander, just thankful Rack wasn't being Raging Bull or Rocky III when he'd pretend to box and spar his way among the evening crowds.

'Wiv, eh?'

'Yeh. Clitheroe's in the ginnel. He's got the cell phone.'

'Right. Where's Bling?'

'Who?'

Rack sighed. Too many useless drossies on the team, that's what, so he had to do every fucking thing. 'Get me a limo, Dab. Massive, one of them long white things.'

'Straight up?' Rack had never sent Dabbo for anything like this before.

Rack halted and gave him the stare. 'I'll wait here.'

Dabbo ran in a panic to obey. Rack watched the girls over on the Yellow, over on the long station ramp. He was pleased to see the girls hard at it, in and out of punters' motors like fiddlers' elbows.

240

The new massive car park there, big as a city, did a roaring trade of an evening. He wondered if Grellie kept her Yellow string under strength for any particular reason. He didn't like thoughts like this, because they signalled something wrong.

Was it time Martina did her finance review, or was that next month? He guessed it was time to appoint another key – a top goer like Bonn, boss of three other goers. If things were left to him, as Martina and Posser really ought, he'd make Bonn pick which goer would get the enviable promotion. Except, Bonn would go red and look aside instead of yelping with glee at the power that would give. Rum bloke, Bonn. Too much schooling in that fucking seminary, too much reading, and far too much thinking. He needed to have his own bird to come home to and knock about a bit, like God intended. It's what women liked, though you'd not to notice when they pretended different. Even Mama, his brainless mother, knew that was true, and she was thick as pig shit.

He leant on the pedestrian railing to watch the traffic, whistling that tune from that musical about somebody's wagons, a cowboy film with hardly any shooting. Rack knew he would have made a brilliant cowboy.

Twenty minutes, along came a giant white limousine with as many windows as a mill. He embarked, beckoned Dabbo in. Time for a bit of decent blood. Blood cleared things up. Rack often found that.

Chapter Forty-One

B&S ('bedren and sistren') – brothers and sisters; folk of a like ethnicity

Clare met Dr Elphinstone by the ICU. She disliked the new uniforms of the Intensive Care Unit nurses, that too of physiotherapists who tried to adapt their own plain whites to simulate them. Females were too group-conscious, Clare believed, noticing similar events in her student days. The ICU sister, a plain woman called Felster, shared her opinion and corrected transgressors without success. Arguments about status in hospitals came from auxiliaries, technicians, and therapists, who would kill to call themselves real professionals.

'Got to make a decision today, Dr Burtonall,' Terry said. They fell in step along the corridor, heels muffling as they reached the business section. They entered the changing room to get protective clothing. Clare also hated the design of the cover-all boots, everything new in the wrongest design to save a few farthings, some cack-handed rule from Admin maniacs.

Clare glanced round as they changed. Nobody junior present, so they could speak. 'Still nothing from any family?'

'Not a soss. I've given up hopes. The police say they've had no joy.'

'And Admin?'

242

Terry gave her a wry smile. He was good at those oblique glances you could never quite judge in Edwardian novels: quizzical, ironic, wry, sardonic. 'Are you serious, Clare? They'll rediscover the patient's file just when it's all over.'

She smiled. 'The usual, then.'

'Anything to disclaim responsibility.' He grunted, stooping to haul on the ridiculous coveralls. 'I often wonder what sort of minds they have. I mean, do they choose the job because they need doctrine, or are they trained into it by each other?'

'The child, though.' Clare felt she wanted to escape from spiralling round grievances about useless staff today. 'They re-did an AVPU score?'

'Yes.'

Terry straightened. Clare noticed her male colleagues never checked their appearances in the mirrors, while it was the first thing females did. Was the urge to create a visual impression inflexibly drilled into the female, or was it instinctive? Or did all human beings start out with it, and males simply get taught not to bother? Doubtless sociologists were beavering away at their idle trade on this topic, soon to write that best-seller tirade proving the obvious. Social scientists had lately shown that people preferred beauty, would you believe, and even the most learned journals had published their stuff.

'I haven't seen it yet.'

'That's why I asked for you, Clare.' He gave her a grimace. He was good at those, too. 'Prejudices are roaring about the hospital. Religion's raised its ugly head. You'll have seen the pickets by the front gate.' He smiled more openly. 'I can get you their handouts if you want.'

'Another time.'

Together they walked into the ward with that slithery shuffle imposed by their footwear. This latest Admin achievement made it literally impossible to reach across a coma bed without ripping the damned garment at the waist. Further cost-cutting triumphs were rumoured to be planned by Admin. Terry Elphinstone called Admin the HSBU, health service burden unit, but he was veering towards a political life in some rebellious mini-party soon to seek election. Clare couldn't care less who ruled the Finance Subvention Team as long as they showed a bit of common sense.

The girl was in a side section, no longer podded in a closed unit of her own. The routine of 'special-ling' – allocating a nurse to continual watch – had long since been discontinued in the interests of economy. Expense had to be cut, Admin ruled, and now coma patients were left alone in the mesh of electronic monitors. Clare thought of the modern practice as callous, simply leaving coma patients to get on with whatever life they had left. No relatives, of course, and no nurse, though she noticed the nurse attending the NS, the nursing station, occasionally glancing through the console screen as she and Terry entered to stand beside the coma bed.

'Gadget city,' Elphinstone muttered. 'Would you rather have a nurse on special?'

Clare sighed. 'We speak as if it was the Dark Ages, and it was only eight years ago.'

'No bitterness.' The consultant physician handed her the record, no more than a handset, its screen permanently polarised for better viewing in the hooded illumination of the ICU section. 'The AVPU was equivocal. Response to pain wasn't tried. The only response was to vocal stimulus.'

'Houseman's observations?' Clare asked.

Elphinstone glanced over her shoulder. 'Yes. He's new, three weeks only on the house. From Manchester University.'

'It's probably wishful thinking.' The tendency of new young doctors to over-estimate clinical responses of incoming head injury patients – A for Alert, V for response to vocal stimulus, P for response to pain, and U for lack of any response – and score too optimistically, was well-known. 'I made that mistake a dozen times, until I realised I was just willing the patient to have less damage than I could see.'

'We all did.'

'Now, though, on the GCS?'

'I'm afraid I can't push it above 3.'

Clare scrolled the miniature screen through the Glasgow Coma Scale rapidly, searching for any doctor's note registering improvement in examinations of the comatose girl. 'I wonder if there's a less inflexible series of observations, Terry. Like, what if we brought in somebody entirely new to the case, and asked them to score without a GCS numbering scale?'

'I have,' Elphinstone said quietly. 'You're she, Clare.'

'Of course.' Clare felt the weight of his request. The GCS was a means of registering the re-activity of patients on a numerical scale. It could be used by nurses and doctors alike. The motor response had six grades, 6 down to 1, verbal response 5 down to 1, and eye opening 4 down to 1. The simplest interpretation was to make a sum of the scores. The lowest of each category being 1, a score of 3 registered the comatose patient as unresponsive.

'Poor girl.'

'The hospital spokesmen are itching to go,' Elphinstone said in a mutter, not wanting the words recorded on the continuous DVD. 'I'd like to tell them to get stuffed.'

'I'll give her a general examination, Terry, then enter my findings.'

'Thanks, Clare. Want me to stay, send a nurse?'

'I'd rather you stayed, please. The duty nurse is in her last hour. She'll be scribing the night report in her immortal prose.'

Elphinstone went to sit beneath the bank of consoles while Clare began the clinical examination. At the end she recorded her findings in painstaking detail. Together they left with a backward glance, just to check, and went to collect the radiographs and electroencephalogram traces. They made quite an armful. The consulting room on the same floor was vacant, and they sat at the long desk to scatter the data and compare findings.

They scored the patient NFU, not for resuscitation. The ethics committee would review their opinions, and advise the consultant concerned who would make the final decision. Clare felt a traitor. Terry Elphinstone felt as bad. They left the hospital separately, knowing paparazzi were staking out the premises and would give teeth to photograph them drinking in a bar or emerging and chatting as they went. Newspaper photographers were not above sketching in cheerful grins on the sombre faces of doctors, to give subeditors something to crow about. Any falsehood was worth printing to gain attention.

Chapter Forty-Two

G-man – Grenadian (West Indies)

Bling was toking up on the casino, first after the third St Helens traffic island on the Liverpool Road some way out of the city, when a huge obese Grenadian came and whispered.

'Rack who?'

'Some mad lole, looks about four years old. Come to say sorry.'

'Sorry's for parole and probation, Jaskie ma man.'

'He's in some great tanker fing.'

'What's he say sorry 'bout?'

'He say gelt. Means money.' The fat G man quivered with anxiety, went for it. 'Only, I'd see him, Bling.'

Bling looked his surprise at the Grenadian, and nodded, rising to go through the layered smoke as the metal music thumped and screeched. The crowd parted to let him pass, the Grenadian waddling after. Four others separated from the mob and trailed Bling to the curtained entrance.

The Trinidadian was a foot taller than the

youth who waited in the foyer. Rack didn't need to be told the outer doors would close and remain so until he left. Several girls – he liked their glitzy raiment and jewellery, and every one wore a ton of make-up, real class – quietly disappeared, leaving the giant and himself alone. Rack wondered how he'd look in a long leather coat almost down to the floor like this enormous well-shaped black geezer, only he reckoned he could wear better style that that. And the glimpse of gold teeth, like a fucking gilded graveyard, meant this Windy had no sense of style, no 'rim' as they spoke among themselves.

'Who you, man?' Bling saw the lad's confidence, and wondered if he hadn't a vague notion, dredged up from memory, of who this little turd actually was.

'Rack.' The youth smiled, standing there. 'Came to say sorry, that's all.'

'I axing whaffor.'

'Oh, that bloke Mr Iffy.'

'Who he?'

'Iffy? Runs a couple of tower blocks and doss rentals near the edge of the city centre. I thought it were the middle syndicate's, and I sent a couple of lads across to lean on him, get what's due. First I heard of him tonight, see.'

'No, I dun' see.'

'I didn't realise Mr Iffy's shelling to you, like he says. I just didn't want you taking it wrong, see?'

'He paying me?'

Bling held up a hand, but the silly young bastard took not a blind bit of notice and started foot-tapping and humming and rocking to the thumping music from within, that wooden way loles did when they full in theysels. Bling thought hard. He had no memory of any Mr Iffy paying him dues for a rental scam. So why he saying he is?

'Why he sayin' he is when he in't?'

Rack paused, still affable. 'Eh? Isn't he? Only, my lads said he's already paying you. I called my lads off, seeing he can't pay both, right?'

'Why you here, man?'

'I came to say I wasn't trying to muscle in or anything. No business of mine, Just so you know your manor's OK by us.'

'Wait.' Bling stared down at the youth, who seemed unfazed by the casino, the honchos, the bro pack, the scene. 'This Iffy. What's he got?'

'Money. Small rents, but he's clinging to mucho back payo if he's kept your end all this time. See you, friend.'

Bling watched Rack go, nodding to the hulking bros on the door so they stood immobile. He beckoned. His fat Grenadian leg man appeared.

'This Iffy bin milkin' my herd, G man. We see him. I be there this time.'

'Now, Bling?'

'One hour. Find where an' what.'

Iffy saw the cars pull into his yard. His four were already standing in a cluster by the far gate. The walled yard was a size, originally intended for loading barrels on drays from the brewery. The whole building had been converted into flatlets with two so-called penthouses on the eighth floor. He had decided to play hell, when insolent architects ordered him to erect fire escapes on two sides abutting the passing streets. He halted, terrified, feeling for his cell phone.

'You Iffy?'

A fat black man, huge and quivering from his enormous flab, came and stood too close. Iffy could detect the man's odoriferous breath. What, garlic, spices in mad mixtures, maybe impossible dried meats gone bad and cooked in oceans of oil? He recoiled.

'Yes. What do you want?'

His four men stood mute and still. Only then did Iffy see that several black men were standing close by them. And his men were slowly turning round to face the wall as if on some order.

'Your bank accounts. Your cards. PINs, your reffos, bank codes. Give them all.'

'I...' Iffy went for it. He started to sweat heavily, though the night was cool. 'The banks are closed until nine o'clock.'

'All of them, Mr Iffy.'

'Takin' too long, G man,' a deep bass voice rumbled from the nearest black motor.

'See,' the fat hulk whispered, as if imparting a confidence to a friend, 'my boss want those tings now. You give, unnerstan'?'

'I only have two or three with me,' Iffy said desperately, shaking so badly he couldn't open his case. The fat man took it with a sigh of regret.

'Your famblih in our care, Mr Iffy, see?' The fat man showed Iffy his cell phone, where Iffy's wife and three children were smiling at the camera. 'Ten minutes ago, they come to help us ... wid our enquiries.' He snuffled, and Iffy realised the fat man was laughing, snuffling like a hog, his layers of pendulous fat quivering.

'My family?'

'They want you to give me all those numbers, see? Den you go home, live happy ever after, see?' He stopped laughing. 'Or not, Mr Iffy.'

Iffy gave over nine bank cards, credit and withdrawal numbers. The fat man chose three at random and gestured one of his men over. The man trotted off and returned five minutes later.

'They's OK, G man.'

'Mr Iffy? They's all OK? Tell yez or no. Any lying here, you going take the wet walk home, really, yeh, really?'

'I've given you them all correctly.'

'No more, like in your pocket? In yo' sock?' More snuffling laughter.

'No, sir. That is all.'

'None in yo' wife name?'

'No. That's all.'

'OK, righteous man. Home you go.'

Iffy looked about but could not see his car, a customised Chrysler classic version. He'd only had it a year.

'My car,' he said, feeling shell-shocked. 'Is my car...?'

'Ah, iz borrowed. You walk home.'

Iffy wondered about night buses. He'd never ridden on a bus since he first came to the city. Was it the 86 that passed by the end of his avenue? He almost said thank you, and left the yard, starting walking alongside the disused canal. He began to worry about hoodlums and junkies, who were said to infest these areas. Once thriving communities, they were now derelict, yards and footpaths

251

littered with broken glass, springs, tattered remains of discarded furniture. Somewhere fires burned among the rubble and refuse. He was sure he heard rats scurrying among the debris.

He died on the bridge leading into a safer district, a Chrysler classic running him down as he crossed into the lighted street opposite. His last thought was, that's my motor, coming for me to take me home! He died so glad that the terrible episode was finally over, and he would ride home in peace and somehow restore order to his world in this calamitous night.

Chapter Forty-Three

rim – Rhythm-in-the-Midden (variously pr.) the most fashionable (of music, clothes, clubs)

'Look, Vern, I'm not muscling in. You know me.'

Hassall found the IOIC, the Yoik in station slang, stirring a drink made from mangoes and carrots. On his face was an expression of distaste. Vernon Taffy was a florid man, features purple as a Victoria plum. Hassall wondered how Vern managed to stay fat when he wheezed and sweated simply moving from desk to files.

Vern's glance was sardonic. Aye, he knew Hassall. 'I have to drink this gunge twice a day. It's supposed to cut my weight down by a pound a week.'

Hassall was intrigued, having health problems

of his own. Was it everyone these days, or just in his age group? 'And does it?'

'No. Improves my appetite so I eat like a bloody horse. Anything I can help you with? The answer's no.'

'The perv's death. That biochemist. He's here, isn't he?'

'No. Farnworth General. Friend of your pal, that doctor who fiddles your physical so you can draw your undeservedly high salary for doing sweet sod all.'

'Mind if I come?'

'Yep, I do. I'll let you know what he says when I'm back.' Vern didn't want the unfit, rumouredly diabetic Hassall making eyebrow melodrama with some young quack he fancied in his old age, while some incomprehensible scientist poured out hieroglyphics.

'I'll say nowt, Vern, arrive and leave with you, OK?' Hassall wheedled, knowing his friend's mind.

They compromised, and left to catch Dr Clare at Farnworth General by coffee time. Hassall noticed his friend failed to drink the mango-carrot drink. He would irritate Vern Taffy, when they returned, by reminding him and waiting until he'd drunk every last drop. Hassall's missus knew Mrs Taffy, a useful conduit for the more discerning.

'The section you see,' Dr Roundel told the thirty-five millimetre image when the two policeman had seated themselves and Clare had slipped into the gloaming to join them, 'is provided by the pathologist. They have a different histopathology

253

unit in the North-East.'

Hugely obese but heavily muscled, Dr Roundel was the best scientific brain in the district, according to Clare, who had particularly asked for him to do the toxicology.

'Does it matter?' Vern Taffy grumbled quietly, wanting this eerie stuff over and done with. It should have been emailed or couriered through, save him a time mine. Instead, he had to waste two hours while some weirdo dobber bored everybody sick.

'It does to me,' Dr Roundel said in his episcopalean timbre, surprising Taffy who thought he'd been inaudible to the speaker. 'I'd like to know how they selected this particular set of coordinates. Alignment tells a hell of a lot, unless you're too bored to bother.'

'Sorry, Charles,' Clare said meekly. He was her friend, and had rights of his own. 'I was too late to prep our visitors. My fault.'

'Ever read the original?' The scientist seemed tired. 'No?'

Hassall realised they were being asked a direct question. 'Er, no.'

'It escapes students these days.' Roundel shook massively and the trio in the small projection room understood that it was his silent chuckle. 'Reading the originals.'

'Er, which would that be?'

Roundel sobered and used the light-arrow of his torch to indicate the sliver of missile embedded in the sectioned flesh of the victim.

'This is a piece of hardwood, the sort you can get at any hardware multi-shop. In fact, it could

254

even be a splinter trimmed off some larger piece. Sashes, window frames, model-maker suppliers, everybody uses it if they're any sort of craftsman, and even if they're not.'

The multi-coloured section was heavily stained. 'Ordinary haematoxylin and eosin stain, the usual rubbish. I like metachromatic stains myself – methylene blue is the commonest example, but the North-East omitted to send us some un-stained paraffin histology with this. And they kept the paraffin wax blocks of tissue themselves.' Roundel added drily, 'So impressed by the gravitas of the forensic and legal urgency of this case, you see.'

Clare interceded quickly to prevent any nasti-ness. 'Charles, this sliver of wood was the missile, then?'

'It's where the poison was, yes. *Maximiliana regis* is the original wood, a small South American palm tree. Described as bearing huge ostrich-like plumes. Produces a truly tough wood, decorative sometimes, but it's only use otherwise is marine work – like shoving palm stems under riverside huts and whatnot.'

'Charles,' Clare interrupted. 'You mean you think otherwise?'

'Meaning except for poisoned arrows. The Guiana Indians made – still do make, I believe, though you'd need an anthropologist from the Archaeology School, but don't tell them it was me sent you.' He did his monstrous silent shake of mirth before recovering. 'Macouchi Indians there were pretty kind to Mr Waterton back in 1812. It's a famous, if now seriously neglected, chronicle of travels recorded by an adventurer. Highly educated, he left us good descriptions. He bribed the tribes rotten. Indefatigable, he was, riddled with malaria and enough parasites to sink a ship. Why the hell he didn't die of Yellow Fever God knows. Superb vaccine for that nowadays, incidentally.'

'The poison, though?'

'Oh, the Wourali plant, *Strychnos toxifera*. Never seen it myself, but it's some sort of vine thing, swarms up other plants to get enough living space. They use roots. Pharmacognocists are plenteous in pharmaceutical firms if you want to root them out.' More shaking at his impossible pun, then, 'Stedman originally described the Cocofera palm by name, so young Waterton had already heard of it. And some earlier intrepid geezer, Keymis, had located the vine in 1596, believe it or not. I often wonder if they'd no blinking homes to go to, wandering about like that. Thank God they did, or we'd know nothing.'

'This poison, though,' Hassall said, prompted by Clare's interruption. 'Is it available now?'

'Oh, common, Mr Hassall,' the scientist said. 'It's the one anaesthetists use still in a purified form. Synthetic, I shouldn't doubt. Called curare. Nick it from any physiology lab anywhere in the world. Knowing the lax security in Anat. and Physiol. Units in various medical schools, I'd say you could just walk in and lift a ton.'

Hassall watched Dr Roundel do his shake at lax security.

'Thank you, Doctor,' he said. 'Very interesting about those arrows things. Curare, eh?'

'The dose takes minutes only. Check the effects with a medical doctor, like Dr Clare there. Every public library should have Waterton's *Wanderings in South America*. The poison's modern derivatives are used in virtually every hospital. And in experimental medicine, of course. Undergraduates, post-grads, sciences and medics. They'd all have access to supplies.'

He seemed disappointed by Clare's smiling thanks and that his session was being ended so quickly. 'And animal units,' he called as his audience left. 'And veterinary surgeons, and any high street vet. Vet nurses use it...'

'See you Tuesday, Charles,' Clare said over her shoulder. 'Free for a drink after the Clinico-Pathological Conference on Ethics?'

'We'll need one after that carry-on, Clare,' Roundel said sadly, standing by the multi-coloured screen of poisoned arrow's tip embedded in human tissue. He was sorry it was ending so quickly, He'd only just got going. 'See you.'

Chapter Forty-Four

dobber – fat idler

'OK, Bonn?'

Rack was waiting as Bonn left the Time and Scythe. He came down the stairs instead of in the lift, as if it did him good, like them women in leotards on running machines and hauling weights in the Bouncing Block down Moor Lane.

'Thank you for waiting, Rack,' Bonn said, like it was Rack's idea to be polite instead of Martina's inflexible rule you durst not transgress or you'd get her ice-blue eyes. He and Bonn fell in step and turned down Mealhouse Lane.

'OK, mate. Fancy a cuppa?'

'No, thank you, Rack. I shall sit a while in the Volunteer, then have tea in the Valiance Carvery.'

That place was no great shakes, but Bonn seemed to like its space. Another thing: Bonn always went in through the Bridge Street entrance instead of the front door. He seemed to think it was more polite, which only showed what a twisted burke Bonn really was. Rack was glad he didn't have Bonn's brain. It'd stop you doing anything straight. It could make you ill.

'Look, Bonn,' Rack said. 'Isn't it time you got your own bird?'

This again, Bonn thought. 'I don't quite understand, Rack.'

Rack thought Bonn knew well enough what he meant. 'See, a bloke who doesn't have his own tart, it does his head in. Don't get me wrong,' he said quickly, in case Bonn interrupted – he never had yet, but there was always a first time. 'You get plenty of humpo with the money women, but it can't be the same, right? With your own bird you could do anyfink, give her a good hiding, try things out. Have a good row, a real up-and-downer. Stands to reason you'd feel better.'

'Rack, please moderate your language.'

Rack wasn't going to give up. 'Don't you shag Martina? You live in Posser's house, and she's a gorgeous looker even if she does limp. Say to her, real tactful, "Look, Martina. I'll have you as my bint, forget your gammy leg, OK?" She'd jump at it, and Posser'd be glad. You are really dim, mate.'

'Thank you. I appreciate the thought.' They walked as far as the Foundry Street fork, where Bonn paused. The stander was only trying his best. 'Rack. I must have seemed somewhat laconic.'

'Yeh.' Rack didn't know if Bonn was narked or saying sorry, which.

'I apologise.'

Rack was relieved. 'OK, wack. Just wondered.'

'I shall swim at the Bouncing Block later.'

'Here, Bonn. For fuck's sake – sorry. Don't pay to go swimming. Martina owns the whole frigging gym, OK? No wonder she gets narked. Not even the ordinary goers pay. It disses us.'

Bonn hesitated. It caused disrespect to Martina, Rack, the other standers and employees of the syndicate's extensive arms and enterprises if he paid an entrance fee to the gymnasium? However simple it might seem to some, it actually was a grave moral problem. Was it fair, to use the swimming pool and make no contribution to its running expenses? Further, would it lead to other forms of exploitation – for that is truly what it was – and cause him to begin having tea at the various tea rooms and hotels in the city centre and not even pay? One abuse inexorably led to another. Soon, he would be tempted to demand meals, drinks perhaps, other facilities, and not pay a penny. Others, as Rack said, always avoided making payment. It was quite in order, in fact exactly what Martina instructed her keys, goers, and standers to do. Yet he still felt uncomfortable, as if it were stealing. Which it actually was. He had a credit card, courtesy of Martina's diligent Miss Hope in the control centre. It remained unused. There was no doubting Rack's concern. Would Rack get in trouble with Martina?

'Very well, Rack. Thank you for reminding me.'

'There, mate!' Rack was hugely delighted. Breakthrough! 'Oh, Berenice Six-Six-Nine, top floor, Amadar Royale in Liverpool Road, noon tomorrow.'

'Ah, noon is rather unusual, Rack.'

Rack shrugged. 'It's what was asked for.' He grinned. 'Hey, Bonn. Berenice sounds like bare knees.' He fell about, laughing. 'Get it? Bare *knees!*'

'I would not have thought of that, Rack.'

Bonn walked on the pavement, north side of the Square, to the Valiance Carvery. He decided he would make a donation to a charity equal to the amount he would have otherwise paid for admission to the Bouncing Block swimming pool afterwards. Except here too was another moral difficulty: which charity was sound, and not ruled by a self-indulgent bureaucracy eager to milk contributions for themselves, plus every perk from motor expenses to holidays and monstrous index-linked pensions?

The assassin replaced the receiver, and pencilled a note: Amadar Royale Hotel, off Deansgate, Liverpool Road, top floor, 12.00 noon, pseudonym Berenice Six-Six-Nine. At times like this, moments reserved for rewards, the skin positively glowed. Tilting the mirror and adjusting the metastable lamp – of course, with the new bulbs, sixty watts of electricity ran only eleven – facial features seemed to become even more alluring than usual. Peace was in the apartment air – the word flat seemed so mundane, too ordinary. No, this was celebration time.

How often had the TV news gone over the same details? The description of the woman – fairly young, walking quickly away from the stumbling, drunken man, pausing as if to turn back and help, but thinking the better of it and hurrying on – had not been too flattering. The age given was doubtful. One insolent yobbo among the bouncers said the figure was that of quite an old bird, but wasn't sure. That would have really hurt.

Celebration. Newspapers would be jubilant in their hysteria. Already editions were out, shown in graphic close-ups, grim newscasters holding the front pages for the cameras to focus. Why did those illiterates always print the same ignorant boldtype screamers? ASSASSIN STRIKES DOWN PERVERT was one. Most annoying was JUSTICE BY UNKNOWN SLAYER, if you please. Tomorrow's lot would be even sillier. The loudest tabloids would give it gavotte, with supposed analyses of motivation of the common people who now had 'had enough' of incompetent judiciary, The broadsheets would go for waffle, bringing out archaic column-inches dredged from tiresome records in Albemarle Street and that simply awful place in Colindale run by the halt, the lame and the blind.

Tomorrow, the reward. The assassin had resorted to similar pleasures three times before.

One such reward was in Leeds, a goer called Wayne from Australia, quite amusing but with the emotional opacity of a brick though quite bright. The second had been in Birmingham, a mulatto – was one allowed to use that term still? He had been unrelentingly jovial and became rather tiresome, though satisfactory in other ways. The third reward was in North London, which turned out to be something of a mistake, an anxious Indian youth who seemed bent on proving he was as good as anyone else about whatever it was he thought he was doing. The assassin wondered about the key with the enigmatic name, booked less than an hour since.

Bonn seemed, if lexicographers spoke truth (did they ever?) to mean 'good for nothing'. Strange. In the ancient Breton, 'simple', perhaps even 'wasteful', or was that in error? The assassin was too excited, thinking of the pleasures to come, to speculate further. Derivations could wait. Would the young man have wisdom? Or would he be mesmerised, too thick to do more than simply listen, nodding, wondering what the hell he had got himself into?

The assassin watched the news, giggling at the bumblings of the senior police, why did they always need desks when speaking to the public or the news media? Some mental barrier, perhaps?

Thinking of the delight to come, the assassin dared a glass of wine – a red, little tannin, thank heavens, and none of that revolting bovine albumen French vintners insisted on – and wondered about the key who would bring pleasure to the hotel room at noon next day, It would not end in physical intercourse, not necessarily. It would depend on the feelings generated, the possibilities emerging as they enacted the encounter. It would seal the death of the pervert.

Then the news changed.

The assassin sat forward, glaring at the screen.

The Farnworth General Ethics Committee announced their decision of the coma girl. 'It was thought in the patient's best interests,' the announcer intoned, smug face showing her satisfaction at presenting momentous news in her South Surrey drawl, 'to begin the legal processes that will result in withdrawal of life support. She was first admitted...'

The assassin sat back. The scene cut to an outside camera, where Dr Clare Burtonall was shown walking, another smug bitch, across a hospital car park to a great old maroon Humber SuperSnipe, the sort you didn't see about any more. A legend below gave her printed name. The assassin's job was clearly not yet over. Tomorrow, the assassin would need the *General Medical Register.* Bitch.

God rest the poor girl, the assassin thought, tears welling. Very well, it would be pleasure at noon, for a task well done. Then on to the next task, the sequel, of another execution yet to be performed, on Dr Clare. Death should be in the hands of morality, not by the whim of folk who thought themselves God Almighty because they had dozed for a few years in medical school.

Life was simply one damned thing after another, the comedy writer HL Menken said. The assassin wondered if the great American linguist was trying to be witty. Did it matter?

263

Chapter Forty-Five

prole – average person, run-of-the-mill

'Berenice.' Bonn opened the door just enough.
  'Bonn, I presume?'
  'Yes.'
  Berenice Six-Six-Nine went confidently in, appraising him. This was the most costly goer in the north? Worth so much?
  Average height, no designer clothes, only run-of-the-mill shoes, hair looking almost combed. He seemed awkward. Berenice hoped no complaint would become due. She had been so looking forward to her reward, so deservedly earned.
  'I can offer a drink,' Bonn said, diffident.
  Berenice once had drawn a swashbuckler of a youth in Wolverhampton. Yuri had rushed in practically kicking off his shoes and advancing with passion so overwhelming it proved wholly refreshing. Berenice preferred that. It was a form of assault, sure, but that's what was paid for, right? Service, after all. This Bonn could 'offer a drink'. Well thank goodness for that at least.
  The riotous Yuri gratified Berenice, perhaps because his behaviour was so different from the norm at work, that school of rituals and tidy systems. Still, proof of the pudding.
  'I'll have coffee, Bonn.'
  'Ah,' he said, full of doubt. 'If you wish, except...'

Berenice waited to see what he would do, this expensive instrument standing there. He hesitated a moment longer, then came to recover the coat she had dropped on the couch.

'Yes?'

'Except, nobody will drink my coffee.'

'Nobody drinks it?'

She was almost amused. The expense of hiring this Bonn came to mind. In some up-market hotel in Bristol once, before an independent vigilante career became a real possibility, while meeting a supper companion at a quite splendidly ornate lounge bar, a startling cry had sounded, and a droll figure sprang out of the foliage by the reception area. The Tarzan-O-Gram caused laughter among the hotel guests. The figure wore a loin-cloth of leopard skin, and bellowed a girl's name. A hen night, of course. The usual mayhem ensued. The Tarzan carried off a screaming bride-to-be, she shrieking with delight, to applause and cheers of friends. Berenice sensed disappointment, though. The youth acting as Tarzan had seemed so casual, merely doing a get-it-over-with job. The feeling seemed to be general too among other guests, for Berenice heard remarks afterwards.

Bonn, meanwhile, was saying nothing. She studied him. No Tarzan he.

'Why not?'

'It does not prove suitable.'

She sat, slightly irritated, as he took the coat into the bedroom – there's confidence, Berenice thought with an inward grimace – and returned. His anxiety was contagious, but Berenice was beyond sympathy. This was a *reward*, for Christ's

265

sake, not a social endurance test.

OK, so he made terrible coffee. Was he going to turn out a taxi with a wheel missing?

He did not take one of the armchairs in the sumptuous room. Berenice felt their immediate lack of rapport, and speculated on the possible reasons for his feeble reception. Was she emanating something, perhaps from the recent success of executing her fourth perv? It might be possible, except this non-coffee non-maker seemed concerned, as if his ineptitude was the most almighty problem. No, she decided to insist.

'Try me with any kind.'

'I have it nearly ready. If you could be specific, I should try.'

'That's good to know.'

No answer. Pay a king's ransom, and discuss how to make coffee?

'What's this specific? You mean type of bean, ratio of grains to water? What?'

He sighed. It was only a minimal exhalation, but an honest heartfelt sigh. 'Yes, please.' He glanced round to the kitchen. Berenice heard something bubbling, presumably Bonn's extensive coffee-making preparations back there. 'It's the same with other drinks. They provide so many kinds. Like for other drinks.'

'Do they now.' Berenice reached for her cell phone. This was nonsensical. All that effort, the killing, the stake-outs, the God-horrendous expenditure of buying accurate addresses for the perp and his protectors, and now the whole evening lay ahead with nothing to show except a lonely dinner in some restaurant while others looked across and thought, hello, somebody dining alone over there, no partner, a failure.

Then Bonn spoke, seeming to find in her gesture a reassurance.

'I think it's quite like murder.'

Berenice felt blood drain, cheeks tingle, and she froze. *What* did he just say?

'It's what?' she managed, throat tight.

'I apologise. I mean a moral problem. It is almost as severe as the worst events that happen out there. In the city.'

Berenice suddenly wanted the coffee problem back. 'Coffee is?'

'Making for another.' Now he did sit, perching on the arm of one of the armchairs opposite.

'How do you work that out?'

He almost smiled. She observed puzzlement. How come they send out somebody so socially inept? Clients who paid the highest fees were bound to be the most demanding. They should not have to struggle to discover what the hell a goer was talking about.

'The best upbringing is to sit down to meals together,' he said. 'I've heard so.'

'So they say.'

'I often try to imagine it. With someone like you.'

'With someone like me?'

Did he mean with just anyone? Perhaps he was too young for the game he was supposed to be playing here. God, he only looked twenty.

The half-smile almost showed. It was shyness, and evidently unpractised. 'Before you came I tried to draw you.'

Berenice looked about for the drawing. None.
'It was your name, Berenice. So lovely.'

It was difficult to avoid his expression. She attempted to read it. What did he know, to mention murder?

'I like it.' He added, 'I trust I do not give offence.'

'No, of course not.' Berenice felt exhausted. Endless doubt, when he should have been ... doing what, exactly? For he seemed unprepared to do anything. And why her growing wish to reassure him that all was well, when the cell phone was waiting to make the complaint?

'Berenice the Guardian,' Bonn said, rising now with purpose and moving to the kitchen. He called over his shoulder, 'You'll have my version of coffee, and like it.'

'There are several Berenices,' she said, meaning it as a corrective.

'It wouldn't be the daughter of Mithridates,' his voice came through the kitchen door. He seemed unabashed, now on course, doing something. 'I wouldn't want you to be Agrippa the Elder's daughter, so she is out for absolute certain. And I truly felt somewhat against the King of Egypt's daughter, because she got up to no good most of the time.'

'Oh?' She listened. Was this one so costly simply because he was educated?

'Not Ptolomaeus Legus's wife, either.' She heard water begin to percolate and scented coffee. He was pouring. 'That particular Berenice was a problem. All that funny business over her son being raised to the throne of Egypt. There is only so much you can take, after all.'

'There is, is there?' Berenice had chosen the pseudonym and the numerical suffix with great care, hugging herself at the self-entertainment and the delicious concealment the choice had given her. Her private fable was despoiled now by this invasion.

'You would be gentle. You, I believe, are Berenice the Guardian.' He returned carrying a small tray, frowning in concentration as he placed it on the table before her. 'That's the reason I drew you in lead-point.'

'Can I see?'

He considered this. 'Perhaps. Later.'

No agreement in there, Berenice realised, with annoyance. Not meaning yes and perhaps later *on*. He meant that maybe he might let this fantastic work of art be seen, probably scrawled on some scrap while he waited for her in the hotel's grandest suite.

'What if I insisted?'

This took him aback, and he looked. He was now beside her, and she realised his eyes were blue, though why did that matter?

'The colour of eyes,' Bonn said, judging the cafetière as if it had just appeared. 'Brown-eyed individuals are said to feel less pain. They say.'

She wore contact lenses. Was he quick, or observant? Worse, could this one be discerning? 'Did your family have their meals together?'

'I do not remember.' He anticipated a rebuke by saying, 'I only mean to say there is no way I can know.'

'You were adopted?'

'I do not know. It must be so comforting.'

269

'Don't ... clients take you out to dinner?'

'I try to make various arrangements.'

She watched him press the cafetière filter. He did this simple gesture with a concentration so fixed it would have been laughable if he had not mentioned murder. Before coming into the hotel, Berenice had made sure, watched for the signs. A youth, idiotically dressed, had arrived first and loitered about the hotel foyer, plus two more in the corridor, and a final one by the lifts. So she had been correctly informed. She had hired from a professional outfit. They took precautions. Berenice had deliberately given the hotel receptionist a dazzling smile and asked for the suite number, so she would be remembered. She had played this game too often to be caught, and had been perfectly ready if it turned out to be some sort of cheap scam. It had happened, but only once.

'I am always afraid this will fall to pieces,' Bonn was saying.

'You have done it before, though.'

'Yes. Except I had never seen one until...'

'Yes?' Until he had been freed from gaol, perhaps? Left a reformatory, or juvenile prison?

'Until I left school.'

'You know the Berenices of history, Bonn.'

Meticulously he poured her a cup of coffee into, she noticed, superb Royal Doulton. No expense spared. Scammers would have stinted, because scammers always do. She felt herself relax, in the ascendant at last.

'I like to read.'

'During those non-mealtimes?'

He smiled. 'I erred with your sketch.'

270

'Do you make drawings of all your clients?' Risk was tiresome, now entering these dull proceedings with this average, truly oh-so-average, youth.

He seemed surprised she should ask such a question. 'Certainly not. It would be improper.'

'The same with photographs, voice recordings?'

'Of course.'

She accepted the cup. 'Yet you have a ... stander, is that the right word? One in the hotel foyer, and two others in corridors.'

'They are selected for their obedience, I am told, and are invigilated to ensure performance.'

She raised the cup to her mouth. He seemed honestly interested. She observed his lips move slightly in synchrony with her first sip, and felt a glim of humour. His was the response of a child who sees something done for the first time. Yet, she thought, frankly amused, he surely cannot be so new to this game. Could it be that she felt to him like his very first time? Intriguing, but unlikely, Her previous experiences with goers proved their lack of any sensitivity. To them, performance was all.

'There is sugar,' he said when her expression changed.

'Your coffee is execrable. Sugar wouldn't help.'

He did not sigh at her judgement. 'Why did you mention murder?'

'The news. I wish they would not display newspapers for sale so the headlines show.'

Curious choice of words, Berenice registered. A goer in Southampton, supposedly a student, once told her he was picked for his carefree manner. Bonn was not stilted, just somehow con-

271

fined. She speculated on prison. Had he done time? If so, for what crime?

'That's surely the point, to encourage people to buy?'

'Yes,' he said, and that was that, so the world merely did what it did and could go on doing it, with all its failings. She wondered if he harboured secret ambitions, just as her previous hired goers, and asked. She wanted to know if his aim was to stay out of the hands of police.

'Ambition does not signify, Berenice.'

'Everybody has ambitions, so *you* must have. Is this your perfect life?' Berenice knew her natural belligerence was rising. Soon this might come to a sweep-out, leaving him to explain to his superiors why she demanded a refund for a truly wasted evening.

He considered. 'Well?' she demanded harshly. An outburst would soon be inevitable.

'You make it so.'

The simple truthfulness shocked her even more than his incongruous mention of murder a few minutes since.

'I what?'

He did not say it again, just nodded as if to some inner interrogator.

'Do you mean me?'

'You, Berenice.' He seemed sad. 'The pity is, you will not believe things could possibly be thus. Hearing me reply that way, you instantly opt for disbelief. You tell yourself I must be dissembling just to please you.'

'Do I?'

'I fear so.' He stared at his coffee cup, glancing

272

from it to the cafetière as if judging if he ought to try some, then sat back a little in rejection. 'I think that is the response you will make.'

'And why *thus?*' she demanded, bluntly adding sarcasm to show she could be angry if she wanted, and under these circumstances. The one who pays the piper...

'I am apprehensive, Berenice. You will take umbrage.'

'I promise I won't.' She wanted to get to the bottom of this, before she let fly and dotted his Pleases Agency in the eye by an imperious demand for satisfaction.

He appraised her. She felt his sorrow, and for a fleeting moment wondered if it was going too far to report him for being inept. But, Christ Almighty, she was paying through the nose for this gunge. She had a right.

'You give bliss.' He worried for an instant that he had said this before to someone – he would not let himself remember her supposed name – and cautioned himself against routine words in prayer. Wasn't there some Quaker, Society of Friends, admonition that spoke harshly against 'vain repetition', as a wrong condemning communal prayer? He would have to reason the comparison out, in his lantern hours. 'Bliss is indivisible. It comes only from the woman.'

'Men don't give it, then.' She cracked a cynical smile. It felt like a gangster's snarl. Maybe it was.

'I have no way of knowing. I wonder, though, if the lady knows the effect she has on a man.'

'Well, yes. Of course she does. Magazines are full of it, aren't they.'

Silence while he thought. 'In charity, I am obliged to believe the woman does not know. If she does know, and deprives her man of that ecstasy, then she is the instrument of sorrow.'

'Any woman?' She had not thought this far before. 'Like, any at all?'

'Yes.' He spoke with simplicity, yes it was raining, yes it was early afternoon.

'Is everything you think of so obvious?'

'Nothing else.' And smiled, and just when it seemed it wouldn't quite make it, seemed to take over his features and the smile came so wholly she began to smile back before she caught herself. She was going to sue the pants off the Pleases Agency, Inc., dithery old telephone voices and all. 'There can be very little else left, considering the nature of bliss.'

'Is it every time?'

'Of course. Think of grace.'

She almost asked if he meant somebody by that name before she realised. 'Grace, as in holiness?'

'Not quite.' He inspected her cup and would have shrugged. She knew he understood a shrug would do nothing, and thought with a small feeling of triumph, I'm starting to get the hang of this odd creature. Grace, though?

'Sorry about the coffee,' she found herself saying, quite as if she were responsible for the spectacular failure.

'I did warn you, Berenice. I could have prepared all kinds of other drinks.'

'Grace.' If she was going to blister and demand the National Debt as compensation, she could afford a few minutes more of this idle chat.

274

'It is the sole prerogative of women. They are ignorant.'

She exploded, sitting up. 'Excuse me!'

He waited a few moments. 'Your lack of thought about this causes the distress, Berenice. It was there when you entered. Your confidence is admirable, your lack of comprehension not. Especially when grace is your gift.'

'What about you men, then?' Her anger showed. She shifted restlessly, furious at having let herself in for this. Any second, he would bluster his way out and she would zap him for insolence, report him for anything she could think up and ruin his spectacularly *perfect* life leaving him without his precious self-indulgent prattle.

'We are the test you enact.'

That stopped all thought. 'Test? What's this test?'

'Survival, murder, life. Or any of their opposites.'

Jesus. The opposite of murder? Her brain felt wooden, unable to plan the way back into the conversation.

'I don't understand.' She'd almost forgotten his name. That's what happened when you avoided using a name just because you were fuming in a rage.

'No, you don't.' His sorrow returned, and she felt it spread into her from his proximity. She almost reached over to pat his hand consolingly before she caught herself and thought, what the hell do I think I'm doing? 'Giving bliss must be divine.'

Divine, now? Did he simply mean good, the way some queers used it? Or as in paradisical? She saw his gaze on her, and realised this was his idea of

275

asking a question, and realised too in the same instant he was waiting on her answer: was giving bliss, that indivisible ecstasy that to him was perfection on earth, divine? Or did she not believe it to be so?

And she understood his sorrow, for the first time actually seeing something of what he meant, that a woman conferred the ultimate bliss.

'I don't know,' she said with the nearest she could come to humility. She, mistress of life and death, saw in that moment that she was only mistress of death, its purveyor, and a bringer of final sanction. She had never thought of giving anyone bliss.

'I don't know,' she said again.

He held the quiet until her eyes began to prick, quite as if feeling for tears. She blinked angrily. Was this the opposite of power, or a lessening of achievement, simply moving the markers by which she operated?

'It is hard to feel, I suppose.' His smile might never have been. 'I only sense the brilliance, the totality. Sometimes I have actually wondered how the lady must be in herself, knowing she has given so great a gift. It must feel to her like the opposite of inflicting death. In fact, no greater gift seems thinkable.'

'Who taught you all this, Bonn?' It was a beginner's question, foolish, and at her stage in life. She cursed herself in case he thought her stupid.

'I found it,' he said.

'You found it to be obvious? That what you meant?'

'No. I try to say what I mean.' He looked sadly

276

at the crockery. 'I should have guided you better. I'm a very poor guide.'

'I think I should leave.'

'Of course, Berenice. Thank you.'

This was her first sweep-out. She accepted her coat, and he bussed her fleetingly at the door.

'Goodbye, Berenice.'

'Goodbye, Bonn.'

She walked away down the corridor, conscious with the acute sense of the vigilante that somebody flitted silently from the stairwell even before she reached the lifts. Another shadow, among all the bright chattering lounge guests and the illumination of the foyer and reception area, was gone just as swiftly when she went outside for a taxi.

It seemed unnecessary, just right now, to phone the Pleases Agency, Inc., so she had a quiet dinner alone in the first hotel she came to. She postponed making her threat to the morning, when she might feel better. More firm perhaps? She felt something had been stolen from her capacity for feelings. Was it resolve, resolution? Yet how could it be? Pure certainty had always been in her nature. She was a creature of absolute conviction. What had happened? How could she now go back, after all she had done, to working out what to do? Ridiculous. Perhaps Bonn would have to be punished.

Chapter Forty-Six

san – boss, chief

The Palais Rocco was in uproar when Martina arrived on the balcony. Two minders preceded her, making sure the lights were not on full glare and enough space was left where she wanted. The length of the dance-floor stretched below her position. She nodded for a minder to draw the table closer, preferring to give commands by tilts of her head, an eyebrow, rather than issue dictates. A woman could sound too rebuking, or too conciliatory, and she rarely wished to be tarred by either of those brushes.

The feeble band was warming up. A tall, bespectacled double bass player, a keyboard man evidently the worse for drink – this early? – an elderly trumpeter in a grey suit, waistcoat and all, with a plethoric saxophonist whose red countenance shone like a cardinal's, the combo was hired for the regional semi-finals of the Mogga Dancing Championships.

'Keyboard's called Quopper, boss.' Rack slid into the next chair, suddenly rabbiting as if they had only parted a moment since instead of almost a week. 'He's always sloshed. As long as he doesn't smoke the fire alarms don't go off, and he can really play.'

'Has anyone been in?' Martina scanned the

crowd already thickening about the staircases and the fringe of the dance-floor. The mogga dancing would start soon. Non-competing couples used the time to practise elementary steps while the floor was free.

'You mean Bonn,' Rack said, glad he was tactful. 'Not yet. He's going to hospital.'

'Hospital? Bonn?'

'Don't get your knickers in a twist, boss. He's going to do summert to that little bint they're going to...'

He didn't know how to say it. It went against the grain to let some local hurt girl die, like what they were going to do up at the General Infirmary. He wondered if he should tell Martina about the street girls' tears all over the Square about the girl, wanting bloody gavotte dolled out to somebody. That's what a san was for, as they saw it. Some tarts were gathering excitedly at a neighbouring table, rosettes and bags of rose petals at the ready. Rack loved being really sensitive. He knew birds liked tact, being gentle.

'What, Rack?' Martina ground the words out, hating his coyness. He was trying to speak like Bonn. She should be told everything without having to beg for scraps. This morning she had taken particular note: Bonn had had his usual breakfast, hardly a word. She too had been quiet except for please-pass-the-marmalade. As if they were an old married couple, so long wed they communicated by osmosis and sense rather than words to get by.

Rack turned to face those ice-blues and said, 'Oh, fuck. What now, for Christ's sake?' and thought a bit, then, 'Just telling you, boss. Bonn's

279

gone to hospital. The stringers are in sort of...' He petered out. Martina's eyes radiated a laser thing that shut you up. He sometimes tried to do it in front of the mirror, but his eyes didn't work like hers. Christ, she looked like she could kill. What had he done wrong? He'd only come to keep her up to date with things on the street. Now she was acting like she wanted blood running down Moorgate, but why?

'Are in what?'

'A strop!' Rack got to the word with a yelp of pleasure. Some of the nearby girls laughed and looked at him. He tilted his baseball cap and winked roguishly at them, shoving out his dazzling watch so it flickered on and off and played a tune. They giggled, gave a glance at Martina as if to check she didn't mind, saw her expression and swiftly turned their attention back to the dance-floor.

'I take it,' Martina said, 'you mean the last rites.'

'Them, yeh.'

'I was not told.'

'No, well, like you don't go to church or anyfink, like it's not your bag, OK?'

'So you said nothing.'

'Well, like I knowed you wus busy wiv accounts and things, and all them rentals...'

'In future,' she said, looking at the stage and permitting her hand to make a small transverse motion to end talk.

'Boss, you're a right fucking bitch today.'

His way of talking grew odd, he realised, when Martina gave him the ice. It was like somehow her look got into his words so they didn't talk the same as usual. Down in the Smoke, before he come north among these fucking loons with his daft Mama and his useless gone-to-glory Papa, there was probably a posh word for it. Bonn would know. Rack would like to ask these things, but by the time he got to see Bonn again he knew he'd have forgotten what the fuck he wanted to ask. It was because he had so many important things to remember. People like Martina and Bonn had fuck all to worry about. He was the genius who kept Martina's city from falling apart.

'Tell me in future.'

'Right, boss.'

That was another thing. Nobody else called Martina boss, not even Grellie or the goers or even the keys. No street girl would get to talk to Martina unless she sent for them, and then they knew it was the wet walk home or promotion, one of the two. Like this afternoon, with that slinky bint Rack liked and had used once or twice, except she had a liking for spices that left him squiffy. He hadn't ever had a meal with her, only a shag now and then. He had a theory about curry powder getting into the bedclothes. She was up to Martina later, poor stupid cunt. Lucky he had a replacement, arranged with Grellie as soon as Grellie said the spicey girl Devvie had got to go.

Rack allowed everybody to believe rumour, that he and Martina were related, second cousins or something, which would explain why a brilliant brain like Rack would work for a bad-tempered cunt like Martina, and because he was kind and took pity on this lame relative who ran the syndicate while her dad, Posser, was sick on Brad-shawgate North. It was logical. Rack prided himself on being logical and part of Martina's family. He'd started the rumour, of course, which was why it was so good and worked well good.

'She is under surveillance.'

'Watched, you mean, boss?'

Rack belched. He'd had a bowl of peanuts earlier and they always tended to repeat on him. He'd have a word with the scatterbrained bints running the Butty Bar. He'd had a quick nosh after leaving the Rum Romeo Casino in Meal-house Lane. That meant another serious job, mega-trouble, finding out who was cheating by giving out el cheapo monkey-nuts instead of the real thing. Rack wasn't sure how you could tell a good peanut from a dud. Still, he could blame them, stir the shit so they stopped him belching every two minutes. It was embarrassing.

Applause interrupted from below, as Hiplips emerged in a glowing butterfly cape, electric lights rushing round the hem from his tall winged collar to his rainbow lamee cat suit. He wore a dark mask that emitted light in lasered streaks, and talloned gloves of glowing scarlet.

'Looks a right fucking mess, dun'ee, boss?' Rack dragged himself from the vital peanut problem to make his peace with Martina. He didn't want her staying in this strop. She was in a right fucking mood as it was, what with having to shunt Devvie off this afternoon. He decided tact would be the only way, because bints liked a bit of the old high-way-gent stuff. ''Ere, boss. What you all steamed up about Bonn for?' Here came the tactful bit.

'The little bint in the Farnworth General's pegging out, see? The docs are doing it, so Bonn can't do a thing wiv her, see? He can't shag her or anyfink. She's no threat, see what I mean? He'll just say a dickie or two, and everyfink's Sir Garnet, innit?'

He hated his mixture of Cockney and northern when Martina went into one. He blamed her. He'd thought it was going to be an easy day, just a fire to arrange for some do-it-yourself warehouse on the outskirts, after he'd found out from Sonz who was bugging Dr Clare's pad. Then maybe send Akker to stitch a bump-and-dump car theft scam being run by three Greek cousins from Atherton, and off to the snooker knock-out final at the Shot Pot. He had money on Holy Sass, a Rasta with a deformed hand. Rack had a theory about deformed hands as long as odds were 13-8 against.

Martina sat in a blind fury. Luckily, the nearby tables, all full now of spectators clapping in happy anticipation of the competitors and laughing at Hiplips's mad outfit, could no longer hear what Rack said. They would not hear her reply, either.

'Be quiet, Rack.'

'Eh?' He stared as the lights dimmed. The dancers paraded onto the floor to wild applause. The combo, taking its time from the trumpeter, struck up *The Entrance Of The Gladiators*.

Martina moved her gaze. Rack relaxed and shrugged compliance. In a moment she would tell him to get after Bonn and make sure the lead key returned not only in safety but without his visit having been noticed by media, paparazzi or public or hospital staff. That, Rack decided, was OK. It's what bints did, get themselves worked up over sweet fuck all. He could make time, tell Akker to do the warehouse fire without Rack because he had a busy day ahead now what with one thing and another. The peanuts really rankled.

'I hopes they play sommink decent, boss,' Rack said. 'Sommink I can sing to.'

She did not answer, just stared at the faces along the balcony.

'I've got a good voice because I'm the right shape. It all depends on the chest, see? It's nipples, see?'

Nobody listened. Hiplips shed his cape to roars and stepped to greet the dancers as they lined up.

'Darlings and tramps!' Hiplips carolled, twirling. 'The regional semi-finals of the mogga dancing championships begin ... now!' In roars, he curtseyed and danced a few dainty steps. 'Six bars of any dance, followed by six of any other, to one continuous melody played by our Palais Rocco Combo of Delights!'

He cupped his hand and listened. The crowd chanted, 'Oh what a sight!' This was a favourite catch-phrase, invented for openers. He gave a scornful gesture at Quopper, who grinned and raised a glass from the keyboard.

'They all owe me money!' Hiplips squeaked, and got a salvo of laughter. 'Now! Four judges will report as each couple is eliminated. The nine couples will be reduced by one after every tune is played in full. Capeesh, tout le monde?'

'Yes, Hiplips!' the ecstatic spectators yelled.

He grinned delightedly, and did a shimmy,

spinning with balletic grace and waltzing his way to stand before the stage. He gestured, and the band struck a slow foxtrot.

'Rack.' Martina kept her eyes on the dancers as they immediately moved into the marked rhythm. 'Get over to the General Infirmary and see that Bonn...'

Rack's seat was vacant. He had gone. She did not look towards the exits. He would already be on his way. He had better not be late. The syndicate must not be embroiled in stupidities like this girl. Those things happened or they didn't happen, no way to put clocks back, however hysterical street walkers became. They had their jobs to do.

Rack had a bike take him to Askey's shop, The Triple Racer in Bolgate Street. Askey turned himself out like the long-dead comedian, right down to the seemingly bulbous forehead, thick horn-rimmed specs and dapper suit. He was a little bloke who kept secrets and told only Rack what went on. Messages could be given him, to reach Rack within minutes from anywhere in the city. His couriers, pedal-cyclists or on motor-bikes, lounged about on the steps hoping to get some panic command to take messages or documents to city companies. They lived for speed.

'Hospital,' Rack said. 'Me.'

'Tello,' Askey shouted out of the window hatch, and Tello fired his scooter.

'And get Dizzie from the Ball Boys, Askey. I've teed him up. He'll be ready. To the hospital now, now, now.'

Rack jumped astride and they were off, Rack

285

shouting in the courier's ear about the way motors ought to be built, one wheel instead of two to go faster.

In the hospital, Bonn walked down the corridors. He knew from the newspapers where the girl was. He held flowers, freesias and carnations. He had spoken to Information, and they told him he could leave the flowers at the nursing station on the same floor but that access to the sick girl was not allowed.

Speaking to her doctors first had seemed sensible, but there were ways. For all he knew he would be refused entry if his intentions were known, so it was better simply to take a chance. If he were unfortunate and got expelled, he would think again. A few visitors were in, even at this late hour. One newspaper had said the girl would be taken off her life support systems late tonight. The stringers had been adamant. Somebody had to give the poor girl Extreme Unction, though exactly what they meant they hadn't been able to say.

One girl, Lee-Ann, said it should be Catholic, 'like with oil and musty stuff,' as she told him. Her aunt in Barbados had died, and the priest had done the last rites. The family was pleased Auntie had gone to Heaven. Her partner Beckie, however, stuck out for hymns in the hospital garden because that's what signified the end of life. Three argumentative stringers from Green in Greygate said prayers wouldn't work unless the perv was topped, asking everybody was the perv who got killed in Newcaste-on-Tyne the girl's real weirdo or not. Bonn said nothing to anyone, simply caught the bus from the Central Gardens, buying flowers from Bee the flower lady and sitting in clear view as the Number 8 moved off into the crystal-lit city night. Word would spread that Bonn was going to do the girl's last prayers. Several girls would be miffed, thinking he'd need a girl along to come back with, on account of feeling sad. Grellie must have overheard somebody going on about it and Bonn guessed, from her sudden appearance at the newspaper vendor's stall at the Manchester Road junction, she'd learned he was on his way to hospital. She must have fined the first three who were short on strides, accusing them in her typical manner of not working hard enough, and threatened to fine ten more if they stayed idle. Bonn had overheard from walking straight into that mess, stayed put on the bus when Grellie stood looking at him in mute appeal as it pulled out. He never knew how the girls all knew.

Inevitable, thought Bonn, in this city centre. There seemed no reasons for any events, and certainly none for the consequences. It was as if motive vanished when the city took on a mood. He once had been told to sit in on the trial of a girl by Rack, Posser, and three older women he failed to recognise. The girl had knifed another girl who, word was, had seemed her rival, but over what or why was impossibly vague. Rack had tried explaining it was inevitable. The city and its streets were simply unknowable. Heaven knows what Martina would think, but what could one do?

He went up in the lift to the Intensive Care Floor. A suave young doctor, who almost looked too much like a doctor actually to be one, seemed to be waiting.

'Good evening.' Bonn read the name off the security tag. 'Ah, Dr Kildare. I wonder if I might...'

'Only for three minutes. This way, please.'

'Ah, I wish to know if I can–'

'This *way*, please.'

Bonn followed. The doctor seemed to have three security tags. He nodded to the nurses at their monitoring station, lights hooded on desks, and to the security man. He signed the entry list almost without looking, opened the door and gestured Bonn inside, saying, 'Three minutes with your sister, then out. Understand?'

Sister? 'Of course.'

Bonn found himself in a gloaming more apt for an aquarium than a sick room. In a tangle of tubes, a cocoon of some plastic thinness, lay a girl. She seemed transparent and shrunken, much younger than the fourteen years she was said to be. He heard the doctor's quiet voice instructing the security guard to tap on the door to say when the patient's brother's time was up.

Impossible. Bonn's vision blurred. He approached, wanting to touch her hand, somehow press reassurance into her fragile form. Out of the question, he supposed, but would it matter if she was about to...? He could not formulate any question, and brought no answers. In the ultimate dilemma of religion, he symbolised, and actually was becoming, religion's final evidence of the loss that all prayer signified. The request he brought, the plea to some almighty power, proved its own denial. The truth of that impotence was in his arrival. What purpose had he in mind when agreeing to come? Do what? Undoubtedly the girl child was dying, or dead, or just maintained by chugging machinery working like leather bellows powered by electric engines. Did that mean she was unconscious, or comatose, or maybe simply in a suspended state where she flickered in and out of consciousness and was able to hear whispers from somewhere beyond?

What would it matter, then, if he reached through the plastic tenting – he did so – took her small hand and said, 'I am your brother, love.'

And realised he did not know her true name. She had used a dozen false names in the exercise of her, what had it been, work? Play? Career?

'I am here, love. We'll be going on holiday soon,' he said quietly. 'The place you've always wanted to go. Do you remember it? There's a little puppy. I'll bring him. He's too small to walk yet, so he lives in a basket. You shall feed him every day, until he grows big enough to play out.'

He ran out of things to invent but pressed on, hearing footsteps along the corridor.

'You can decide everything. If you don't like something, then you needn't do it. If you want something, you shall have it. Whatever you say, love.'

And one final lie came as he heard the security man tapping on the door, saying quietly, 'Three minutes.'

'And I'll stay with you all the time, if you want. Can I? Will that be all right?'

He felt nothing, but liked to pretend. The words came in a rush, and he gave the words of Extreme Unction, following the Latin softly. He blessed her, reaching her brow as the door hissed ajar, and stepped quickly back.

The doctor was there making a hurrying gesture, his chin giving direction. Without a backward glance Bonn left and walked down the corridor.

'End door, go right. Downstairs.' It was a whispered instruction and meaning go quickly, don't delay. Bonn obeyed, trotting down the steps as lifts clashed and voices seemed to be calling.

To his surprise the doctor was still with him when he reached some kind of car park. Glass crackled underfoot, a glass was smashed nearby, then two more suddenly in quick succession. A female called out some demand. Someone came running, in the distance cars started. The doctor – strangely now lacking his white coat but carrying a bundle in a dark bin-bag – was shoving him along to a stone balcony by the end of the car park. No lights, which Bonn thought strange.

'Over the side.' The doctor – was he actually a doctor, or some impostor? – thrust Bonn towards the balustrade and said, 'Over, mate. Fast, OK? Give. Give!'

Stupidly Bonn stared, thinking, what, a tip? And realised he was still carrying the flowers he had intended for the girl. He relinquished them and climbed over. Hands grabbed his ankles, and he was guided to the ground one level below the car park terrace.

'Get on.' He stretched astride a pedal cycle and the rider shoved off, Bonn holding the man's waist to steady himself. The courier was powerful, used to his job, and they swished through the darkness, no lights, along a pavement, and then

290

suddenly through a yard and into a small terraced house. He dismounted at the rider's command and followed to the front door, where another cyclist beckoned him onto the saddle of a spare bike. Bonn mounted, wobbling, pedalled after the rider down the ill-lit street and then into a road.

'Lights,' the guide called over his shoulder and, when Bonn could not find the controls, swore and stopped, put Bonn's lights on and resumed.

Twenty minutes later they came into the main stretch of the old City Road, long since ignored by most motorised traffic since the A-Sixties were built for speed. There, Bonn was told to alight and found himself in a taxi heading for the city. He got out in Victoria Square at the Rivergate. Several of the street walkers were there, and halted seeing him arrive. They offered no greeting, except for one who began to say a shy hello but was swiftly shushed by the others.

He went to the Volunteer and sat in the pub. Rack brought him a drink, some kind of beer.

'OK, mate?' Rack said, flinging himself down. 'You know who won that fucking snooker after all? It wasn't Stappo, you know, that Jamaican bugger. It were Prosky, that Ukranio from St Helens. Well?'

'Excellent,' Bonn tasted the beer and managed not to grimace. It would have been rude not to accept.

'Excellent?' Rack was up in arms at Bonn's taking the wrong side. 'I told them to get it different. I'll fucking do Stappo, useless prat. I tellt him it were to be a black ball game, and what did the fucker do but try to be too fucking showy?'

291

'Please, Rack. Language. There are ladies present.' None was in earshot.

Rack settled back, pleased, but continued his grumble. As long as Bonn was ballocking him for talking ordinary, things were more or less on track. 'You liked Kildare?' he asked with pride. 'He's an actor. I reckon I ought to take some of them blokes on permanent, though he catches a different tram, know what I mean? I mean he's queer as a bent giraffe. All actors should be gardeners. Know why?'

'No,' Bonn said, thinking of the poor girl. 'I suppose it's their genes.'

'No!' Rack said triumphantly, everything making sense again. 'They use the wrong petrol, see? It works like this...'

Bonn realised Rack had an immense store of charity somewhere within, and listened in appreciation. Gibberish had its uses to both speaker and listener, if both felt correctly. Listening, his eyes filled. It was perhaps the beer, to which he had never been accustomed.

Chapter Forty-Seven

garms – attire, stylish dress

Sonz's bugs worked. Better had, Rack thought.

'Them's the calls that Dr Clare bint made. Times in the right-hand column.'

Sonz didn't know Rack could not read, so was

well narked when the chief stander crumpled the paper and shoved it into his pocket. Sonz was already pissed off because Rack told him not to smoke. Where was the harm in a fag?

They stood at the rear of the City Attire College show, where a huge marquee extended the audience area for the catwalk frolics about to come. Movie stars would attend, plus local celebs. Today was only a rehearsal, but still off the fucking wall. Rack had never seen so many thin tarts. Like Ethiopia. Jesus.

'See,' he told Sonz, well into theories, 'the reason they're thin is they get made sick. It's treadle machines, see?'

'Treadle machines.' Sonz nodded slowly, never knowing what the fuck Rack was on about. He did leckie, plugs, switches, wires, devices. Electricity was sane, pure logic. He'd tried to buy a photo of Faraday, who'd invented it, but shops in the mall thought him barmy. They'd never heard of him. Give Sonz a series of flexes and trannies, he was happy, finish. He listened while Rack talked crap.

'They sits, legs working ten, twelve hours a day, see?'

'Rack? What yer got clobber on wrong for?'

Rack was instantly proud Sonz had spotted his gear. Coming to the designers' school, he'd used his brains, getting Grellie's Green stringers to help him dress fantastic, just the job to go among the barmy sods showing off their fancy glossy today. He'd decided on a hooped football jersey, black and orange zig-zags. Left arm through the neck hole, his head projecting through a slit near

293

the arm sate, and the dangling empty arms tied in a knot with diamonte handcuffs. He knew he looked great, because he alone, among millions, could carry style off.

'Who says it's wrong?' Rack gave Sonz the bent eye.

Sonz shrugged, instantly into any lies that would come to his rescue. 'Not me, Rack, I meant that pale bint as we come in. I don't know gear, see?'

'She's another illiterate. Like these two cunts.'

Two girls danced down the catwalk to a reggae thrup, some old bint screaming orders, ballocking them because they weren't moving right. One wailed back a complaint.

'Here.' Rack grabbed a passing bloke. 'Where's the new frocks, then?'

'They won't be brought out until the night.' The bloke wore make-up. Rack let him go with an expression of distaste.

'Queer,' he decided as the bloke rushed off. 'Here, missus.'

He grabbed the older woman who'd stopped shouting and was going backstage muttering angrily to herself, 'Bitches, bitches.'

'Missus, who's boss here?'

'Of what? The exhibition, the show, the college? What?'

'This thing.'

'It's Fender Malvoliante.' She shook herself free and started to weep. 'It's always me. You just see. Some little thing goes wrong, Fender blames me. He's so lacking in understanding. Yet you'd think, wouldn't you?'

She shed tears while Rack watched her in surprise. He saw her give a surreptitious glance at his own garms and thought, yeh, this old cow's got an eye for class. She must be some sort of designer, right? She must really be boss of this show, so she'd know a thing or two about what was right. He felt proud in his exotic clobber.

'Don't you worry, Ma,' he told her. 'Just send Fender to me when he comes, right?'

'Fender's already here.' She tapped her waist, where three cell phones hung like a cobbler's shop. Rack admired it and saw Sonz looking.

'Tell him I wants a quick word, OK?'

'Whom shall I say?'

Rack loved that whom, which sounded like zoom, sort of space-age. He liked this old bint, and didn't like this Fender fucker who blamed her and made her skryke when she never done nothing wrong.

'He'll know, love.' The old woman went, looking back.

'That reminds me,' Sonz said, itching for a fag, 'I been meaning to ask. Did you get somebody else bugging that Dr Clare?'

'Me?' Rack eyed Sonz, wondering if this was the start of a rebellion, because he was fucking going to have none of it.

'Only, her frigging phone's like a Continental telecom.'

'Somebody else planted her flat?' How many was this?

'Like the fucking Tube map. Never seen so many superfluous wires. See, I always reckon leckies don't work things out on the job, see? They just go with some kind of bluey.'

'Bluey.' Rack realised he was talking like Bonn, never asking a fucking thing, and corrected himself. 'What the fuck's a bluey?'

'Blue-prints. Paper drawings. Electricians turn up at a site-station, see, and just do what their blue-prints say. They don't see what a bastard the job actually is, see?'

'You mean this Dr Clare bint, she's already bugged?'

'Two. One in the place, one to somewhere local.'

'Can you find out where?'

'Already did. Some flat across the street. It's called Raglan Road.'

'I know it's called Raglan fucking Road. I fucking sent you, didn't I?'

'Oh, yeh.'

'You done good, Sonz,' Rack said, worried now but not showing it. 'Pick up more about who done it, OK?'

'Right, Rack.' He wondered how far he could push it, so said, 'I'm dying for a fag, Rack.'

'Then piss off. Shot Pot after six.'

'Right. Ta-ra.'

Rack began thinking, watching more skeletal tarts frolicking their stupid way down the improvised catwalk. A bloke came, seeming frantic. Rack stared, never having seen such a monstrosity. The bloke's trousers seemed in tatters, and his shirt was made of strings loosely tied in bows – fucking *strings,* fucking *bows.* He wore much gold, and a necklace that somebody had made out of watches, real watches that ticked and told the time. Rack reckoned a good thirty watches must have gone into making that useless fucking thing. The man was barefoot.

'You want me? Are you the contractor? Marquee? Catwalk? What?'

'I'm Rack. Here,' Rack said, strike while the iron's hot, 'Why're your bints all so thin?'

The man gaped, checked the appearance of a passing file quick-stepping along the raised shoring to that loony music. 'You really think they should be, like, *obese?*'

'Nowt wrong with something to get hold of, know what I mean?'

'Is it the crash?'

Rack didn't know what he meant. No screw for Martina's syndicate from a whole fucking college, for Christ's sake, then Sonz's news about others bugging Dr Clare. And now this?

'Well, where I come from,' Rack said lamely. 'Look. There's a mob going to lift your designs, see? I can take them out before they get here, see?'

'Mob?' The tattered man in all them watches looked, then his brow cleared. 'You mean...?'

'Sorry it's bad news,' Rack said, trying to look as appalled as the bloke did. Whatever the man thought he was being told, it was right, because Rack truly did want to worry him, then get the fuck out of this lunatic dump with all these files of twitching bints who hadn't got an ounce of tit to bounce between them. They needed a good meal. He could send them to Posher Nosher, maybe get Martina's syndicate a percentage on it.

'They're not...' The watches man didn't look as if he could afford a razor, not had a shave for weeks, and looked in off the fucking road. 'Not the ones who did MacAnyhow's third Soho show?'

'It's confidential,' Rack said. The idiot was looking Rack up and down like he wanted to take Rack's clothes to bits. 'Look, my three lawyers are outside. If you want our contract signed – you get the certificates, insurance, all the VAT chits you need to take it off expenses, see? If you want to sign, we'll take the mob yobs down before they're out of their vans, see? You need not even lock up of a night, not once you're on the books.' Rack nodded at the marquee entrance, where his three hired actors from Liverpool – all in sombre suits, homburg hats and carrying black briefcases – stood staring in at Rack, as instructed. Fender was immediately less casual.

'You can do that?' He fingered Rack's shirt, which really pissed Rack off, but anything in the cause of getting this college's money on a proper footing, start the gelt flowing where it belonged.

'We done it for Lukashti Mutu Babberone,' Rack said, getting fed up. 'You know, that Nigerian design school going to New York...' Rack rolled off three other names, making them up all on the spur, then closed with, 'But you don't tell anybody, OK? Just decide quick, because we've two others in the north.'

'Why didn't MacAnyhow hire you?'

Rack stared the mistrustful sod down. He hated being argued with. It was like people didn't have any fucking ears.

'We don't do that far south,' he said. 'It's divided up. How many teams d'you think I've got, for fuck's sake?'

'Right, right.' Fender stroked at Rack's sleeve bands, now really pissing Rack off. 'Do they have

298

to be different colours? The bands?'

'Why?' Rack asked darkly, now mega pissed off gigantico with this cretin.

'Only, I might do something with fur, if I get it patented in time. I'll think something really macho, but not on those hopeless Balkan girls. They try sanctuary piss, can you imagine, when I'm rutty-slutty?'

'Fucking loons,' Rack said, wanting normal back. This place was fucking insane.

'I'll do it. Send your butties in, tell them to ask for Fender's benders.' He left, tittering. Rack watched another moment of disgust, trying to work out the theory for watches round your neck, and decided to leave it.

He went outside, and told the three actors, 'You lot piss off. Go to Reels, ticket agency corner of George Street, side entrance. Get your money and hop it to the 'Pool. Don't even stop for a pint.'

Rack belled Askey, the boss of the Triple Racer, to send a biker over to Thrimbleby and Thrimbleby, lawyers who did the syndicate's rubbish contract work, wanting their scrawlers over at the City Attire College and to ask for Fender's benders, lawyers for the exhibition. He was on edge, wondering about the recent hiring of other small flats in Raglan Road, and why he hadn't heard about any. He also wondered what the fuck Akker was up to, dawdling all fucking week and never lifting a finger. Once she heard, Martina would go into ice fucking mode. Just what Rack needed, a week of wholesome street blood.

He didn't even say hello back to two of the Yellow girls coming off troll. They hunched up

299

and scurried on past, not wanting to know. They done right, Rack thought, everybody stay out of my fucking way until things got sorted.

Chapter Forty-Eight

shroomer – addict (fr. mushroom-taker)

St Michael's had seen better days. Its sham façade was sham even for the 1840s, with its once-grand steps now touching the traffic. Congregations had dwindled to a remnant, double figures counting as a pretty good week. Its one priest was defeated by the tides of time and drifters who encrusted his side chapels of a night and raised fires in his vaults. It was an unusual evening if the fire brigade was not summoned by passing citizens worried by strange glows flickering in the partly boarded-up windows. Bonn knew of the priest. The sign announced *Confessions – 6–8 or by arrangement.*

He entered the church. He had served mass here, when the parish asked for a visiting acolyte. Always short of numbers even then. He knew the connecting doorway to the presbytery from the vestry, and made his way down the length of the church and into the cloakroom. He turned right and knocked. No answer, so he called ahead and continued down the corridor. As a little lad, he had been challenged here by two belligerent housekeepers in pinafores. Now, the dusty place echoed. Religion had a deal to answer for.

'Father Tomkinson?' he called. He tapped on every door as he went.

'Hello?'

'Father Tomkinson? I came to ask your help, if I might.'

Bonn entered a stuffy rather gaunt room, tall ceilings and an arched window, with paint flaking from the walls and the doors shiny with lack of care. Faded, Bonn thought, the whole church was on its last legs. This parish was dying.

'Hello?' The old priest was reading some gigantic leatherbound tome. Bonn recognised Scheller's *Lexicon Totius Latinitatis*, a set reference work from his own seminary days before that institute had closed for lack of ordinands. 'I've hardly strength to lift this, let alone have sight enough to read.'

'It is dated, Father.'

'Since that irascible band of sinners in Oxford took over the Latin lobby you mean?' The priest sighed. 'I mustn't grumble. It gives me pleasure to re-read old references. I alternate between this and Collier's *Great Dictionary* which,' he grinned unexpectedly, 'as you see over there is two volumes bound into one. I use that stand.'

He indicated a hard-wood book-stand in the form of a desk lectern. It held an open volume larger still. 'A mohammedan in the parish gave it to me, a kindness, when he heard I could no longer even lift the wretched books I wish to read. So generous.'

'Indeed.'

'Do I know you?'

'I once served mass here, from the seminary school.'

301

'So many of you did.' The priest grimaced. 'And now so few. You'll have left the faith, then?'

Bonn was taken aback. 'Yes. I am afraid so.'

'Don't be.' Father Tomkinson sighed, glancing round as if he heard voices. 'Do sit down. I guessed you were either someone who knew the pathways of the church, or one of the junkies who inhabit the crypts from time to time. You sounded questioning rather than questing, the give-away of the genuine caller.'

'Not questing, then.'

The priest laughed, scratching the sounds out and shaking with the effort so his spectacles dangled. He repositioned them.

'I apologise. You do not ask, only posit some proposition! I recognise the training of the incipient cleric who has been through the mill of religious tutorials. Salesians, weren't they? Disputes for the sake of no disputes at all! Still, hardly doing wrong, even if their brand of logic reads now like a social-worker's night-school course that it is indistinguishable from TV chat sessions. How may I help?'

'I wish you to give absolution to a girl, fourteen or so in years. She is about to die in the hospital.'

'*About* to die?'

'Yes.'

'As by arrangement?'

'Yes. She ... she is going to be taken off her life support systems.'

'Is this you, my son, making your confession?'

'No.'

'You're sure?'

'Yes.'

302

'And I don't suppose it would matter to you, if you were or if you weren't.'

'No.'

'The clear answer: yes, no, no, yes!' The old priest sighed, smiling. 'How marvellous to encounter one who replies as God intended words to be used! Would they let me go on a formal visit?'

'No. She is under security control.'

'Is that why you are here?'

'No.'

'Then why?'

'I visited her, and gave her the last rites.'

'You gave her Extreme Unction?'

'Yes.'

'Why?'

'I felt obliged to respond to the request of others. I ought to have thought, but failed to.'

'I see. You are not a relative?'

'No.'

'Those who requested that you act so – are they?'

'No.'

'Then how is it they demanded you perform the last rites for this unknown girl?'

'They feel strongly.'

'The girl is the child prostitute in the General Infirmary?'

'A young girl in that place, yes.'

'If I, as a legitimate priest, would not be permitted to visit, how did you manage to?'

'Access became available.'

'These solicitous friends of the girl's. They can only be prostitutes?'

The huge volume in the priest's lap would have

the answer to that, if Bonn felt able to make any kind of reply. Prostitute? Once, the old word prostitute meant, to 'place before', to cause to stand, to be lewd in the cause of lust. Did that entitle him to answer that the girl he had absolved and given Extreme Unction to was nothing more than one who shagged, who sold her body and her time, to stand against a wall while some punter rammed into her and spent his seed into her orifices to obtain relief that would last maybe a night or two? There were so many synonyms of the word, almost as many as for the male penis. Had any the right to make assumptions? The poor girl had been found cast like a broken shell by a roadside, which was all he knew, or had the right to know.

He said nothing.

'I shall, by proxy. I trust the Almighty will know His own. Will you stay?'

'No, thank you.'

'It will take no time at all.'

I know, Bonn thought, but did not say. The Almighty will know His own? The terrible quotation was the Roman Catholic bishop's, who had given his army the command to exterminate everyone in the city of Albinensians, whether heretics or faithful.

He thanked Father Tomkinson and left the way he had come, his footsteps echoing. Reflexively he reached out a hand to the holy water font, but withdrew before his finger-tips touched the surface, and emerged blinking into the cold breeze in Hathaway Street, shivering at the chill.

Chapter Forty-Nine

Blues Brothers – police (after two popular entertainers)

The assassin had a clearer idea of destiny, now she had struck down Grobbon. He was relatively simple, the kind of industry she never shirked, and it was done. Tiresome in the execution, of course, in the fantastic detail needed, but the sense of achievement was so real. Thrills did not come cheap.

She positively glowed, reading newspaper reports slowly and with relish. This was her one misfortune, the need to collect emblems, notes of her triumphs. Four executions was hardly an insignificant total. She had box-files on a shelf in open view, because who came here? And she always cleared evidence of her successes away before any guests arrived.

Dangerous to simply down-load the newspaper columns mentioning her executions. Computers kept sly hold of whatever you read, typed, stored. Even if you deleted the retained documents, a disc only pretended to erase. Any thick ploddite could untangle PCs these days.

She lay on her couch before the fire. Gas, of course. Simulated logs, of course. All very modern. Warm enough for the cat she might have bought and loved, in other circumstances. She steeled her heart against pets. She would have been overjoyed. But no. Father had insisted on duty, to be served at all costs. And she was engaged in restoring righteousness to life. Good heavens, even the ignorant paparazzi could see that. One headline read IS THERE A VIGILANTE OUT THERE? And at least three tabloids – she hadn't the time to study them all – printed grave editorials giving tacit approval of her crusade. The same three actually used that word, crusade. One had gone on, second paragraph:

The question before us is clear. Does society have a right to take matters out of the hands of police? The answer is a resounding yes. Sooner or later society will snap. How often has this newspaper warned the Crown Prosecution Service that the real risk comes not from criminals, for we know their evil ways. It comes from ordinary people. Only last July we warned the city that vigilante actions would become inevitable. People will act when Law does not.

Only a few weeks ago, a convicted Midlands criminal pervert calling himself Blendix was released on declaration of a mistrial, yet another example of the judges failing to give punishment to those who deserve it. Blendix made his way north, doubtless to assault yet more innocent children. Parts of his body were discovered by a hungry mumper – a tramp living rough in churchyards – who was bin-diving for fast foods in a skip. This happened in the very centre of our city! Police reports released yesterday prove that Blendix was the same man who was killed on the M18 motorway by a driver who failed to stop and whose van has yet to be traced. This paper asks, are the two events connected?

The worst aspect is that some strange ancient tropical poison was used in the case of 'Toofy' Grobbon. Video CCTV records in Newcastle drew a blank, even though Grobbon, recently released on a technicality, was murdered while under police protection. Clearly the police are unable to do what the Law requires. Can citizens be blamed if they complete the sentence the Law should impose?

The Law is failing all of us in society. Who suffers? We do. Our children do. Society suffers wholesale because police do not do their job, and because the lawyers only protect the criminal, never the victim. THEY FAIL TO PROTECT THE LAW-ABIDING!! This newspaper continues to campaign against inefficient councillors, police, and useless judges, and will continue...

She laid it aside. One photograph, a cutting from a local rag, showed two doctors walking from the Farnworth General Infirmary. Dr Clare Burtonall was named one, Dr T Elphinstone the other. Both seemed embarrassed at photographers' attentions. There was a suggestion of hurry, as if to escape notice. Well they might try to keep out of sight, the assassin thought. The first notion, how to execute them, was to use a car. She had done it before with Blendix on the M18 motorway. True vermin. You saw enough dead foxes and rats on motorways. One more verminous creature was a mere incidental. Removing his hand – a home-made guillotine, commonly used by skilled modellists such as she now could claim to be, was simple to use, even though she had almost forgotten the blade's shield-guard. Imagine having to go back and hunt the motorway's verges for it!

307

And placing the plastic-bagged hand in the bin, as a clear warning to the city's pervs, had been a brainwave. She laid aside her clipping.

Last time she had indulged, she was Berenice Six-Six-Nine, with that strangely ineffectual yet intriguing Bonn. Did she deserve another little reward? She pondered, arguing temptations to and fro. Men would hire someone for personal pleasure without giving it a single thought, 'no worries', as Australians always concluded. Why then should a woman demur? God, hiring sexual comfort was as simple as buying a new lipstick, to read some magazines these days. Further, she had not had any consummation with Bonn. The encounter had somehow run into the sand, and she did not yet know why. She had had to solace herself alone, in ways she had learned. Fine, it was now socially acceptable to think of these things, to buy instruments of pleasure and reach fruition by dreaming frank, even horrific, sexual pleasures. Sure, shops were everywhere now, all aimed at providing the means of gratification. Yet you couldn't really think of solitary acts as fulfilment.

The afternoon she left Bonn she had felt miffed, as if under a cloud. She had always been a good girl at school, done the homework, been attentive in class, attained whatever goals teachers set. Father was pleased, and saw that she had a truly worthwhile career, not like her two wretched sisters and that pathetic brother who did nothing all day except tot figures in a builder's yard and issue electric plugs. She deserved a reward for so much devoted effort. Easy, to book some temporary lover. Those frail-sounding old women on the Pleases Agency, Inc. telephones gave the impression of having hats decorated with cherries and pastel chintz veils.

Bonn, though. She would execute the first of those two doctors, then reward herself by hiring a goer to provide whatever she might think appropriate. The doctors clearly deserved to die, for they were about to deprive that poor child of life by withdrawing life support. Easy, the assassin thought, to switch off the only link with life the poor injured child had. Oh, sure, so very, very easy. Yet they didn't want to take the consequences, did they? They would shelter behind Law, and when challenged bleat their usual inane excuses, that the Law let them to do it. They would murder. They forget morality, Berenice the Protector thought, working herself up to a fury. It was high time they were made to remember.

If the police and the lawyers wouldn't stem the evil tide, well, she would. She had decided to become Berenice Six-Six-Nine. The telephone call would be from a public phone box, of course, and the gadget she carried would disguise her voice adequately.

And her reward? Bonn, get to the bottom of the discontent she had felt when leaving. Yes, he was strange, and yes, he was different, but why? Something was unexplained, if not inexplicable. She would consider this Bonn as an abstract problem, then decide what to do, which of the doctors must die first.

Chapter Fifty

shodder – plain-clothes policeman

Grahame was a morose Scot who replaced the SOCO because of some family trouble. He was discharged for 'involvement' – in various parts of the north you didn't specify the kind of graft. He didn't know enough of the local scene to refuse Hassall a place at the CCTV viewing.

'See this bloke?' Grahame said, swivelling round to check that all agreed. 'He goes in. That doctor isn't. D'you follow?'

'Get on with it,' Hassall said quite audibly. Younger element looked round. He was tired, and the old urge to smoke had recurred. He wanted a drink. Diets and exercise were all very well, but doctors didn't have to stick to the regimes they prescribed.

'Both impostors, d'you follow?'

I follow that you've seen too many phoney TV serials, Hassall groused. The DS was a fulltime slogger called Bateson, a player of rugby and wishful scholar hooked on night-school law courses.

'That squirt with the flowers takes them out, see? Ducks out the back way. Somebody smashed the bloody lights and the cameras there, so nothing after he goes down the stairs. Must have gone over the balustrade into the street and scarpered.'

'And the girl?'

'The young intruder seems to have torn the laminar-flow plastic containment capsule, and then done nothing. That's the–'

'The bubble,' Hassall said, thinking, Give me strength. How long did this burke serve up there in sunny Glasgow, and doing what? 'The doctor?'

'No record. Left no dabs. Probably–'

'That new-skin spray.' Hassall rose, irritable now because the stuff was invented in the chemical works down the road, what was it, two furlongs. 'It's standard issue hereabouts. We going?'

'To where?'

'See the legit doctor.'

They left, DS Bateson thinking he'd got two testy old gits here, no mistake. Something to tell the lads in the snooker club, give them a laugh.

Dr Elphinstone had heard the news. He took their names, watched the video monitor until they held up their IDs then admitted the three of them to the doctoral staff house. By then Hassall had made his peace with Grahame, chatting amiably on the way over, making an effort so the Scot could leave off his dour act. He did not pry, let the SOCO do all the asking, though he was too high and mighty to take up Hassall's offer. Twice he said he didn't need his hand held. Hassall set him straight, said he was doing something on the side for the Inland Revenue, a separate report for druggos in the city centre. Grahame was suspicious, but Hassall's act, a lazy ageing part-timer working his cards out, started to convince.

'Dr Terence Elphinstone?' Grahame gave the world his stern look, shoving into the hallway the

311

instant the door opened.

'Yes.'

'We want to show you some stills and ask if you've seen these images before. Upstairs?'

'For what?' The doctor was puzzled. 'Is it Mr Hassall?'

'Same old same old.' Hassall told him the original SOCO was temporarily absent. He introduced Mr Grahame and DS Bateson as if there was all the time in the world, Grahame seething at the delay. 'Gan we come in, Doctor, or are you entertaining blondes?'

'Certainly.' The doctor led them down the corridor, through two pairs of reinforced fire doors and into the doctors' common room. 'This is our spacious accommodation. Make yourselves at home. What stills?'

'These.' Grahame barked the word, embarrassing Hassall still more. The SOCO almost threw a brown envelope of stills at the doctor, whose eyes stayed on Grahame just a moment longer than necessary. Grahame was pissing off a possible witness, Hassall sighed inwardly, noting that Bateson was trying to smile agreeably to lessen the hairiness.

The doctor took out the photographs and went to tilt the standard lamp to catch more light while he slowly inspected them one by one. Grahame perched on the edge of his chair as if about to leap.

'Take your time, Dr Elphinstone,' Hassall put in, needing to make this as casual as he could, with the aggressive sub showing all the tact of an axe. 'The question is, do you recognise either of these two people?'

The doctor tried the stills again with spectacles, and shook his head. 'Neither, I'm afraid. Why?'

'They were in your unit!' Grahame barked. 'Seeing your patient.'

The doctor nodded slowly and had a third go, without success.

'Early today!' It came out as an accusation.

Hassall rose and took the photographs, passing them to the DS to replace in their envelope.

'That's all, Dr Elphinstone. Don't worry. Only, had you been notified about any visiting doctor standing in for your housemen or registrars?'

'No. I'm not sure if Dr Burtonall has, but not me. Usually it's on a rota. Why do you think they took the risk, coming into hospital like that? I mean, the cameras, the security. What for?'

'The lay youth passed himself off as her brother. The supposed doctor had fake documents saying he was a locum for the duty registrar doctor.'

'It was slick!' Grahame snapped, all belligerence.

'It wasn't quite,' Hassall put in amiably. 'It was just lucky. Except the security cameras malfunctioned outside, no lights. We were just unlucky. Thanks for the help, Dr Elphinstone.'

'Is there anything you want us to do?' The doctor sounded uncertain at the discordant attitudes of his visitors. 'Only, I have the call number of Security. He's fulltime, after that business with those protestors.'

'We have that, and whatever else we need!' Grahame almost snatched the envelope from Bateson and marched ahead. Hassall followed while the DS spoke a few mild words to the doctor.

As they left, Hassall was pleased to see Bateson glance at the security lights over the doctors' mess entrance, and give a look along the narrow street for parked cars. One car, marked for the hospital, stood in the small car park, and the police car was the other. They drove away. Hassall decided to ask after the original SOCO's likely length of leave, get rid of the irascible Scot as soon as he could. He hadn't the authority to shunt the sub sideways, of course, but there were ways of helping an incomer on his merry way. For the very best of reasons, of course.

Dr Elphinstone had just settled into his book, intermittently watching football on television, when the buzzer sounded. He clipped the catch to View, and saw a police uniform on the fuzzy screen. A gloved hand was holding a cell phone, and the policeman seemed to be talking into it. The doctor glimpsed another large envelope, and buzzed the outer door open.

'More photographs?'

He looked up as footfalls sounded in the corridor and the door opened. The mask startled him. In that instant, a swift succession of silly explanations raced through his mind. Some game, the housemen fooling about the way they did when one or other had finished his six-month internship? Some All Hallows malarkey with the wrong date? No envelope now. Where was it?

The policeman – was it a man, though? Surely the figure was too slight? The policeman held a weapon, holding it out as if making a diffident offering for the doctor to accept it as a gift. The

314

gloved digit tightened, and Dr Elphinstone started to rise, saying hesitantly, 'No, look, there must be some–'

The weapon moved, and the world ended.

Chapter Fifty-One

calco *(cal*orie-*co*unter) – one who diets to excess

Hassall thought Dr Clare looked particularly tired tonight, setting him wondering how many of these extra-curricular appointments she allowed in, say, a week. He was about to sit himself down but Clare gestured him to strip behind the screen.

'Full examination, please, Mr Hassall. It's over four months.'

'Full? I only came for–'

'For a full examination,' Clare said firmly. 'I shall estimate your age.'

'Age? I told you. I'm–'

'My estimate might differ. It's your functional age I want. Down to underpants, please.'

'I'm in a hurry, Dr Burtonall.'

'So am I, Mr Hassall.'

Miserably he divested himself and hung his clothes over the screen.

Without delay she gave him the standard blood pressure, ophthalmic and cardiac examination, and asked him to stand while she assessed his percentage of body fat, height and weight. She did a number of other estimates, murmuring the name of each instrument with instructions to him: 'PEF – peak expiratory flow; please exhale to your maximum using this mouthpiece.'

The whole series was exhausting. Twice, not quite joking, he demanded to know if she never ran out of gadgets. It took the best part of an hour, including time for him to recover.

'Doctor, what's this in aid of?'

Finally she let him position himself before her. 'Nearly done. Now I shall give you a potted version just to show you elementary tests you can do on yourself any old time anywhere, to estimate your age. It should prove there's no magic in medical machinery.'

He tried to laugh. 'I'm beginning to wish I'd not come!'

'An estimate of your seeming age is vital, Mr Hassall. Never mind what your birth certificate says. We think it provides a more reliable means of working out your bodily function. It suggests the reliability of symptoms and whatever tests we use on you.'

'What does it mean?'

'By comparing it with your chronological age – your years – we get a firmer measure of you as a living entity.'

Hassall almost said his real reason for coming tonight. He had things to ask Dr Burtonall. Evidently she was not yet aware of Dr Elphinstone's killing. He had ascertained that she would be next on call if Dr Elphinstone were unobtainable for any reason. Something was amiss. He glanced at her phone, and saw the comforting red glow of the dot, so malfunction was not the reason.

316

'Don't look so worried.' She smiled. 'This lot are tests you can perform with the aid of a stopwatch. First, your skin elasticity.' He sat down as she indicated. 'Put your hand flat on my desk. I shall grab as much skin on the dorsum as I can without hurting you. Now I let go.' Simultaneously she clicked her stopwatch and they saw his skin resume its normal contour.

'I time your skin at over forty-six seconds.'

'Is that good?'

'One test alone means little. Only the combination with other tests gives any significance.'

'Is that not it?' Hassall felt vulnerable, wanting to dress and get down to his reason for the visit.

'Most GPs do a battery of ten tests. Let's get on. Skin fold is my next.' She smiled and got him to stand, arm extended. 'I measure the thickness of the droopy bit of your upper arm, using this caliper. It won't hurt. You can do it yourself, using just your finger and thumb to judge thickness of the skin fold. It's simply a very rough way of measuring body fat. Fanatic slimmers go to pieces if they find it more than an inch – that's two-and-a-bit centimetres. Less is good. More is bad.'

'Is mine good?'

'Terrible, Mr Hassall!' Clare said cheerfully. 'Next, your waist-to-hip ratio. All these things you can do yourself, remember, to keep a check on your progress. Hope you're remembering all this.'

'Oh, certainly.'

'Waist divided by hips. Most GPs like it to be 0.8 or below. Yours is bad news. The reason I'm telling you,' she said, suddenly serious, 'is, you'll only go home and worry yourself into an early grave if I don't. Get Mrs Hassall to do it for you every couple of months. If she wants to learn these, I'll take her through them, all right?'

'Yes,' Hassall said gloomily.

'Near vision comes next. Ruler sticking out from your cheek, held in one hand. Yes, like that. Take any card and move it along the ruler. No!' She caught him as he turned for his spectacles. 'Reading glasses is cheating, Mr Hassall! Slide the card along the ruler until the letters go blurred. How near to your eye can you read the address on the card?'

'There.'

'All it is, is a crude estimate of how far your age-driven tendency to longer vision has got to. Doctors use various points-scoring systems, but ten centimetres is jolly good. Yours is way over thirty, not too bright. Now, the counting test. Just count backwards from one hundred in sevens. Start now, please.'

'Er, hundred, ninety-three, er, eighty-seven – no, eighty-six...'

Clare clicked the stop-watch as he reached the end. 'Thirty.'

'How am I doing?'

'Weakly. Now, my highly technical candle test.' She lit a candle, smiling to make a joke of the proceedings. 'You sit fifteen centimetres away, candle on a level with your mouth. Huff the candle out. If you purse your lips,' she said with mock sternness, 'the test won't count. Mouth staying open, and ... *blow.*'

He failed to blow out the flame. 'I can do it if I do a proper puff, like pursing my mouth. Won't

318

that do?'

The end of the instrumentation phase was worrying him. Clare smiled, guessing he thought this part a pantomime.

'I'm doing these as any ordinary PT instructor would do them, Mr Hassall. Of course, if there is a significant increase in your actual age when compared to your performance age, then I should be inclined to send you to our Age Assessment Unit, but quite honestly these elementary tests give as good a rough estimate as most. And you can do them yourself any time, which doesn't worry you sick the way a hospital visit would.'

'Is that it?'

'No. *Ten* tests, remember? Look in the mirror. Can you see a faint whitish rim round your cornea? The arcus senilis has been known since the Ancient World. No ring at all, is best. I've already accurately recorded yours. Rough guides advise giving five points for no arcus, then docking a point for every quarter of the circumference, down to complete encirclement which gets one point only. You can invent your own point-scoring system, but often they all reach similar conclusions.'

A phone buzzed. She smiled. 'The answer machine'll take it.'

'Please answer. I'll wait.'

Clare looked, and slowly lifted the receiver. 'Hello?' She listened, eyes on Hassall, and after a while nodded. 'I understand. Thank you. I have ... I have a patient with me now. I'll come straight in. Thank you.'

She paused, looking at the receiver a long time.

319

'You knew when you came, Mr Hassall.' She meant Dr Elphinstone's murder.

'Yes.' He felt stupid, standing there in underpants and bare feet. Every time he undressed he tried to suck in his belly, whether in the bathroom, or before Dr Clare. 'I didn't know whether to say anything.'

'You were investigating, Mr Hassall. You wanted to see if I had any clue to who killed Terry?'

Terry, then, Hassall thought. So did she know him better than a clinical relationship might suggest? He honestly didn't know the answer. Maybe it was in his mind, maybe not.

'I was stupid to assume you had come for your medical, Mr Hassall.' He would have expected a bitter smile. 'There are three remaining tests. Hair greyness I have already recorded – no greyness is best, complete greyness loses points. Then the two reaction tests.'

She instructed him to balance on one leg, the other at a 45-degree angle, and timed him to the point of overbalancing with his eyes closed and hands akimbo. 'We make three timings,' she said, flat-voiced, 'and take the longest.' He lasted thirty-four seconds, a poor score. 'Over seventy seconds scores best. Below thirty gets least.'

'He was killed soon after we called on him,' Hassall said. 'I was there just before,' Hassall said. 'The new SOCO – scene of the crime officer – is a cilops from the north. He rather gave your friend a ballocking, sorry.'

'You are right-handed, Mr Hassall,' Clare intoned, ignoring what he said. 'When I drop this ruler I hold vertically above your hand, try to

320

catch it.' He complied, she made three trials and wrote the result. 'You missed it twice, then caught it at twenty-five centimetres. The further it falls before you catch it, the worse the pointage. Fifteen centimetres is our shut-off for max points. That is it. Those are the rough elementary screening tests for age most on-the-hoof evaluators use. I'll sum your count while you dress, Mr Hassall.'

In silence he came from behind the screen and stood at her desk as she finished. She came round to show him the arithmetic.

'I'm afraid it's as I thought, Mr Hassall. Your performance age is over your chronological age. There are ways to record this – ratio of age in years to points scored, and so on – but I never find maths much value. The best thing is to keep the whole result in mind, and then try to improve your score over, say, six months. It can be done by exercise, getting your body-mass index to something reasonable, diet.'

'Well, I am trying.'

'You've stopped smoking?'

'Of course.'

'Exercise?'

'I walk a good three miles daily, and every third day do the grass until I sweat, or the rowing machine.'

'Drinking?'

'I found controlling that the worst. The rest, well,' he shrugged, convincingly, he thought, 'it's pretty easy.'

'You are allowed twelve alcohol units weekly, Mr Hassall. We doctors used to think that changing from beer or spirits to wine conferred advantage, but we now believe swapping to wine does little good. Whichever suits you – wine, beer, or spirits – stay with. Women should have less, of course,' she added with a faint suggestion of bitterness that momentarily surprised him.

'I'll be at the Farnworth,' he said awkwardly. 'Thank you.'

'Please remember that cigarette smoke does linger on the garments and in the hair, so its easily detectable by anyone, Mr Hassall.'

He coloured, made for the door, and paused. 'You haven't noticed anyone, say, observing you in the hospital grounds? Behaving suspiciously, loitering anywhere?'

'Not really, no.'

But she had hesitated, and Hassall wanted to pry. He remained at the door in silence, then nodded and moved out, closing the door as if on a sick room. He supposed that one lie deserved another.

Inside, Clare felt tears start, wondering how soon she could see Bonn. It was desperately urgent now. Book him, she thought in rage, I have to book my lover.

Outside, somewhere in the Central Gardens, Hassall would be smoking his silly head off, as he probably had been when he should have been guarding poor Terry from some killer. Patients always lie, her old professor had said. If they say their smoking is ten a day, double it to get the truth. Lies were the norm, no longer the exception. She had lied when Hassall asked her about somebody watching – she had no evidence, though, only felt a presence, perhaps from glimps-

322

ing somebody too often for coincidence. Subliminal. That wasn't evidence to tell a policeman, was it? Surely not.

Chapter Fifty-Two

yah-bah – methylamphetamine (a stimulant drug)

Hassall went to the desk. The Bouncing Block gymnasium had a strange reputation. Even as he waited for the gorgeous slender scented lass on Reception to notice him, he was aware of the plush surroundings and the exotic flora and fauna of the place. Two muscled hulks minced by, pausing every two paces to study themselves in the mirror. They were talking about body oiling, androgenic steroids, better definition of their lats, whatever they were. A group of women descended the stairs, chattering of the number of lengths necessary in the Long Pool to shape their bellies. Hassall had never seen so many mirrors.

'Mr Hasssssall?'

He had never heard his name pronounced with so many letter esses, either. He looked round, surly, into the features of a bronzed Adonis.

'Jeremiska, Mr Hasssssall.'

Hassall did not offer to shake the limp hand.

'We knew you were coming. We almost baked you a cake!' Jeremiska seemed of indeterminate gender, wore exotic make-up on his tanned features, with enough eyeliner to camouflage a ship. He wore a narrow loin-cloth. Hassall was repelled by the nipple rings and assorted iron-mongery studding the man's bellybutton.

'Hello, Jeremiska, darling!' one of the passing women carolled. The apparition stared at her, and called after, 'Hello, Dawn, sweetie!' adding immediately to Hassall under his breath, 'Shame about the *legs*. I've told the poor bitch, but what can you do? She's on yah-bah, like the rest.'

'Register, sir?' The desk maiden deigned to notice Hassall.

'No, ta, miss.'

Jeremiska tittered. 'Put Mr Hassall down as C virgule O Dr Clare Burtonall, Valerise!' He beck-oned Hassall, who followed.

'What's virgule, Jeremiska?' the girl called.

'It's the proper way of saying a forward slash, dwaaahling! Like when you piss against the wind!' Jeremiska whispered, 'Valerise always has that effect on people. Ignorant cow. Has difficulty with our pool attendant. Do you really *dream* there can be a surgical operation for her degree of bad breath? Doubt it myself. This way, sweetie.'

Hassall paused and growled, 'Look, lad. Don't call me sweetie. Hassall, OK?'

'Oooh! Very well, be like that.'

They entered a suite of changing rooms, where Hassall was told to change into a jogging suit and trainers. He obeyed, and came into the massive gymnasium. Several people were already on various machines. Hassall eyed them with hatred. Jeremiska was gushy and urged him onto a walk-ing machine.

'I shall set Intro, with a nil slope factor! All rightee? Go!'

The machine moved, Hassall walking on the moving tread. Dials marked his speed, steps, calories expended, heart rate. He settled down, feeling ridiculous.

'Fifteen minutes, Mr Hassall!' Jeremiska twittered, moving off, fluttering his fingers at other clients. 'Then it's the pool for you, thirty minutes of water-walking! Oh, you'll enjoy it!'

'Aye, right.'

Hassall was relieved when the showy git turned his attentions to others, and looked round. On the next machine, a youngish woman was moving with alacrity, her breathing steady. She smiled.

'Your first time?'

'Aye. Sent by my quack. I've to slim down.'

'A bully? I sympathise.'

Hassall eyed her form. There didn't seem to be an ounce of fat on her. 'You can't need much whittling, miss.'

'Thank you. No, it's cardiac for me. I've been coming here for three months. I have special duties that require fitness.'

'School, eh?'

The woman seemed surprised. 'Well spotted. I'm a teacher, but PE isn't my subject, no. Sedentary job, you see. Everybody's always on about risk factors.'

'Wise lass.' Hassall was becoming breathless. The woman kindly reached across and moved one of the controls. The pace slowed. 'Ta, love. Stay close. I may need you again. I hope that queer doesn't leave me on this damned thing longer than he's supposed to.'

'Oh, he's innocent,' the assassin said. 'The body builders are the least of the city's worries. Don't you think that?'

Hassall was too winded to converse, and went back to silent endeavour, him and the machine, watching the clock above the window showing how much longer his torture had to go. His companion smiled, clicked her controls to a gradual stop, and went through to the glass-enclosed lounge where she lay to rest. A glass of barley water was served and she drank, listening to the conversations of others who had finished their stints.

She thought of the five she had executed, in protection of the nation's children. Her duty, her lifelong task, was as urgent now as when she had begun. The first incident, though nothing like as serious as some, had concerned a child missing from her school. The little eight-year-old boy eventually was found sadly wandering the by-pass, evidently fired by some childhood dream of becoming a pirate. Near thing, though. He was found by a doctor and his wife going out for the evening and taken to the police station. That set the assassin thinking. A chance encounter at one of the modelling society's monthly gatherings with Hal and his special golfing buddy in Suffolk, and several chats later she had financial backers. Her public image – dedicated primary school teacher, contributor to the hospice movements and sundry other charities – served her well. Difficult, of course, to get in the swing, so to speak, even though she was a meticulous capable woman

326

who – this was the essential part – would go to endless efforts to achieve a good result.

The hand in the skip had been a brainwave. At once a warning to the city's perverts and a signal that the good people were now on the attack, it had been gruesome but thrilling. No routine communications with Hal and his pal, for security. The money was passed at the model society's assemblies, and she went innocently about her business, which was the defence of Good against Evil.

Blendix from the Midlands had been easy. The first, however, had not been quite so elementary. Oh, it sounded simple enough. The pervert, a fortyish police liaison officer with social services, lived on a river barge moored off the Nottingham reaches. She had planned it quite well, though she'd left mistakes. She had laid the fire to start the minute he got home one evening. Harrowing and risky to keep watch – an essential part of the plan. Once she had made certain he was there alone, she had ignited the rope, swung it on the deck, and that had been that. The weapon she had taken along, in case the perv tried to escape his fate, turned out to be unnecessary. Much relief about that.

One was by poison, a quite frank cyanide business in a drink at his home, and she hadn't even had to visit the place. Somehow unsatisfactory, for reasons she could not explain. Because, maybe, the police regarded it as a plain suicide? It had not been understood as much of a warning to the community of paedophiles. The rest were seen, guardedly, as ominous warnings, vigilantes taking the law into their own (and far more just!) hands...

327

'Smiling like a Cheshire cat, miss.'

Hassall flopped down heavily on the next lounger, red of face and breathing heavily. He declined the barley water with a weary shake of the head.

'It's good for you,' the assassin warned. 'Otherwise they wouldn't keep on about it.'

'Every blinking thing is, these days.'

'The trainer will be along any minute to complain. You must drink half a pint after every session. It's a condition.'

'Aye, I know all that.'

'Did I hear you at the desk, your doctor sent you?'

'Correct. She thinks I won't last long if I don't get fitter.'

'She's right. We're starting an anti-obesity drive at our school.'

'Teacher's hell of a job.' Hassall eyed her.

'Only little children, but you can't start too early.'

'I've to go to a school later on today.' Hassall mentioned the school. He had chosen it because its school hall was the location of the modelling society's exhibitions, some old caretaker called Entwistle there the club secretary. Dr Elphinstone's death was caused by a spherical lead bullet, nowadays only homemade by enthusiasts. No one more enthusiastic than a modeller.

'That's my school!'

'Want a lift?'

'Certainly not!' She smiled. 'Watch out. Here comes your fitness man.'

As Jeremiska wafted up in his glittering caftan,

she smiled and went to the pool, pleased with herself. She could have reached school in a police car! Problems start in social chit-chat, though. She might have let some remark drop that could have alerted him. She had survived in her vital quest by not being deceived by apparent innocence, and nobody looked more innocent than the overweight, bumbling Mr Hassall.

Also, there was the remote – very remote, admittedly – possibility that Hassall's presence here was not quite as coincidental as it seemed. Killers could make mistakes, as could police, but executioners had to lay plans that were perfect at all times. Security was as much part of her duty as execution.

Chapter Fifty-Three

leaner – pimp

Rack, slumping into an alcove in the Rum Romeo Casino's din, was seriously pissed off. He was narked at Bonn, Martina, at Grellie and the girl he liked, all curry powder and spice, called Devvie that Martina said had to go. He waited for Devvie, Martina and Grellie, fed up to the balls. He'd only just got Devvie motoring, and here she was doing wrong. Chances were it would be the wet walk home. Only Martina could decide. Birds who went off the rails always did it for some bloke, at first. Then they got hooked on drugs, seriously lost

329

the plot, and overboard they went. More ways than one, Rack thought, chuckling at the notion of overboard into the water, and the wet walk home. Get it? He laughed aloud. Clever, that. He'd try to remember it, to tell Bonn. Second thoughts, better not. He always wanted a drink before one of these carry-ons, but knew not to touch a drop until after.

Here came Grellie among the tables, pausing at the blackjack table, but only for show, like she was casual instead of going somewhere. Punters exchanged a word, offered her a drink. She was already moving before they spoke. Clever girl, Grellie. Rack seriously wished Bonn'd take her on. Rack had asked her a couple of times but she'd given him the sailor's elbow. He'd got nowhere. For Bonn, Grellie would do anything, get him really normal for a change. She'd start him chatting like a bloke ought to, and stop the daft cunt thinking all the frigging time like it was a sodding job.

Grellie advanced through the throng, shoving hands away, talking to all and sundry, smiling, using her luscious shape. Women have an unfair advantage, because they can do anything and get away with it, the shapes they were. Blokes have to toe the line. It was a right fucking liberty.

At a blackjack table, the assassin placed a bet – a fiver chip – on her two cards, jack of hearts and a two of clubs. She watched the lovely girl who smilingly declined drinks offered by the bettors. Beautiful, the assassin thought. Now, if anybody was tempted to have a lesbian fling, there was the girl to start with. What had they called her, Grellie, was it? Strange name, but everybody seemed to know her. A prostitute for certain, but so? They were said to be the best les lovers, or so the one female friend the assassin knew for certain – ignore how she'd learned *that* little fact – had said. Strange. The assassin observed the girl's sinuous progress among the crowded tables. Obviously leaving for some street trolling, the assassin guessed a little enviously. Deep down, she suspected that all women wanted to be a prostitute, experience the madness of selling yourself to be used...

Hang on. What was this? Grellie plumped herself down at a recessed table.

There against the back wall, the seating was shadowed, hooded lights offering partial concealment. A youth, wearing quite mad garb consisting of a pilot's leather helmet, goggles raised to his brow, a diamonte-studded waistcoat, a bright electric-yellow shirt with billowing sleeves, and enormous cowboy boots, and flashing sleeve restrainers. He waved to the girl called Grellie, and started his bow-tie revolving with glitzy lights, grinning. The girl seated herself opposite, almost ignoring the brass-thick youth. Even in the talk and at this distance, the assassin heard him bawl, 'Wotcher, Grellie. Seen Bonn?'

The assassin's throat tightened. Bonn? There could not be many Bonns in this cold northern city. Had she seen the youth before? Could he have been one of the loungers in that hotel when she had met Bonn and left without getting any kind of reward, reward she so richly deserved for having rid the world of a pervert who preyed on

331

children? She saw the rough yobbo raise a hand, and instantly the nearest two waitresses changed direction, one even leaving a customer from whom she was taking orders at a roulette table. Both hurried to serve him. He ordered for himself and Grellie, who shook her head, no. He had authority, this loud-voiced scenic youth in aberrant gear, whoever he was.

Tonight she would meet Bonn again, already booked. That gave her time to change her mind – not that it would have been any the cheaper, for all expenses had to be met beforehand, and there was no question of a simple cancellation fee. Criminal. Still, the assassin reasoned, a man hiring a prostitute had to pay whether he achieved orgasm or not. She supposed they worked on the same principle. It was probably fair. Her gaze drifted over the far side, touched on the alcove, and was surprised to see a new girl seated there, almost as if she had suddenly appeared. A blonde, quite lovely from this distance, seated slightly askew as if she had some kind of... The girl moved to adjust, and the assassin knew. There had been a girl in school who had had polio and had limped ever after. She too had made that slight shift when seated. The blonde girl was lame. The blonde seemed to say nothing, but the others stooped to pay heed, so the blonde was boss.

Grellie stiffened at something said, taking bad news on board and trying to explain her way out of a problem. Looking for excuses? The colour-decked lad just listened, when it was clearly against his nature to stay silent. He almost bounced in his seat, but the blonde girl made a

332

simple palm-down gesture and he stilled instantly. The assassin was impressed. That degree of power, over some callow youth who was never still, and a gorgeous young prostitute who clearly had caught everybody's notice drifting across a huge casino, probably the largest gambling place in the city centre. What power did she have, and how?

'Card?' the croupier asked.

The assassin nodded. A card came, ten of diamonds. Bust. The assassin sighed, and passed her cards across.

'Tough luck,' the punter opposite said.

For one moment the assassin almost relented. Should she keep the conversation going and discover who the three were exactly in that alcove, the blonde girl, the brassy youth, and the exquisite Grellie? No, stay firm. Odd how diffident the yobbo and that Grellie girl were the instant the blonde girl appeared. Body language always reveals the pecking order. Tonight, the assassin thought warming within, she would meet Bonn again, take no nonsense from him, and possibly get her just reward. She had a right to payment. And an explanation.

Then she saw Hassall enter.

The policeman came across to the bars lining the approach to the stage, perched awkwardly on a stool and ordered. It must have been a truly bad day, for the paunchy man ordered a pint of something and downed it almost in one, nodding straight away for another. He turned from the bar. The assassin had paid her ante for the next round and bent over her hand, two of spades and five of clubs. Hassall bought cigarettes and lit up, quite illicit if you believed the city by-laws. He chatted to the bar man. The assassin was relieved. She would let him get into his conversation then slope out unnoticed. She might leave by passing the alcove holding the three interesting parties who seemed so influential at the Rum Romeo Casino. Maybe. Or would that be too risky, with Hassall ogling the scenery? The barman seemed to know him, which boded ill. She wanted to hear their conversation so far off.

In the alcove, Martina frowned at the waitress who brought Rack his drink, only a ginger beer but still spinning things out. The girl faded.

'Devvie,' Martina said.

Grellie felt inclined to support the girl. 'The lass has worked well so far, even if she's patchy in her strides. She makes up for slow nights by extra strides on her quick.'

'And her thefts?'

'She nicks from the casino,' Rack said, feeling really down. He knew that tone. Martina wouldn't let up on this, so he'd have a load of right drossy work to do later. Grellie was wasting her time, but, typical bird, was in there batting for the doomed girl.

What is it about females, Rack wondered, that makes them keep rabbiting, yak-yak, until the cows came home when anybody could see they were wasting their time?

'Say on, Rack.' Martina kept her eyes on Grellie. 'Thefts.'

'Never here. Only ever in the Lagoon, Waterloo Street, and lately the Rowlocks Casino.'

'More,' Martina ordered as Rack paused to slurp

his ginger beer. Grellie defiantly stared into Martina's ice-blue eyes, keeping it up as Rack resumed.

'She does it three nights a week. Remember the goon who does them TV slots, dances in the shopping malls until they found out he was a queer who kilt some druggo, made out he was on a ferry from the Isle of Man and hadn't gone there at all? Well, that nerk got one of his pals to start up a talent contest, sending them on one of these knock-out shows – you phone your vote and they become super stars, know it? He's tall, has a squint–'

'*Rack.*'

'Well, she does a ticket scam. Not on her own, o'course. Uses three Barboes, one white and two black. They're not ours. I reckon one is a part-time leaner. They bring duffo chalk in from Jamaica or somewhere up the fucking Amazon.'

'How?' Martina's eyes stayed on Grellie, who gave in and looked at Rack.

'Dunno how they gets it in, boss. They spins a kilo a fortnight, word is.'

'And the money?'

'She stashes it in Leeds. I think it's stocks and shares. I reckon we should hire 'em in, maybe think about it.'

'We can't beat them, so we join?' Martina asked quietly.

Rack winced inwardly then gave a great grin. 'Nah, boss, just joking. Having a laugh. I knowed you wouldn't go in for that, don't I?' He laughed, pretended to shoot an imaginary gun from the hip, going blam-blam-blam and blowing on the smoking pistol before miming shoving it back into his non-existent holster.

'And?'

'She shags two of the three, the white and the old black geezer. What the fuck is the use of that?' He was instantly into indignation, demanding if Grellie would behave like that or would she see sense and do what was natural instead.

'The other?'

'He comes and goes, boss. I reckon he's the muler, y'know?' He explained, 'The one who brings the chalk in, see, through the Customs?'

'The Rowlocks?'

'Always there, with a bit in the Lagoon. Not so easy there for Devvie, because it's only ever cards, see? It's a bit down market and she fancies herself.'

'How much did you know, Grellie?'

The girl had slumped during Rack's account. She now seemed tired, and nodded. 'I knew hardly any of this, except she's been shelling out bunce right and left. Four shops in the malls. That means,' she added bitterly, 'maybe twice as many. Girls who start their own game never do things in ones and twos.'

'Papadops owns half the Rowlocks, by arrangement.' Martina raised a finger for silence as she deliberated how to put this. 'Posser and Papadops knew each other once, so the Greek gentleman is kept on. It was his place, the Rowlocks. I must see to it that Devvie ends her contract, and the three bringers must go.'

'Who does them?' Rack asked.

'Who, then?'

'Papadops'll want to do it himself, make sure

he's still in the ring, see? Greeks,' Rack continued airily, 'are like that. I know them. It's their fishes. They have different breeds in their sea, see? These fishes have a kind of celery growing on them down deep, and when they're caught–'

'Let Papadops in on it, Grellie. No, Rack.'

Rack halted, narked at Grellie being told to do the dirty, when dissing the city centre was down to him, not some bint. He wondered how to put it with the tact for which he was famed, and said, 'No, boss, you're fucking wrong there. It's down to me, straightening is down to me, not some bint like Grellie.'

'Rack.' Martina held him in her blues until he shut up. 'I want Grellie to do it. That way, Papadops'll know I mean to leave the three men to him. Is the white man a Barbo too?'

'Talks like it, boss.' Rack glared at Grellie.

'They all must go. Grellie, see to it tonight.'

Grellie nodded, now truly exhausted. If Bonn ever got wind of this, it would be the end and she would never see him again. More than likely, Bonn would simply walk off and take whatever flak came his way. Martina must know that too, the conniving bitch. And Rack.

'Rack, see to Devvie. You understand?'

'Yep, boss.' He did an exaggerated salute. 'This is no easy assignment!' He looked from one to the other. 'Who said that? No points, boss! No points, Grellie! John Wayne in that war picture! Don't you remember?'

'That's all. Grellie?'

'Nothing, Martina.'

'Rack, anything?'

'No, boss.'

'Then get on with it. One thing.' Martina took a slow breath. 'Who is Devvie, incidentally? Tall girl, wears head-bands with beads, in the Green?'

'No, you silly bitch, boss. Short, half goojer, talks sort of Accrington. Reckons she can dance.'

'I place her.' Martina nodded, and told them they could leave. They knew to go straight away, leaving Martina to limp out at her own pace when nobody was looking. 'Thank you,' she said to Grellie.

'See you, boss.'

Grellie said nothing, but walked from the Rum Romeo with a face of stone, Rack bouncing beside her explaining some theory about how women died different from men due to their smaller feet.

Chapter Fifty-Four

kleptocracy – full-time exploiters, in group

'This place,' Bonn said to Rack as they drew up at the top of the street.

'This is it.' Rack drew on an imaginary cigar and flicked pretended ash from the car window. He put on a Hollywood hood's drawl copied from some B film. 'I cased the neighbourhood, Caponey.'

'Very well.'

The street was in semi-darkness, terraced houses abutting on pavement. Further down, a high wall of an infant school showed, with one nearby shop still illuminated, a congregation of youths smoking and lounging there.

'Upstairs, just over the doorway with them lights.'

'Very well.'

'I'm your stander, tonight, Bonn. I've got Tickle and Dolby round the back, an' two others for heave-ho if any locals start creating.'

'Thank you, Rack.'

'Know how long it is since we had a right rumble, Bonn?' Rack sounded wistful. 'It's three months.' He cackled a sudden laugh. 'That Danish git started up in the Royal and Grand, di'n' he? I slammed that bar down pronto and gets you out through the fucking window, everybody in the lounge hootin' an' hollerin', great.'

'I was grateful for the rescue, Rack.'

'I miss it when things are, like, smooth.'

'Perhaps because you enjoy it so much, Rack.'

'That's right!' Rack sounded surprised. Maybe Bonn had more brains than what Rack thought. 'I don't go looking for trouble.' He went all pious, because Bonn didn't think scrapping was sort of decent, which was well strange.

'Berenice Six-Six-Nine. You shagged her before, not long since.'

'I see.'

Rack nodded and clicked Bonn's door for him. 'Two hours. I'll be around. Oh, Bonn?'

'Yes?'

'That girl Devvie's leaving tonight. She'll be on the nine-fifteen train.'

'You don't know where, exactly, Rack.'

339

Rack guessed it was meant as some sort of question. 'No. She's going to get her own set-up, she tellt Grellie, God knows where.' He smiled and shrugged, the girls beyond him, never no motives to speak of.

'Please convey my best wishes, and remember to thank her for all she has done for Grellie and Martina.'

'Right, right.'

Rack watched Bonn cross to the door and knock. It was opened almost instantly but the light wasn't on so Rack had no idea who was there. Dolby would, though, because he was on the roof and carried more electronics than the National Grid. He'd have warned if anything was amiss.

Rack sighed. He didn't like these jobs where circumstances changed, like Bonn being booked out here in the sordid sticks among dingy streets with only old gas-lamp to light the way. It took a fucking army to guard a key in these dumps, when one stander in a hotel corridor was quite enough for a posh hotel like the Amadar Royale or the Royal and Grand, or the Worcester Club and Tea rooms, all of which Martina owned so could be worked cheaper and no worries. Those were all in Victoria Square where they belonged, not out here in this shivery place that should have been bulldozed a century gone.

He drove off, parked on a spare patch of cinders round the side turning in the darkness, whistled and got a couple of taps on the car roof. He grunted, let his eyes adjust to the gloom and stepped out, ready for assault, but it was only Hookie from the Shot Pot, black as Newgate's knocker and the size of a tram. His teeth shone white in the darkness.

'Nice wheels, man. Where you get them?'

'Found under a bush, Hookie. I got a cramp job on after this stander's done. I want you wiv, OK? Extra bunce for the trouble.'

'How much? I mean, yeh, but how much?'

'One large. A bit wet, mebbe.'

'OK.' Hookie shrugged.

'I got to get Bonn down the city centre first when he's done, OK?'

'OK, Rack.'

'Get in the car here, no lights, no smokes, no CD, no sound, OK?'

'Jesus, Rack. OK.' Hookie slid behind the wheel and sat. Rack eeled to the street he had just left, certain he was unnoticed by the gaggle of yobbos lounging in the block of yellow light from the window of the corner shop, and moments later was inside the door Bonn had just entered. It was locked, narking him because it meant this Berenice bitch was a suspicious cow. He made sure he locked the door behind him and floated silently in.

Berenice Six-Six-Nine seemed to move to shake hands, but Bonn was unsure of this, for the instant passed. She gestured for him to go up the stairs first. He complied, chiding himself for noticing the one gaslight, the faded and stained wallpaper, the dust accumulated in the corner of each riser. No carpet, and one old newspaper left time-faded on the landing.

'In there, Bonn.' She sounded breathless, but it was only emotion made her so.

341

'Thank you.'

He opened the one door from the small square landing, and entered a room that was gaudy by comparison. He stepped to one side to give her room to come in. She examined his face, hoping for some revelatory expression, smiling and evidently pleased. Rude, of course, to show amazement, for the room truly was an astonishment after the tatty stairwell, the crumbling edifice of the terrace, and the generally unclean hallway. He made trite remarks, how pleasant, she had worked wonders, something of that kind.

'I can see you're stunned,' the assassin concluded, advancing past him and inviting him by gesture to seat himself facing.

'You caught me out.'

It seemed the right thing to say because she gave a squeak of a laugh and clapped her hands.

'I lived here once.'

Once? Perhaps she had been born in this very house. Bonn's mind raced, constructing a past for Berenice: the poor little girl whose father worked – where? – at the canal docks or mills, perhaps, a lone child with a defeated mother in a neighbourhood laundry, clogs to school with all the derision of growing up a teenager longing for better clothes and posh schooling.

'And you came back.'

'Yes.' She hesitated, quite as if caught out about to make some unwise revelation. 'I rent it. I don't suppose it will be here for long. At least I shall have it for as long as it stays.'

'If you own it...' Bonn was almost trapped into asking an outright question, and that would never do. To him, social chitchat was simply that, and no place for questions. Questions were an intrusion, a frontal assault on the privacy of another, and so intolerable. Everyone out here – he thought of his freedom, once out of the seminary – seemed to find direct, even personal, questions acceptable and nothing like the brawling jousts he once imagined them to be. It had been a shock, far worse than the physical encounters for which he was paid. Those latter were, to him, acceptable as eating, dressing, having a bath and admiring some painting like the pre-Raphaelites or the modernists of the Salford Art Gallery, or even the Bolton-le-Moors watercolours of de Wint, or Valette. Sexual congress was desirable, very like the air one was fortunate enough to breathe, or experiencing lovely free rain and liberating winds of an autumn, sensations he had once thought beyond his destiny.

'Yes?' Berenice asked expectantly.

She wore a loose dress caught at the waist with a leather belt. It was woven from thin strips, and multi-coloured. Her hair was beautiful. She wore spectacles. For some reason he could not define he suspected they were a disguise, and he felt a gremlin of suspicion alight on his shoulder to whisper that she would normally never dress in such high heels, with fish-net stockings, have her best – were they best? – three-string choker of pearls on. She wore two rings, the gemstones catching at every passing light.

The room was beautifully appointed, other women would say. Three doors led from the sitting-room. All seemed new, the carpet plush,

343

the furniture evidently expensive. The walls were panelled with seasoned heartwood, and the lights hardly there yet the room was in a full glow. It was clever decorative art, he realised. Unable to explain the reason, he found himself thinking of Dr Clare's ex-husband, the developer Clifford Burtonall, now one of the city's principal shapers and designers.

'No one can take it from you, I meant. I must seem impertinent.'

She gestured at the lovely room. 'I think I have taste, Bonn. I assumed when I decided to ... well, rent for a while, that I could use it as a refuge. Not so. City planners try to commandeer the neighbourhood.'

'Some might be glad.'

'Some might not!' She spoke harshly. 'Planners assume an illegitimate authority just because they can. We let them get away with it. This street is an instance. Those lads idling about out there. I know they could be better off in some gardened leafy suburb, but only on paper. Would they really?'

'I don't know, Berenice.'

His use of her name calmed her. Bonn remembered where he had seen similar light fittings before. Mr Burtonall's splendid office, fifth floor, George Street. He must have cannibalised old houses, re-used their light fixtures. Had Clifford, Clare's ex-husband, been here, to rescue this old terraced house from dereliction? If so, why? Commerce alone, or some darker reason?

'I perhaps am wrong, Bonn. You seem to be so well-adjusted, a breath of fresh air.' He was about to make a polite disclaimer when she went on,

344

'Did you get in trouble?'

'In trouble.'

'Last time. When I swep' out, like the lady in the play.'

What lady? In what play? Presuming she meant her previous booking with him, he shook his head. 'Not at all. I cannot.'

She waited, eyebrows raised. He realised she was an attractive woman. The thought came, more suspicions again, that she would normally dress frumpy and bulbous, perhaps yet more disguise. But why would any woman do that, when their natural inclinations were towards display and exotic showiness of attire, of cosmetics, of elegance? He had speculated the previous few evenings whether the tendency of women was to competition among herds of their kind, in a sort of I'm-more-beautiful-so-look-at-me exhibition. Only three nights before he had alighted from a motor in the Square when two of Grellie's walkers, one from the Yellow, the other Red, had fought, actually fought, screeching and pulling hair and scratching, as appalled commuters called for police. It was Rack's sudden arrival that stilled the whole business, and they had been whisked away to some dire punishment Grellie would decide on. Rack had been laconic for once, telling Bonn, 'Something about a fucking frock, what d'you reckon to *that?*' It transpired one girl had spoken unfavourably of the other's dress.

'Only, I felt bad afterwards.'

'You had no reason to.'

'I wanted to, so badly, Bonn.'

'I was in error to speak as I did, Berenice.'

She purred at her name, and folded her legs under her on the couch. 'I ought to be rushing about getting you a drink. Instead I feel restful. Do you mind?'

'I have no right to mind, Berenice. I am here at your behest.'

'Did you start out to be, to do what you do?'

'I was about to catch a train,' he surprised her by revealing. This was unusual for him. He realised he had only ever given this account to Dr Clare before now. Berenice was ingenuous, in the modern sense.

'To where?'

'I was unsure. I had never bought a train ticket before.'

'In this city?'

'Yes.'

'And what happened? Don't tell me!' She guessed. 'You were taken on by a lady bent on pleasure, she picked you up and you realised your worth, that you could make a living by just being kind, and maybe more, to bored women who had no need to watch the pennies. That the scenario?'

He worried about the use of that scenario term, and how in fact she saw him. How on earth could he query her at this point in the conversation? She was adapt at questions. The sense of jousting came to him. He prepared to defend himself from advancing lances. It was at this juncture in debate among seminarians that surrender always came as a tempting option. He had long since got over it, and eased himself further into the armchair, readying his mind.

'No.'

'Then what?' She hugged herself. 'I am enjoying this, Bonn. I have only ever felt this kind of ... satisfaction, delight, once or twice before. I can't think of the word.'

'Power.'

'That's it! Yes, power!' She stared at him. 'Please go on.'

'I was having tea. It took such desperation, actually speaking to a waitress, saying please could I have some tea. It was tea-time, you see,' he put in, as if setting out a Boolean proposition. 'I suppose I was trying to find refuge in some pattern of normality, or what I guessed might be usual. Outside, I mean. I did not know how to cope with the tea things. A lady was watching. She spoke.'

'And that was it!'

'No.' Bonn found it hard to go on. Berenice seemed to be enthralled, actually clapping her hands like a little girl in delight at his tale. 'It now seems so mundane, a simple misunderstanding.'

'What happened? The waitress?'

'I realised the lady was under a misapprehension. She seemed to regard me as someone else. I...' He caught himself in time, and changed it to, 'She called me by a name not my own. I wondered if it meant something that had passed me by, like so many other things. You can do that, thinking folk mean something else, quite as if you are not interested in new Jaguars, or whatever.'

'True.' She was in rapture, eyes shining, lips apart. In freer circumstances Bonn would have found her reaction disturbing. 'What did the lady do?'

'Someone came.'

'The management, moaning you were using the hotel lounge to pick up loose ladies?'

'No. The one who came was a male.' Who, Bonn cautioned himself, was one of the Pleases Agency's goers, and who had later joked about the incident with Rack. Only once, and had never since broached the subject.

'I see.' Berenice exhaled slowly. Her excitement shed her years. 'He was the one the lady was waiting for!'

'Yes.'

'How on earth...? Whatever did she say?'

'The lady laughed and appeared pleased. She left with him.'

'Is that it? Did she not say anything?'

'She did.'

'Please tell me.' She patted the couch beside her. Bonn took this as an invitation to move across.

'She said that if ever I wanted to... It would be unfair to say more.'

'Won't you at least tell me who she was?'

'That is out of the question, Berenice.'

She laughed, touching his hair. 'So stern! Am I being told off?'

'I would not presume.'

'Unless I wanted you to?' She added at his puzzlement, 'Told me off. Rebuked.'

'It is as the lady wishes.'

'But not that lady, the one who misunderstood!'

'No! I did not understand, you see. I had no ... learning.'

'And you have now?'

'I fear not.'

She was enormously amused. 'I am so entertained! The transition must have come about somehow, Bonn. You looked up agencies in the phone book, or did you wait until the lady came down?' She giggled at the pun. 'And accosted her as she left the hotel? Waited for her in the car park, made a suggestion? What?'

'I was not alive to those concepts, Berenice. Even what occurred – I mean this, being here, speaking with a beautiful lady who has invited me – is beyond my understanding. No. An elderly man, seated in the hotel lounge, addressed me. He explained he ran an agency, and asked if I were interested in work.'

'Did he tell you what it was?'

'No. I gathered he was trying to clarify what had taken place, the incident with the lady. I thought it improper, in public.'

'And still do?'

'Certainly.'

'Poor thing. However did you manage when you... You must have begun sooner or later, or you wouldn't be here, well, answering, when, you know?'

'I cannot grasp the purpose.'

'Of what? Money?' She seemed about to make a joke of the topic but held off. 'Sex?'

'Not that. The way a woman comes to it.'

'Comes to it?' She frowned for the first time, and he watched as her features changed.

'Women are a pattern of heavens,' he said, a mere frank observation. 'They are so alive, so eager to reveal and be revealed to. An excitement. Yet they never seem convinced of their worth. I can not understand it.'

349

'Of course we know our worth.'

'Not really, Berenice.' He shook his head. It was at this point he became doubtful, worried he was following some ordained path that his brain could no longer analyse, instead of genuinely offering his own thoughts and not those instilled into him by some learning process he really ought to forget.

'We women are all on about it, especially these days when every city ought to be called Gangchester. Freedom means a right to demand that others fund you because you're dissatisfied. Everybody else has a duty to give you more, when you haven't earned the right to a single damned thing!'

'I mean women.' Conversations could get out of hand, like last time. 'I cannot see what a woman gets out of it.'

'Out of what?'

'Sexual congress.'

'Sex is for everybody. Both.'

'I wonder why women bother with men,' he said, reflecting. 'At first, I believed women were simply being kind. It was only later, one by one, I came to see they wished to do whatever they procured a goer for.'

'Goer.' She said the word a few times, trying it out.

'I cannot see what women get.'

He felt saddened by her lack of comprehension. His own bafflement was probably far worse, deeper and more unassailable. There seemed no future in the argument, and definitely no way of excavating the archaeology of his attitude. That his lack of understanding had only come since he became a goer – heavens, was it eighteen months? – offered no route in to the core. It was a simple plain inability to understand why women hired him, what they wanted. Likely, it would never be resolved now.

'For me, Bonn, it's a reward.' She raised her eyebrows in surprise at the turn the conversation was taking, but pressed on, 'That's probably why I was so cross with myself when I swep' out.'

He would have to look up the origin of that phrase. Was it in Oscar Wilde, or something more commonplace?

'I wonder if I had caught the train.'

'You did not even know which train, Bonn.'

She was rearranging his hair and frowning at it with concentration, withdrawing to check on his looks as she did this and that. It had always been a thatch, and he never bothered it. Dr Clare often did the same, and said he should have somebody see to it. She even offered to make an appointment for him to visit a hairdresser and become 'really stylish', an assertion that still puzzled him, for what on earth would be the purpose of that? Teeth were enough trouble, for visits to the dentists took time and needed a drive out of the city to somewhere he would be unknown.

'That is my meaning. I would be in some library, or possibly trying to follow some banking code and studying for a night-school qualification in law or history.'

Her fingers halted. 'Why did you say that?'

He shrugged to show he was disarmed, fearing he had struck a nerve. 'Any job.'

'You must be well paid, Bonn.'

351

'Others see to it.'

'Do they pay you into a bank? Secret accounts in foreign funds?'

'I never enquire.'

'Your clothes, shoes. You never wear a watch, no rings, nothing designer-label. Is it to disguise?'

'No. I would feel embarrassed choosing.'

'You are looked after. They do that to prize horses. Racing horses, and those at stud.'

'I have heard so.'

'Two followed you. One in the car and one who went next door.' She laughed at his expression. 'There's nobody there now. The old man next door used to work in the mills until they all closed. Then canal work, until they all went under computer control. The other side is a deaf old lady who can't be touched.'

'Can't be touched. I hope she welcomes the status, Berenice.'

'You are too grave, Bonn.'

'I do not think I am.'

'Jolly inside, is that it? You are unwilling to show yourself, you as you honestly are?'

The image was profoundly lowering. She must have felt his sudden upset for she quickly went on, 'I don't mean it's all put on. I don't feel it is. I mean you state things, rather than come out with them. Maybe you are too restricted, is what I meant.'

'The deaf old lady is sacrosanct. I find that pleasing. Because of the youths outside by that corner shop, at a loose end. They might have been tempted to mug her and steal her things, buy drugs or whatever. It is the way of the city.'

'Not with her. They know not to.'

'She has friends, then, sons who work locally.' Bonn was aware no cars had passed along the street since his arrival, and had assumed it was Rack's doing.

'Something like that.'

'Camouflage. Your entrance is a disguise. It works well.'

'I make sure of it.' She paused. Her fingers moved to his mouth. 'Did I offend? About the race-horses?'

'You can not offend, Berenice. The lady has the right. I am here for her purpose of being here, so it is her right to give, say, do, ask. I can't do hair, though I should try if asked. I cannot design a dress, though I should try if desired. I would probably make a hash of cooking a meal, though ... and so on.' He relaxed, aware of his ineptitude. 'I know how limited I am. This is the reason I am unable to understand.'

'Do other women think the same as I do?'

'I have no way of knowing. And I could not say even if I knew.'

She was smiling now. 'Is this like a confessional?'

That term again. 'At least as honest, and certainly as trustworthy.'

'You don't keep a diary?'

'Certainly not! That would be the ultimate transgression.'

'Like Fingal O'Flaherty Wills's clever crack about travelling with a diary?'

He found a smile starting, as if to share hers. 'Oscar Wilde's use of his middle names might have offended his ancestors, maybe. Something sensational to read on the train, so he always travelled with his diary. A remark like that is almost too clever by half.'

'Where do you come from, Bonn?' she asked, with affection. 'Is it your real name?'

'I think I invented it.'

'No other?'

'I could not invent two, for the one person I suppose myself to be.'

'The old man. Was he the proprietor of Pleases Agency?'

'I presumed so. He was very pleasant.' Bonn felt the limits of his conversation coming close. 'I was disturbed.'

'By the sex? Did he explain what you would have to do?'

'I made my own progress.'

'You seem innocent.'

'That cannot be, Berenice.'

She wanted him to smile, really smile as she knew he could, but he was too... The French criticised those too intellectual to respond with emotion, though they should talk! She watched him, trying to think how far passion, if he was capable of achieving passion, could carry him. Confession on the one hand, while testing the boundaries of passionate involvement on the other? Was this the reason he was priced more highly than any of the other goers at the Agency, that he invited this feeling in his other ... what are we, she thought, clients? Women? She wanted to tell him about herself. It would be a mistake.

He seemed prompted, as if suddenly the thought had somehow osmosed into him from her own mind, and looked at a small Congreve clock, quite still, on the bureau. It caught his attention.

'Lovely piece of engineering, Berenice.'

'Miniature.'

'Your friend is very talented. Except...'

She could never take criticism, and asked sharply, 'What?'

'The physics of the rolling ball on an incline might be the same for a miniature version, I suppose, as for a larger. As in the original Congreve design. I know too little physics.'

'A small weight falls at a speed equal to that of a large one.'

He considered. 'Thank you. I meant only to praise.'

'A friend did it.'

'Please pass on my approbation.' He sighed. 'How brilliant, to construct something of that kind. Changing the shape and use of inanimate objects is akin to creating. You would be reaching across time to touch the mind of others. Almost god-like.'

'Do you do similar, by what you do?'

'Of course not.' He hesitated, in case he had gone too far. 'I have no understanding, which is where we began.'

'Yet you come on trust. Here.' She turned his face by a hand on his cheek so she could see him. 'I could be anyone.'

'You are Berenice. That is enough.'

'Is it? Truly enough for you to come? Oh, I know those guardians you bring with you—'

'They bring me, actually. I do not even know the address. The city is where the Mysterious

Orient begins.'

'See?' She was suddenly shy and shielded her face. 'I'm becoming fond, which will never do.' The moment passed and she felt a rise in confidence. 'I feel willing to confide, which means I must not.'

'That's the spirit.' His lightness made a joke of it.

'Do others?'

'Other ladies are not my concern, Berenice. I am here.'

'Are all the others like you? I don't think they can be, or you'd cost the same. I meant do they observe confidences.'

'I never ask them.'

'Don't you all meet for a chin-wag? Men are supposed to talk about women all the time.'

'The opposite is true, Berenice. There is no meeting place. No other goer has ever told me anything about his ladies, nor ever asked me for any opinion of any I have met.'

'Techniques, then? This is the way for that one, while the other always prefers a different way of making love?'

'No. I should leave, if anyone asked.'

'Other goers must think you up-tight, a recluse even.'

'I would think it impolite to invite confidences. The lady must be protected.'

'Why?'

'Because she is who she is. No explanation is possible, or even necessary.'

'It is an implacable attitude, Bonn.'

'No other is justifiable.'

356

'I had dreams of booking you, and wreaking all manner of savage lusts on you.' She threw her head back and laughed, honestly laughed, the way she had thought herself unable to do. 'Can you imagine?'

'Yes.'

She came to, dabbing her eyes, looking. 'You can? Is it a common dream, then? I mean, do we all think like that?'

'I forget.'

'You won't say.' She nodded wisely. 'I suppose other ... clients think themselves entitled to enjoy some reward, or want to kick over the traces and really go to the dogs. Is everyone like that?'

He was taken aback by her sudden seriousness. This seemed to be the reason he was brought here, for her to bring this up. The incongruity of her abrupt explosion of laughter was startling enough to make him feel they were back at the introduction stage, on her dingy staircase.

'All people harbour doubt. And everyone must wonder at the condition opposite to the life they themselves lead.'

'Like what?'

He let her harshness go unnoticed, and felt her tension. She was almost threatening.

'A lady in a mundane job. I can see such a one wondering how it would be, to go, say, gambling in Las Vegas and risk her all on the throw of dice. It might explain the bank clerk who steals a million and lights out to Spain, or a lady who becomes a street walker.

'Those little people might secretly want to do something desperate. They might be sick of hearing of criminals getting away with murder, perversions, doing unspeakable evil to those who are utterly defenceless, while the lawyers do nothing about it.'

'They may be.'

'It's the age of the criminal, Bonn. Whoever commits crime can escape the law. As in this city, every city. The time of the vigilante must come sooner or later, and people will applaud.'

'Some.'

'Some,' she said flatly, 'but not you?'

'No. I should be sad.'

'Sad for whom? The criminal, if somebody took the law into their own hands?'

'For the victim.' He felt enveloped in sorrow, not quite following what Berenice was saying but acutely aware of her distress.

'Some justice would have been done in her name, at least!' she cried. 'Can't you see that?'

'The victim is often ignored by the law, yes. But by all others too. It is our way. I would give a great deal to know if we were always like that, or if our attitudes were new and only lately invented.'

She looked him over as if he had just walked in, her gaze travelling his length and touching on his face at last.

'What do you want to do?'

'Come.' He rose and stood, hand extended. She placed her hand in his and he raised her. 'There is time, I suppose still. The clock has not struck yet.'

'It doesn't strike.'

He smiled, so slowly she wondered at his stillness. Then she saw his expression ease, and the smile spread so it almost took over his entire features, and she could see the pleasure in him. She wanted to be a part of his pleasure, a trusting element in the shaping and achieving of it in a place she had never been.

'I know,' he said.

She followed him as he led, correcting the direction when he chose the wrong door, and they went into the bedroom. She let him fumble for the light, and then saw he had gone for the bedside lamp instead of the wall switches. He turned, lifted her and gently placed her on the bed, and sat on the edge. He frowned with concentration, eyes on her face searching for agreement as he took off her shoes and undid her belt. She moved her body to help. He began with the buttons on her dress, so serious that she had to smile. A child at his building blocks, first the reds, then blue, then the gaudy yellow. He tried to fold the dress after removing it, doing so badly it was comical. He did not know where to place it, once he had made it a clumsy parcel, and put it on the bedside table beside the lamp.

'Shall I do the rest?'

'If you wish, Berenice.'

His attention did not waver. His frown did not change. He simply watched, even turning his head to see as she undid her brassiere and lifted her arms to escape her petticoat, looking to see where the crackles came from as the nylon frizzed on her skin.

'I want what you do to others, Bonn.' She wanted the covers turned back before he started on his own clothes. He nodded, still examining her hair, her skin and then her hands. 'Exactly.'

359

'Very well.'

'Exactly as if I were one of the ordinary women.'

'Very well, Berenice.'

Hardly the words of a vehement lover, she thought, but then I am Berenice Six-Six-Nine, so who am I to complain at the cloaks of others?

Chapter Fifty-Five

freezo – no-charge sex with a prostitute

The assassin came to. Her very bones felt sore, her skin and buttocks afire. She had cried out for abuse, and it had been so right. What had she said, told, offered? She could barely remember. His teeth marks were already stiffening. She lay prone, her face in the pillow. She wondered if men felt the same exotic willingness to be forced and compelled to beg for sanction.

She gagged momentarily, smiled and turned her face for air. And saw Bonn seated by the bedside, about to stand from putting on his shoes.

'I am reluctant to leave, Berenice.'

'I'm glad. Thank you.'

'I wish you so well.'

'You have to go?'

'Yes.'

'Please be careful out there.' She could hardly move. The bruises were bound to show. Cheap at the price. The price! She almost laughed at the notion of expense, for how could cost matter after what she had had, and learned. Her rib cage hurt where he had crushed her as they loved. Was love a misnomer? She wanted time to work out what she had done.

'Do men need to think this kind of thing through, Bonn?' She almost called him darling, the ultimate incongruity.

'I do not know.'

'You answer like a robot.'

'I am afraid of being misunderstood.'

'Because you misunderstand yourself, perhaps?'

'No.' He stayed serious. 'Truth is already there, in duty.'

'Bonn?' He paused in the act of moving away. 'Did I say too much?'

'A lady has no need to concern herself of that.'

'Confessional? I remember asking that.'

'Hardly, Berenice.' He too did not smile. 'A lady has a right, to trust.'

'Trust can be bought, then?'

'Not quite. It ought to be innate. Relationships are not a collusion, like that writer says.'

'Which writer?'

'You might not know him.' He went to her and pressed his mouth to the marks he had made on her bruised throat, her breasts. 'God bless, Berenice.'

'I wish I were,' she said in a whisper.

'You wish you were...'

'Berenice Six-Six-Nine.'

'With me, you are always she.'

'Can I stay here?'

'As long as you want, of course you can.'

'It was against your wishes, Bonn.' She turned

361

enough to see his questioning expression. 'Hitting me when you came, like I asked.'

'Your wishes became mine, Berenice.'

'And that's what you do always?'

'I cannot say.'

'Thank you.'

'Goodbye, Berenice.'

She slipped into sleep as the door closed. Sound-proofing the stairwell and the rest of the house had cost a fortune, well worth it. She wondered how soon she could afford another episode, perhaps not quite the same or leading to the same climax, with Bonn. Maybe a more innocent tryst this time, with less carnal input? She smiled at the pun – it seemed to be happening oftener and oftener. She must control the tendency to pun, in case that odious Hassall and his repellent team, including that morose incompetent Glaswegian, picked up on any thought linkage.

She needed more money. Seeing Bonn again was essential, to discover what she had blurted out while he performed the abuse she had craved. The odd thing was, she almost feared what he now believed of her, yet had come to no conclusions about him.

Look him up somewhere? The reference libraries in the city were still excellent, but that was likely to change in the coming cut-backs. A problem for later. For now, rest, then the other doctor who had murdered the girl child by cutting off her life support system in ICU. As Dr Elphinstone, so with Dr Clare Burtonall.

She slept, replete.

Devvie and her friend Errol dressed for the occasion. Rack sent someone Devvie had never met before to tell her she was due at one – *one!* – hour's notice at a hotel to talk about promotion. She wailed, 'One fucking *hour?* To get *ready?*' It was left to Errol, great lanky talker, gold teeth like how did he manage to hold his head up with that weight, and enough bling to prove he was the wheeler who mattered in the city. Up and coming Errol. Devvie milked the funds and chipping in only half her strides to Rack's money girl Kay in the Rum Romeo, so was worth as much as the other two girls Errol's pal Wintrobe already had on his big snow-powered milk train.

Life was sweet. Except for this sudden dash on Rack's stupid say-so.

'We gotta go, Devvie hon,' Errol ordered. 'Promotion, right? In the Last Pull, out on the Liverpool stretch.'

'That's a hundred frigging miles!'

'Six.' Errol turned from the mirror. 'Gotta, or Rack'll give promotion to Carlotta.'

'Who the fuck is Carlotta?' Devvie hissed through barred teeth. 'That accountant cow? I'll scratch her eyes out.'

'It's heap biggo,' Errol ruled. 'They make these special arrangements, it's big. Maybe doing accounts for part of the syndicate, know what I'm sayin' here?'

They raced to big it up for the important promotion interview, and hared down the Liverpool Road in Errol's big new red De Lorean copy he'd had made. Custom tooled and noisy, it proved you'd arrived among the loles, make them

363

all stare and shake their heads like they ever do.

Rook, erstwhile sham doctor in the General Infirmary's ICU but now a plain messenger in a threadbare striped suit, took out his false buck teeth and vowed to get his hair tinted back to normality before the day was out. He stood in the rainy night to watch them zoom off to Rack's fake appointment. Rook sighed. Hell of a way to make a living, character work on the spur like this, but Rack paid on the nail – well, thirty days, but never late and no taxes. And Rook just knew that one day there'd come his chance, and he'd make the West End among Theatre Land's glitterati, who ruled the world of stage and celluloid. He knew his acting was good, truly good. His one sorrow was, he could put none of this character work for Rack on his CV. People wouldn't believe him anyway. Rook left the message with Fat George that they were on their way.

Errol and Devvie made the Last Pull Hotel with ten minutes to spare, Devvie swearing she'd kill that Rack once she got promotion. She kept on to Errol, find out who this bitch Carlotta was. If she was some Balkan whore, the like of which Rack was into these days, Devvie vowed to use her newly promoted powers and see that dear Carlotta took the wet walk home. Serve the cow right, competing for a job that was rightly Devvie's, whatever it turned out to be.

They parked and raced in. Some massive convention was going on, suited goons wandering and braying with tags and a registration desk. All of them were computer warriors, talking gibberish like it was the only language the world had.

Quite crazy. Errol asked, shouted, demanded and Devvie did her wail, all to no point because nobody knew what the fuck they were talking about until some tired-looking git, drab in a long gaberdine mac like it was pouring inside as well as out, came and said, 'You wanting the interview room? Seventh floor, back stairs. Go that way.'

They stopped shrieking, and rushed. The man shook his head. The crowd forgot them and carried on boozing and cruising, surrounding the scores of model robots on the ground floor where the convention action was.

Errol went ahead of Devvie, through the swing door and into a service corridor, where metal doors led into busy kitchens and the long branching side-corridors lost their carpets to bare flags. They were conscious of the sudden stillness broken only by the hullabuloos from distant kitchens. A dog-leg caught the end of the corridor where a service lift stood. They buzzed. Its doors opened immediately. They entered, and Errol dabbed seven.

'They better pick you, hon, after this.'

'They will.'

The doors crashed back, and they entered the plush corridor of the main hotel. A maid was sorting linen. She took no notice until they asked for the committee rooms. She told them it was the wrong floor, one down. Six, not seven.

They re-entered the small service lift and touched the control button. The doors slid to. Nothing happened. The maid turned immediately and signalled with a raised hand to Akker at the far end of the corridor. He nodded and checked his watch. He spoke into a cell phone, the waitress waiting patiently, humming a new song she had learned the evening before at the Palais Rocco. She loved Hiplips, and even had a laugh when her boyfriend, whom she partnered at the mogga dancing, mimicked the instructor. He had his shrill abusive voice off pat. They had a real laugh about Hiplips.

Akker clicked his phone away, always the same pocket in his drab gab. Lolaine, the service maid, had done two of these jobs before, but only one with Akker himself, who was like the boss of wet walks they said in the city, if folk ever dared to talk. Lolaine was proud to be picked. It meant money, and she needed plenty to put down on a house in Darwen, where the prices had shot up even for a small two-up two downer with a new loo, built in the 1870s and feebly restored. An arm and a leg, her bloke Commo kept saying, but he was a planner and they wanted children the minute they got wed come November. A winter wedding, but so? Too many superstitions spoiled the broth. Lolaine had this aged auntie who kept on about portents.

Then Akker raised his hand and dropped it, as if chopping. Lolaine stabbed the rod she had been given at the controls of the service lift. The straight metal seemed to flow into the slot and stayed there. A sound began, increasingly a whine going up in pitch. She gave a shiver, counting to the number she had been taught, and listened.

The whole building gave a slight shudder and then there was silence. She stepped away and peered down the corridor to Akker and copied his earlier gesture. All done. He mimed taking out the rod. She obeyed, and placed the metal between two sheets, leaving the trolley there as instructed.

She left by the main staircase, carrying a small stack of pillowcases, really regretting that Akker had ordered she wasn't to take them home. She didn't dare disobey, because of what happened to her friend Joanie the previous year. Only one place to deposit the pillow-cases, in the ground floor linen cupboard. She wondered what would happen to the metal stick.

Akker went down the service stairs and encountered nobody. Best to attend to everything himself, so he came on the sub-basement unseen. The entrance there was from the car park. Nobody was about, shouts and applause sounding on the ground floor where those maniacs who invented robots were hard at it, putting their machines through their paces. He shook his head at the foibles of mankind. What people got up to, honest to God, some nights it was like everybody on earth was a maniac. He tapped a switch on his remote and the small service lift doors parted. They were in a right mess, the two of them smashed beyond recognition from the crash of the falling lift. Devvie's legs were asplay and the bloke's head was almost off, blood smearing the service lift walls. Akker felt utter distaste. The CCTV camera was dislodged from its fixtures. As a precaution, he made sure its fittings were severed. If only folk knew how they might end up, they'd take more care over what they did. Life was complicated enough without death.

He dropped a couple of sach doses of white powder between the girl's legs – nice touch, that, showing where she might have concealed the rest of her drugs – and stuffed two in the top of her stockings. He liked that, too, because a girl who wore stockings still had class. It showed she wasn't all whore. He wore gloves, of course, but remembered to bag them and hold the plastic freezer bag in his hand away from his clothes. He was pleased the CCTV cameras showed no signal when he tested them, and went upstairs to make his way out through the roaring crowd.

If anybody noticed me, he thought, they deserve a frigging medal. He was keen to get back to the city centre. He hated countryside, because there terraced streets began to thin out. The worst bit was the artificial skin he had to spray on his finger-tips, to prevent dabs the police forensics might lift, should they give up enough of their valuable boozing in the police clubs to bother their tiny heads. The false skin felt tight after a couple of hours. A bloke could get truly narked at not being able to feel a damned thing.

He thought of Devvie's luscious thighs, rucked skirt and stockings. He swallowed. It really was time he got back to civilisation, report to Rack and ask for a bit of spare. Except Rack might shell him onto some new bint, and they could prove troublesome if they learned he was a freezo, on the house. No. Best to simply turn up at the working house in Bradshawgate and pay. If they let him fork out for some tart, word would get back to Rack and he'd go into one and want to know why Akker hadn't asked for a girl on the side. Akker then would tell Rack he didn't like to take advantage, which would make Rack glee up and bung him extra. All this was a maybe, but all life was only a complexity of maybes.

His regret was not shagging Devvie beforehand, though it was forbidden. The only tanker who'd ever done that found himself taking the red walk home the following night, serve the silly fucker right, endangering everybody like that. It was self-indulgence, which hadn't ought to be allowed. Akker knew him, Denbo, from his own same school in Burnley. RIP, Denbo.

Rack always knew best, even though the lad was thick as a plank. Akker walked to the main road, only two hundred paces from the hotel, and was collected by a night driver from Walkden on his way home to Lancaster. Neither man spoke. The driver had a plastic shopping bag ready for Akker's rubbish, and a blanket for him to sit on. Lancaster was hell of a way, but Rack always insisted on details and the drivers were extravagantly well paid. The man dropped Akker at the Volunteer where, Akker knew, a whole crowd of pub regulars were in place ready to swear blind that Akker had played darts all evening coming fifth in the darts championship. That was Rack's little joke, for Akker had thrashed the bastard twice the previous week, 501 up, end on double top. Rack had some nerve. Akker wondered how some folk could sleep at night.

Chapter Fifty-Six

swerve – illicit carriage of bonded goods for profit

Arthur and Evadne Burtonall were as unmatched a couple as existed among middle-agers. Parents of Clare's ex-husband, they still kept in touch after the divorce, occasionally inviting themselves round to Clare's for coffee and a chat. That is, Evadne decided she would come, and her benign husband came too. Clare often wondered whether her erstwhile father-in-law hoped to dampen his wife's vehemence. He was given to smiling apologies while Evadne told Clare where she was going wrong, her duties to Clifford.

They arrived in the pouring rain. Clare let them in, finding herself apologising for the weather. She made them a coffee and offered wine – it was gone nine – before Evadne started on the inevitable litany of reproach.

'Have you reconsidered, Clare?'

'Reconsidered what?'

'I think you know very well what.' Evadne had the trick of slitting her mouth. Clare saw it as rolling out the guns for a salvo. Certainly it couldn't be for some revelation, and apology was not in Evadne's vocabulary.

'No, Evadne. What?'

'Clifford.' Mrs Burtonall tasted the coffee and

laid it aside. Not improved, then, Clare thought. 'Has it occurred to you that he might be willing to consider reconciliation? These things happen, Clare.'

'No, it hasn't. In fact, I'm surprised you bring it up.'

'Surprised?' Evadne cooed sweetly. 'Should it not be your duty when wrongly separated?'

'Maybe, if separation was wrong and not inevitable.'

'Inevitable to whom, dear?'

Dear, that poisonous epithet, was never far away when certain minds met. Clare wondered how other women got on with their mothers-in-law, extant or simply ex.

'To me, Evadne. And just as irrevocable now. Did Clifford suggest you come?'

'I wish to bring you both to your senses.'

'Implying I'm deranged?'

'The faults were certainly not Clifford's, Clare!'

'Look,' Arthur said reasonably. 'Maybe we've all got off on the wrong, foot. Why don't we think how not to make matters worse?'

'Arthur! It has to be said.'

'Why?' her husband asked calmly. He would have winked at Clare but he was in Evadne's firing line and would get hell all the way home.

'Somebody has to! And you wouldn't say a word, if it was left to you!'

Arthur sighed and went to the window to check the weather, one of his gambits. He looked out. 'Still raining. That person's gone. Drowned rat by now.'

'Person? What person?'

371

'Somebody was looking at the addresses on the door. They left sharpish. Maybe some thief. Junkies are everywhere these days.'

'Did you get a good look at him?'

'No. Maybe he thought we were police.'

'Young or old?'

'He wasn't old.'

Clare thought of Bonn, until Evadne offered, 'I thought it might be a woman visitor.'

'All the more reason to be worried,' Arthur said. Worries about disorder was another constant.

'Except, she might have buzzed.'

Evadne returned to her purpose. 'Clifford would reconsider, Clare, if you would bother to meet him halfway.'

'Clifford was a crook. I shall never trust him. I'd never agree to a reconciliation, Evadne. Tell him that.'

'I see.'

'We needn't have talked of this at all,' Arthur said. 'Least said soonest mended.'

'Least said, and people get away with never doing what's right.' Evadne went thin-lipped. 'It's time you considered what stage your life *is*. Make a new start with Clifford and simply see how you get along, Clare.'

'We are getting along very well, thank you, Evadne – apart.' She wondered how much Arthur knew.

'So any kind of reconciliation is out of the question, then.'

'Of course.'

'Have you not even thought of perhaps meeting him, for a meal as friends, try a holiday together?

Think of the serial killer out there. And your ridiculous wish to become a martyr, serving the city's tramps and ... and street people. Think at least of your own safety!'

'What brought this on, Evadne?' Clare asked, suddenly curious. 'Is Clifford in difficulties again?'

'I resent the implication!'

'Resent all you like. He proved to me that he's a vile criminal, and a dangerous man to do business with, let alone marry. No, thank you.'

She thought of the person snooping outside. A million innocent explanations, of course, so no need to worry. She was safe in the flat. And the two students on the floor above were in, because she could hear the music centre thumping. The girl on the ground floor, another student, was always practising her speeches. Clare would not be alone, even after Arthur and Evadne left.

'Clare. I think there will come a time in your life when you will regret having said that.'

'I doubt it.' She tried to sound definite and quite sad, failed on the second count but remained steadfast on the first. 'Assure Clifford that he must live his life without me to defend him as I did once before.'

'Very well.'

They left after a few minutes, Arthur grimacing apologetically from the door. Clare went to the window and looked to see them go. She couldn't resist looking up and down the street. Pity it wasn't quite as well lit as it ought to be, when the nights were drawing in and the rain falling. She saw the car pull away, and drew the curtains to shut the evening out.

Chapter Fifty-Seven

mumper – one who sleeps without shelter

The Senior Liaison Officer was in a paddy. He called his five senior subs to Central, and when somebody demurred ('Pressure of work') pulled down enough seniority to set them all moaning. Except Hassall, who was glad to be roped in because he heard things on the grapevine, literally when he was almost three sheets to the wind and making the Volunteer's regulars shut up after he'd blundered in earlier.

'The question is linkage,' Argent intoned. He sounded like the clapper of a sonorous bell trying to chime deeper, and only succeeded in seeming querulous. His stature, thin and cadaverous, worked against him. He ought to have had the dimensions of a rugby player or Italian tenor, and instead looked like a Praying Mantis. 'How many? We know of the Skip Mincer, a perv. Then another perv in Newcastle-on-Tyne, discharged from here.'

'The two at the Last Pull?'

'Devorah Maine was a lass who moved here about five weeks since. Worked as a streeter in the city centre but we can't get a fix.'

'Her bloke Errol Worrelson was done here, two years back, pimping and cannabis possession.'

'Got off with a caution.'

Same legal counsel, Hassall thought, Mrs Horsfall, but he made no offer. And Devorah could abbreviate, street walker style, to Devvie, sort of thing the stringers did.

'The Don't Kill The Innocent pickets will be out today,' Argent boomed even deeper. 'They took umbrage about the dead girl and the Intensive Care Unit who did the deed. The Ethics Committee chairman will do a talk-over on the six o'clock *Looking North* cut-in after the main TV news. Six twenty-eight, it comes on.'

'And the doctor?'

'Gram,' Argent snapped, and handed over.

'Like a fucking classroom,' some CID shodder muttered, earning a reprimanding glare from the SLO. They gave attention to the Scot, who brought a massive file to the desk and slammed it, his chin corrugated in a grimace.

'Dr Terence H Elphinstone, murder of,' Grahame said, eyes ranging the faces.

'Police officers for the consideration of.'

The same grumbler got a titter. They had all been bored witless by the Customs and Excise classifications used at Hendon.

'Best of order!' Argent called.

'The doctor was killed by shots at close range from a customised weapon, possibly even home-made. The ballistics boys will let us know soonest.'

A quiet mutter, 'Easter?'

Argent stood glaring, and perched on the desk to keep his eye on the group.

'The incident occurred minutes after Dr Elphinstone was visited for the purposes of interrogation

375

by three police officers, all here present. He was unable to offer much information and the interview was terminated after fifteen minutes.'

'Can we have a transcript, please?'

'They are available in the door stack. Take one as you leave.' Grahame cleared his throat. 'The perpetrator arrived soon afterwards, using our recent visit as a possible means of urging entry as,' with grave portent, 'a pretence that the previous visitors had sent documents for Dr Elphinstone's perusal.'

The group gave a theatrical murmur of suppressed amazement as if this'd never occurred to any of them. Hassall stirred, sickened by the childishness. Jokers all. Grahame looked his suspicions. Argent raised a warning finger to cut the malarkey.

'This is important,' he said. A woman officer at the back started to get the giggles and pretended a fit of coughing.

'CCTV was defunct when the alarm was raised. The tapes were dismantled and part of the camera missing. It viewed the doorway. It failed to.'

The gasp of horror was more audible this time. Hassall shuffled his feet in embarrassment, wanting out. This whole session could have been done with a handout.

Grahame unrolled a display drop. The officers mimed exaggerated interest, openly nudging each other and giving murmurs of pretended awe at the lines and arrows. The SOCO didn't know if they were taking the mickey. Argent, who did know, was red-faced.

'The above is the sequence of events in chronological sequence.'

'A sequence is a sequence,' the officer next to

376

the choking policewoman said gravely, causing her to convulse.

'A sequence in chronological order too!' his neighbour said. 'Phewee!'

Hassall rose, tapping his wrist to the SLO, who knew he had a health difficulty. He'd had enough. He went through to the Observation Display room, inevitably nicknamed 'Odeon', making sure he collected the handouts as he left. He caught the technician still winding up the previous showing, and asked could he see the pictures again.

'It's my eyes, Con,' he lied. 'I'm having difficulty. Bloody doctors gave me these sodding drops. I could hardly see a bloody thing in there.'

'You want any run through?'

'If it's not too much trouble. I could do it myself if you're pushed.'

'Not likely.' Con made light of Hassall's request. No technician was willing for others to fumble with his stuff. 'I'd never get anything straight again, Hasso. Sit you down. Five minutes.'

Hassall waited patiently. The room darkened. He saw the doctors' mess car park, the outline of the residence building against the sky glow. Grahame, himself, and DS Bateson, were admitted by a vaguely-seen Dr Elphinstone. The CCTV remnant showed nothing for a while, then its real evidence made a jerky disappearance in milky fuzz, the only sound a strong hissing.

'Con?' Hassall called, turning. 'Can you get anything before it vanishes?'

'Been over and over it, not a soss.' The technician began rewinding. 'Anything else?'

'Can you blow up them stills?'

377

'The Infirmary, that ICU ward? Hang on.'

Hassall could remember them all. In fact, he'd had copies struck and had brought them in this morning.

'A different screen. Turn a bit right, OK?'

Hassall obeyed, and a white screen crashed down. The corridor leapt into view, the phoney doctor, the youngish man walking beside him, both only imperfectly seen. Profiles were never satisfactory. A downward view from, say, a ceiling mount would have been much better, the way security people always recommended.

'Too much white light from every angle, see?'

'Aye. Seen any of these before, Con?'

'No. Except in that doctor's own scan.'

'Scan?'

'CCTV outside the Infirmary. Car park. Maybe that was the same geezer, dunno.'

'Can you show me?'

'Back to the old one?' The technician was getting fed up.

'You're brilliant, Con.'

'Yeh, yeh. You should have been in earlier. I ran them all then.'

'Bad night last night. I tried, though.'

The CCTV from the hospital showed, fluorescent and greenish, everything blurred. Hassall had to ask Con to run it at normal speed instead of galloping through the frames.

'Slow it, eh? Just a few frames, Con.'

The technician got it down to acting pace. Hassall deliberated, called for it a second time.

'That's not the only entrance, is it?' he asked.

'No. Four. Two CCTVs broken, vandalism.

One got nicked the week before.'

'And them coming out?'

'Nothing. The back one was lifted, the side one broken, somebody smashing them for a lark. If only they knew what real damage they did when they played about being hooligans.'

'Maybe they do.'

'Deliberate?'

'Mebbe.' He rose and thanked the technician for his efforts. 'Here, Con. One thing. Why did you call it the doctor's scan?'

'I think one of them's the quack. Big old Humber SuperSnipe, rottenest colour on the island, innit? Purple. Trust a bird, eh?'

'Where?' Only Dr Clare drove an old maroon-purple Humber. He had not seen her in the CCTV footage. 'She isn't in it, is she?'

'Yeh. You look.' Grumbling away at the time, Con got the room dark and started up the same run. In the darkness, the same young bloke came walking across the car park towards the hospital entrance. He did not seek the shadows, except for one sudden instant when someone emerged from the front entrance.

'Again, Con, please?'

'She doesn't notice him, see?'

'Got it.' Hassall was tired or he would have spotted the slight change earlier.

Coming to a distance of, what, forty paces of the Infirmary doorway, the young bloke abruptly altered direction. *He turned away.* In fact, Hassall thought, his entire persona altered. He suddenly shambled instead of walking. He slouched with a stoop, his whole manner seeming that of an indigent moving with little hope among the parked cars, as vagrants looked for vehicles with the keys still in the ignition.

The woman – definitely Dr Clare – walked unseeing among the cars to the bottom left of the picture.

'We got views of the car park, Con?'

'You mean for identification? No. I reckon you could ask that doctor. Maybe she noticed something, eh?'

'Maybe.' He saw the footage to the end. The stranger moved in that new idle fashion round the edge of the car park then smoothly resumed his normal gait *when Dr Clare had gone.* He knew Dr Clare and she him. The entrance was not within the camera range, and the other CCTVs had been damaged beyond repair.

'Ta, Con. Do you do the externals?'

'If you mean Raglan Road, no. Helen Tate does those. Won't be in until five.'

'Can you let her know I'm interested?'

'Good luck with Helen,' Con said.

'What's that mean?' Hassall blinked as the lights shot on. He had to hold a hand to protect his vision. Con was grinning.

'Barbary lass is Helen, at extra work.'

'Aren't we all!'

He was sure he'd seen the young bloke before somewhere. Not sure where, but the entire north of the country was like a village, in a way of speaking. Find one person out for definite, you had the coat-tails of the others. Haul a little, taking care how you did it, and soon you'd have a whole bunch, with any luck.

Chapter Fifty-Eight

UB – Uniformed Branch (police), also Useless Bastards

It took time to set up, but Heghorn engineered it well, for a sprog. Two uniformed beat officers – gold dust, with Hassall having to moan through eleven phone calls, begging like a supplicant with a broken bowl – and three interviews where the UBs enjoyed themselves being smug at the CID's expense. 'Uniform bastards paying off scores I'd never even heard of,' Hassall told Heghorn once they got going. 'They'll crow they've solved the ozone layer if it comes off.'

'It shouldn't be, Mr Hassall,' Heghorn said as they waited.

'It's called life,' Hassall told him. 'I'll be in London Road Main Line, that station caff where the beer's kept cold for visiting Yanks.'

'That barmaid,' Heghorn tutted, which surprised Hassall because he didn't think the newcomer had it in him. Grahame had got wind of the pull, of course, and came roaring in. Jesus, but he was a sulky sod, Hassall thought, as the morose Glaswegian glowered demanding what was going on. Hassall said he'd welcome him at the interview.

'If it comes off.'

Hassall wondered if Grahame had been a bully

at school, or only when he reached adulthood where he could exercise the chest-jabbing technique he seemed to have perfected. Bullypath, maybe.

'I'll call you in exactly two hours and...' Hassall consulted his watch, still awaiting repair from a time he'd keeled over in the bathroom and his missus called a duty GP. It had been his first warning his health was not quite tickety-boo. He couldn't be bothered to mend his watch. '...and forty-six minutes. Did Drewett find you?'

Drewett was up for Deputy Assistant to the commissioner, who was visiting the three city precincts.

'No. Where? When?'

'Dunno.' Hassall made his cell phone bleep by leaning on it slightly. No call, of course, but it allowed him to get shut of the aggressive bore. Grahame dithered, then left. Hassall immediately put the cell phone away until it was urgently needed in the same fashion, and followed DS Heghorn to the car compound. He had no intention of co-opting the bullypath in the arrest of Skally, or they'd be there until the planet ran out.

Skally was hard to find, but Heghorn pinned the louse-ridden mumper to a corner 'buildings' littered with derelict cars and rotting mattresses among puddles and cinders. A buildings was the local term for a vacant lot where once terraced houses had stood, now cleared and left derelict as the city councils lost interest in corrupt neighbourhoods. The accompanying uniformed ploddites acted their part somewhat over-enthusiastically, but that was in order. Hassall waited in his motor round the corner until Skally was hauled into the police car. Hassall went across and talked through the car window.

'Good day, Skal. OK are we?'

'Morning, Mr Hassall.' Skally had the most mournful face you could wish to clap eyes on. He was tattered, grubby, stinking to high heaven. The UB lads hated mumpers, swearing they could actually see fleas leaping. His beard straggled, his ears were matted. The lads said they saw greenfly in his matted ears. His shoes dribbled watery stains that nobody was willing to investigate. He was one long unravelling cardigan.

'Can I get him out, Mr Hassall?' the police driver complained. How the hell the uniformed branch made a grouse out of a simple request was a miracle to Hassall. Words were OK, if you let them get on with being just ordinary, but the UBs invariably managed to inflex any syllable with complaint, approval, hatred, misery, anything to get an edge. It got on his nerves.

Hassall ignored the whimper. 'Skally, what were you up to three nights back?'

'Nothing, Mr Hassall. Just doing my thing.'

'Nobody in this city is ever just doing his thing, Skal. Not the lord mayor, not the city council and especially,' he added, wanting Grahame to learn how aggressive he too could be because he was recording this little chat on a Sony digital in his waistcoat, 'not you, you idle git.'

'*What*, Mr Hassall?' Skally asked in alarm, eyes woeful because Hassall never came on belligerent. Hassall was usually good with informers.

'I'm losing patience, Skal.' He tapped his

383

pocket where the digital showed, and winked. 'I'm not just acting, understand?'

Skally's brow cleared. 'Yes, Mr Hassall. I never did nowt, honest.'

'Three nights since, Skal. Really think this time. Were you hanging around the doctors' mess up at the Infirmary?'

'No, sir.'

'Not sir, if you please, Skal. You're not in the army now.'

Skally had been a hero in some foreign brawl where snow and landmines coincided. He had been a brilliant innovator, and invented a new way of excavating booby traps in ammunition dumps. Nobody had worked out what made him turn to scavenging garbage. He earned some decoration after desperate warfare in some desert, and always watched the Poppy Day parades from a pub window. He never marched, and saved up drinking money so the pubs wouldn't throw him out during the Cenotaph service. Hassall twice had stumped up for the vagrant so he could get drunk during the Armistice Parade, in tribute to Skally's dead pals.

'Can I get him out, Mr Hassall?'

'Leave your vehicle,' Hassall ordered the driver, who testily went, pointedly leaving his door ajar. 'Stand away some distance.'

That would set Grahame's ulcers a-popping, the implication there was no observer to the interview. Hassall smiled at the thought, then told himself off for being as theatrical as that load of police clag in the nick talk room this morning.

'These stills, Skal. Take your time.'

The mumper took the glossies and flicked through them. Hassall knew he recognised the subject instantly.

'That's Bonn, Mr Hassall. I don't know her.'

'Bonn?' Hassall had heard the name.

'Bonn. He's key goer, so I heard. Women pay him a fortune to get shagged, see? It's like his proper job.'

Hassall wondered whether to take Skally in and do this down at the nick, but it always meant too much palaver. 'That goer scam?'

'That's it. I honestly don't see him around. Doesn't shop down the malls. Not trendy. The girls love him.'

'Well, they would, a job like that, eh?'

'No, Mr Hassall. The street lasses, them stringers. They walk round him. They wanted somebody topped for that kid. They begged Bonn, but he never does owt like that. The docs pulled her plug. It were in the papers.'

'Where's he live?' Hassall slowly shook his head as he spoke. Skally got the meaning and looked at the policeman's digital.

'I don't know, Mr Hassall.'

'You sure of that?' More false aggro for the stand-in SOCO to admire. God, but bullypaths were boring fuckers. Hassall played the scene out by inventing something that would show he was on the ball and give Skally enough to pretend to his mumper mates that he was questioned for being innocent again, the sort of swinish thing the police were continual at, for fascist reasons.

Hassall considered. 'Now, Skal.' This was the real cloaky bit, so Grahame would think Hassall

385

was into major terrorism wonder-work. 'Heard anything about some ammunition floating around the city? Your background and all. I'm told you can smell ammo at a league-and-half.'

'Yeh. Thought you'd come round to it,' Skal astonished Hassall by saying, corrugated teeth in a grin. Hassall saw his mouth was ulcerated, the lips having lately bled. He was worried on two counts. One, his invented question was meant only as flannel, and now here came loose bangers, and Skally the ex-army explosives man wouldn't get ammunition wrong. Two, Hassall didn't want to lose his most valuable grasser from some sickness, Skally looking on his last legs. 'Somebody's bought two shells. Yank, see? Things they used in the Gulf. They set them off with a couple of wires and a mobile phone in them Middle East places.'

'Is that right.' Hassall tried to sound convincing. What to say now? 'Thought as much. Where'd it change hands?'

'Not yet. And some marksman stuff's doing the rounds.'

'Heard about that,' Hassall said, wanting to shut the mumper up. Now, he was worried sick about everything. Skally's lips were bleeding badly, blood on his chin. 'You poorly, Skal? You look bad.'

'I'm not, Mr Hassall.' Skally had the vagrant's continual fear of illness.

'Go to the doctor's.'

'They won't take you if you've no address. You've got to have an address to get seen, and you can't get an address if you're a dosser, see?'

'Go to Dr Burtonall down Raglan Street. She sees no-homers. Just walk in. Say I sent you.'

'You sure, Mr Hassall? I keep getting slung from the Infirmary. It's the law.'

'The law's wrong, Skal. You know that.'

'What if the quack slings me out?'

'She won't. Make sure you go. I'll check and ask.'

'Right, Mr Hassall. Can you give me a lift there?'

'Leave off, Skal.' Hassall took his photographs. Heghorn was waiting at the edge of the buildings.

'That him, Mr Hassall?'

'Make sure he gets down the city, Raglan Street. And give him this gelt.' He passed Heghorn a note. 'He's sick. Tell him to eat.'

'Right.' Heghorn waved the driver back into the car after passing the vagrant the money and talking a little while. A UB swore and complained. Skally shuffled off between the UBs. 'Where to, Mr Hassall?'

'You did all right there,' Hassall said. He didn't like praising anybody. 'City. I need to check on a lame lass.'

He wondered whether he could get away with trying his digital recorder when he visited Martina's. No, too chancy.

Hassall guessed he was the only one in the city's division who knew how restricted the police resources were. This was an instance. In two hours, he had the methods and site of the Pleases Agency, Inc., and was more or less coming to terms with the notion of wealthy women getting themselves seen to. Their business, after all. Blokes did it with the stringers, so why not women with whoever? He pulled a few past incidents, failing to find any Bonn, no faces, no descriptions. It was a system operating on word-of-mouth publicity, though it was in the phone book plain as day.

He gave it much thought, until he felt time making a sly exit on him, then acted.

The Granadee Film and Television Studios at the south-east corner of Victoria Square occupied most of what was old Greygate. Hassall knew Grellie's Green stringers' beat ran from Quaker Street to the west and as far north of the square up to the Vallance Carvery beyond Bridal Street. 'God knows how they make pictures here,' he told Heghorn, 'what with the traffic noise. I mean, it's London and The South, isn't it?' He nodded to the exit signs saying just that, pantechnicons and HGVs roaring their way through from the Liverpool motorway.

'It needs a by-pass, Mr Hassall.'

'Don't we all.' That made Heghorn glance at his superior. It sounded unlike a quip.

They walked in and Heghorn did the necessary ID.

'He's at the read-in,' the girl receptionist said. She smiled at Heghorn, who smiled back. She ignored Hassall, who was beginning to dislike these youngsters more and more. 'They can't interrupt that. It goes on to six o'clock.'

'Get him out, please. A serious traffic violation.'

'He doesn't have a car.'

'He tell you that, did he?' Heghorn didn't include Hassall in the conversation. He sighed. 'Look, Sally.' Her name was on the desk. 'I've got to report or...' he checked his notebook '...Jeremy Hughston will have to come down to the station.'

'Well, if it's serious.' The girl crossed to a phone

388

to make a discreet call. She looked back at Heghorn. 'What name did you say, please?'

'Jeremy Hughston will know me,' Heghorn said with confidence. 'Just tell him it's the usual.'

'Has he had a car accident?' the girl asked, wide-eyed, cupping the receiver.

'Privileged information, Sally.'

Hassall thought Heghorn was doing well so went through to wait among advertisements. They were for TV episodes which Granadee prayed would enable it to keep the franchise instead of greedy Midland combines claiming it. Eventually a worried actor came hurrying in. Hassall rose without a word and passed him, ostensibly on the way to the toilet then casually going downstairs into the underground car park. Cameras followed him, as everywhere in the city these days.

He waited inside the final doorway. The actor and Heghorn came down in the lift.

'That girl. Still with you, Jem?'

'Hello, Mr Hassall.' Hughston was nervous, eyes everywhere. Heghorn went to speak to the uniformed security man in the entrance booth at the bank of CCTV monitors.

'Get her to me soonest. What's her name?'

They both knew Hassall hadn't forgotten her. She did voices for soap operas, no fewer than three TV networks.

'Seffa. She's working here the day after tomorrow. Will that do?'

'No, Jem. Now. Get her here smartish.'

'But she's in Leeds. Voice-overs take for ever, Mr Hassall.'

'Get her.'

'Now?'

Hassall raised his eyebrows. Jem brought out his cell phone.

That evening, Bonn was booked by a Ensilla One-Seven-Three, Miss Charity arranging it. Credit cards were perfectly acceptable. The time was nine o'clock, somewhat later than usual, but Ensilla was particularly pressed for time, being a busy banking executive from Leeds, about to fly to Rome later. She was able to give three references. Suite 418 was arranged at the Amadar Royale.

Twenty minutes to nine, Rack left the Volunteer. He had Average along because he felt uneasy about Ensilla One-Seven Three. Twice he'd had Miss Charity run the call through for him. There was something odd, but he couldn't quite finger it and told Tickle to be on stand-by just in case. He imagined he might have heard the lady's voice before, and made sure he was ahead of Bonn to dip-and-run the Amadar hotel. It was in the kitchens, making his way through, that he encountered DS Heghorn, who called Hassall.

They spoke by the one unused serving bar beyond sight of the hectic kitchen staff.

'Look,' Hassall said to Rack without preamble. 'I think you know me.' He saw Rack reach for a cell phone. 'No briefs, lad. Nothing's going to happen. You're not going to be charged. I want ten minutes with Bonn.'

'That bint,' Rack said, knowing now.

'Aye, lad. That bint. She'll be up there soon. I've two plainers along, see she gets there in one piece. No names, no pack drill, OK?'

Rack felt around the edges of his mind for tricks. It felt sane. 'OK.'

Hassall eyed the youth, wondering what the hell the lad thought he was up to dressed like a Yank rugby player in padded shoulders surmounted by the cockerel helmet of a Victorian peeler, a string of medals on his chest with gauntlet gloves and cowboy boots. His arms were bare, and huge magabaga beads were tied about his calves, clacking like massive castanets as he walked. Young people were beyond him. He thought of retirement.

'How d'you want it played? Get Bonn down here for a quick chat, or me go up to the fourth floor?'

'He won't get took?'

'No. Promise.'

Rack nodded, because he'd be the one who made certain Bonn didn't get took in. 'You follow me in the next lift. You want your bint to stay?'

'No. I'll owf her when I come.'

'Then what?'

'I think your bloke might have witnessed somebody I want and am going to get.'

'When?'

'Infirmary that night.'

Rack thought, and was surprised. 'OK. No record?'

'That is correct.'

Rack looked at Hassall a long moment, nodded and left. Hassall heard the lift crash, gave him five minutes then followed alone.

In Suite 401, Bonn was standing by the window when Hassall knocked and entered. Ensilla One-

391

Seven-Three turned out to be quite a plain woman of thirty or so. Hassall had only seen her once before, when she had been thickly made up, in doss-house clothes and alighting from some motorbike side-car on a police job. He could not help staring. People were different from their voices. He'd imagined some femme fatale, and here was somebody homely, destined to look after a family hurrying in for their teas. She was dumpy and smiling. Hassall said hello.

'Ta, Ensilla. You can go.'

'Thank you.' She looked uncertainly at Bonn, who went with her to the door and held it while she left.

'Goodbye, Bonn. I'm so sorry about this. It wasn't my idea.'

He closed the door on her. 'Mr Hassall.'

'How do, son.' Hassall sat heavily. 'This was the only way I could see you without breaking heads all over the city. OK, is it?'

'If my ... acquaintance thinks so, yes.'

'You're all so bleeding young,' Hassall marvelled. 'That daft lad out there. He knows twice as much as the United Nations, to hear him. And you, trusting him, to yak here with some copper. Its well weird.'

Bonn dwelt on the question. Hassall gave up waiting. 'The night you went to visit the sick girl in the General Infirmary.'

'I remember. You consider me a possible witness.'

'You were camera'd going in. That's the last record, except for still photographs in the corridor with that phoney doctor. You were identified.'

392

'I recall the instance.'

Recall? Instance? Hassall blinked. 'You went to say so-long, eh?'

'No. To give her a blessing. Extreme Unction.'

'A what?' He thought. 'Some sort of...?'

'Sacrament. She was about to die, everyone said. The media were agog. Religious groups petitioned the courts, even parliament.'

'Who's this everybody who wanted you to go blessing the lass?'

'I am not at liberty to say.'

Hassall eyed the young bloke who had resumed his position by the window, looking out into the dark city. Some signalling device, was it? To show watching eyes he was still in 401? He wouldn't put it past that mad yob in the kitchen, who seemed to be the main organiser, to record every syllable. Hassall got the idea this Bonn would stick to whatever he thought proper. No sweating news out of him, whatever Hassall might try. He gave up that tack.

'I accept that you went to bless her, then scarpered. My question is, did you see anybody in the car park? It looked like you noticed somebody leaving the main entrance, those steps, y'know? You ducked aside, for a short delay. It was a doctor, we think. Did you see anybody else?'

'I noticed no one else.'

But he'd paused, so he must know Dr Burton-all. How, though? Was he her patient, maybe?

'And anybody in the ICU?'

'Only the nurse at the desk, whom I would not be able to recognise now. And the doctor who admitted me.'

'OK. Watch this.'

Hassall undid a flapped pocket and brought out a video. He slipped it into the TV compo and searched for the controls. Bonn made no move to help.

Hassall clicked it on and after cursing the controls managed to show the grainy recording of a CCTV.

'Only a much-edited chunk was shown on the news. We kept back most of it. This is it in its entirety. Say if you can recognise anyone in it, OK? I'll repeat it as many times as you like.'

Bonn came round to stand by the couch, Hassall peering at the screen from the armchair.

'It's outside the disco where the perv was killed. The one who got off from having hurt that girl. Those two bouncer blokes, we've cleared. They're known to the Newcastle police. This load of girls is going to the disco – see them? The three lads are still at school, all trying to look twice as old so they can get into the disco.'

'I follow.'

'Now this woman comes down. See her? She hesitates, then decides to cross over like she's a bit scared of the disco. A lady alone, it's wise to avoid trouble, right?'

'Certainly.'

'She passes close to the victim. She seems almost about to ask for a light for a cigarette. Now watch.'

The victim made a small jerking movement, brushed at something near his thigh, looked hard at the woman passing him, and moved on.

'See that?'

'He was stung,' Bonn said. 'He would have

394

called out to the lady, but she was respectable and the guardians by the illuminated doorway would have assumed he was accosting her and taken action accordingly.'

Guardians by the *illuminated* doorway? Christ. Hassall glanced appraisingly at Bonn, who was concentrating on the screen.

'He starts to stumble a bit. See him? He seems to go giddy. Less than two minutes, he wobbles like he was drunk. He stops, looks round like he's heard somebody say something. We've checked, but no speech is on the tape.'

'As if the lady touched him with something malevolent. A needle or a knife. She had opportunity, and proximity.'

That's it, Hassall thought. The perv was looking for the woman who'd stung him with 'something malevolent'.

'You ever see her before?'

'I cannot tell from this.'

'You must know many women.'

'I would not be at liberty to tell.'

'You didn't see her in the Infirmary that night?'

'No.'

'You see, son, she might have somehow approached Dr Elphinstone after we'd called on him the night he was killed.'

'I follow. I did not notice anyone of her description at the Infirmary when I went there.'

'Anything else you can tell me?'

Bonn took his time, then, 'No. I cannot.'

'The thing is, Bonn, this killer is a serial. She'll do it again. And again. She's judge, jury, hangman. It won't do.'

'I follow.'

'She's done it before, we think maybe twice or more.'

'I follow.'

'And I needn't say that–'

'Threats are unnecessary, Mr Hassall. I understand your concern.'

'Could you tell me a little of your background? Parents? Origin?'

Bonn looked directly at him, and with sadness.

'No. I shall leave now. Goodnight.'

'Hang on, son. Just a couple of things more.'

Bonn opened the door, went past Heghorn who was standing in the corridor, and walked away. He caught the lift to the ground floor. Hassall thought, was that sheer fucking insolence, or simple resolve?

Chapter Fifty-Nine

tinny – purveyor of illicit weapons

Late that evening, Rack came round to 13, Bradshawgate North. The Victorian terraced house was much larger that it appeared from the street, and the activities in Numbers 11, 15 and 17, given over to working houses were incredible. The staff, over thirty fulltime working girls who served the clientele, worked continually. Lauren was the money girl, but the suprema who ran the houses was Melissa, a shrew of a housewife from Fleetwood who had learned commerce coping with old fisher folk there. She could be sweet, and always was to Martina. She adored Posser, who occasionally slipped in for coffee and a sundowner. Nobody dared tell Martina of such sins, sick old Posser getting his two tots with Indian tonic and ice, against stern Dr Winnwick's strictest orders.

The chief stander wanted to get this over with. He had waited until Martina and Posser would, he guessed, have had their evening meal. They would have been primed by Bonn, who had gone over Hassall's questions as soon as he and Rack met up in the Volunteer. Hassall and the rest of his neff crew had gone from the central district.

Posser and Martina had two homes, Number 13, and a similar terraced house for private gatherings to do with business – lawyers, would-be buy-outs, investors full of dazzlingly bright ideas for cutting their way into the city's sins, and petitioners who wanted franchises in the syndicate's domain. The second dwelling was more façade than actual home. It was almost sterile, and Bonn never stayed there. His place in 13 was a room on the top floor, practically a garret, sparsely decorated and hardly furnished.

Rack entered and stood sheepish and dejected, before Posser saw him at last with a start.

'Heavens, Rack. You startled me, coming in like that. Help yourself.'

'Feels everything's a dog's breakfast.'

'My fault.' Bonn brought his own armchair a little squarer so they all faced inward. Rack took the couch facing the fire, and Posser was in his usual chair opposite Bonn. Martina sat, legs folded, on the carpet near her father. The two housekeepers, neither of whom lived in except when Posser was having a bad time, had excelled themselves tonight, leaving out a selection of small dishes on two butler trays within reach. 'I have already explained.'

'Look. It's nobody's fault.' Posser puffed on his atomiser to get going. 'It's just that times change. The plod are desperate. Look at the news. They're on the rack. This domino is going down the list, and everybody's out to get the plod. Isn't there somebody getting out next month?'

'Yeh,' Rack said, brightening. 'In the Smoke. Some perv for that French girl, the one on the train, and some kiddie in a park.'

'There you go,' Posser wheezed, starting a coughing fit that Bonn tried to end by banging his back.

'What now, though?' Martina asked Rack directly once they were settled. 'With this Hassall onto us.'

'We always knew he was,' Posser managed to say, leaning back while Bonn wiped the old man's damp forehead.

'You knew him before, Dad?'

'Aye. He's a duckegg, but something of a buffer between us and them. He picks bones, scours, listens. Never got higher, though.'

'What is he nagging us for, then, Posser?' Rack tried to sound cool because you had to respect Posser, who'd started the whole syndicate after thinking up the Pleases Agency in the first place. Also, he wouldn't last long. Rack knew he had to be tactful so he said, 'You won't last long, the way you sound, Posser.'

Martina turned her blues on Rack, who wondered if she was narked because she wanted him not to be so twinkle-toes about Posser being poorly and that.

'Mr Hassall was doubtless worried about public opinion.'

'There's been questions on the news, politicians and newscasters on the go.'

That finished Posser for the whilst. Martina moved her gaze from Rack at last, who wanted to ask Bonn what the fuck he'd done wrong, but Bonn cleared his throat to show he was going to say something if people didn't mind too much.

'He came prepared.'

'Tell us again, Bonn.'

Martina's use of Bonn's name was like something forced from her, Rack saw. He couldn't help thinking they must just nosh their teas in silence, never a fucking word, when all the time Martina was crazy about Bonn and Bonn badly needing his own tart to use and knock about a bit when fancy took. He decided to tell the stupid pair they should get shagging each other like sane folk, even if it was just for Posser's sake, who was soon going to croak. You could see that, with half an eye. His own theory was that too much brain did your fucking life in. Bonn was too brainy for his own good, and hell of a sight too fucking thinkish for Martina's. Trouble was, she was clever, for a tart, and that made matters twice as bad. Where was the sense in two clever people, a prick and a cunt, under the same roof and not having it away on the fucking stairs? Even Grellie's stringers could see it, and they had the brains of a wart, not a think among the lot, except for some.

'Mr Hassall sees this as the malice of one serial killer who will murder again.'

Bonn slowly reiterated the conversation with Hassall. He did not even falter when he came to the CCTV footage of the murder of Grobbon, went straight on with a simple description. Only Martina picked up on something in his manner.

'The question is,' Martina said, 'what has it got to do with us? You have outdone yourself, Bonn, responding to what a few scatterbrained bimbos wanted you to do, that mumbo-jumbo over the dying girl. That's undoubtedly what landed us in this quandary with Hassall. Are we involved any other way?'

'No,' Posser wheezed. Bonn dabbed Posser's forehead. The old man looked ashen, his breathing clamorous.

'Except for that quack, boss.' Rack explained, 'We pay her, right? For the homeless and the tarts, routine checks an on-demand stuff, like you fixed, right?'

Dr Clare's remuneration was fee-for-service without retainer, virtually freelance.

'So?'

'So she's nearly pay-roll. Hassall'll pick up on that. The sod's a sieve. He'll sniff round her, mebbe guess she's one of Bonn's uppers, regular.'

'Indeed.'

'Yet so are many other women,' Posser managed to say. His lips were bluish. Martina signalled that it should be ended and Posser got to bed. She nodded when Rack moved to go.

'Come back tomorrow, Rack.'

'OK, boss. Thing is.' He halted, drawing an imaginary six-shooter on some rival gunman, 'I reckon we find this serio and blam whoever it is. See my plan?' He became expansive. 'Then it all vanishes like snow off a duck.'

'Good idea, Rack,' Martina said for quickness, wanting him out. 'Do nothing yet.'

'Right, boss.' He darted from side to side down the hallway shooting his fingers as he went into the darkness of the street.

With Bonn's help, Martina got Posser undressed and into bed. His tablets, his one half-ounce of permitted red wine on Dr Winnwick's instructions, then she switched on his baby-alarm and they returned to the living-room.

'I shall stay downstairs reading, Martina.'

She seated herself, aware of his short-comings, his inability to think he too had rights. God, if killers and perverts had rights in gaol, a free man with any resolve at all should be able to assert himself instead of blathering like a teenage schoolgirl at her first dance. Yet she had lain under him and been filled with gladness, the few times they had made love. She dared not consider the hopes she might harbour within, for herself and for Bonn. It would be too damaging. Her dad had expectations for her and Bonn. He said as much, been enthusiastic at Bonn's willingness to come and live with them when Bonn's old spartan room, Mrs Corrigan's cramped terraced house in Waterloo Street, was sold. Posser of course had bought that terraced house through a nominee, but kept that fact to himself.

401

Bonn had a book. Martina said nothing as he opened it and started to read by firelight. He would be her choice. She could command him, the way she knew he was sometimes commanded by uppers who hired him. Only one month since, she had given instructions to Miss Merry, head of the Pleases Agency booking ladies, to double Bonn's fees. Not a single upper had demurred. They just paid up. Was it simple innocence, or perhaps a knowledge of evil, that attracted them? He must have studied both in that wretched seminary. She blamed all religions.

'The doctor, Bonn.' This was the crux.

'Dr Burtonall, Clare Three-Nine-Five.' He had been ready, slowly closed his book.

'Yes. How is she connected?'

'I am uncertain of details, Martina. I suspect she has Mr Hassall as a patient. She also acts for us, our street girls, the goers, and vagrants, any of whom might have said something inadvertently, or perhaps confirmed some clue Dr Burtonall suspected.'

'Does she talk about these things to Hassall?'

'I doubt it. She has strong convictions on confidentiality.'

'So strong and unshakeable,' Martina said in an ugly voice, 'that she swam into our ken because she protected her husband Clifford from complicity in murder by falsely providing him with an alibi. He, remember, made a fortune from city developments.'

'She divorced him,' Bonn gently reminded.

'And became rich from marital division of the spoils. Women give their all in love, do they not –

until they find it profitable to sacrifice account-ability!'

'I wonder if there is some other connection, Martina.'

'Besides Dr Clare?' She waited a long while before asking outright, quietly, 'Is there, Bonn?'

He made as if to shrug but prevented himself. She wondered if he thought a shrug would become an unspoken lie, on his ridiculous scale of morality that so often trapped him.

They were seated across from each other beside the fire, bookends, adversaries.

'I am unsure.'

'But you harbour suspicions?'

'I do.'

It felt like pulling teeth. She felt as sad as he seemed. Sorrows was a word made for him, but sorrows at what? Lately, Bonn was paid through the Ball Boys Disco counter, on the nail every tenth day, an absolute fortune by any measure. She herself oversaw his investments, and Mr Doveo of her city firm of accountants made sure there was no come-back from the Inland Revenue, all above board. Everything a man could want. Baffled, she yet marvelled at his capacity for being troubled. If somehow she could dig deep into his mind, would she find conclusions to reach and believe? She doubted it. And his mystic adoration of women surely must have some foundation in grief from early childhood ... correct, or not? Nowadays, you explained any emotion by trite psychoanalysis, whether in sitcoms or serious novels, documentaries or high-brow films. They were nothing but dross, and their statements silly to the point of embarrassment.

'What are they?'

'I am in doubt, Martina.'

Then he did a strange thing, unprecedented. He rose and crossed to sit himself beside her on the chaise. She looked her surprise. What did he want of her?

'I might have stumbled on the perpetrator, Martina. Or one in the perpetrator's circle of acquaintances.'

'Who is it?'

'That is my difficulty.' He stayed looking at the fire. She wanted some artist to happen by, perhaps start sketching quickly so as not to miss the contours of his features, stencilled as they were from the firelight. Not handsome, 'average everything' as a key called Zen once told her. Early days, back then, when Bonn had merely seemed an unexplained newcomer. Now, an enigma.

'You mean what to do?'

'Yes.'

'Is it one of mine?'

Mine, not Posser's any longer, signifying she only deferred to her father as a token of respect.

'One of yours.' He paused. 'One of mine.'

This was it now, Martina told herself, down to the end play. 'A client, one of our uppers?' She was shocked. 'A woman bribed the serio?

'No, Martina. The question is this: is one of our clients the serio.'

'She did it herself?'

'I cannot say.'

'Why are we talking round her, if it is she?' Martina rose and walked a pace, not making the

404

sideways movement to disguise her limp. 'Bonn. Think of Posser.'

'Posser.' He was startled.

'And me. And, heaven's sake, Rack, the girls, your other uppers, the keys. We've had a killing before. The keys and goers are vulnerable. You remember.'

'Yes.' A key had been stabbed, killed in the street within reach of a city hotel. Retribution had followed, and serious blood flowed on Martina's orders.

'We are all vulnerable to a serial killer. Who is successful, Bonn, don't forget. How many more will she do?' She was still unable to grasp the idea, talk of a woman serio as if she fitted every known pattern.

'Of us, you mean.'

'Exactly.' She saw his wounds open, his mind a display. 'Posser would be the easy one. The girls in the house next. Has she ever visited Number 11? 15? Used any of the street stringers, if she's that way inclined?'

'I know none of this, Martina.'

'You avoid knowing, Bonn.' Martina returned and sat beside him. She took his hand. 'It's hard. Why else would you risk everything to bless – whatever, anoint – that child? You could have been arrested by the security. They might have put you on trial for being the damned killer yourself. The plod are stupid – and desperate – enough. All for some idiotic reserve.'

'The girls–'

'Leave the girls out of this! You could have prayed for her in a church, for God's sake! The

405

girls could have organised some service instead. It was stupid.'

She calmed and gave him time. He stared into the fire, open hand to protect his eyes from the heat. It was exactly as Posser sat reading when he read by firelight as the nights drew in and the embers glowed red. She thought, do all men do the same? A woman would simply move aside from the fire, switch on a reading lamp. They were like children.

'Have you not thought, Bonn, of the true consequences?'

He looked, almost surprised she was there. 'Consequences.'

'Your hospital visit was safe thanks only to Rack.' And myself, she thought in anger.

'Rack was very efficient.'

'And?' Her eyes filled.

'And what?' He almost winced, waiting on her answer.

'Consider, Bonn. The ripples from your visit might have spread to the serio. They might have...' She stopped. His expression cleared and he understood.

'You mean Dr Elphinstone.'

'Yes.' She embraced him, tears down her cheeks. 'I don't know. It might have started her thinking she had to move on the doctors.'

'The doctors.'

'You see, darling,' she said, speaking without any sense of incongruity, 'I think the Right-To-Living lobby, and the Life-At-Any-Price people, is camouflage for her. She executes perverts who escape the law. She uses the religious movements

406

to cloak her activities, laying the blame on them. It's a possibility.'

'So it is,' he said dully.

'And it disperses police efforts. They are confused, so many people, sects ranting about perverts and laws and religion and moral duties they don't know a thing. Hence Hassall's guesswork.'

'So Dr Elphinstone dies. And the perverts die. And...'

'And Dr Burtonall will surely die. She was the counter-signatrix, remember. I have seen the papers.'

He raised his head and stared at her. 'You saw them.'

'I took no special pains, merely got Miss Wilberan – you know her, recruits aides for our legal flannel – to pass herself off as a Right-To-Living notary. She photographed the medico-legal documents. Bonn. If I could do that in an hour, how easy would it be for somebody more dedicated, less scrupulous, than Miss Wilberan?'

'I see.'

'Keep silent, darling, you put many in jeopardy. Me, Posser. If she *is* one of your uppers, then she will have Rack, and the other standers he takes along – who is it currently, Tickle? Prole? Kazak?'

'Among some, yes.'

'And, darling,' she said gently, weeping inside for him, 'we are in the telephone book.'

'Yes, there is that.'

'Hassall will be knocking on our door soon.'

He thought a long while, his head now slumped on her shoulder, her arm on his neck. 'I require a say in the ... in the outcome, Martina.'

She spoke with pity. 'No deals can be done, Bonn, not at this juncture. Not with anyone – you, Posser, Rack, the girls, the casinos, not even me.' It would be immoral, she could have added if she had been so inclined to that degree of risky extravagance.

'I have always tried evasion. How disreputable I am.'

'Think so, if you like. The choice is black or white. If you want, Bonn, give up the week's block in which she might be, then Rack can get Akker in and Hollow and Gerbil and Warman.'

Bonn wondered at the names. He recognised none, only Akker. Did she have so many evildoers on strength? Four killers, for one?

'They decide, then.'

'If necessary, Bonn.'

'I'm so tired. Promise you will do nothing until I am certain.'

'Of course. Promise.'

He took a long while, then, 'I think maybe Berenice Six-SixNine is...'

She held him, her face chilling with tears. 'Come to bed, darling. Sleep with me tonight.'

'Very well.'

'Very well,' she said, trying to mock his dull tone in an attempt at lightness of heart, and failing. 'Go on up. I'll make us a hot drink. Read for a while.'

'Yes, Martina.'

He went alone. Martina went into the kitchen, and started the kettle. As soon as she heard an upstairs door go, she reached for her cell phone and spoke briefly.

Chapter Sixty

slider – a cat burglar

Fat George, newspaper vendor at the corner of Bolgate Street near Askey's Triple Racer, listened to Askey's couriers Dort, Fazz, Gitter and Zers argue about who'd done most needles. This was their topic. Fat George was ready when Rack came swinging by. Rack was the world's greatest ballroom dancer right at that minute. On the way over he'd been Maradona, world's greatest footballer, and a World War I air ace.

'Wotcher, Rack.'

'See that twist, George?' Rack spun again, grinning.

'Aye, great.' Fat George thought Rack a loon, but Rack was the syndicate's boss stander, so there you go.

'Want a place sussed, George.' Rack waited while some civilian bought a paper and left groaning at the football results, like any of them mattered. People always amazed Rack. 'A slider.'

'Without trace? Use Gommer. He's about.'

'Is he drinking?'

'Not for months.' Fat George added by way of explanation, 'His dad's got a job selling picture books.'

'Oh, right.' Rack stared. 'What the fuck's that to do with a suss job?'

'Eh?' George served two girls with the *Evening News*. 'Gommer reckons it's posh.'

Rack was still mystified, but hadn't time. 'Get him, half an hour. Gotter be dark.'

It was early morning. Rack went to Askey, with his calf-lick, bulbous forehead, titch frame and heavy specs. The newsagent was relieved to see Rack come waltzing in.

'Rack, tell them what's what.'

The four bikers started yakking. To needle meant going illegally down a one-way street and not getting nicked. Fazz and Gitter were almost brawling.

'Is it any time, Rack?' Fazz demanded. 'A needle counts whenever. Finish.'

'No!' Gitter yelled. He already had a black eye. 'It doesn't count if you're not on a legit courier run. Right, Rack?'

'Yeh.' Rack thought them stupid. They lived to sprint around the city, spent the day bragging how fast they'd done this or that journey. 'That's right,' he said, to shut them up.

'See?' Gitter shouted. 'I'm right! So I'm in the lead.'

They ran a weekly championship, who did most needles. The prize was a pint of the Volunteer's lukewarm lees. Rack leant on the counter, Askey eyeing him uneasily as the couriers returned to bragging on the steps. They were still arguing.

'Three places, Askey,' Rack told him. 'Slider.'

'Gommer's good, Rack.'

'Is he sober?'

'Aye. Got religion, though, because his dad's in a bookshop now.'

More fucking mystery. 'Good enough to get me in?'

'Best slider yet,' Askey said doubtfully. 'Do as he says, though. Oh, can you tell Bonn ta for that trolley chair for my sister?'

'Right.' Askey's sister's legs no longer worked. Rack's theory was, you got bad legs from bad shampoo. Bonn sent things to help her move about. Rack reckoned he knew twice as much as doctors and Bonn. He wouldn't pass the message because it sounded poncified. 'One's a school. After hours.'

'That's not common, Rack.'

Rack was pleased. 'A first, eh, Ask?'

Ten minutes later Gommer came astride a courier's bike, and was flung onto the pavement, puffing as if he'd done the pedalling. He was a sad bloke, his face littered by acne among other scars.

'Ball Boys, Gom. Ready for off in half an hour.'

'Right, Rack.' The slider looked at Askey's clock and said after Rack had gone, dribbling an imaginary ball down the street and back to being Maradona, 'Why didn't he send word to be in the Ball Boys?'

'You might have been sloshed, Gommer.'

'The Word of the Lord runs in my veins, Askey.' Gommer made the Sign of the Cross and closed his eyes devoutly.

'Aye,' Askey said. 'Pray away, son. Three sliders is a lot on one night.'

'Let us pray,' Gommer said.

'Aye, right.' Askey went to answer the phone and shouted through the hatch, 'Next lad. Get St

411

Alban here to the Ball Boys Disco now-now.'

The school emptied in a massive rush. Rack explained to Gommer what was needed and left him to it. It was always the best when you trusted your slider.

Akker was up, with Vimto who'd done time for being a tinny, meaning a seller and provider of weapons. Rack had fixed a couple of strawmen, to alibi himself at a cake shop a mile or so down the road. The strawmen were good, reliable women – strawmen were always birds, being more willing and sticking to their pre-scripted perjury however the plod wheedled or threatened. Rack's strawmen knew their job. They were not to smoke, had somebody to look after their children at no notice, and loved the pin money. Any time, any distance. Rack normally had a habit of using the waiting time for a bit of frolic with one, but not now. Tonight was blood, the ultimate mogga dance.

The two strawers watched a drossy re-run while Rack sat with an imaginary bow and arrow at the window, behind curtains for the Seventh Cavalry to ride into the trap.

'Women always feel fat, see? You do your teeth wrong.'

'That so?' one, Varla from Wolverhampton, said, hardly listening because until Rack used the voice you needn't bother. She had thought Rack would have bonked one of them tonight, but he seemed wound up in whatever they were sup-posed not to be doing.

'I'm too fat,' Andreena commented, eyes on the television. 'I hate this presenter. She got her nose

412

broke once. It riles me. Whyn't she have it done?'

'The BBC'd pay for it,' Varla said. 'They have surgeons.'

'I hate her. She's mad after that footballer on *Sports Quiz Night.*'

Still no cavalry, Rack thought, and just listen to the silly cows. Not a brain in their heads. He had three cell phones and two signallers out there. More than a war, for Christ's sake. Still, it would end tonight. If only Mama knew, she'd be lighting candles all over St David's, stupid mare hooked on her religion. She still believed he was a computer buff for ICI, his cover tale.

That made him think of Gommer. Gommer had actually come to Rack eight months back, fresh from a drying unit after being a wino a whole year. He actually showed Rack certificates, spread them onto the table at the Shot Pot, not knowing Rack couldn't read. Rack was impressed. The parchment was well scrolly. Gommer was a special man back from the Balkans once that war was done with. Rack had asked him straight out, 'Were you in the Kate?' and had to explain, 'Kate Karney, army,' because Gommer was thick, being local and so didn't talk proper. And learned yes, those were army certificates.

Rack took him on, pay on the day. He never took doers on pay-or-play because that would cost the syndicate a fortune. They had to stay fit and ready, like now.

Twenty past seven, Rack got the whistle and went without a word, taking two of the cell phones. He left the third for the straw lasses.

Varla said, 'I thought he'd have wanted to do a

bit with one of us, Andreena.'

'I think it's a bad time for him, Varl.'

They watched telly.

People were trickling into the school, all lighted windows.

'School in the day, becomes a night school at night, see?'

'Right.'

'She's a teacher like you said. Which you want? Her classroom does French seven-thirty till nine. The place shuts at quarter-to-ten.'

'Where else does she teach?'

'Some workshop.'

'Is it used at night?'

'Nar.' Gommer grinned. 'Safety rules. They're tacked up everywhere, no using machinery. Law won't let night schools, see? Only kids in the daytime. It's near the school-yard, bike sheds stuck on. Which yer want?'

'Workshop first. Been in?'

'Nar. You said not.'

Rack was satisfied, proving he'd outwitted the slider by his brilliance, checking Gommer had strictly obeyed. If Gommer had gone blundering in everywhere, he'd have known Fat George and Askey told him wrong, and he'd've had to blame the fucking lot, Gommer included. His magic mind had proved him right all along. Being right was down to him, being wrong was the fault of others, and they deserved getting done over. He felt good about tonight. It was all coming right.

They went into the main entrance, bold as brass, checked some timetable of classes as late-comers dashed in past them, then went through to the school-yard. Rack let Gommer go first. That was how they met the night-school caretaker.

'Hello, lads.' The old man was the best sort, Rack could tell instantly, which was just as well because he was truly narked Gommer had let him in for this, a fucking witness. The old man carried a bucket and mop. 'Lost, are we?'

'Trying to get out the back way,' Rack told him. 'I didn't realise my old teacher was teaching. Thought they'd be different.'

'Pity. I'm Harry Entwistle. Just do a bit of looking-after.' He looked sad. 'I know how you feel. I'd still be scared if Sister Hyacinth turned up here. Taught me at St Elphige's when I was eight. Who was it?'

'Mr Joachim,' Gommer said quick, surprising Rack because he thought nobody knew he couldn't read and anyhow Gommer never talked first.

'Maths, eh? Not many takers.' The old man said confidentially, 'If they get fewer than six, they have to close the subject down. He's already on six. Won't you reconsider?'

'Can't face it,' Gommer said. Rack stared at him thinking, Christ, Gommer got fucking clever of a sudden.

'This way.' The caretaker took them to the top of some stone steps and pointed. 'Through there. The back gate can be unclicked but shuts heavy. Make sure you pull it to, against vandals. We get all sorts round here.'

'Thanks, mister.'

They went. The school-yard was empty, the

415

street lights over the wall showing. They walked casually, slowly, by the wall, keeping in the shadow, talking rhubarb-soda-water-bubble-rhubarb the way movie extras did. One saying that over and over sounded stupid, two like a mob, words indistinguishable.

'Here,' Gommer said, and they halted. Nobody about still. 'It's a workshop. That old bloke helps your lass to make toy trains and such here. And kids make toy engines.'

'Get us in.'

'Push the door.'

Rack went inside, Gommer holding Rack's waist like skaters, step by step, the way of sliders who'd to take along some duff git on a job in the dark.

'Lights, are there?'

'None we can use. Here.' A slit torch, the flashlight low and constant, shone its sliver of light round the workshop. A midget model of trains and sidings, a station half-built, with trees made from sponge and little lead figures waiting for dinky trains, the panorama of miniature spectacle was laid out on a long bench. Unfinished.

'See them little lathes?' Gommer sounded full of admiration. 'I could do wonders with them. Cost the fucking earth.'

'What's that box say?' No need to conceal his ignorance now.

'Some exhibition society, model railways. Next month.'

'What's she do, then? Just makes little engines?'

'Looks like it. It's labelled, Stockton-on-Tees. The steam engine's LNER. It's an old railway.'

'Anything we'd need to know?'

416

'Doesn't look like it. Unless,' Gommer added, worrying he'd taken a risk in speaking too bluntly, 'you think so.'

'Have one last shufti, then we scarper.'

He waited for the slider to go round, poking and lifting and peering. Even though he stood a mere few paces away in the confined space, he couldn't hear Gommer's movements. That was class. Rack felt proud of having chosen right.

They left through the gate as directed by Mr Entwistle, and were picked up by Vidgey in his grocery van at the corner of Wimpole Street. He dropped them a mile away from the mark's house. They walked the rest.

The house was a disappointment, and Rack said so. 'I thought teachers lived better than this. Has it a garden?'

'Neat, with a shed.'

'She in?'

'She's staking that quack out. I tellt you.'

'So you did,' said Rack, replete with cunning because he'd tricked Gommer a second time into revealing he was no longer an alky. Rack felt really impressed with his own genius. He was dying to tell Bonn about all this cleverness, and then Bonn would really admire him.

They went round to the back alley, and climbed over the pathetic wooden fence into the garden. The shed stood far from the house, with a side door almost touching the fence.

'Easy for somebody to slip out, eh?' Gommer whispered. Rack hissed disapproval, the usual way to say shut up when doing a slider job. Gommer touched Rack's arm and a shed door opened,

417

making the gloom intensify in a rectangle ahead of them. Gommer assumed the skater's grip, and together they shuffled silently into the shed's interior. Gommer did his torchlight. Rack thought, Is this *it?* Jesus. It was an ordinary shed, for Christ's sake. Plant pots, a few trays of soil, nothing to speak of. Gommer touched his elbow, releasing him, and he saw.

A flap came down from a wall. Still nothing more than simple planking, an elementary shed after all, cheapest possible construction. It certainly wasn't worth all the effort. Except for a tray that Gommer silently lowered from the left-hand wall. It was a complete workshop in miniature. The small lathes, the tool racks, the strips of metal, even batteries ready for action.

Gommer tapped Rack three times, the slider's silent question to ask what now. Rack tapped him twice in answer, go on, do whatever you think. Gommer showed what bothered him: cylindrical tubes, the bulbous sphere in a recess, the connection with a small electrical box-shaped black thing. Gommer did his three taps, then a double. Rack slid his hand on the slider's arm, the signal to go. Gommer switched off, and Rack turned. He waited until Gommer gripped him, and they skated in slow silence from the shed.

They left over the fence, and walked to where Vidgey was stocking up his grocery van from another vehicle.

'My brother's,' he told them. 'Brings cheapo from Somerset. Give us a hand, lads?'

'On your bike, Vidgey.'

He obeyed immediately, and they were driven

418

back to the city centre in grand style.

'See, Rack,' Gommer explained as they went to the Ball Boys Disco for a drink and alibis, 'she's got a shed that looks fuck all but can make anything.'

'And them tubes and that copper ball?'

'See the midget air-pump? It pumps the copper sphere up. Fix it to them tubes, load them with the little balls I showed you – they're lead, cast in them moulds, make them by melting lead piping, do it on a candle if you're stuck – and you've a ready-made gun. Silent except for a pop. We used real ones in the Balkans. I made five for night work. Our lads were great. Yanks hate them.'

'Can they shoot?'

'Yeh. She's a clever bitch. That sphere's just a trial prototype. She made several other ones that lie flat instead of round. See the black ones?'

'Er, no.'

Gommer was disappointed, but didn't say so because Rack could get well narked. This sort of thing proved Rack was thick, brains of a brick.

'Well, there were five flatties. Load them with a lead ball, you could shoot somebody and nobody'd hear unless they were a couple of steps off. Get it?'

'Yeh. Work for arrows as well, would it?'

'Course it would.' Gommer was thrilled he'd seen it with his own eyes. 'Reckon I could really go for a bird with them brains, Rack.' He spoke wistfully. 'Imagine that – talking about miniature engineering all fucking night, then a beer and bed, eh? Paradise.'

Rack thought Gommer mental. Gommer

419

thought Rack dim as a Toc H lamp. The watcher across the road fixed his bicycle's dynamo at last and cycled to the railway station. He made one call there. When he emerged, his bike had been stolen. He didn't even falter.

Chapter Sixty-One

duff-duff – conclusion (fr. drum sound signi-fying conclusion of a soap serial)

Clare Three-Nine-Five was early for once. The children's survey for inherited Garrod-type Enzyme-Deficiency Diseases was going badly. Part of her research finance had been withdrawn – in the words of Admin, 'the furtherance advant-ages of subvention-sharing become extendable, enabling extra-hospital participation', meaning Clare's funds were cut. That meant a quarter of the GPs in the city would complain to her, first thing tomorrow morning, asking why was it always northern cities, places with the worst infant mor-tality and morbidity, got penalised. The incom-petent Admin staff promised to hold a meeting with Dr Agnes Ferram, Clare's special friend, who would fight a losing battle all along and still lose. Tomorrow, in short, would be hell. Agnes would start smoking again in the Ladies (Staff Only) and set the fire alarms off and she wouldn't care a tinker's. The children's survey would be doomed. Admin would be pleased, because then they would have all that funding free to use for new office carpets, central heating, and computer systems they didn't know much about.

She booked Bonn and asked for a suite on the fourth floor of the Amadar Royale, where she and Bonn had met so many times before.

Nine o'clock, she arrived. The stander was taken aback, but evaporated as Clare came from the lift and reached Suite 419. All was well. She entered, stood a moment, and surveyed the place. Freesias – exactly as the first time she had booked Bonn. She smiled at the memory. He had been so mild, so accepting, and had not demurred when she left without a single sexual innuendo. Was there such a thing as platonic love? Now, she thought not.

Coffee and tea were laid. The place was lovely. Once a bank in the old Victorian days when the city's cotton manufactures clothed the world, the Amadar Royale had been cleverly re-done. It functioned well, exactly as the Café Phrynne, place for lone ladies to encounter the Pleases Agency goers and keys. She smiled at her slick use of street language. It had taken time. Only when she realised, thanks to Bonn's innocent reasoning, Clifford's evil, did she throw over her loyalty to her husband. That led to the divorce, and her freedom. And the eternal reproaches of Evadne Burtonall.

Bonn entered. 'Freesias, Clare. I associate them with you.'

'Thank you for remembering.'

'Favourites.' He took her hand, gingerly. 'I was amazed at the colours in the seminary. Fuchsias. Of course, they are not an indigenous flower.'

'We have colours in ours.'

421

'Of course. Their stridency does not match extraneous ones.'

'No.' She eyed him. 'What's wrong, darling?'

He sat, looking with his usual intensity at – into? – her features. He seemed to have abandoned his usual offer to bring her a drink, ask after her well-being. She still wondered how much of his speech was drilled, the ritual prepared for him as a script provides words for an actor to say. From time to time she was convinced he responded as he truly was, prepared texts kept only for other clients. Hateful word. Now, the belief weakened a little.

'What is it, Bonn? Has something happened?'

'You hinted you were being followed.'

'Yes. I'd almost forgotten I told you of Arthur's mention of a street lurker at the door. I was a little concerned.' She told him of the students in the building. 'I'm quite safe, as far as anyone is these days.'

'Suspicion only, then.'

'Well, yes.'

'Nothing at the Infirmary.'

'No. Why?'

'The murder of Dr Elphinstone. The lobbies picketing the hospitals. The disturbances, the poor girl.'

'The Ethics Committee made the decision to withdraw life support systems. Nowadays it's not the doctors' option. It wasn't just me and Terry.'

'No, Clare, yet they killed him. Have you got a security unit?'

A *direct* question, from this theologian? 'Personally, or the hospital?'

'Either. Both.'

422

'Neither, not really. There are security people on the door and the gates, and one in the car park.'

'So nothing.'

'Well, not that I know.'

'I think it's time you took precautions, Clare.'

She moved and sat beside him. Tonight he seemed unreal. This wasn't romance, in fact she wasn't even certain it was anything to do with love.

'Have you heard anything? Should I tell the police?'

'They will do nothing except leave you more vulnerable.'

'What, then?' She was becoming alarmed. 'I've never seen you like this, darling. Have you found something out?'

'I would tell you if I had.' He weighed matters for a while, then went on, 'Clare. I think the serio – the killer – will make further attempts. I hope people will take...'

'Matters into their own hands, Bonn?'

He winced. 'I was trying not to say that, Clare.' A thought, then finished, 'Will prevent it. I don't know if they can.'

'What should I do?'

'I can have somebody go with you.'

'I came alone.'

He shook his head. 'No, Clare. Someone was not far away, making sure you got here safely. I can see you reach home safely. After that, you are as vulnerable as your friend Dr Elphinstone.'

'Are we safe here?' She glanced involuntarily at the windows.

'Yes. While we are together.'

'This seems absurd.'

423

'Dr Terry would have said the same. And the pervert Ricky Grobbon, who died so strangely in Newcastle under night-and-day police protection. Remember Tennock, the mumper who found the hand of a murdered pervert from the Midlands. The deceased was a known paedophile.'

'There are more.'

'At least two. This serio does not stop.'

'You know who it is, Bonn,' she said dully.

'I worry for you. For others.'

'For that Martina, too, in your syndicate?'

'Yes,' he said honestly. 'And her father, who is sick.'

'Among others.' It seemed a mortal cruelty that she was merely one of many, even in this.

'Yes, Clare.'

'I want you to marry me, Bonn. You said once you might be willing.'

'I would be.' Then, 'I should continue the trade in which I am engaged.'

'Why?'

'It is a revelation.' His gaze fixed on distance, perhaps to a vision he once had and continually recaptured when forced to explain belief. 'I had no notion of its existence. Now, I know love can be as real as breath. It is in everyone, exactly where it is supposed to be. Religious teaching is not too far out, Clare. It is simply not understood by those who teach it, because none of them practises it. They give it lip service. We out here are left to learn the love present in life.'

'You *forgive* the perverts who torture children?'

'They fail to see.'

'Should you not go to the police, if you suspect,

what did you call him, the serio?'

'She,' he said quietly. 'She.'

Clare drew back the better to appraise him. 'Female? The killer is a female?'

'I am uncertain. Others are trying to make sure.'

'And will they then tell the police?'

'I do not know.'

'Bonn.' She took his hand. 'What if I walked out of here and told the police this? That you knew the killer, that your friends were trying to track him – her – down?'

'You would not be able to, Clare.'

She cried harshly, 'Don't try that I'm-sad-so-leave-me-alone trick, Bonn. I won't let you. What's to stop me telling the police now? Using the phone?'

'Try if you must, Clare.'

She looked at the door, round the suite, her handbag with her cell phone. 'Is there nothing we can do?'

'Yes. Leave the street folk to do their best to protect their own.'

'And me? Am I one of their own?'

'So far, Clare, yes.'

She sank back on the couch. 'I feel exhausted.'

'Come and lie with me, Clare.' He added when she looked, 'Please. It would mean a great deal.'

She had never heard him ask before. The demand before now came from her, leading or inviting the union that followed. Her mind was in a turmoil. 'After what you told me, that your street friends are hunting for some serial killer? You'll just hope they'll find her before she kills again?

425

Kills you? Me? Your director Martina?'

'Yes. Please.' He stood, and extended his hand.

She rose too and shook her head. 'I can't, Bonn. I can't. It would be condoning wrong. What if the killer gets away, just because you won't tell the police?'

'The police have not found the serio, Clare, because they cannot.'

'It's your duty, Bonn. Mine. Tell them, and they can do their job.'

'No, Clare.'

'You want me to sleep with you while they – your friends – get on with hunting the killer, instead of phoning Mr Hassall? Is that it?'

'Almost. Perhaps. I do not know.'

'No, Bonn. I won't.'

She left him then, standing there with his hand still outstretched to the vacated couch. She glanced back and almost hesitated, but continued out into the corridor. She'd be safe at least until she reached the police station. Bonn had said so, and she trusted him. Hurrying, she thought, is this jealousy, that he includes everyone he knows into his circle who must be protected, Martina, that stander crew who guard him, the prostitutes? It was intolerable. She was unsure, and was on her guard as she reached the foyer, said a smiling goodnight to the receptionist, and asked for someone to accompany her down to the car park because she was nervous on account of the dark nights.

The uniformed foyer attendant complied, and waved her off in her maroon SuperSnipe as she drove out.

Chapter Sixty-Two

cackle – deception by words alone

Bonn caught the morning bus, Number 8 from Central Gardens. He wanted to visit the grave of Father Crossley. He carried no flowers.

'Morning, Bonn.' The assassin seated herself next to him, smiling. She looked remarkably fresh, even younger than before. 'You remember me. Berenice.'

'Good morning.'

'Going to see friends?'

He did not reply for a moment. 'A grave.'

'I thought I saw you last evening. The Amadar?'

'Reasons baffle me, always did. I am no nearer, for all my wondering what they actually are.' Apart from two children with their mother on the back seat, they were the only passengers. Berenice must have learned where he lived. He was not concerned.

'Why visit a grave at all, you mean, that kind of thing?'

'How, rather. A pilgrimage to express regret, perhaps an apology for successes missed. Hard to tell.'

'Or to gloat.'

An odd interpretation of a sentiment, he thought, if sentiment it was.

'There always seems to be better things one can

427

do with one's time, Berenice, until one is actually there at the cemetery. Then comes guilt, that one is really somewhat bored, standing in a churchyard looking at a stone.'

'Think how you might feel if you were responsible, Bonn.'

'St John's, Farnworth,' he explained. 'Near the Manchester Road end. A priest, my tutor at a seminary school.' Her knowing hardly would matter now. Concealment would be purposeless.

'I thought you...' She'd been about to say *you people,* meaning you hired cicisbeos, you Jeremy Jessamys, you hired fucks. 'I thought you never discussed your personal circumstances.'

'I do not.'

'May I come with you, Bonn?'

'I like privacy, Berenice.'

'That woman you see is a doctor, isn't she?'

'I do not recall, Berenice.'

'Dr Clare Burtonall, who drives a massive old maroon Humber. Ugh!'

'I cannot say.'

'You mean you won't.' She was smiling a hard smile. He was reminded of the three-colour paintings of De Lempicka, those connecting greys and opaque whites done with ochre over thinned grey. They would make one shiver, if one were concerned by these things.

'Cannot.'

The bus wound its way. He liked the Number 12 more, though the old 8 was more direct. Was that a reason?

'I want to make an offer, Bonn.' He looked round at this, making sure those children were

428

not in earshot. They were playing a game of I Spy, squealing and arguing who had seen what first. Their mother was having a hard time spelling so as to convince. 'I want to see you personally in future.'

'I do not follow.'

'Surely you must have been asked this before? I am not personally wealthy. Two gentlemen friends, both military, fund my activities, a kind of interest, a hobby. I accept it for no other motive than philanthropy. It has legal overtones, and I think you would have to be guided as to how they relate to modern life. I could tell you more about me, if you would consent.'

'I do not follow, Berenice.'

'I want us to become, what do they say, an item.' She gave a soft laugh as if by way of a disclaimer. 'I should see you did not lose by the arrangement. It could go as far, or stay as close to your chest, as you like, and I would go along.'

'Yes, I have been asked before.'

'What, marriage?' Immediately intrigued, she made an elegant gesture to help her question along. 'Allow yourself to be bought, in sole employment? A kept man for a lady's plaything?'

'Ladies using me for the first time respond differently.' He spoke looking out of the window as if at an abstraction. 'One might be baffled, finding herself unable to grasp what she actually wants. Another might see herself as abused. Or find herself so empowered by the gigantic achievement of going out and behaving as she always imagined a man does – paying a prostitute for sexual congress – that she can't quite come to terms with it.

Others can be overwhelmed by guilt or shame. Or become what the trade – I mean other goers – call a flitter, and move like a night moth from one, to another, to a third and a fourth, deliriously carouselling around all the goers in the Agency. As if she becomes a marathon runner, striving to outdo other runners for ever and ever, or has leapt on some mad sexual merry-go-round.'

'And I?'

'You live to a different beat, Berenice, and have yet to explain: To yourself, as much as to me. Of course, you never need explain at all, not to either of us, or indeed to anyone.'

'Think, Bonn. You have a remarkable position. You have the gift, the stigma of sorrow. I don't know you enough to say what the sorrows are, but they must be the things making us females seek you out. If I, with all my talents – I'll tell you what they are when you agree to come in with me – can achieve what I have achieved, just think what we could achieve together.'

'I am not poor, Berenice.'

'You mean you can't be bribed?'

'I suppose not, though money has no bearing.'

'Would you agree to consider, though, if I could get my backers to agree to my taking on a partner?'

'I can't say.' He had almost filled up at the thought of betrayal, and brought it into the open. 'Think what betrayal might incur, Berenice. Supposing your, what did you say, interest or hobby, involved robbing banks, or some scam that was wholly reprehensible. Or think of, say, some activity that might damage people's lives. I might find it necessary to betray you. Betrayal is the modern idiom, Berenice. You cannot be too careful. In fact, you might ask yourself if you would be willing to accept a special friendship on those terms. You know nothing of my likes, dislikes, my inabilities to cope.'

'I should be willing to try.' She was curious. The bus was now stopping regularly, people getting on and off, short journeys. They went through a street market that for some reason gave Bonn a momentary smile. 'If you would.'

'Life is trials in a succession, Berenice. It is a quotation, I think. Pompous. Like somebody wanted to compose an epigram, so his name would be in the reference works, something to put in the prefaces of novels.'

'I should be able to give you all kind of assurances, Bonn.'

'I should not.' He gazed at her as a group of five lads came on arguing about fishing, saying that the lodges round Affetside were hopeless, the fish deformed because of pollution. He listened in surprise. Was that true? He would have asked, if he had been alone, and learned of the disturbing phenomenon. 'I could never promise to think in a certain manner, so far ahead of events.'

'Isn't there trust?'

'Yes. It is never, never unconditional.'

'Like love?'

'Yes, Berenice.' His sorrow was evident. 'Like love, never unconditional. We think so. We like to pretend so. We use silliness words as a code, like "commitment". The sole references in that expression are to a legal contract and its enforce-

431

ability, not to morality. Think how many creaking old roues have gorgeous young wives. Like the American comedian says, "When do you ever see a beautiful starlet with a poor truck driver?" Never.'

'Where am I in all this, Bonn?'

'If you mean in me, Berenice, not anywhere.'

'Are you looking?'

'I wonder.'

An elderly couple boarded and came down the aisle, seating themselves opposite. The lady carried a bunch of flowers. A flower stall was usually placed outside the entrance to St John's churchyard, Bonn remembered, worrying if he would be thought improper or too mean if he were to buy a bouquet from that barrow. He did not have to pay, not for anything, though he carried enough money for such minor costs. The girl Kay in the Ball Boys censoriously checked that he had spent only coppers during the weeks when all the other goers, and especially the keys, rattled up expenses for clothes, hair salons, skin care, manicures, fantastical meals and wines.

'Let me, Bonn. I think we would be superb.'

'If I agreed to think it over, understand that I would never meet your backers. I could not face that. Discussion over agreements is appalling.'

'Right.' They waited in silence, the old couple talking over their visit to the churchyard and smilingly explaining to Bonn, who glanced across at some remark, 'We're going to visit a neighbour. He was in the war, you know. Lived alone, but he was well liked. Last month. We felt guilty not calling on him.'

'Well, you do feel that,' his wife added. 'It's here now.'

They rang the bell and started to get up. Bonn shook his head at Berenice, and they stayed on until the next stop then alighted. Bonn watched the bus leave.

'That would leave you in my hands, though,' Berenice said.

'I know.'

'You'd have no comeback if there was a question of what was legal and what wasn't.'

'I know.'

'That's what trust is, Bonn.'

'I know.' He looked into her, and his direct sadness was even greater now than it had seemed. 'It puts on you an intolerable responsibility, Berenice. That is its terrible power, and the sorrow it imparts.'

'I shall book you tonight, Bonn. We can decide the details.'

'You do realise I haven't yet agreed to join you, Berenice. You do know I will agree only to meet later and discuss whether or not I will comply. If I hear your suggestions and then retreat, that will be the end of it. I do not want to fly under false colours.'

She smiled. 'I see that seduction, as a means of getting my way, is out. I'd hoped differently. It will have to be intellectual, right?'

'As the lady wishes,' he said courteously, and they parted. He walked back to St John's churchyard, leaving her at the bus stop.

Chapter Sixty-Three

the Cyclops – the Crown Prosecution Service

The police station in Charleston had a curious mix, to Clare, of different indolences. Two people sat on a bench in a corridor. Three uniformed officers laughed at some remark nearby. Everyone seemed to know everyone else except the supplicants, if that is what they were. Civilians among military? If so, what was she?

Unwilling to wait, she told the desk officer her name, and said she was in a hurry. He took her through to an office. Not Hassall's? She dwelt on the words she might have to say. It would become, must be, some revelation. Bonn would never cope, the reasoning, the purposes, of the thought processes, would never even get started. She was unsure if she felt contempt, hatred, jealousy, or a mixture of all those plus uncountable others. Above all, she felt dispossessed, but not in the same way as when leaving Clifford. Did any of those reasons apply now? Though of course she and Bonn were still linked. This urgent issue of survival could only be resolved by the police – it was what they were for, what they had the means to achieve. Once it was over, she and Bonn could settle their own arrangements. She had to do this for herself, and for Bonn. Doing nothing, as he seemed ready to, was intolerable.

434

Their first meeting, 'for the purposes of', as Admin accountants might well record it, had actually been their fifth or sixth. It was however the first time she had been confident, surprised to find herself so and knowing the outcome. She had burned to ask that still-unresolved question of whether Bonn saw her as a 'client', that odious term she so hated. When she had asked, and implicitly agreed, that he should become her live-in partner, she had reasoned that surely those other women didn't have much excuse. Sexual repletion was their sole purpose and ulterior motive, whereas she had reached a totally different level of intimacy they could never attain. And surely that was not possible for Bonn, not with each client, was it?

Broaching the subject, in bed in that hotel suite, he had looked along the pillow and simply replied, 'I love mouths.'

'Everybody's?' she had said, immediately wanting to erase it. 'Sorry, Bonn.'

'No,' he said unexpectedly. 'Some mouths are beautiful. They make me love all mouths.'

Then she had uttered the most terrible problem of all. 'How much is tact, and how much what you mean?'

'I mean all of it,' he said, and placed his mouth on hers. And later, when she had told him how puzzled she was that men liked breasts so, he had replied, 'Women are the puzzle. They cannot see the obvious.'

At the time she had laughed. She had laughed at what for him was a truth, an incomprehension he felt as naturally as breathing, and still could not find answers for. Had she been stupid?

Oh, there was the revenge element, of course. She had wanted to exact revenge on her husband Clifford, who had betrayed her with his criminal activities, and used her as his alibi. Wouldn't any woman feel the same? And it was natural to find motives for infidelity, for that's what using Bonn actually became, when she had learned to love the youth, so much younger than she. She had actually asked outright, she remembered, as they lay together after making love.

She had speculated, rambling on while he listened, only moments afterwards, 'Imagine me lying here, maybe while you ran the bath for us, me throwing out casual questions. I would never know, would I? I mean, would your replies be evasions? A careful gush of platitudes? I simply wouldn't know.'

And later added, 'Could there be a greater recipe for disaster?'

And he'd said, quite calm, 'Which of us would be the unknown, Clare?'

His way, they had come to stay at a distance. She had gone on, same encounter, 'Does it become a mere carnal activity, grinding out repletion like a product?'

'Yes,' he had said instantly with a trace of sadness that moved her, until she cautioned herself that it might be his trademark trick, to lace confession with sorrow. 'It does become like that, Clare, in some women. They keep score, mark their mind cards, keep record of methods, levels reached.'

He went on to say that those clients had learned to use, with his usual lingering sadness. They behaved like an absolute beginner at the mogga

436

dancing, not knowing what on earth is going on and why the lady was striving for varieties of sex. A woman of that kind, overcome with the realisation of her new power, could fling herself headlong into clienthood. He had actually used that word. He said they'd called such women trippers, and said it was fine, even if it was the road to addiction. 'It has no turning,' he told her with care, 'no place to sit and wonder how far she has travelled, and why she is travelling at all.'

'Do they give up?' she asked.

'It's as if they see only possession.'

'How on earth do they cope?'

'One or two want the possession to be total, permanent union the only way.' As he'd spoken, she could have sworn he was sincere, but then warned herself that he was a magician at his trade. 'If they are wealthy, some eventually see the light, and resort to hiring occasionally as the need arises. If they're not wealthy, it is harder.'

'Why?'

'They can't understand why they can't buy me completely.'

'Not even when they're impossibly rich?'

Then they'd gone into making love, and she had cried out for him to knead her flesh harder, telling him frankly, 'That isn't hard enough, Bonn.'

Could there have been a more impossible conversation between two lovers? She felt close to tears, waiting here for her police interview.

'How do, Dr Clare,' Hassall said, entering and plumping himself down in a chair, carefully or accidentally beside her rather than on the opposite side of the desk. 'What can we do for you?'

437

'I want to report a possible item of information.'

'You sound like a news sound-bite. Isn't that what they call it?'

'I wouldn't know.'

'You look pale, Doctor.' He smiled at his quip. 'You aren't going to keel over on me are you? Send me out for a glass of water while you rifle the filing cabinet for police secrets about the Lord Mayor?'

'No, thank you, Mr Hassall. I asked for you because you know my history, about my erstwhile husband and everything.'

'Ta for that.'

'I hope I didn't intrude on your day. The desk sergeant said you were in an important staff meeting, and he grimaced.'

'The worst kind.'

'Mr Grahame, you mean?'

'Very astute. I suppose medical training makes you fast on your toes, eh?'

'Not really.'

'Cheer up, Clare. Things can't be that bad.' He sighed heavily. 'Think of some old git who has diabetes Type Two and wants to hide it from his employers, and has difficulty finding a quack who will cooperate in the deception. Now, *that's* hardship, young lady!'

She managed a smile at his description of himself. 'Oh, I'm sure there's some compliant doctor who could be bribed, Mr Hassall.'

'Watch it,' in mock threat. 'Or I'll get the rubber truncheon out and call the lads.'

'I think I know someone who might know the serio.'

That stilled him. He let down his chair with a

small thump. Until then he had been rocking it on its two back legs.

Serio. A criminal's word.

'I believe so.'

'You want this recorded?'

'No.'

'Hang on.' He left, returning within minute, carrying a small rectangle. He handed it to her. She stared. 'Digital,' he said. 'I can't understand how they can get a load of chat on a small thing like a postage stamp, but they say they can.'

'Thank you.' She put the sliver away in her handbag. 'His name is Bonn. He is a–'

'I know of him, Clare. Did he admit it?'

'I was not cross-questioning him.'

He grinned. 'Tooshay, madam. What'd he tell you? Isn't it hard to revert to normal talk when you're usually in interview mode? No wonder them TV folk can't talk proper once they start interviewing. Like editors, I suppose.'

She would not be deflected by his claptrap, and moved impatiently, wanting to have it over and done with. Betrayal was a special activity and could not be hurried but, once started, it had to be got through.

'I met Bonn. He said things that made me believe he might know details of the serio. I can't exactly remember how he put it into words, but he might know details that would lead to her.'

'Her.'

'Her. He might think it's a female.'

'More exactly?'

'I'm unsure. Maybe I have run it through my mind too many times to know any longer. I should

439

have come straight away, but I was afraid. Last night I locked the door, made sure I had the necessary emergency phone numbers by the bedside, charged up my cell phone. I made a hundred unnecessary phone calls to make sure people were at home.'

Twenty-three, Hassall registered, which is not quite a hundred, but a convincing enough anxiety.

'Could you tell me more? I mean, it's nothing to do with patient–doctor confidentiality, is it?'

'Nothing like that, Mr Hassall, no.'

'Then tell me what you can.'

She gave him a selection of Bonn's phrases, astonished that, just once, he smiled as if registering, aye, that's the lad all right. Hassall saw how shocked she was by his level of understanding and saw too she was wondering if he had already interviewed Bonn or Bonn's street people. The thought dismayed her.

'I'm dying to know what caused this change of heart, Dr Clare.'

He was serious now. 'I am frightened. That's why I telephoned for a police car to bring me. After Dr Terry. I'm hoping one will take me home when I'm finished.'

'Very wise in the circumstances.' He was grim, planning and plotting away in that affable balding head. 'And afterwards?'

'After what?'

'After I have taken action? After the perpetrator, whoever it turns out to be, is caught and tried? What then?'

'Well, life...' And she saw. 'You mean I would be a police informer.'

440

'Aye, with all the popularity that entails. You might be seen as not wanted round here. Whether caring for vagrants, the prostitutes, the criminals and mumpers, or not. In fact, Dr Clare, you might well be hated.'

'And lose my hospital post?'

'Ripples in the blood, so to speak. We had a case not so long since. Seemingly trivial, a bloke who told us about some pal, nothing more than a scrape of somebody's motor. He reported it. Didn't even know it was his pal's car that did it. Their wives stopped speaking, children were forced from school, he lost a garage job. The families fought. One sold up and left the district. Divorce followed... Honesty costs, you see. It doesn't come cheap. People don't always recognise the consequences of what they do.'

'I see.' She had not thought this far, and saw horrors ahead.

'I am glad you came. Now, would you be willing to testify?'

'In court?'

'In wherever the investigations take us. Serious matter, after all.'

'I never thought.'

'Time to do your thinking about a formal statement. I have to ask. I'm sorry.'

'So am I.' She spoke with bitterness. She felt forced into this position, and by whom? Bonn shouldn't have dragged her into it. Had he known it would, when he started to speak? Confusion came now. Why had she come? Simply because she was frightened, the serio probably out there about to move on her. 'It seemed so straight-

441

forward. Somebody is killing people. Dr Terry was murdered by somebody who seems to have killed before, maybe more than once, twice... And might be coming for me, or anybody else.'

'It was in the papers about that solicitor. You read it?'

'No.'

'Mrs Horsfall. She reported receiving death threats last week.' He sighed. 'Only doing her job.'

'The lawyer?'

'Got the perv off on some technicality.' He smiled. 'Time was, I used to think I had a fair old grasp of the law. Now it's just shifting sand and I'm as lost as the rest.'

'Did anything happen?'

'No. She has a curious existence.'

Clare waited but he said no more. 'How long will it go on, Mr Hassall?'

'The serio? Until the courts put her – him? – out of commission. The rest, God alone knows. For ever, maybe as long as Martina's people stay around the city.'

'I can't expect life to stay the same after. Is that what you're saying?'

'Different in every way.' He spoke so kindly she felt her eyes prick. 'That's my guess.'

'Does everybody already know that?'

'Plain as day.'

He meant Bonn would already understand, at least this far. She tried to feel, imagine, the changes in her life. Existence without Bonn? It would be impossible. She couldn't do it.

'Do I have to do this interview now, Mr Hassall?'

God, but he wanted a smoke. 'Yes. Unless you

intend to go it alone. That means tell us nothing, leave us back where we were before you came in.'

'Either I speak out and get some police protection, or let you assume I know nothing?'

'That's it.' He leant forward, paternal. 'See, I have to justify every man-hour I use. If I'm going to guard somebody, I'll have to write a report on it, say why, when, how, what for and predict the end. It's like running some baby clinic on NHS expenditure.'

'Can I think about it?'

'You've got to, Dr Clare, got to.'

'Must it be today?'

'Stay here if you like. We can run to some kind of accommodation here, or send you on your hospital work with a special man to stay by your side most of the shift. If you tell us everything you know and let us make an informed guess, we can cover you.'

'How long for?'

'If your information leads us to the serio, why, by the end of the day.'

'Then I shall.' She drew breath. 'I think Bonn knows who, among a handful of his clients, the serio is. Definitely one whom he saw during the past week.'

'Right.' He heaved himself out of his chair and moved to the door. 'Forrester? Get those two in here, if you please. Statement.'

A full hour later he left Clare for a moment, taking Forrester and the two recordists with him. He checked the time on the station clock.

'Eleven-thirty? Look, take care with those transcriptions.'

443

'We'll bring them in one hour, Mr Hassall.'

'Take your time,' he amazed them by saying, and qualified by adding, 'I mean just make sure you dot and cross every letter, OK?'

'Yes, Mr Hassall.'

'Where's Mr Grahame?'

'Now? He's in Ballistics with those lead spheres the pathologist recovered from Dr Elphinstone. You want him rung in?'

'No. No hurry.' He ambled back to Clare, to explain she should stay a while. There would be quite a delay before the typing could be done, and to say he might be able to get a special man to accompany her, but not until much later this evening. Fingers crossed. As two WPCs dealt with Clare, he went through to the police car pound with Heghorn and listened at length to the cyclist who came in an hour later, moaning he'd had his bike pinched while on stake-out. 'Tut tut,' Hassall said. 'Make sure you put in a chit, or they'll have it out of your wages. How did it go?'

Chapter Sixty-Four

straightener – an illegal disciplining, by financial or physical punishment, of one who transgresses

Rack, Akker and Gommer arrived at the house in good time, meaning ten minutes after Bonn met Berenice Six-Six-Nine in the Time and Scythe, Bolgate Street. Gommer had a pause for a brief

444

prayer, which truly disgusted Rack, who kept saying what a fucking way to start a killing and suchlike. Gommer told him, after he'd reached the Amen, that he was speaking out of turn and he had no right because God was God. Rack was livid.

'What?' he said, unloading the missile, taking most of the weight because Akker, being a weakling from Burnley who weighed one ounce wet through, wasn't able to lift a single frigging shell on his own. 'Me? My Mama's a religious nut who prays every fucking meal!'

'Then it should do you some good,' Gommer said, increasing Rack's rage by taking the next missile almost one-handed. 'Religion's not to be sneezed at. You shouldn't say such things.'

'Because its fucking true, that's why.'

'Mama's Catholic, eh?'

'That's right. Me, I'd pull the fucking plug out and let the whole Mediterranean sink down the plug-hole.'

'Religion's the backbone of society.'

'Leave off,' Akker grumbled. He was carrying some flex and a couple of cell phones and three detonators and was well and truly pissed because it was International Bowls on telly which he'd now miss.

'Have you signalled, Rack?' Gommer was a stickler for protocol.

'Shut your teeth. Think I'd forget that? There's nobody in a furlong.'

'No filth?'

'No.'

'How long we got?'

445

'Tickler and Jessop and Deebee're on the Time and Scythe. They'll keep Bonn and the client there until I ding and let them spring. Don't worry.'

'You sure?' Gommer said.

'Worry worry. And shut your asking. Gabby sod.'

'You can't be too careful.'

'You cased it, Gom?' Fifth time of asking. Gommer was well narked at Rack sometimes.

'Clean as a whistle. Just like when we were here before.' He sniggered, because they had been in this same shed, snooping and finding out.

'She's not been back and done something?'

'No. I can test it.'

'We'll wait while you do.'

'Right.'

Gommer lowered his shell and vanished in the gloaming. They heard not a sound, Gommer probably the best slider in the business. Rack and Akker strained to hear, but you wouldn't know he was anywhere. In ten minutes, the shadows thickened as Gommer returned.

'Clean as a whistle.' He chuckled. 'I think.'

'You sure or not?' Rack demanded, showing how on edge he was.

'Sure, Rack.'

'Then let's in and do it.'

'*Introibo ad altare Dei,*' Gommer sang quietly.

'Stop that crap,' Rack said. 'We're in enough trouble without God along to fucking help us out.' Mama demanded all sorts of things from God, and look at the fucking state of her world, and the rest of the world too, if you thought of it.

Bonn and Berenice were talked out. That is, she

446

was worried she was missing something, and Bonn was concerned he had not said he wanted to warn her that he would not be right for her proposed partnership.

They had made love with such gentleness she was concerned. Had she disturbed him? She'd been careful, not given anything away. The previous sex, now seeming so long ago but in fact earlier the same week, was almost a memory. It would serve as a template, she realised, for all similar encounters in the future.

'I once had someone in Birmingham, Bonn. He was lovely, but in the wrong trade, if you follow.'

'No.'

'He was a left-footer. Doubts about his sexuality.'

'He could have been helped.'

'It was pitiful to see. A good lover, though. Gentle, soft. He wasn't one of those who struggled to prove he was a dynamo, leader of some pack.'

'Mhh.'

'You aren't even curious?'

'I have no right to be.'

'You are hard to understand.'

'Berenice. I want the very best for you. That's why I think you should look to yourself, after...'

'After what?' She felt sickened by what she might have revealed to him the last time. She was sure she had disclosed nothing when speaking on the bus to St John's, Farnworth, which had been her test of him, making sure.

'After we made love on your previous booking.'

'What did I say?'

'Nothing that could be evidence, if that's the

joke you mean.' He almost smiled. She melted a little.

'I thought you meant I'd told something of my evil past, or worse present.'

'There can be little to tell.' He needed no answer, and was quite at ease as he went on, 'I believe most people aggrandise themselves. We assume our memories are tragic, horrible, unbelievably bad, when in fact everybody else we know has forgotten everything about us.'

'Do you really believe that, Bonn?'

'Yes. Look at you, Berenice the Guardian. You speak of a partnership as if you caused every famine on the globe, when probably your enterprise – that interest, hobby, you mentioned on the bus – is nothing more than a casual enterprise the Inland Revenue wouldn't even bother with. Or even notice. Please think,' he said earnestly, propping himself up on an elbow, 'and realise you have access to every kind of possible partner just for the asking.'

'Who?'

'Any of the goers in the city. They would jump at it, I suppose. Maybe, anyhow.'

'Are you sure?'

'I know it. A lovely woman like you, those two backers you mentioned. They would see it as really worthwhile.'

'Oh, it's worthwhile all right.'

'You see, if it wasn't, Berenice,' he went on, his eyes shining, 'I think you would give it up, and return to whatever work you do.'

'Teaching,' she blurted out, on the spur.

'Well, there you are!'

'And I should relinquish my hobby, tell my backers I'd changed my addiction to something less compelling, and take up a life of honest toil for the children I teach? Is that it?'

'Well, yes.' He felt the reins had slipped.

'Why do you want me to do that, Bonn?'

'Because you would become more accessible.' He had almost added *of course,* stopped himself at the edge. It would have been an impertinence.

'To whom?'

'To me. To all of us. To the children you teach. A simple life change.'

'Bonn.' She rolled over, smiling, feeling such a sense of glee. 'Are you trying to warn me?'

'I do not know.'

'You are!' And she laughed so vigorously he smiled. 'How absolutely precious! Has some policeman interviewed you, and tried to extort all sorts of confidences from us *clients?*' She made the word a mockery, still laughing. 'And you risk your reputation to warn me against the forces of righteousness? Oh la-la, sir!' She simpered, batting eyelashes at him and hugging herself with glee. 'How very Edwardian! You, my rescuer!'

'It isn't like that, quite, Berenice.'

'Then how is it, Sir Jasper?' She was almost helpless. 'Don't you see, Bonn, darling? God knows what I let slip the other evening, but it must have been the most terrible profound admission of guilt of something or other!'

'I am trying to warn you, Berenice.'

'Then I thank you, kind sir! Do you still not see, my lovely innocent lover?'

'No.' He felt tricked, when he'd thought he was

449

the trickster.

'I am the saviour, Bonn. I am the one who saves!'

'Saves?' Not guards, then?

'I am the lady who rescues civilisation from the forces of evil! I am the saint, and the others are the sinners. The pervs and the criminals must at last face one who rescues the innocent. Don't you see how wrong you are, darling?'

'No,' he said dully, for he did not.

'I would expect no greater understanding,' she said, sobering, her eyes shining with fondness. 'Darling Bonn. Never let your innocence down by suspicion. Never let your innocent soul become tainted by mundanities.'

'I don't understand.'

'I know, darling. Have we time?'

'Perhaps.'

'That, from one such as you, can only mean yes, Bonn.' She drew him close to her, and smiled as they began.

Chapter Sixty-Five

blam – to injure

'Time the old Pilot Ship Casino was redeveloped,' Posser said at supper.

'Dad, finish your halibut.'

Posser ignored Martina, addressing Bonn. 'High time.'

'It's good for your condition.' Martina would not be deflected. 'Dr Winnwick said.'

'I am, love. Bonn? Reckon we should?'

'It is Martina's control centre, Posser.'

'It can still do with improvement.'

'And Martina would need a new centre.'

'Dad, if you don't finish that, I'll call Dr Winnwick tomorrow. I mean it.'

'I can't hurry, for God's sake!' Posser tried his fish, and managed some of the sweet potato. Broad beans were a trial because they took so long. It would have been easier, with only half his breathing left, if she'd got Mrs Emvers to cut it up beforehand. He shook his head when Bonn made to move and do it for him. Jesus, he was like some kid in a high-chair. 'Martina could switch to that place near the Palais Rocco, Quaker Street, near the little car park. Ideal.'

'I don't know it, Posser.'

'It's not far down.'

'There's going to be trouble if you don't eat it while it's hot, Dad.'

'See? Problem solved. Quaker Street, agreed?'

They ate in silence. Bonn realised there was something not quite right. Posser was jubilant, probably knowing that Martina had spent the night with Bonn in her room, but Bonn failed to understand the unresolved argument about the place – which place? – in Quaker Street.

'If you like, Posser, we could send Rack to examine the premises in Waterloo Street, near the Lagoon card place–'

Martina slammed her cutlery down and turned to Bonn, face reddening.

'What Dad means, Bonn, is that I have a small flat near where Moor Lane leaves Quaker Street, opposite side to the Conquistador Bed and Grill. *Now* are you satisfied, Dad?'

'What'd I say?' Posser gasped, coughing. Bonn banged his back and slowly his colour returned to his normal sweaty plum appearance. 'I can't think of everything.'

'The trouble is, Dad, I think you still do.'

'Sorry, sorry,' he wheezed. 'What did I say wrong?'

'You said quite enough, Dad!' She signed for them to resume the meal. 'I apologise, Bonn.'

'I should be willing to help the move, if you decided.'

'Thanks, Bonn. What I meant is...'

'What Dad means,' Martina interrupted snappily, 'with his usual tact is, he wants you to decide, Bonn.'

'Me.' Decide what, though?

'You. It's his idea of matchmaking and trying to force us to take all kinds of decisions we may not even be thinking of, now or at any time.'

'I said nothing of the sort, Martina.'

'You didn't have to, Dad. It's as plain as day. *And* it's offensive. Don't you ever think before you say these things?'

A cell phone rang.

'That stupid tune can only be Rack,' Martina said, answering. Rack was outside, making sure it was all right to come in. 'His phone can play tunes on a recipient's cell as well as his own.'

'I've told him to get rid of it twice,' Posser told her.

'So have I.'

'That lad.' But Posser liked Rack's honesty, so that ended the criticism.

'I'll go.' Bonn rose and went to admit the stander. Martina went through the courtesies of offering Rack a place and a meal.

'Ta, boss.' Rack sat and spooned sweet potato onto a plate, and scraped fish after it. 'I hate them beans. No taste. You like them, Bonn? They're rubbish.'

'Dr Winnwick said they are most nutritious—'

'They're crap, boss. They waste your innards. Know why? It's the water they water them with, see? Should use winter water.'

'What is it, Rack?' Posser asked. Rack could go on for hours.

'That Hassall's been asking about. Talked to three of the girls in Central Gardens all frigging evening.'

Bonn looked. Rack never called the main square Central Gardens. A strange evening, first nonsensical prolonging talk about a possible nothing, and now Rack talking with impossible precision. Why? He started to listen more, wondering.

'He wanted to have them in, but Grellie got their names to the brief.'

'Which lawyer?' Posser asked.

'One of Martina's lot.'

Posser looked away. Rack had put his cell phone on the table, another odd feature. Bonn noticed it.

'How did Grellie manage to get hold of him? And what did Mr Hassall say?'

'It were them three who started you on about

453

that girl in hospital. They didn't want to yak to the filth, so I got the brief to. Hassall said OK, but he still wants a word.'

Bonn had stopped eating. 'It is an odd tale, Rack.'

'Dad, finish your meal. You can't have your evening tot unless you do.'

'In a sec, love.'

'You too, Bonn.'

'Thank you, Martina.'

'See,' Rack went on, 'I reckon with the plod you have to be on the ball... What the fuck's that?'

A noise sounded, a distant crump of sound. It was solid, more a tap on the eardrums than an actual note. Bonn looked across as a window trembled slightly.

'Was that an accident?' Martina said.

'Sounded too far. Maybe on the Liverpool exit.' Rack noshed on, spooning the last of the halibut. 'This is good stuff, boss. Be great with chips, put a bit of bulk on your bones. Boss, you bin getting thin. A bloke likes a bit of meat on a bird. Don't they learn you that at school, useless gits? Know what I reckon?'

'No, what?' Martina asked.

'It sounded more like an explosion,' Bonn said. He rose and drew back the curtains to look out into the night.

'See anything, son?'

'Nothing.' The traffic was still on the Square, visible to the left over the benches.

'Must be motorway, then.'

'At this distance?'

'Sometimes we can hear a major accident out

454

near St Helens,' Martina said. 'Poor people.'

'Amen,' from Posser.

Bonn returned. 'Perhaps no one is hurt.'

'Let's hope so.'

'Want me to find out?' Rack looked in disappointment at the dishes. 'Chips, boss. Tell that lazy cow as cooks for you to get her act together.'

'Rack. The three girls Mr Hassall wanted to interview. You know them well, I trust.'

'Told you, Bonn. Them three who sent you to the Infirmary to do that blessing thing.'

'I should like to see them tomorrow, Martina.' Bonn suggested maybe breakfast time at the Rum Romeo.

'Of course, Bonn. What for?'

'Nothing. Just to ask what Mr Hassall wanted.'

'I can tell you that, Bonn.' Rack guffawed, getting up and pocketing his cell phone. 'Here.' He looked amazed. 'Who turned my cell phone off? You, Bonn?'

'Yes.'

'Oh.' Rack considered, and switched it on. 'Hassall just wants to sniff the birds. Getting too old to pull them any other way.'

'I won't take more than a moment or two of their time.'

'No trouble, Bonn. Here! How would it be if we gave Mr Hassall a freezo now and then, eh? Keep him calm.'

'Do *not* make any such suggestion, Rack.'

'Right, boss. See you. Night.'

Rack left. The front door slammed shut. They sat in silence.

'How about it, Bonn?' Posser said across the

455

quiet table. 'You willing to help with the move, the control centre into Martina's small flat?'

'If it would help, Posser.'

'Thank you, Bonn.'

For once Bonn did not rise to help Martina clearing the main course away. She loaded the trolley and wheeled it out to the kitchen.

'You'll like the pudding, Bonn,' Posser said, taking his time.

'I'm sure I shall.'

'No need to question the girls tomorrow, son.'

'I know, Posser.' Bonn considered, and raised his gaze to take in the old man. 'They will be gone somewhere Rack sends them, safe from questions.'

'Rack doesn't know you spot things. It's his mind, son, too simple. Yet he protects us all.'

Bonn thought of the cell phone on the table as they had finished the meal, and Rack's pointless arrival to sit there while the explosion was triggered, presumably by some cell phone call. They were widely reported to detonate ammunition bombs like that in the Middle East during the troubles there. And the false tale of Mr Hassall's sudden inexplicable desire to interrogate three – a select three – stringers.

He would not show emotion. How odd that he had been allowed to accept Berenice Six-Six-Nine, though, when matters hung on split seconds. He knew he had been made a dupe, used as a simple decoy, keep her away from her home, or school, while it was primed with the explosive that would kill her. Who had placed it? Rack, with other standers? And had Posser, even Martina, given the order?

456

Posser wheezed on, speaking of buying another house further down the terrace, extend the working houses away from the Square.

Perhaps, Bonn wondered, it was time to surrender to the inevitable, do exactly as Posser and Martina wanted? He thought of Clare, and what she might be feeling right now. She must have gone to see Mr Hassall or some other police. But why did they allow Berenice to be killed so? The police must not have been sure of the serio's identity, or they would have taken her in and charged her, and so saved her life. That was the simplest, the most direct.

Now, Berenice would be described as a serial killer who killed herself accidentally, and good riddance. It could be told as such to the tabloids, who would faithfully reproduce whatever babble the police blurted out.

'It had to be done, Bonn,' he heard Posser saying.

'I see.'

'We are a family. You, me, Rack, the teams, the firms, the girls, Grellie's lot. Even the people waiting for their buses in the coach station, and the commuters on the way home. It was best.'

'I see.'

'I won't be long going from now, son. Before the year's out, Dr Winnwick reckons.'

'I'm sorry.'

'You'll stay here, then?'

Penance did not necessarily come from without, nor was it imposed by others for crimes – sins, if you liked – committed. It could be selected, chosen as from a shelf crammed with countless delectables, with every exquisite choice giving as much grief as it gave delight. The more of the latter, in fact, the greater the pain, even the punishment.

'With Martina?'

He thought a long time, then, 'Yes, Posser. I'll stay with Martina.'

'See,' Rack was telling Gommer and Akker as they walked to the Valance Carvery for a slap-up, 'I reckon you'd have got better sound with that Semtex stuff. It's cheap, can't be traced–'

'They fingerprint it, Rack,' Akker said. 'Sorry, but it's new news today.' That was a lie, but it was true they could trace it batch by batch ever since the Czechs came unglued.

'Is that right?' Rack breathed, amazed. 'I must have missed it in the papers.'

Lucky Rack couldn't read, Gommer thought, guessing Akker and his tactics.

'Still easy peasy,' Akker said. 'Two wires and unscrew the nose of the shell. Leave the nose so they'll think it was fired from a mile off. Then a simple call.'

'I'm glad I didn't have to dial it,' Gommer said, worried. 'That sort of thing worries me sick, like would I remember the phone number or not?'

'Can they trace a phone call?'

'Aye. Easy.' Akker never smiled, but if he ever did it would have been now, sort of. 'I left it in the London Road station. Bound to be picked up and used a million times before they catch up with it, if ever.'

'See?' Rack seethed outrage. 'That's why nobody's safe round this fucking city. We have to look out for ordinary people instead of the plod. Know why that is? It's the stuff they put in uniforms.'

'The next bang's due in a minute,' Gommer said.

They went to the Valiance Carvery to listen, arguing.

Chapter Sixty-Six

murray – death (Romany)

The assassin came to against the fence. People seemed to be shouting. Her vision had almost gone, only a world of shadows out there, and she felt blood sticky between her legs, on her face. Her hands found corrugations on her cheekbones.

'Don't go near, Bert,' from some shrieking woman, and 'It's a bomb, is it?' from a man, almost conversational. Maybe he had been in a war somewhere, and knew the sound? Keep the mind clear. That's what one had to do when things suddenly got beyond you. The rule had served her well, and ought to again, now suddenly the world had changed. What had she been doing a moment ago? Going into the workshop at the end of her garden.

She tried to move and almost screamed with pain. Inanities, shouts and talk, continued, shadows on no walls, dark shapes flitting across smoky lamplight hanging in the air. Quite the worst thing was this dizziness. She was unable to make her arms do the right things. Stroke? This must be the same as when some old lady has a stroke, wakes to find speech impossible, and unable to do her hair.

No flashlight within reach. What *had* she been doing? People shouting to get the fire brigade, police. An accident? 'Is anybody in there?' some man yelled, and a voice she vaguely recognised, maybe a neighbour's, answered in a shaky wobble that it was the teacher's house. 'In her garden,' a man was calling. A more solid shadow grew in the air and small beams wavered. It pointed. 'Keep away! Keep away, there!' somebody kept shouting to get the children off the street.

The shed, Berenice remembered, had looked the same, nothing amiss, the traps – hairs across the door, that old trick, a black thread by the lathe and instrument flap so ingeniously concealed, the electronic gadget she had acquired from Hal in the American military – proved that no intruders had entered. It could not have been my devices, Berenice thought. They were safely beneath the flooring, and were voice-activated, what her American military friend called VAVS, meaning a stranger's voice would activate the alarm. Voice secure meant electronics recognised her own voice and set themselves when she entered. 'VAVS are a variation on Friend or Foe, get it?' he'd laughed, showing how it was simply re-set. 'They're so cheap you wouldn't believe!'

Essentials must be intact still. She tried to sit up, couldn't quite manage the movements. That irritating man, who sounded like he'd encountered explosions before, was now saying somebody should check if anybody's hurt but telling everybody keep clear. No help, after all Berenice had done for the idle ignorant public. She might have actually saved the whole street's lives, selfish swine. She thought of Bonn's features, and distantly heard some music, was it *The Daughter of the Regiment,* Donezetti? That piece where Pavarotti gets to high C anyway. Even the orchestra had applauded.

Crawl! She managed to get on hands and knees, and found she could see somewhat, darkness slowly clearing. She was within five or six paces of the shed, so the explosion couldn't have been massive. In the flickering, switching flashlights – couldn't they keep still for a single minute? – she glimpsed the shed. Its wall, the one with the door and the little window, was gone. Shelving, with innocuous non-revelatory bits and pieces, some of her half-completed sceneries for Harry Entwistle's miniature-railway exhibition, had gone too. The interior seemed to be there, and she understood. This blast had occurred near the door.

Poor lovely workshop. She had planned and built every inch. Time to get herself in there and make sure the shed floor was whole. The other side was now cruelly exposed, like catching somebody undressing or on the lavatory. Essential to make certain the workshop would be seen as utterly innocent, when finally the lazy fire brigade and useless police came wah-wahing up, throwing their weight about. She would tell them the tale. Even as she began the painful crawl towards the shed, she was devising her story. Something like

461

the small canister of propane gas had gone up when a Bunsen burner's rubber hose slipped. That would do.

'Then,' she heard herself say, as she moved, making the tale up, 'I recall nothing more until I heard folk calling and found myself on the grass.'

Vital not to let herself be moved to hospital yet. Only once the fire people and police had left. Then she would accept the Infirmary. She almost smiled at the thought of doctors doing her debridement and their pathetic tests while she looked up oh-so-innocently into their concerned faces. She might even find the one she was looking for, Dr Clare. Berenice almost laughed aloud, went dizzy for a moment on the shredded step that had once been her safe entrance to the workshop. It would be very tempting, when she caught sight of her victim in an operating theatre in Casualty, or the Accident and Emergency Unit, to go over the top. Acting was always dangerous, so inviting when some victims-to-be presented themselves.

Blood – she could feel it – dripped from her chin into the scagged doorway, and trickled between her legs. Where were those maddening torchlights when you needed them?

'I think I can see somebody moving,' a man called. None of them was any nearer from the sound of it. Shadows began to wipe the night's dust clouded air.

'Don't go any nearer, Liam, don't!'

'Wait for the police!'

Yes, Berenice thought with sarcasm, let's all wait for the police. Will they do anything? Thoughts came of the next perpetrator needing to be eliminated. That foreigner currently under trial, or that Christian Brother who'd escaped via Toronto after so many cruelties to children? Any number of possibles. She had never had an accident before, nor been deliberately impeded, so pervs exacting revenge were out of the question. Admittedly luck, or the gods, were with her. The value of her crusade was borne out by the many children safely walking to school in the morning, and reaching home without being abducted or molested. Hers was as much sacrament as Bonn saw in the act of love. Indeed, Bonn would be the first to approve of her lone crusade. She knew that. Revealing her true identity was a thrill for the future.

Toppling, she wondered whether Bonn would offer help in a more direct way. She might have dozed, perhaps even slept, trying to reach her workbench. No watch, and no torchlight, everything momentarily dark. Time was happening, but simply unrecorded. Shouts had ended, talk down to muttered babble, with occasional voices calling out more warnings not to go too near. Children, presumably. What the hell were they doing out here on the street at this hour? Shouldn't they be in bed? That was the laxity left them vulnerable to the prey of perverts. Angry, Berenice caught at her mind and disciplined it to think. First, see if she could get upright. She straightened her legs, used her hands to climb slowly upright by shoving her palms onto her shins, knees, then thighs, and stood. Giddy, but in control. That was her guide, control, always in charge. Even when under Bonn and starting to bleat demands the way she had, actually asking for castigation, she had kept control. Only one hallmark of ascendancy in personal relationships. It was this: could you *at any time* regain your authority? The answer must be yes. It meant you were still perfect, as close to a machine as ever *Homo sapiens* could get. She was *always* in control, had to be her life's work.

A flashlight came, switched, then settled, and she could see, thank goodness. A wah-wah sounded, voices were raised, shouted explanations so confused that resigned voices called for quiet, please, while somebody told the tale.

'There! See? There!'

The light wavered slightly then stayed. Berenice saw her own shadow on the pocked wall of the shed, one of the two still standing. Glass jars, her seried box set holding all her screws and smaller implements, had been flung off somewhere but that wasn't going to be a problem. One small electrical thing – a plug socket? – was going zzzz, far right, where her precious let-down hidden cupboard was concealed. That was all right, because the essential thing was to get across there and stop the socket from short-circuiting, or the fire brigade maniacs would hack everything away and all those precious materials and miniature devices would be exposed. Even those ignoramus teams would be suspicious when they saw detonators, plunge activators, the telephonic bugs, switch-keys.

OK, she thought, taking a first careful step, test the flooring before she decided yes, it was safe to transfer all her weight and wait a moment. OK, yes, she would eventually need to revise her own security. Too much reliance could be placed on social camouflage, trust in conformity. Teachers had respectability, sure, however quickly it was dwindling these days. Nobody took responsibility for their own actions, the sense of duty was vanishing everywhere. But sticking to a schedule, being a pillar of society and insisting on strictness meant you were derided, of course. The uneducated and uninformed blamed the worthy people. It was always the case. Even though Berenice knew she held to a perfectly proper life, it was now no longer enough. This accident was nothing more than an unfortunate blip in her precise existence, some spider causing an electrical short, or maybe a burrowing mouse doing unpredicted damage to some container. Obviously her system had been faulty.

Pause. Another step, then a brief wait as her weight carried forward. Safe. Prepare for the next.

Several flashlights now. They moved. Somebody called out to her, 'Lady? Missus? Stand still. Don't move...' Berenice was able to hold the image in her mind of how far she now stood from the fizzing socket. Spirits of turpentine smeared the workbench. She could scent it.

However, if the explosion was deliberate, caused by some malign person intending sabotage, then her whole world would need renewal. Could the police have done this? Were they capable? Doubtful, for somebody in the police would blab, newspaper money would make the police blab. It always did. Criminals, then? Somebody who had watched her unseen, when all the time she had thought she was the huntress? Horrid to think that she herself was the prey, instead of the stalker and the assassin, the noble human being with the purest of motives.

Another careful step. The torchlight returned, held her shadow static against the wall. No creaking in the flooring. Holding the pose, ignore the blood she could feel running down her legs – what, some abdominal injury, could it be? She pressed her foot forward, slowly moved herself to stand there.

Within reach! The fluid showed dark against the benching surface. No cloth to mop it up, the least of her worries. Rid the partially destroyed workshop of that sparking fizzing blip, so the fire people would have no cause to start hacking away at the remaining walls. Police and fire brigades were quite the most destructive of all security teams. Their only response was to destroy, never preserve. Motorway accidents meant miles of security cones, while the police showed off, posturing away for the TV cameras and generally making sure everybody knew who was in charge.

Standing next to the bench, she found she was unable to recognise the socket where the short-circuit was still blueing the worktop. Had one of her multi-gang sockets become misplaced by the explosion? She felt around for the flex. Aware of how slow her reactions had become since the accident, she tried to remember how exactly she had left the worktop. Help was here now, judging by the shouts. Somebody was calling, 'Lady? Are you all right?' She made no answer. Security would be maintained as soon as she stopped the electrical short-circuit. Silence it, leave no sign of anything needing urgent attention from those morons, and she could relax. They could then get on and make their illiterate reports. She thought of them as people who could only write in capitals, half of their words abbreviations for lack of proper spelling. That was what the world had come to.

She wondered, chided herself, and took a decision. Act, or those moronic teams would come barging in. She lifted the three-point plug from the bench. It seemed to be held, still fizzing in her hand.

Carefully she turned it over to see what was fixing it down, maybe nothing more than a piece of wood from the damaged wall. She pulled it gently, so as not to disrupt any electrical connection, felt the minuscule thud of a mercury contact switch in her hand, and in that last blinding flash understood.

Chapter Sixty-Seven

mogga dancing – that type of ballroom competition dancing where each couple changes their dance rhythm to a different style every few bars – usually four or six – throughout a single melody

Clare roused when the alarm went. She stared blearily about the room, recognising her new flat. She heard the loo go and wondered who, then remembered the police woman sent to guard her. The first thing was to let the tea gadget do its thing so she could hear the news and those tiresome morning adverts full of hearty women saying you could buy a car for Nil Percent Interest with nothing to pay until God-knows-when.

Not this morning. Struggling to recall the previous night's events, she plodded slowly through the sequence. The police station, Mr Hassall's endless and tiresomely slow procedures, that wretched statement. Conscience – or was it merely weakness? – had returned as she had gone through the wording. Having to correct the typist's spelling mistakes, and her atrocious punctuation, had caused the whole thing to be done again, while Hassall waffled and barged in and out, humming some irritating song. Oddly, she had the idea he had been waiting for something other than her completed statement, and certainly he had shown no impatience at the recordists' tardiness.

Some time around a bleary midnight, when she was fretting about being on duty at the Farnworth General and Casualty on to her cell phone every two minutes, Hassall seemed to become maniacal, shouting and moving faster than she had ever seen him. Police rushed in every direction, and she had been virtually ignored in the frantic activity. The calls from the General Hospital ceased, and she was left in a kind of limbo. Afterwards there had been no sign of Hassall, and she was handed over to a uniformed woman sergeant. Arrangements had been made for her to return home, and here she was waking into a calm and puzzling morning.

With a woman bringing in tea, saying with a curious kind of brisk opacity, her eyes anywhere else but on Clare, 'Here you are! Thought you

468

could do with this to start the day off. Sleep all right?'

And before Clare could reply she turned aside and left the bedroom saying casually over her shoulder, 'Mr Hassall and Mr Grahame will be along to collect you in half an hour.'

No phones had rung, and the woman did not answer when Clare called. She sipped the tea and quickly rose, determined to act as if she were the only responsible person in the city today. If people didn't like it, that was their hardship. For herself, she would be calm and collected, whatever events presented themselves. She had lost all notion of what rotas she was on, though vaguely supposed some question of Organisation of Triage Services was due to be discussed, if she could get along to the meeting after finishing her own surgery in the city centre. She deliberately avoided contacting her own office. That could be left until she was out of police hands.

Forty minutes later, she and the police woman, no name, were met outside by two marked police motors, their lights mercifully dowsed. The car with its taciturn uniformed driver drove into the old industrial area. A street was cordoned off, several police cars blinking, their blue lights out of time, uniformed blues in the way and a small crowd of onlookers staring at the scene. A house had been reduced to mere rubble. Windows in nearby houses were broken, pavements protected now by striped barriers and incident tape. Two fire appliances blocked the street at a site from which smoke rose in lazy swirls. Firemen seemed to have lost any sense of urgency, more concerned with their engines than the damaged site.

'House went up last night, Doctor.' Hassall was there as she opened the door and stepped out. 'Mind the wet. These fire lads make puddles everywhere. No wonder our council tax is so bloody high, excuse me.'

'Is anyone hurt?' She finally remembered to say her good morning. No ambulances were around.

'Good heavens, they've been and gone. Last night, taking four onlookers, one deceased.'

She looked at the desultory activity. So many official people standing round, everybody either chatting and vaguely disinterested. What for? Normally, she was only called near the time of an accident. These consequences seemed to be merely concerned with tidying up the street.

'I know,' Hassall said heavily without amusement. 'It seems the most boring place on earth afterwards, doesn't it?'

'Why am I brought here, Mr Hassall?' She noticed several plain-clothes officers, two of whom she recognised, paid more attention to a morose stooping man than to Hassall. 'Am I still in detention?'

He smiled then. 'You were never in detention. Police and Criminal Evidence Act refers, amended by Criminal Justice and Public Order Act and other indecipherable balderdash. You were being helpful by making a statement.' He scanned the faces of nearby police officers. 'Not much use now, except for retrospective assessment.'

A pair of firemen came by, having difficulty with the switch controlling the hose on their appliance.

'I felt as if I were being kept, Mr Hassall.'

'Being protected while you gave your account of certain recent events, I'd say.'

'And is that what you will enter in your log book?'

'Not mine.' He nodded to indicate the other man, who was shouting in a belligerent manner at some white-garbed people collecting samples from the debris. 'That hooded lot will be finished in a couple of hours. Non-Intimate Samples, we plod call what they're collecting. I don't suppose you want to stay round here much longer, eh?'

'I don't know why I've been brought here in the first place.'

He put on an air of surprise she was sure was false.

'Why, this is the perpetrator. The stalker. She lived here.'

'She?' Clare stared at the rubble, the site of the explosion, the damaged street. 'The...?'

'The serio. At least, the alleged perpetrator.'

'What happened?'

'Seems like she was making one of her instruments, the sort you helped us investigate with your friend Dr Roundel. Remember, the perv in Newcastle and all that?'

'How can you be sure?' Clare felt sickened, suddenly wanting time to remember what Bonn had said, and what she had written in her statements to the police the night before.

'Oh, I'm never that, Doctor.' Hassall moved irritably as the firemen called for people to shift while they backed their smaller vehicle away from the explosion site. He showed a glimmer of a smile. 'More or less same as you, eh? A profession

471

is an art without certainty. The knack is pretending we know what the hell we're doing every second of every day, when all too often we haven't a clue.'

'Does this mean you are really quite sure?'

'Oh, the serio died all right. It's the sequence of events that bothers me a bit.' He indicated the grumpy man with a nod. 'Unlike him. Mr Grahame thinks it's all clear cut.'

'And isn't it?'

'It'll go down in the log book as that.'

'Whereas really it isn't anything of the kind?'

'Like most diagnoses, Doctor, it's all too often a matter of presuming.' He pulled her away from the kerb as the fire appliance reversed past. 'You start with a presumptive diagnosis, right? Then do your work and finish up with a confirmed one?'

'Yes.' She had avoided mentioning Bonn's name in the final version of the statement, thinking to temporise when she had to sign the definitive version this morning. She was sure it had been left at that.

'Like us, except we have the law pressing us and solicitors moaning and groaning every step of the way. You're lucky you don't. Except,' he added in sudden afterthought, 'if it's a case like that girl who your colleagues pulled the plug on, when the public get all steamed up and rush lawsuits at the General Hospital. Then, we're both in the same boat.'

'I suppose so,' she said dully.

'Want to see the actual site?'

'No, thank you.' She paused before turning away. 'Was anyone else killed beside...?'

'No. Flying glass, nosy folk getting their faces

stung by bits of debris, one bloke got himself flung against a wall by the blast, that sort of thing.'

'How fortunate.'

'Isn't it,' Hassall said heavily. 'Providential, you might say, eh?'

'Can I go now?'

'Off you go, Doctor,' he said, brightening. 'The city's quite safe now things are back to normal. Want a lift?'

'I'll walk, thank you.'

'See you later. Oh, I'll try to be on time for my appointment next time.'

Clare did not answer. She walked away.

Three hours later, she walked into the Café Phrynne off Market Street. Strange how the inner city's moods seemed to reflect the criminal activities, some days sluggishly starting up the day and other times breezily coping with whatever weather and commerce could do. It was nearly noon, and the Phrynne was at its most polite, almost withdrawn quite as if some lady had asked the place to be kept entirely in reserve for some genteel private party later. Clare entered, smiled at the girl on the counter and took a table near one of the alcoves.

Several ladies were in, one or two chatting, one making notes, others reading magazines. Many were single. The place was at its most tasteful. The atmosphere was reassuringly feminine. The usual girl was replaced by a slender pleasant blonde girl in fashionable woollens. Clare ordered coffee from the youth who appeared.

'Blue Mountain is execrable today, m'lady,' he whispered. 'Oh, no. Tell a lie. I mean the Tempest

473

Fugest. The Blue Mountain is actually divine.'

'Thank you. You choose for me, please.'

'Oh, welcome headache!' He smiled and weaved away between tables.

Clare smiled at the girl on the reception counter, who casually drifted over.

'I was just admiring your décor,' she said. 'When first I came here, I told the lady – Carol, isn't it, usually? – how brilliantly clever it was. Mediterranean, I remember, but managing to avoid travelogue yet stopping short of excess.'

'Thank you.' The girl was pleased. 'I'm Liuvka – and yes, from Mother Rooshia!'

They both laughed as the girl made a joke of her charming accent.

'I'm amazed you can change the decoration so well, and so often.'

They chatted about the difficulties of choosing colours. Having established herself as a regular visitor, Clare slipped a note to her before the youth returned with the coffee. The girl drifted off and within moments made an unobtrusive phone call.

Booking Bonn had proved impossible during the past hour, and Clare had given up. The three phone lines to the Pleases Agency were all engaged, engaged. The Café Phrynne was almost a preserve of Martina's syndicate. Admittedly, it was somewhere a casual visitor might be mistaken for an experienced client, though its fetchingly feminine décor and the knowledgeable staff were skilled enough to avoid confusion. Clare had only rarely had to use its services in this way. Now, she felt justified. Liuvka moved by and paused.

'I think the Palais Rocco is open about two, m'lady.'

'Thank you, Liuvka.'

Well before quarter to, she entered the Palais Rocco and ascended the stairs. Where to sit was always a problem for a woman. Was it so for a man, or didn't they care? If not, why should she? Because Bonn would possibly be on the balcony in one of the bays, from where he could look down on the mogga dancers as they practised their moves to the urgings and abuse of some showy instructor. That was the reason she chose a bay almost in line with the length of the dance-floor. She would be visible to anyone else coming to watch. Her throat tightened. Bonn would have no need to come over, say anything to her, even acknowledge her presence. And would he want to, after what had happened?

Yet what had actually come about? She had made a guarded statement, eventually as evasive as she could make it despite the pressure the police put on her, when she began to regret having said anything to Mr Hassall at all. She had done it from fear, but the longer the sessions in the Charleston police station had gone on, the more she had felt the need to protect Bonn and keep his name out of it.

The woman had died, though. Had Bonn been trying to tell her so the police would take action? Or, most sinister of all, so they would take no action at all, on the assumption that Hassall would keep her warning to himself or that the police would collude in letting Bonn's street people

475

create some murderous calamity that would have the outcome it actually did, and the serio die in the explosion? Now, Clare had no doubt. The explosion would be put down to an accidental death, the serial killer dying by her own mistake in handling some improvised weapon. Lucky that nobody else was seriously injured in that narrow street, so the newspapers would have a high old time drawing morals about the serio's 'own sins finding her out'.

Who would have done it, though? As if it mattered, now the city centre was safe again. She felt almost justified, though how things would seem to Bonn was a serious difficulty. Before the serial killing, Clare had felt in control. Yes, at first only by virtue of her purchasing power, the hiring of Bonn, but later on by the sheer conviction that he was becoming hers. They were heading for a lifetime together. Martina was a shadowy rival, true, and a formidable one. Bonn was addicted to his strange life, that seemed so much a part of modern society as women reversed their traditional roles and took over their own destinies. He was a hireling, and acknowledged that, as she was a client, and she too acknowledged her position. Though he had gone along with the notion of coming to live with her for an interim phase. As she understood it, they were to dwell together in her new place. He would still serve the Pleases Agency as before. But that, Clare was convinced, would only last a while, as she and he became one.

Now?

Now, it might be that they were to be as before the killings began. If Bonn came in, as Liuvka had

476

implied in response to Clare's written question about Bonn's movements, and greeted her, or responded to whatever she could manage to say, then they could take matters up. Her call to Hassall and her statements to the police must have damaged the supposed arrangement, yes, but surely not beyond repair? The proof that she had contacted Hassall was plain to see: the police had not taken any action to prevent the explosion, not made any attempt to arrest the serial killer. Instead, they had remained inert, and let the street regime of Martina's syndicate see to her demise. That would explain Hassall's strange inertia, his bumblingly repetitive pedantic insistence on the language of her statements, his querulous rechecking of her phrases as the clock ticked the serial killer's life away and the chances to make an arrest finally disappeared.

Only when the news of the explosions had come in did Hassall and the police act. And she, bemused by the rushing and all the activity, had been simply taken home under protection, to stay and fall asleep while the criminals and the police did their strange dance that led inexorably to the death of the killer.

As ever, her life seemed up to everybody else. The thought depressed her. Was it always to be like this, here in this corrupt city, or was everywhere exactly the same?

'Good afternoon.'

Bonn was standing there. She felt almost in tears.

'Good afternoon.'

'I wonder if you would mind if I were to share

the table. Only, I think the mogga dancing prac-tice might possibly be delayed today.'

'Oh. How disappointing.' She realised he was still standing and nodded. 'Please.'

'Thank you. It always seems the strangest pas-time.' He sat opposite. 'I mean, not quite dancing in time, to such bonny music.'

'I suppose it is.'

'The whole place seems oddly indolent today.' He sighed. 'Moods seem to take hold of a city, just as it can a person.'

'I thought that a few moments ago.'

'Yet, last week, this place was heaving. Now, so quiet.'

'Yes.'

'I suppose everyone will be along later.'

'I suppose so.'

He gave his half-smile at the dance-floor as a couple moved on and began to practise their steps to the recorded music.

'Here they come. Normality.' For a moment they stayed silent, then, 'No explanation for the moods that come along.'

'Yes.' She did not say what might have been natural in other circumstances, that explanations could be uncertain or simply wrong. 'Yes. I thought that too.'

The music changed, and they watched as new dancers took to the floor.

The publishers hope that this book has given you enjoyable reading. Large Print Books are especially designed to be as easy to see and hold as possible. If you wish a complete list of our books please ask at your local library or write directly to:

Magna Large Print Books
Magna House, Long Preston,
Skipton, North Yorkshire.
BD23 4ND

This Large Print Book for the partially sighted, who cannot read normal print, is published under the auspices of

THE ULVERSCROFT FOUNDATION

THE ULVERSCROFT FOUNDATION

... we hope that you have enjoyed this Large Print Book. Please think for a moment about those people who have worse eyesight problems than you ... and are unable to even read or enjoy Large Print, without great difficulty.

You can help them by sending a donation, large or small to:

The Ulverscroft Foundation, 1, The Green, Bradgate Road, Anstey, Leicestershire, LE7 7FU, England.
or request a copy of our brochure for more details.

The Foundation will use all your help to assist those people who are handicapped by various sight problems and need special attention.

Thank you very much for your help.